Smarty Havarti

Smarty Havarti

A Novel

Walter Rice

Drum Roll

This book is a work of fiction and a product of the author's imagination. Any resemblance to actual events, organizations or persons, living or dead, is entirely coincidental.

ISBN 978-0615-50138-3

Published by Drum Roll

For all of you who want to make a difference
and have fun along the way.
The time is now.

Smarty Havarti

He cleared customs easily, but now there was a complication.

The taxi ride from Kastrup Airport to downtown Copenhagen started like a wobbly rocket launch: engine revving, followed by a lurch and a shuddering liftoff from the terminal grounds. The silver Mercedes changed lanes, zip, changed again, zip, then whooshed headlong into the pallid wintry afternoon as the driver aimed his four-wheeled bullet at open country.

"No rush, no rush," said the lone passenger, Jason Stallings.

The driver grunted and gunned the engine as he entered the freeway, throwing what felt like a couple of G's into Jason's chest. The Mercedes, now swerving, now swaying, squeezed between two other cars by bare centimeters, then continued to slice through traffic like an electric carving knife. The cab leveled off its speed momentarily, then cut from the far right to the far left. Like a dizzy politician, Jason thought.

He reached for his stomach and hoped it would stay approximately where it was. "I'm really in no hurry," he said.

The cabbie turned his head back slightly and contorted his face into sharp, cubistic angles, wordlessly relating his contempt for back-seat driving.

Hanging on to the door handle in the right-rear passenger quadrant, Jason watched the speedometer surge from120 kilometers per hour to 140. Quick math: Jason knew a 120 kilometers per hour was almost 75 miles per hour, which had to make 140 a notch or two on the lunatic side of 85 miles per hour. And considering that the freeway was probably built for about 65 with moderate traffic, Jason now saw no reason at all not to sit back and enjoy his last ride on this mortal coil, as the Melancholy Dane might have summed up his plight.

But a speedy half kilometer later, Jason arrived at a new and stunningly clear position: Hamlet be damned. Melancholy was a trivial matter now. Jason could only be transfixed by the driver's apparent death spiral and felt himself drawn relentlessly into the maelstrom. Concrete walls and abutments loomed ahead, and Jason repeatedly tried to predict the point of impact, and how many other vehicles the driver would take out with him.

The taxi surged to 90 miles per hour.

Jason looked to the side, to fields of snow. He had never seen snow move so fast.

The cabbie toyed with Jason's increasingly fragile state of mind. Jason knew now that this had to be one of Copenhagen's mad Russian cab drivers he had heard about, even been warned about in the guidebooks. Speed was the objective, the speed limit a mere suggestion, and the destination, if reached, a happy by-product.

Jason thrust a hand into his carry-on bag, pulled it back with a roll of antacids and popped two tablets into his mouth. He chewed, burped and felt worse. Now he noticed the driver's cologne wafting back to him. It was the heavy-handed drugstore variety some men used in an attempt to cover their lack of hygiene. The cologne started out pleasantly enough, but the sweetness couldn't be hidden and the more Jason smelled it the more disgusting it became. Most likely it was flammable, and Jason thought a better use for it would be as a fuel additive, not that his driver needed any more firepower under the hood.

They reached a straightaway and the Mercedes nosed a little faster toward destiny. Fine, Jason thought, the driver is suffering from delusions and now thinks he's on the Bonneville Salt Flats. Whatever…90, 95 miles per hour on an urban freeway. No problem. No problem at all if you're not intending to live another half minute.

Then they cornered sharply, without slowing down, and Jason and his stomach saw the problem clearly: It took long enough to live thirty-one years—and so little time to end it all.

The irony of it was that, to get here to Denmark, to arrive at this fateful moment, he had left home in Seattle so many hours ago he could hardly count them. It had started with the hour of maddeningly congested traffic just getting to the airport, then moved on to two hours in the terminal where he cheerfully underwent ticket and passport presentations punctuated with a twelve-step program of undignified searches, then nearly four hours on a plane to Chicago. Tack on a couple hours of layover at O'Hare and then a different flight to Copenhagen that took seven more hours. On that plane, he'd slept only two hours even though part of the polar route was dark enough to be night.

All this just to talk with some Danes about the cheese problem. When he'd taken the key account rep's job at Sunny Day Farms a few months ago, he had blithely agreed to "a little travel." So you're the new troubleshooter, his officemates joked. At no point did it enter his mind that he would be going to northern Europe in February to have a near death experience. Oh, God. Just smile and say cheese.

Jason stared at the floor of the Mercedes, now determined to keep his head down until impact. The thing was, he argued silently with the universe and his delirious Russian driver, he couldn't understand why it was necessary to endure so much discomfort before the actual moment of death. Why did he have to die jet-lagged and nauseated? In the winter? On a Friday after he'd worked all week? Why not check out on a fine summer Monday after a decent night's sleep, followed by a cup or two of gourmet coffee with an omelet and toast and strawberry jam? And maybe fresh-squeezed orange juice. Why this way, for God's sake?

And then they began to slow down.

Jason snapped his head up and saw they were entering Copenhagen proper. But not slowly enough. Buildings quickly squeezed in from both sides. He couldn't bear to look left or right, only straight ahead.

And before he knew it they had arrived at his destination, The Hotel Lorentsen, not far from Tivoli Gardens.

Jason got out and planted his feet on *terra firma*. It was an extraordinary feeling. Nothing like a brush with death to change a man's perspective, he thought.

The driver opened the trunk, deposited Jason's suitcase on the pavement covered with a skiff of snow and named his price. Jason paid and tried to tip, but the driver waved him off. "No tip," he barked, at last demonstrating a firm command of two consecutive English words. It was meager, Jason thought, but better than his Danish. Or Russian.

The strange thing was he'd missed the section about taxi tips in the guidebooks. The stranger thing was that he had tried to tip a man who had almost killed him.

The driver removed his Mercedes from the hotel grounds, and the sight of it rushing away gave Jason much relief.

He inhaled some cold Danish air and took his bags inside to the front desk and thought he smelled, what, sawdust? His jet-lagged brain was playing tricks on him, he decided, and he dismissed the thought. The hotel was as modern as advertised on the Web. Ahead he saw a lovely brunette in a navy blue jacket with gold piping and epaulettes. "I have a reservation," he said.

"And your name?"

"Jason Stallings." He put his passport on the elbow-high green marble of the front desk. This passport shtick was becoming a habit. He was now prepared to present his passport to take a walk if necessary. Which he next realized he might have to do.

"I'm sorry, Mr. Stallings," she said with an oh-so-apologetic smile. "We have some sort of conflict," she said, drawing out the last word as she glanced at him, then back at her computer monitor.

"Conflict? What do you mean?" *Conflict* was not a happy word.

"It seems that we're overbooked." She sounded extremely sympathetic. "We don't have a room for you. There's so much going on, the renovation and—"

"Overbooked? Excuse me. I've just traveled nine thousand miles to learn that I'll be sleeping in the street tonight. In the middle of February. This is not at all heartwarming. Could I speak to the manager?"

She shook her head. "I'm sorry. He is—busy. A very important matter."

And Jason's overbooked room wasn't important?

"I see. Then what do you recommend?"

"I can try to arrange a room in another hotel," the brunette said brightly.

"Oh," Jason said, a little surprised. But at this point, a room was a room. "Well, why not. Yes, give that a try. Please." And try really hard, he thought, because he wasn't going to freeze his buns off when tonight's temperature would plunge close to zero. Fahrenheit, that is. Not that he figured the metrically correct Danish hotel staff cared a fig for the American way of measuring intolerably cold weather.

She picked up a phone and immediately made a call—in Danish, of course.

Well, maybe this would turn out okay after all. He was way past tired, but holding up reasonably well. Now that the taxi ride was over, he was no longer nauseated. He thought vaguely of having a drink, but when he turned for a glimpse of the Lorentsen's bar, he instead saw two police cars pull up in front. Four uniformed policemen walked rapidly into the hotel. One of them carried two long sticks wrapped in gray vinyl with black straps and buckles. They waited for the occupants of a third car that had just arrived, a fortyish man in black overcoat and gray rumpled suit and a plainly dressed woman a little younger. Detectives, Jason surmised.

They all converged by the front door and were greeted by a man wearing a blue and gold waistcoat, the companion attire of the desk clerk. The bell captain, Jason decided.

It was good that the hotel uniforms were different from the police uniforms, both in color and texture. The police garb was a lighter blue, and the hotel's fabric was more elegant but less functional. Otherwise, how would they decide which players were on which team? Jason didn't suppose his observation would amuse either the hotel or the police, so kept it to himself.

Meanwhile, the desk clerk apologized for the delay and continued making calls, presumably for the bunk he would be weighing down tonight. When a new hotel customer walked in, a male desk clerk came from the back to check the man in. As the check-in process unfolded without a hitch, Jason noted that there was room for this man, this unworthy stranger with a bad shave and a black leather jacket, but not for himself.

Jason sighed. Another time, another place, he might have raised a stink, but with jet lag heavy on his shoulders and gendarmes at the door, he was not in a fighting mood.

After two uniformed policemen and the detectives went up in the elevator, leaving two uniforms between him and the front door, Jason took a seat in the rather sizable lobby because there was nothing else to do. At least it wasn't going ninety miles per hour. He watched hotel workers go by at two miles per hour, and their pace pleased him. More police types arrived and went upstairs. One of them carried a black case and a camera.

An hour later, Jason's brunette desk clerk called his name. He rose and went forward, as if to receive an honor, maybe a gold-plated trophy for his heroic patience with the taxi driver *and* the hotel. Proudly, she said, "We have found a room for you. In the Kong Jacob," giving the *J* a good, strong *Y* inflection. YAH-kub. "It's not as modern as the Lorentsen, but four-star. Very nice. And the price will actually be slightly less."

"Will I like it?"

"Oh, yes. Very much."

But as soon as he'd asked it, he realized it was a silly question. How did she know? Had she stayed there? Or did Copenhagen's hotel staffs shuffle around the city to the other hotels on weekly visitations to tour the accommodations so they could be truthful and knowledgeable in a crunch time such as this? Jason had no idea what normally happened. All he knew this time was that he did not expect to hear the truth at all, and so he just said, "Wonderful."

"I will call a taxi for you."

Jason stiffened and reflexively thrust his arms out, palms holding back this ridiculous suggestion. "No, please. No taxi. I'll walk."

The desk clerk furrowed her brow. "There will be no charge. We will gladly pay the fare."

He pulled his arms back, not wanting to appear hostile. "The fare is not important. It's just been a bad day for taxis. Really, I can walk."

"But it's too far. At least three kilometers. With your bags." She nodded toward the black rectangular lumps by the chair where he'd been sitting.

Jason looked at his bags as if someone else had recently planted them there. Their little wheels would soon be ground to black powder if he pulled them three kilometers, almost two miles, on hard pavement. Why had he brought all this stuff? Didn't he think Denmark had its own stuff? That it would run out before he arrived and somehow be stuffless?

"We do have a hotel van." the desk clerk offered.

Jason grinned. "Excellent. I'll take it."

"Certainly. But it's not here." That clarification wiped away Jason's grin and reshaped it into a frown. "Not yet anyhow," she added quickly.

"When? When do you expect it?"

"Twenty minutes, perhaps thirty. The housekeeper is picking up supplies and—"

"No problem," Jason said. "I'll wait."

He gathered his bags, found a chair near the front door and went within himself. He was far from home. On business. He had nearly been killed by a mad Russian taxi driver. His room had turned to vapor and would soon disappear with the pale sun into the long winter night. He was jet-lagged and desperately needed a nap. But considering all that, he felt fairly good.

Abruptly, there was a commotion by the stairway. One of the policemen by the front door went toward the stairs. A command in Danish flew the policeman's way, and he turned on his heels back toward the door, followed by a stretcher.

Jason was only six feet away when the stretcher passed. Despite the fairly modern appearance of the hotel, he now assumed it had no adequate service door for this kind of event. It wasn't exactly what the management would want to make public. The long sticks he had seen before now returned. Their black straps, too. He saw a dull red spot on the sheet covering the chest of the stretcher's occupant. If called to testify, Jason would say that he didn't know what it was. But he did know. He saw the thick black shoes. A man. Of average length and girth.

The somber procession trailed out the front door. When had the ambulance arrived? He hadn't noticed. He stared back glumly at the place where he'd first seen the stretcher.

"Hell of a day," he said to nobody.

A uniform was now standing to Jason's right. But it wasn't the police. It was the other desk clerk—*Thomas*, his name tag said—the one who'd helped the black leather jacket while Jason's desk clerk, the lovely brunette, had called to find him a room three kilometers away.

Thomas said, "You're very lucky it wasn't you in that room. It should have been, you know. I'm sorry, I mean it could have been. My English ..."

Jason waved him off. "No apologies necessary." Because instantly he knew that the man in thick black shoes, the man of average length and girth, had lost too much blood and expired in the room that should have been his tonight.

Absently, Jason said, "The room is going to need cleaning now."

"In a day or two," Thomas replied. "After the police search and comb it, and recomb it. After the evidence is taken, questions are asked, fingerprints taken..."

Jason turned to look outside. The stretcher was resting inside the ambulance now, its back doors still open wide, and the rumpled gray suit and his female sidekick were trudging back into the hotel. They turned down a short hallway and then stopped at an important looking door—the manager's office, Jason assumed. The investigation had already begun. Jason looked back outside. The stretcher was still visible. Despite all the rushing today, no one was in any hurry now to whisk away the unfortunate man in his thick black shoes and stained sheet.

Jason thought about the lunatic cab driver who had nearly killed him, and he thought about the horizontal man out front who had been killed in a room overhead, a room that he, Jason Stallings, had been scheduled to occupy. Death was certainly rubbing shoulders with him today.

#

The Kong Jacob was a stately pile of red bricks that was old enough to have a history. Jason guessed that history was probably burnished with stories of royalty and luminaries, but he didn't care much. Still, the hotel embraced him like a long-lost American cousin, accepting his passport and credit card, apologizing for its renovation—hadn't he heard that the Lorentsen was also renovating?—and dispatching him efficiently to room 123 on the second floor. Even though he was by now hugely jet-lagged, he found the room number reassuringly basic and was amused by the deliberate mismatch of the floor with the room number. Just like England. As Mark Twain once wrote, "It's un-American."

Jason's room was long and narrow with the long side parallel to the hallway. The bed was on the left end, a sitting area with TV in the middle, and the bathroom around the corner perpendicular to the rest of the room and in another wing of the hotel. All three areas had windows overlooking a courtyard with dining tables. There was no snow in the courtyard, no sign of weather at all. The six-story hotel flanked all four sides of the squarish courtyard and was capped by a plastic skylight held up by metal braces. Jason estimated the skylight to be twenty times the size of his room. This wasn't the modern Lorentsen he had been expecting, but he found it mildly interesting.

The plumbing was adequate. The toilet flushed, and then shut off at just the right moment. Hot water ran into the sink on command as Jason tried to wash the fatigue from his face. But the exposed pipes, though painted a clean, fresh white, were twisted and gnarled like the limbs of an old tree. There seemed to be three possibilities: the hotel's age, a pipe fitter's bad dreams or Danish code. Not entirely convinced, Jason decided to go with the first possibility.

The hotel exuded a lavender perfumed scent, probably piped in through its air ducts. Jason had noticed that in the hallway, and his room was no different. Still, he could also smell fresh paint, not from his room, not even from his floor probably, but from somewhere in the hotel. At least the renovation he'd been told about could explain that. Like the smell of sawdust at the Lorentsen. But he wasn't going to complain to the management. After the recitation of apologies, there would be the lingering question of how he had smelled something no one else had. Had he been poking around unauthorized areas? Sticking his head into air ducts? No, he wasn't even going to raise the subject.

Jason knew the smells were far more apparent to him than the average person. For almost three years now, his sense of smell had been heightened. It had started shortly after he had a heatstroke halfway into the eight-mile Bloomsday Run in Spokane, across the state from Seattle. It was about eighty degrees that day, and uncharacteristically he stopped to walk about fifty yards. He ran another fifty, felt bad, and then walked another fifty. When he started again, he fell, remembering only the bite of rough asphalt on a knee before he lost consciousness.

Jason looked down at the dining tables in the covered hotel courtyard. The sunlight coming through the skylight seemed to be waning already, easing Copenhagen into Friday night. He drew away from the window and unpacked part of his bags. There was something a little too domestic about taking out everything. It wasn't as if he were moving in. He straightened up and breathed through his nose. The air freshener in the room he was meant to smell. The paint he wasn't. He could blame that on eating some bad lettuce—and what happened after the heatstroke.

The medics had taken Jason to a hospital, where the nurses cooled him down and he quickly recovered. Jason thought he might be dead for a while, but surprised himself by walking out of the emergency room. A friend drove him home and told him not to run for a few days. They even laughed about that. The nurses said Jason would feel better the next day, but he didn't. He was ejecting at both ends and had the strength of a wet towel. So he went back to the emergency room. The staff looked concerned and ran tests. He had hepatitis.

In time, he recovered from that, too, but along the way his sense of smell took a wild ride. Coffee smelled like burning rubber, so he didn't touch it. Soap was weird, too, reeking so much of a chemistry lab that washing his hands was an ordeal. Foods were either absolutely flat or too strong to bring near his nose. When he started feeling better, all that went away, but he was left with the ability to pick up faint but real scents that others didn't detect at all. Sometimes this was useful, but often was only annoying. So he learned not to say too much about what he smelled unless he was fairly sure other people also noticed.

In the bargain with the heatstroke, Jason became more sensitive to cold weather, something he didn't fully appreciate until the next winter after the race. And the natural follow-up to that, he thought with amusement, would be a wintertime trip to Scandinavia. It was cold, all right. No disappointment here. He hefted a sweater out of a suitcase. Of course, he had planned and brought extra clothing and even bought a long wool coat and special hat for this trip. There would be little need for those back in Seattle. He just hoped they did the job in Denmark.

He turned and eyed the bed. He started thinking: Old hotel, lumpy mattress, the last thing he needed. Still, the bed invited him over for a tryout. He yawned but resisted nature's forces long enough to set his travel alarm. Five p.m. sounded about right. Just a couple of hours. Then his head hit the pillow, his eyes clamped shut and he surrendered to the inevitable.

\#

Though he was certain he could have slept right through till morning, Jason forced himself out into the increasingly cold, and now dark, late Copenhagen afternoon. For a week he would be under the sway of Danish time. If he were going to do business with the cheese people in the daytime, he had to be awake then. On the sidewalk outside the hotel, he adjusted the charcoal gray hat around his ears and huddled under his matching overcoat and then took off. He walked a few blocks and turned into the west end of the Strøget, which the guidebooks assured him was a five-block long shopping area containing some of Copenhagen's finest stores.

The air was bracing, to say the least, so Jason was wide awake now. But even half asleep he would have noticed the Burger King sign. From the Kong Jacob to the Kong Burger in less than ten minutes. It really was a global village.

Hunger was stirring, but Jason was looking for something a little more Danish. And not pastries. He kept moving. It occurred to him later that the cheeseburgers might have Danish cheese, which brought his attention back to the reason he was in Denmark: the havarti export problem. And why all the trouble? Well, he would think about that tomorrow when he went to the warehouse and talked face to face with some of the cheese people. The cheese people. He really had to think of something else to call them. Maybe tomorrow he would work on that, too.

But now he had to do a little shopping for his mother. He reached a gloved hand into his coat pocket and took out a scrap of note paper with a store name and address headed by the word AMBER. His mother was thorough. And luck was with him. He spotted the shop a half block ahead, and it was still open since Friday night was the night Copenhagen's stores kept later hours. This was way too convenient. Copenhagen was a great place to buy amber, he'd been told, thanks to the Danish forests millions of years ago that had made the amber. Petrified tree resin. Jason didn't know how many millions of years, but he was fairly clear on two points: There wasn't much of a forest left now in this country of farms—farms with cows that produced milk for Danish havarti, he hoped—and however long ago the amber began to form, it was definitely pre-Denmark.

It didn't take long to find an amber bracelet trimmed in sterling silver that would suit his mother's tastes, and his credit card. In fact, he had barely spent enough time in the store to feel that his wool coat was too heavy.

Back on the street, Jason's coat was in its element, so to speak. With the shopping detail taken care of, his mind turned to dinner. He found a fairly quiet restaurant that looked normal by his American standards and had a *rodfiske* dinner. The *fish* part he figured out, but had to admit his ignorance of Danish to the waitress. She took it in stride and explained it in English. *Rod* was *red*. Red fish. Translated or not, it was tasty, and he felt well-fed.

Fearing he might fall asleep during dinner, Jason had ordered coffee and steered away from wine, but now it was about eight o'clock and surprisingly he felt more awake. Maybe he would stop for a drink someplace on the way back to his hotel. He had the time and not much else to do tonight. And so far, his sense of direction was holding up, so he felt confident he could find the Kong Jacob again.

Checking out side streets, he found a sizable Irish pub just off the Strøget. As he approached it, he wondered if there were more Irish pubs outside of Ireland than in Ireland. Somehow an Irish pub in Denmark sounded more farfetched than one in Seattle, but that didn't stop him. He walked up four steps and headed in to an empty table by the big front window. That's kind of different, he thought. A window on a bar. If the cigarette smoke wasn't too thick, people could see in from the street. It was a refreshing notion.

He took off his North Pole hat and coat and settled in, undaunted by the stale smell of cigarettes. In a minute a young guy in a long-sleeved T-shirt and jeans came by looking like a waiter and said something in Danish. Jason thought of ordering aquavit, the homegrown Danish liquor, but backed off. Instead he said, "Scotch on the rocks," and that seemed to do the job because the waiter headed back toward the bartender. While Jason was waiting, he looked around. There was a large poster by the door with a picture of a band named Street Dog. Picking through the Danish printing below the picture, Jason figured they would be kicking off their Friday night gig at nine.

The scotch arrived and Jason paid. He sipped and felt the customary jolt of the smoky liquor, which knew nothing of international boundaries. This was almost too funny, and the alcohol hadn't even gone to his head yet. An American ordering scotch in English at an Irish pub in Denmark. Throw in this afternoon's contact with the rushing Russian and Jason felt like a United Nations all by himself.

He sat alone and sipped. For a few minutes he just enjoyed being in the present moment, doing nothing, feeling no urge or pressure to do anything. Simply being.

Then a voice broke through. "May I?"

Jason looked up and saw a tall, thin man reach for an empty chair across the table with one hand while holding on to his drink with the other. He was about six feet two with short brown hair and a fairly long nose. Jason thought at first that the guy only wanted the chair, and said, "Sure." But then the man sat down and looked him in the eye.

"You're American," the guy said. "Me, too."

"Oh." Jason was still a bit stunned. Did he have a sign up? *American. Need table partner.* "Yeah. Right. Just got in from Seattle."

"Great. I'm from California. Bay Area. Been here a few days. I'm, uh, Greg Hunt." He thrust a hand across the table.

Jason shook it and said, "Jason Stallings."

Hunt looked around, and Jason decided he was in his mid-thirties, four or five years older than himself.

Hunt turned back to him. "This place is something, huh."

"Very interesting," Jason replied, though he hadn't really decided yet. The walls were decorated with framed shamrocks and pictures of green Irish hills, and he presumed there was a fortress of Irish whiskey at the bar. It was a transparent attempt at atmosphere, not offensive but too ordinary and expected to be inspiring. Anyway, the Irish angle wasn't strong enough to keep the conversation going, so Jason switched thoughts. "You here for the band, Greg?"

"What?" It was getting noisy now as stage time neared. "Oh, the band. What's their name? Meat Dogs?"

"I think it's Street Dog."

"Right. Dutch group, I heard." Add another one to the U.N. roundtable, Jason thought. "No, I didn't really come for the music," Hunt went on, "but I might stick around a little, listen to a few tunes until I get tired of hanging out."

Hunt took a swallow of his drink, and Jason suspected this wasn't Hunt's first of the evening. The California man put the glass down and reached into his jacket pocket and took out a pack of cigarettes, popped one loose, grabbed a lighter from another pocket and lit up. "You smoke?"

"No, never have."

"Everyone smokes in Denmark," Hunt said. "It's nice for someone like me. Crazy, but nice. Not like California. You can't smoke anywhere in California anymore. Is it like that in Seattle? No smoking here, no smoking there, do-gooders trying to tell smokers what to do and where to do it. You know, it drives you stark-raving mad."

Hunt's face twisted in disapproval, and his volume rose with every word, which could have been a benefit of sorts if Jason had really wanted to hear what he was saying. The din in the pub was giddy and growing like a balloon on a helium machine. What had happened to that quiet little time when Jason just wanted to sit and be in the moment?

He watched Hunt alternate between pulls on his drink and puffs on the cigarette. Pull and puff. He tried to dodge the exhalation of smoke but only partly succeeded.

"You married or anything, Jason?" Hunt asked.

Jason sat back. "No, not married." Absently, he ran his fingers around the rim of the glass. "Not even close."

"Girlfriend?"

"Not really. Kind of a dry spell just now, I guess."

"Too bad." Hunt paused. "I've got a girlfriend. Right here in Copenhagen." A quick puff, then, "Not many guys from California can say that."

"Sounds exotic. What's her name?"

"Gitte. She's a looker, all right. Blonde hair just off the shoulders. Wonderful smile, classic figure. Something to die for, I tell you. Smart, too. Maybe too smart for me."

Jason didn't say anything, and Hunt filled the space with a burst of nervous laughter. "She's something," he said, nodding in agreement with himself.

"Meet her here in Copenhagen?" Jason asked.

"Nah. San Francisco. Like I said, I've only been here a couple of days."

"Is she here?" Jason looked around for a blonde, but saw too many. "In the pub?"

Hunt put his lips tight together and shook his head slowly. "Not tonight. But soon I'll be seeing Gitte," he said with determination.

"Well, I wanted to see her, too," Jason said, trying to lighten things up with a mock serious tone. "After that buildup and all. Is she dropping by later?"

"I don't think so." Hunt look distracted, then snapped, "The time isn't right."

Well, thought Jason, that was one subject he wasn't going to touch again.

Hunt drained his glass, glanced at Jason's, which wasn't quite empty, and said, "I'll get us another round. What're you having there?"

Jason told him and Hunt sprang to his feet and pushed his way to the bar because the servers were tied up with the crowd beginning to come in for the band. Jason thought momentarily about skipping out and heading to the hotel for a long night's sleep, but he saw Hunt glance back at him from the bar and so just sat there. After all, he was in no hurry and the guy was buying him a drink. When Jason was ready to leave, he'd tell him to his face.

Hunt brought back the drinks. "Thanks, Greg."

"No problem, man."

"So, Greg, I take it you're not in Denmark for business."

Hunt looked up in surprise. "Business? Hmm, not really. Vacation, I guess. Must be. I quit my job. You?"

"Business," Jason said. "I can't think of any other reason to come to Scandinavia in the winter. Except maybe a girlfriend."

Hunt raised his glass in appreciation of the joke, and they both laughed. Hunt asked what kind of business, and Jason gave him his card and told him a little about his food broker job for Sunny Day Farms and about the Danish havarti import problem he'd come to untangle, but it was obvious that Hunt was only responding with polite nods and had no interest.

They sipped a little and then Hunt coolly asked, "You ever think about killing a man?"

Jason recoiled and looked squarely at Hunt. "Well, no. Never crossed my mind."

"It's crossed mine." Hunt was matter of fact.

Maybe Jason should have asked who the victim might be, but he had no taste for that line of questioning. He thought of the dead man back in the first hotel, but that was the past and Hunt seemed to be talking future. Or was it just the booze talking? Jason couldn't be sure.

"Seriously, I've thought of it. But I can see you haven't. It sort of makes you sick, doesn't it? A little nauseous?" Hunt didn't wait for an answer but rocked his chair back on two legs and spoke philosophically as if he were contemplating something risky but legal, something on the order of skydiving. "I think it must start that way for everyone. You walk away at first, but then you come back to it. You play with the idea, poke it with a stick, find out if it moves away or springs back at you. Roll it around like bread dough, make a ball and then flatten it, see if it rises, see what it tells you."

Jason was stunned by this rather elaborate description of how to sign on for murder. But he recovered enough to ask, "And what has it told you?"

"Nothing," Hunt almost shouted.

The Irish pub grew even louder in Jason's ear, and he felt a heavy wave of jet lag. He should have left the first time, or never come into this place. He took a big swallow of scotch, but it didn't help.

Hunt lit another cigarette and started in again, tempering the discussion for a moment. "Well, it's only a conversation we're having. For God's sakes, we're in some stupid Irish bar in Denmark. You think anyone back home is listening, that maybe somebody will find out? And what if they do? We're just talking."

Jason was too tired for debate and could have got up and walked out without a word, but he decided to offer some rebuttal. "Sure, it's only a conversation. Only words. But everything starts with an idea. Some things you take action on, but a lot of ideas just fade away. They don't work out. Maybe they're bad ideas, so you forget them. I think this is a bad idea, Greg."

"I think this is a bad idea, Greg," Hunt said derisively. "Well, maybe. We'll see."

They sat there not speaking for half a minute. Then Street Dog began to tune up, strumming guitars, tapping at drums. Da-dum, da-dum-dum-dum. The discussion was over.

Jason stood up and reached for his coat. "Well, I'm jet-lagged and need to get some sleep. Say hello to Gitte, and thanks for the drink." Half of it was untouched.

Hunt nodded. "Sure."

And Jason was out of there.

Strangely, the freezing night air felt good. Jason looked back, half fearing Hunt would follow him, but he hadn't. It was one thing to have a drink or two with a crazy man in a crowded bar, but another to be tracked down on a dark street. Jason hadn't given Hunt his hotel name, and he didn't know where Hunt was staying either, except probably not with his beloved Gitte. Anyway, neither he nor Hunt had much of a clue about where to find each other, and that was fine with Jason.

With a weary feeling, he hurried along, trying to stay under the lights. His long day that had started a continent and nine time zones away was tightening its grip. And the cold air that he'd found refreshing moments ago was now beginning to sink into his bones. The only comforting thought was that his hotel wasn't far away.

A minute later a startling jolt of energy raced up the back of his neck. He turned his head to the side as if casually looking at a shop window and then let his peripheral vision give him confirmation of what he'd already sensed. He really was being followed.

#

The man in the long gray coat had been waiting patiently in the street, watching the Irish pub and one American patron in particular. Using a zoom lens, he had taken photos through the bar's big front window. But then the target's drinking partner had walked out and headed with purpose down the Strøget. Time to decide, stay or go. The man in the long gray coat discreetly snapped more photos from a distance, then almost casually began to follow the drinking partner.

The one in the bar, a somewhat reckless but mostly known quantity, could stay there. This was Target A. The walker, now Target B, was different. Too little was known about him, and that was cause for concern. The meeting in the Irish pub might have been nothing. Or it might have been an early sign of trouble. Even an innocent connection could interfere with the larger game. A's contact with B might have been arranged, though the plan appeared to be clumsy at best. And why was B there at all? This wasn't making sense. The whole thing smelled of a ruse. The man in the gray coat was not going to be tricked. Never. So he followed Target B to see what he could learn. Knowledge was so much better than trust. Only a fool relied on trust.

Shortly, a black hat and coat hurried past, seemingly drawn toward the target moving along the Strøget. The man in the long gray coat blinked, disappointed and surprised that he'd been caught off guard. Why hadn't he noticed this one before? Was he losing his touch? No, it was only a momentary lapse. No one else would know, and it wouldn't happen again. He pulled his shoulders back and took a deep breath of the frigid air. So he would have to follow them both, Target B and now Target C.

His supervisors treated him like a machine, but he knew better. Without a doubt he was as hard as steel and could perform delicate and demanding tasks with flawless precision, but sometimes in the gaps he recognized real emotions. Now was one of those times, and it was far from welcome. He could feel hot anger rising to defy the cold night, anger that surged from deep within his torso and up to his now flushed face. He didn't blame the anger, he blamed the cause of the anger. These stupid people were complicating his life, and he didn't like that at all.

2

This time Jason did a full head turn. It wasn't Hunt following him, it was a woman. She was a blonde Scandinavian type in a black hat and black coat on a black night. Maybe it was Gitte. He wished she would go back and have a drink with Hunt and rock to the melodies of Street Dog.

Jason passed Burger King and was soon at the end of the Strøget. As he turned toward the Kong Jacob, he stole another look back. The blonde was still behind him but a little closer now. Oh, well. Another three blocks and he would be at the hotel. He slowed deliberately, testing, and she slowed. So she didn't want to get too close. As he wondered what that meant, he resumed his normal pace and she picked up hers. She was now about thirty yards back. Would she maintain that distance or try to edge up?

The rest of the way Jason's curiosity about this woman struggled with his desire just to turn in for the night. As he neared the front door of the hotel, he glanced back one last time and saw that the woman had closed another ten yards. Now he could see that she was about his age and very nice looking. Under some other circumstance, he would like to meet her. Instead, he hurriedly pulled open the door and entered the lobby. He took off his hat and went straight to the elevator and punched the up button, then just as quickly swerved to the left and found the stairs. The Kong Jacob's elevator was slow, and by the time it arrived at the ground floor, she would be there and he wouldn't.

It was a short dash up to his room. He slid his card key into the reader and went inside and closed the door. Then he stood by the door with the lights out. This was probably nothing, but he admitted being a little spooked. He'd been in the country less than eight hours, but Denmark seemed to be full of surprises: a dead man in his first hotel room, a crazy man in the pub, now a woman following him with suspicious determination. Then he chided himself for trying to evade a woman who didn't even look threatening. When he thought about it, he didn't even know for sure that she had come into the hotel after him. Maybe she'd gone down the street to something else. There could have been another hotel, a café, her apartment.

He took off his coat and heard footsteps in the hallway and a door, or doors, opening and closing. It became quiet again, and then something in the hallway sounded like small footsteps. The low carpet would have hushed any jarring sounds, but this definitely wasn't a heavy man slapping heels and soles into the floor.

All right, Jason thought, what was the point in being afraid? It was silly to be so cautious. He was safe in his hotel room, and he wasn't about to be jumped if he just cracked open the door, was he? No, this was a highly civilized country. He turned on a lamp in his room, opened the door and peered out.

Well, that was some luck. After he had tried to evade the woman, here she was practically at his doorstep. The blonde in the black coat was standing across the hall one door down. She turned to him and said something in Danish.

#

Once Jason had walked out, his drinking partner sat in the Irish pub just tapping his fingers on the table they'd shared. A few minutes later when the band started, it got really loud, and he didn't see any reason to hang around. People were eyeing his table as if it were prime waterfront property. To hell with it. He gulped his drink, glanced at his drinking partner's half-consumed scotch, and knocked it back as well. Then he put on his coat and left, stumbling a little as he went down the steps. The band was getting on his nerves. Meat Dogs, Street Dog, they could eat anything they wanted if he didn't have to listen. Is this the best the Germans had to offer? Or was it the Dutch? He wasn't sure now.

It was well below freezing, but he'd had three and a half drinks this evening and thought he probably couldn't feel it as much. The so-called experts said that was a bad thing, but what the hell did they know? He put on a stocking cap he'd bought in Tahoe, jammed his hands into his coat pockets and started walking back to the Commodore Hotel. He had gloves on, but they weren't thick enough for this climate.

He looked up the street. It was a fair walk. Maybe he should call a taxi. But there weren't any taxis on this street, no cars at all. No cars *allowed*. How in the world did the locals get around this place?

He laughed to himself and noticed a passerby stare at him. He sure had scared the wits out of that poor guy from Seattle. What was his name? Jason Rollins? Skallings? He couldn't remember. It was on the card in his pocket if he really wanted to know. But now he wondered if he had handled the guy right. Maybe he'd said too much to Jason even if he had given a false name. Greg Hunt, he'd said, instead of Craig Huff. Maybe that was too close.

He knew he was just trying on his new-found freedom, trying out his bravado, riffing on nonsense. What did that hurt? Most people spouted nonsense all day long and didn't even know it. At least he recognized it. Talking with this Jason guy was like being an actor. It was fun, gave him a rush. High octane. He had an audience and, God, he could hardly stop himself. Of course, there was an element of truth in his nonsense. If Mr. Square Jaw out there didn't get off his high horse and just deal professionally with the business at hand, Craig might actually need to think about an extreme approach. Ha. Wouldn't Jason's eyes pop out if he heard that? *That's a bad idea, Greg.*

Enough of that grim sideshow, Craig Huff thought. It was Friday night and time to party. All right, even if he had been cryptic, he'd gotten carried away and probably spoken a little too intensely about dealing with Square Jaw, but what he'd told Jason about Gitte really was true, not complete but factual as far as he'd gone. It was the other stuff that was such a jump into the unknown. But in between business classes he'd done a little theater in his college days, so he knew how that went. Now, instead of working from a script, he was improvising like a wild man. Back home, before he'd taken the money, everybody probably thought he was the mild-mannered accountant. But what did they think of him now? Criminal? Con man? Lunatic? What did they know of the real Craig Huff? He felt he could be dangerous if he let himself go. Would he? Not tonight. Tonight other things were on his mind.

He trudged along, thinking now that he had underestimated the distance to his hotel. Had he already passed it? No, surely not. He'd only gone a couple of blocks.

Huff's mind zipped back to Jason's face, that surprised look he'd tried so hard to conceal. Jason...yeah, Mr. Seattle. He knew the type: a young businessman, a food importer, his card said. So probably all he wanted to do was finish his work and fly on to someplace warmer. He felt a little sorry for the guy, getting sent to Denmark in the winter. What a break.

Yeah, except that Huff had sent himself to the same place. Talk about perverse. It would have been a no-brainer to jet down to Mexico or the Caribbean if it hadn't been for certain other interests—Gitte, for one. The money was in a Cayman Islands account now, so that's probably where they would suspect him of going, that is if they were smart enough to follow the money. Follow the money. What a load of crap. Besides, he had enough of his own for a while to avoid tapping into the big stash.

Still, he had to be on guard for foolishness. There was too much at stake. He'd talked with Mr. Seattle because he was already homesick for the good old US of A. Something about the way the guy dressed, he had to be American. Sure you could speak English just about wherever you wanted in Copenhagen, but it wasn't the same.

He checked his watch. Gitte would be home from her office dinner party in a few minutes, or so she'd told him. He would call then. Would she invite him over?

He'd met Gitte Benneker last summer by chance at Pier 39 in San Francisco on a carefree Saturday afternoon. She was on her summer holiday to the states. Twenty-six years old and all alone in America. Well, not strictly speaking. She'd flown over with friends, but later they'd gone their own way. By that Sunday afternoon, he was so taken with Gitte that he called the boss and arranged for vacation the next week so he could show her the sights of California, or as much as they could see in a week. Of course, the romantic time was fantastic. He couldn't get enough of her, and it seemed she had the same desire for him.

Maybe he should have thought more about it then, about the contingencies, the long-term implications. She wouldn't think about moving to the United States, at least not seriously. She said she couldn't get a green card. She was only an office clerk with no special skills, and why would such a big, important country want her? Besides, they'd just met. She put on her little smile and did that squint that absolutely melted him. Shouldn't they see how things went?

They had email, of course, and frequent phone calls. He'd suggested texting, but she didn't want to do that. So it was email and phone calls. The email turned out to be less frequent than he had expected, and most of the calls he initiated. But he didn't mind. In fact, over the months, he hardly noticed he was driving down a one-way street.

Now here he was on her turf. Why hadn't he seen this coming? Smart guy, he should have been able to figure it out even before getting on the plane. But the truth was that Gitte had her own comfortable life in Copenhagen, even though it was probably frozen solid from November to March. Was he taking their relationship much more seriously than she was? No doubt, but it was a painful pill to swallow. He should have known from the start that a summer fling like theirs usually had the lifespan of an insect. Which was about how he felt if he let himself get too far into the idea. But maybe he was just too down on himself for taking things this far without knowing where he was going. He hoped he was wrong. He owed it to himself, and to Gitte, to give this a chance.

She was probably still in shock at actually seeing him in Denmark. He couldn't blame her. He could see now that she'd tried last summer to tell him in small ways, but he hadn't listened, had steamrolled over her objections. So she'd gone home and put a lot of distance between them, but still hadn't had the courage to speak up forcefully. What did she really think? And could he change her mind? Those were the critical questions.

Huff could see his end of the Strøget ahead. There was some kind of a statue, a horse. It was only a couple of blocks now to the Commodore.

His future with Gitte gnawed at him and wouldn't let go. Had his showing up in Denmark forced the issue? He hadn't told her that he'd quit his job and given up his apartment, that the Salvation Army now owned more of his stuff than he did. Nor had he told her that he had enough money for another five years without working, maybe longer if he didn't get extravagant. Would that scare her? He'd simply told her he was on vacation. That was safe, he thought. Don't give her too much else to think about, wait until the picture became clear.

But this was pretty much all he thought about. The Gitte of last summer and the Gitte of now. Compare and contrast. It was like some never-ending essay exam. He'd passed the Erotica Museum a while ago, but ironically now that he was actually here in this so-called libertine country there had been precious little sex. His first night here they'd fallen into bed, maybe for old times' sake, and it had been great. But that was four nights ago, and there hadn't been a repeat. He thought he was a patient man, but this situation was stretching him like a rubber band. Sure, she had to get up and go to work in the morning, but still. There was a limit on how much he could take.

When he got to his hotel, he relieved himself first. Too much scotch, he knew. Should have played it cooler. And his sinuses were plugged again. He found his saline nasal spray and gave each nostril a couple shots. Between the drinks and the icy weather, he couldn't catch a break. Was he ready now? He took a deep breath. Ready. Get with it. So then he phoned.

"*Goddag.*" Hello. The voice was so feminine, almost faint.

"Gitte, it's Craig."

"Oh, hi," she said, switching to English, with a mild accent. Her voice was stronger now, but flat.

"How was the dinner party?"

"Oh, it was nice, I guess. You know, it was one of those office things I had to go to. If I had missed it, people would be asking questions for weeks on end. I don't deal well with that."

"Sure. I understand. Can't get you in trouble." Huff waited a few seconds for her to say something, but she didn't. So he went on. "Are you tired?"

"Yes, Craig, a little. It's been an...unusual week"

"I know what you mean. But it's Friday night. You can sleep in tomorrow."

"That's true. Maybe I will."

He waited for Gitte to invite him over, but she didn't. This wasn't going well. He had to make a move. "Gitte, would you like to come over now?" he asked.

"To your hotel? The Commodore?" She paused. "I don't know."

If he tried hard, he could almost filter out the weariness in her voice. Okay, maybe she didn't want to sleep with him. Try something else. It would be unbearable if he couldn't see her tonight. He'd really been counting on this. "I was thinking of a drink. In the bar. We could talk." She hadn't even been to his hotel.

"Well...maybe."

She was caving, Huff thought. "Sure, it's only a ten-minute cab ride." Make it sound like nothing. That was it.

"Hmmm. All right."

All right, all right. Eager now. "Good. If you call for a ride now, you could be here in, what, twenty minutes?"

"I suppose. Craig, do we have to be so precise? What if it's twenty-five minutes? Thirty minutes?"

Oh, oh, he was pushing too hard. "No, I didn't mean it that way, Gitte. I just wanted, well, to know when to look for you." That's it. Nice upbeat turn.

"All right, then. I'll call for a taxi. But I can't stay long."

She had to throw that zinger in, Huff thought after they had hung up. It was her out. Then if she said it again, it wouldn't be a surprise. Well, he would ignore it.

\#

Jason eyed the woman in the hotel hallway outside his room and said, "I'm sorry. I don't speak Danish."

Her face lit up and she laughed a little. "Well, that's a relief. I don't either," she said in English, very *American* English. "I was trying to say I'm sorry for disturbing you."

"You're not Scandinavian?"

"No, I'm from—Pittsburgh."

"The Steelers," he said.

"Don't forget the Pirates."

"I'm from Seattle," he said.

"Mariners." She pointed up like a game show contestant happy to get the correct answer to Sports for two hundred dollars. "Who could forget that season? Tied the all-time record for victories, right?"

That was several years back, Jason recalled, so she must know her baseball. Better than he did. He vaguely knew the Pirates had won the World Series more than once, but hoped she didn't ask him which years. He'd rather talk football anyhow.

She took off her black winter hat, revealing not blonde hair but brown hair overlaid with yellowish strands and sexy wavelets down to her shoulders. Now that Jason had a better view, he found her really quite pretty, not threatening at all. About five feet six and an inviting smile. There was more to this than he'd first thought.

A head popped out of another door. "We're making too much noise," she whispered. "Shall we go downstairs and talk?"

"All right."

"I'll just put my coat in my room. It's right here."

She went into the room in front of her and came back in a white turtleneck and dark blue pants that showed off her trim figure, and they went down to the bar on the ground floor and found a quiet table. There were only eight or ten people in the bar. And since it was Friday night, Jason wondered if the bar was ever busy. He wasn't complaining though. He'd seen enough action for one night at the Irish pub. They settled in on opposite sides of a booth, and Jason made eye contact with the bartender. Then he turned to the woman. "I'm Jason Stallings."

"Danni Rossler," she said and shook his hand. "That's Danni with two *N's* and an *I*."

Her handshake had a nice, soft touch, Jason thought. Firm but not aggressive.

He smiled and said, "I thought you were following me back there on the Strøget, Danni with an I."

She nodded. "Yes, I was."

He leaned forward and gestured with his hands. "I mean you were *behind* me, but you weren't *following* me. I see that now. You have a room here at the hotel."

"I was behind you *and* I was following you." She smiled, seemingly pleased with the clarity she'd offered.

But Jason wasn't clear. "It's semantics," he said, a little perturbed that they were disagreeing already.

She laughed. "No, I was really following you. I was *pursuing* you. And happily you walked right into my hotel, right onto my floor."

"Happily. I see. And here I thought I was walking into *my* hotel. But why were you following me? Pursuing me?"

"Because you were talking to that man Huff. Back in that Irish place."

"Oh." Jason was taken aback, but now the bartender was at his side in a red and black brocade vest. He was a stone-faced, balding man in his mid-fifties who looked as if he'd rather be doing something else on a Friday night besides opening beers and pouring shots and keeping the bar wiped clean and dry.

Jason looked at Danni for her order, and she shrugged. "I don't know. What are you having?"

He'd had enough scotch for one night and didn't really need another drink at all. But here he was in a bar, and when in Rome…or Copenhagen… "I was thinking of a whiskey sour."

"Why not. Make that two," she told the bartender.

After the man had gone away, Jason said, "First of all, the guy's name back there was Hunt, not Huff. Greg Hunt, I believe. And second, if you were in the pub anywhere near that table, I would have noticed you. You're very striking. The classic Danish blonde. From Pittsburgh."

She smiled and said, "Thanks for the compliment. But I have to confess I didn't get that close. I didn't really hear you. Actually, I was outside."

"Outside? It was freezing. Worse than freezing."

"I was wearing a heavy coat. Anyway, I saw you both through that big window."

Jason thought about Hunt's assertion that nobody from the United States would ever find out what was said at that table. The man was close to being wrong already, and if Jason said much to Danni, Hunt would definitely be wrong. "Well, I guess you were entitled to look. Besides, I don't have anything to hide."

"Maybe you don't," Danni said. "But he does. You don't know him? I mean, you never met him before tonight?"

"Right. Never saw him before tonight. He just invited himself to sit down at my table. When he found out I was American, he stayed and talked."

"Probably lonely already."

"What?" This woman wasn't making any sense, Jason thought.

"Anyway, *you* are wrong about the name," Danni said. "If he said Hunt, he's lying. It really is Huff. Craig Huff, not Greg Hunt, or whatever he told you."

"You're sure?"

"Absolutely. Now what else did he say?"

The whiskey sours came, and it appeared that the citrus in the drinks might be less sour than the bartender's face. Jason figured the man's feet must hurt. Jason said, "*Tak*," thank you, and the man brightened a little.

After the bartender left, Danni and Jason clicked glasses. "To Denmark," Jason said.

"To success," she said.

"Success? In what?"

"Oh, that's a long story. Maybe we should get back to Craig Huff. Now what did he tell you?"

"Oh, some crazy stuff. What difference does it make?"

Danni tried her drink. "Hey, this is good."

"I thought you might like one." Jason sipped his drink. "A whiskey sour is all about balance. You need the whiskey for a foundation and a strong flavor, and you need sweetness to tone it down. And then you add the citrus for more flavor and the acidic or sour taste, and then magically you have balance."

"Very interesting. So you think I'm out of balance?"

As far as he could tell just by looking, she had the utmost physical balance. Nothing whatsoever seemed out of place. But he wasn't about to answer her question that way. Until he got to know her better, a little caution would be in order. "Not at all. But you know, considering that we just met, you sure do ask a lot of questions."

"I need to ask questions. And I need to warn you that Huff could be dangerous. You shouldn't get involved with him."

Jason raised his hands. "I'm already out of the picture. And I have zero objection to not getting involved with him."

"You're patronizing me, Jason."

"No, I'm not," he said. "Frankly, I found the guy a little disturbing, even as a casual drinking partner. Anyway, you act like a woman with some serious reasons for being so inquisitive. I could tell you some things, but first I'd like to know why I'm telling you. What's your interest in all this?"

"All right, I suppose that's a fair question," Danni conceded. "I used to work with him. He gave his notice abruptly, left his job about a week ago, and then a large sum of company money turned up missing. He told people he was going to do a little traveling, see the world."

Jason got the picture even if there was some annoying static. "So instead of the tropics, he starts with northern Europe in February. And then you show up here in the dead of winter. Makes sense so far. How'd you know he was going to Denmark?"

"Hmm. Well, I talked to his landlord. Huff dropped some hints. And then he got rid of all his furniture and most of his belongings. He called the Salvation Army, and they came with a truck and hauled away almost everything."

"Sounds like a man who doesn't plan to come back."

"He's got to be desperate," Danni said.

"Is it just you tracking him, or do you have help?"

Danni looked at the ceiling, and then back at him. Her shoulders slumped. "Jason, there are some things I simply can't tell you. But let's say that I was sent to find out what he's doing and get the money back. I've been in Copenhagen two days, and tonight's the first time I've spotted him. I thought finding him on the Strøget was my best shot, at least for now, and I feel lucky that I saw him at all. But now that you've seen him, too, I was hoping you could help me out." She gave him a plaintive look.

"How much money, Danni?"

She shook her head. "Really—"

"A hundred thousand? A million?"

Danni sighed. "Somewhere in between. Actually, I'm not totally sure, and neither is..." Her voice drifted away. "But more than two-hundred-fifty thousand, maybe even three hundred."

"Beats my paycheck. What kind of business are you in?"

She didn't answer right away, but finally said, "Electronics."

"What's the company name?"

Danni shook her head.

"Can you say where it is?"

"The United States."

"That was helpful. Why were you chosen to go after him?"

"You know, you're really pushing. This is a very important company matter. If our competitors found out..."

"Okay, okay." But Jason was confused. Huff, or whatever his name was, had told him in the bar that he was from California, and now Danni was saying they were in the same company and that she was from Pittsburgh. Maybe this would make more sense after a good night's sleep. Anyway, she was probably some kind of security agent just doing her job, and it didn't matter in the long run because after tonight he was going to steer clear of this monkey business and stick to working out the havarti problem and then go home. Jason thought a second and said, "He told me he had a girlfriend here."

"A girlfriend?"

"He called her Gitte. Said he'd met her in San Francisco."

"I had no idea. And you believed him?"

"I don't know. She wasn't there in the flesh, so it could have been just a story. He was kind of bragging. Maybe he was only trying to impress me. But let me tell you, the way he talked about her, I wanted to meet her."

"Okay. What else?"

"He said he was unemployed."

"No argument there. What else?"

"He had heavy things on his mind." Jason raised his eyebrows, waiting to see how far he should take this.

"Well, if I had stolen three hundred grand, I'd have heavy things on my mind, too."

"Well, yeah. But I don't think that was it."

"Then what?"

"Better have another shot of that whiskey sour, Danni."

"That bad, huh?" But she followed his advice.

"Maybe. You can be the judge. Anyway, Hunt, or Huff, asked me if I'd ever killed anybody."

Danni gasped.

"I know what you mean," Jason said. "It struck me the same way. I don't know, I may be too tired to think about this tonight. I just flew in this afternoon, and I probably should be asleep right now, but I'm staying up to get on Danish time, so if I sound a little incoherent, let me know."

"You're doing fine. Did he say he had actually killed someone?"

"No, he didn't suggest that he had already done anything. But there was something weighing on his mind, something besides the girlfriend, I think. I wondered if it was just the booze talking, so you know I'm not convinced he could kill someone." Danni brightened a little hearing that, but Jason went on. "At the same time, I'm not convinced that he couldn't."

Danni turned away and shook her head. "I knew he had jumped off track, but I didn't know he'd gone that far."

#

Craig Huff paced around his hotel room, turned on the TV and found nothing to soothe him. He studied the time, walked around some more, washed his face, looked back at the TV, checked the time again and finally went downstairs to the bar.

It wasn't the Irish place, that was for sure. Not too big, somewhat dark, a few people there but fairly quiet. No Meat Dogs with big amps, not even background music. He ordered a Tuborg and a plate of smoked salmon with cheese and crackers. All this booze, he needed to eat. He'd had some other appetizer early on at the Irish place but somehow missed dinner. The beer came, and by the time the bottle was in his hands, twenty minutes had passed since he'd talked with Gitte. She was late.

Well, he half expected she would be. When the appetizer arrived, he worked on that. It helped occupy his mind, and the salmon tasted good, though he realized now it would have gone better with wine than beer. His mind went back to Gitte. Did she have trouble getting a cab? Or maybe she had stood him up. A wave of panic washed over him. He hadn't thought of that before. Surely she wouldn't drop him cold. He nursed the beer, but it didn't help. He began to sweat. He hadn't noticed until now, but everyone in the bar seemed so frivolous, so uncaring, just laughing and joking as if nothing mattered. Shut up, he wanted to shout. Here he was in a make-or-break situation, and they were content to party on. Idiots! They didn't have a clue.

He should call her. She had a cellphone—he had seen her use it—but he didn't have the number. She'd given him only her apartment phone, said the cellphone, or mobile as she called it, was company property and she had to be careful how she used it. Now that he'd given it some thought, the whole phone thing sounded wrong. She hadn't been straight with him. He wanted that number. He didn't want to call her apartment phone again and seem insecure if she hadn't left. That would be bad. And if she was already on her way, then calling the apartment was pointless. He brought the beer bottle to his mouth again and let the fizz play against his tongue. Couldn't seem like some low-life guzzler. He ate more of the salmon, the cheese. A little bite here, a little bite there. Had to stretch this out. Wait for Gitte.

After another fifteen minutes, he saw her come in, straight, long blonde hair bouncing. It cheered him up right away. He wanted to give her a big kiss. But when he got to his feet, there was a surprise. Another young woman was with her.

"Craig," Gitte said breathlessly. "I hope you don't mind, but Cabrina dropped by, and, well, we both decided to come over." She glanced at Cabrina and back to Huff and shrugged in an innocent schoolgirl way as if this were something that just happened and there was no helping anybody or anything.

Huff tilted his head. "Cabrina?" He had doubts about the story already. So Gitte had brought protection. Did that mean he was to be feared? He was no animal, she had no reason.

The women were already taking off their coats. "Sorry," Gitte said. "I'm so bad at introductions. Cabrina, this is my friend Craig Huff, from the U.S."

My friend. Huff felt that, a sharp twist in his chest.

"And, Craig, this is my friend Cabrina Jorgensen." She pronounced the last name with a *Y* sound.

Huff looked at Cabrina. She was probably two or three years younger than Gitte and a couple of inches taller at about five feet seven. Her figure could compete with the best, and her long cinnamon-colored hair was magically captivating. Not one strand was out of place, so she must have brushed it in the taxi. Her makeup was moderate but pristine, and her green sweater and short gray pleated skirt with black tights were sporty and sexy at the same time. So far this week, Huff had seen Gitte mostly in black pants, as she was tonight, with a blue sweater, so this was different. Gitte was pretty, but Cabrina was a knockout. Still, Huff wasn't pleased that Gitte had brought her. He knew one thing: Gitte wasn't going to make a fool of him.

Neither Huff nor Cabrina offered to shake hands, so they simply nodded at each other. Cabrina didn't seem exactly shy, but she wasn't forthcoming, either. Huff realized that Gitte might be the only one in the room who truly knew why Cabrina was there. He broke the ice. "Hello, Cabrina. Glad to meet you."

"Hello." She looked around. "I've never been in this hotel," she said in perfect English, apparently answering a question no one had asked. Huff and Gitte looked at each other, silently wondering what she meant, but they let it pass.

"Well, look," Gitte said, "can we sit? I did too much standing at that party." The bartender came by to take the orders, and the women both considered an appetizer like the one Huff was finishing but then decided they weren't that hungry and just went with glasses of white wine, some French Sauvignon Blanc he'd never heard of. But that was okay with Huff because at least they had ordered wine, and that meant they would be staying awhile.

The women sat across the table from him, Cabrina straight across. Huff didn't know how that had happened, but he didn't think it was right. Gitte didn't seem to care. Instead, she talked about the office party, and it was quickly established that Cabrina hadn't gone. She didn't work with Gitte, they were just friends. "I'm in food service," Cabrina said. Huff figured that was a euphemism for waitress.

The longer they sat, the more Huff realized he had been thrown into an odd and unexpected situation. He had invited over his girlfriend, the woman he'd flown half way around the world to see, and now that she was here, his attention kept being diverted by her friend Cabrina. She kept smiling at him in a strange, soft way, and she casually reached out and touched his hands or forearms three or four times to emphasize a point of conversation. Meanwhile, Gitte kept her hands tight around her wine glass and didn't gave a hint that she was aware of what Cabrina was doing. Of course, she couldn't see what was happening under the table. Cabrina's knees brushed Huff's twice, and Cabrina knew it and just smiled.

Well, it was hard to stay mad at Gitte. Putting everything together, Huff was sure none of it was accidental. Cabrina didn't seem like someone who flip-flopped around as if her arms and legs were only loosely attached. She exhibited poise and control. She knew where her body was and what she intended to do with it. So it was all calculated, but to what end?

As their glasses went dry, the evening took another turn. Gitte said, "Why don't we all go to your room, Craig? We can have some wine sent up and relax. These chairs are *sooo* hard."

Gitte threw him her famous squint, which melted him as predictably as ice on a hot stove.

"Wonderful," Cabrina chimed in.

Huff waved the bartender over, got a wine list and let the ladies choose. He thought Gitte would make the selection because it had been her suggestion, but then she said, "You decide, Cabrina. You're better at these things." Cabrina didn't hesitate, picking out a mid-range French Chardonnay. Huff was nonplussed at first, then realized it must have been her food service background at work.

After Huff had signed off the bill to his room, they took the small elevator three floors up. He held Gitte's hand while less than an arm's length away Cabrina faced him and gave him the craziest suggestive stare. Huff couldn't believe his good fortune to be in the company of two classy ladies, but he really liked Gitte and didn't understand why she was doing this. Was she really planning what he thought? Good things come in threes. Right. Small, medium, large. Tic-tac-toe. Blah, blah, blah. Craig, Gitte, Cabrina. Or maybe it was just three blind mice. He was jumping to conclusions and getting himself all twisted up. Better just relax.

As the elevator slowly rose, he wasn't sure how he felt about this. No matter how captivating Cabrina was, he wondered deep down if he wouldn't be betraying Gitte, even if she gave him that funny squint. Or was this the real Gitte he was only now getting to know? And how could he betray her if it was her idea?

Once they were in his room, time took its time when he wanted to move on, and it raced ahead when he wanted to slow down. A knock on the door brought the wine before he thought possible. The businesslike waiter opened the bottle and poured a taste for Huff, who nodded his approval. After the waiter had poured all the glasses and left, Gitte said, "We should toast."

"To what?" Huff thought of *love*, but maybe that was too much to hope for. He didn't want to ruin the mood.

"To adventure," Cabrina offered.

"I like that," Gitte said. "And to mystery. You can't have one without the other."

"How's that?" Huff asked.

"Well, if there were no mystery, you would know exactly what was going to happen," Gitte answered. "And if you knew what was going to happen, then everything would be predictable and there would be no adventure."

Cabrina got up and clicked glasses with Gitte. "Well said. To mystery and adventure."

They all said the Chardonnay was pleasant with just the right touch of oak. Gitte thanked Cabrina for ordering a good wine, and Cabrina thought nothing of it because she'd had it before. "I knew we couldn't go wrong." Huff actually thought the Chard wasn't bright enough or balanced enough to compete with Napa. And despite what he'd said, it wasn't even buttery enough. But he kept his opinions to himself. Nobody had come to his room to hear about French wines finishing second in *Bottle Shock.*

Gitte kicked off her shoes and sprawled on the bed. She told the others that she very much liked the idea of having her needs met by an obedient staff, but Huff said she would atrophy if she did nothing and Cabrina laughed. "The wine has already gone to your head. But good luck in finding someone to wait on you."

When Huff put his wine glass on an end table and started kissing Gitte, soft jazzy music floated over them. Without his even noticing her, Cabrina had gone over and turned on the TV to the menu channel. As they were getting in sync to the music, Cabrina then switched off the two lamps closest to the bed, leaving on only the one at the far side of the room. Huff appreciated the cozy new ambiance and wanted to draw Gitte out, so he asked her to dance. But she wouldn't let herself be pulled off the bed. "I don't want to move," she said. "If you want to dance, dance with Cabrina."

He went with the flow—and mystery and adventure. Cabrina removed her shoes and told Huff to take his off as well. Then she put her head on his shoulder and held him tight in a dreamy slow dance. Huff soon felt himself relaxing, intoxicated with Cabrina's perfume and the molding of her body against his. But unsure of his pleasure, he glanced back at Gitte. There was nothing to worry about, he saw. She was lounging catlike on the bed with a smile of deep satisfaction. As the second song blended into the first, Cabrina put her arms around his neck, and at the end of the dance she tiptoed up, kissed him squarely on the lips and spoke in the most sultry voice he'd ever heard. "Thank you, Craig."

Huff squeezed Cabrina in return and then separated himself and went back to sit down next to Gitte on the bed. "You should have warned me about your friend."

"She's something, huh."

"Dynamite."

"I thought you'd like her."

"Of course. But, Gitte, I like you."

Behind him, Cabrina held the bottle. "More Chardonnay?" She refilled everyone's glass without waiting for an answer.

Huff took a drink of wine then put down his glass, impatient to get Gitte involved. "You want to dance now?" he asked her.

"Not yet. Maybe later I'll just watch you and Cabrina again. But now..."

Gitte took off her sweater and bra, then pulled him down and made him feel wanted in a way that he hadn't felt since their days in California. His anxiety dropped away like heavy chains. He was so in love. Later, without knowing how much time had passed, he felt Cabrina at his side, brushing his arm at first, then sweeping upward and rubbing his shoulders before trailing gentle kisses across the back of his neck.

How the rest happened, Huff remembered in short sections like a movie that kept getting re-edited.

His mind was operating on two simultaneous but conflicting tracks. One part monitored the sensory impressions with his two partners, checking for overload, but moving cautiously ahead. Another part knew he was only an actor in Gitte's play. And now that he was in the midst of it, he couldn't believe the script. The stage directions revealed themselves little by little, but the motivation escaped him. If only he were stronger...

His physical strength was greater than theirs combined, but that wasn't the issue at all. In the face of this deep, magnetic attraction, he could no more resist than fly. He felt himself pulled between Gitte's arms and Cabrina's charms. He wanted to stop and sort things out, but the rapids of time and desire washed him on.

In a moment of clarity, he surfaced and resolved to give his affections only to Gitte. But when he burrowed his face into her softness, she told him there was a nice surprise if he turned around.

Cabrina was behind him but what difference did that make? He turned and his jaw dropped. She wasn't wearing a stitch.

Gitte said, "She wants you, Craig."

"Gitte, I, I..." Huff's head swiveled between a half naked beauty and a fully naked beauty.

"It's okay, Craig." Gitte smiled and kissed him. "Don't worry. Just enjoy yourself."

Bodies shuffled magically, and Huff didn't know how the change had happened. It shouldn't be happening, he thought, but Cabrina's force drew him in and he suddenly lost track of Gitte. His focus was on Cabrina, and he couldn't help himself. He would get back to Gitte later. The pleasure, and the anticipation, almost overwhelmed him.

When he finally turned, Gitte was fully dressed standing by the door with her coat. She did a slow wave and said, "Bye, guys. Have fun."

Huff wanted to stop her but was too confused. He lifted up part way to see Gitte's coat going out the door. Cabrina pulled him back down and spoke sternly. "When you have a naked lady in your bed, pay attention."

Afterward, while he lay there fighting off sleep, Cabrina finished getting dressed and then asked for taxi fare home. "Sure," he said. "Look in my wallet."

She found the wallet in his pants pocket and took out a hundred kroner. "Okay?" she asked, holding up the paper money.

"That's fine." That was only about twenty dollars. No problem. He looked at the ceiling, still recovering, though he figured that might take all night.

Cabrina turned away from him and put the wallet back and then came around and opened the desk drawer and took out a hotel pen and notepad. She wrote something and told him, "This is my home number. Call me tomorrow night about seven thirty or eight." She stepped over and kissed him one last time and was gone.

3

Even though the sun was sleeping in, Jason managed to roll out of bed around seven-thirty. He felt better than he had last night, but being in a different country was still a little unreal and he wouldn't have been totally surprised to learn he was on another planet. Or maybe Copenhagen was just some elaborate movie set to fool unwitting visitors.

When he heard the busy little sounds of knives and forks tapping on plates down in the courtyard, he realized he would have to hustle to meet Danni for breakfast at eight. But through sheer will power he showered, shaved and found clothes that weren't rumpled beyond his normal high standards. That meant that his shirt should cover his back, chest, and arms and that his pants should reach from his waist to his shoe tops. Danni had suggested that the first one ready knock on the other's door, so when Jason heard the little rap, he knew who it was. Being first in this case was not a point of pride. He opened the door.

"Good morning," Danni chirped. "Are we ready?"

"Awake," he said, "but readiness depends on the objective."

"Breakfast?"

"Then let's go before I fall asleep." He stepped out into the hallway and pulled the door shut. "Tell me they have coffee."

"The coffee is hot and strong. Rough night?" she asked as they walked down the hallway toward the stairs.

"Oh, was it night? That must be my problem. And here I thought this country had its clocks all backwards."

"You'll get used to it," Danni said.

"You're speaking from experience?"

"Not exactly, but that's what I'm told. At least it's getting better for me."

"Well, I'm an optimist," Jason said. "I figure that by the time I'm over jet leg it'll be time to fly home and do it again."

They went down the stairs, took a couple of turns, and walked into the courtyard, which doubled as the Kong Jacob's breakfast room. Floodlights illuminated the tables of white linen, but the skylight was turning brighter with a hint of sunrise. Several tables were already occupied, but Jason and Danni easily found an empty one and magically someone delivered a coffeepot and glasses of orange juice. "How did they know?" Jason asked.

"They just do. They're very efficient."

Jason sipped his coffee and was heartened to learn that its restorative powers were as strong on one continent as another. "Did I tell you I have this medical problem?"

Danni looked concerned. "No, you didn't mention it."

"Caffeine deficiency." He nodded solemnly. "If I don't take it orally at regular intervals, at least during the early hours of the day, then I have to fall back on injections."

"Oooh. Sounds painful."

"It can be. The problem now is not the supply, because this is very good coffee, the problem is that I'm confused about what constitutes the early hours of the day. Take some of these people here. Obviously, they got up and started their day before they were sure the sun would come up. I mean, they could have been wrong."

"It's faith. Pure faith."

"I'll have to work on that. Might build character."

They decided they were ready to eat now, so went to the buffet tables and helped themselves. There was plenty to choose from, and most of it looked good. Other than the cuts of nearly raw pickled herring, which Jason and Danni avoided, everything looked fairly American: bacon, eggs, croissants, oatmeal, milk, cheese, yogurt, pastries. And there was plenty of it.

Back at their table with full plates, they ate silently for a few minutes, and then Danni said, "There are a couple of things I forgot to ask you last night."

"Fire away. Just so you don't take me downtown for questioning."

"Why? Have you done something wrong?"

"Probably. I just haven't been told yet. Anyway, I want to make sure I get that one phone call. To Seattle."

"Very funny." She poked at her scrambled eggs. "Well, one thing I was wondering is if you know where Craig Huff is staying. It could be really important."

"No idea. Copenhagen, I presume. But I didn't ask, and he didn't tell me."

Danni put her fork down. "I should have asked you last night, but I guess I already knew the answer. Anyway, I was hoping."

"Sorry. It didn't occur to me it would be meaningful. We didn't talk about it, which seemed like a good idea at the time. I didn't bring it up because I didn't want to tell him where I was staying and I didn't especially care where he was staying. He didn't seem terribly stable."

Danni nodded and looked a little sad. Jason was worried that she was taking all this too personally. Must be her first big case, he thought. He would try to counsel her on the wisdom of keeping some distance from her work if he didn't think she would stonewall him again. No, he wasn't taking that road today.

Jason sipped coffee and then looked up at Danni. "You know, the way you're going about this ..."

"You don't like my style?"

Jason opened his eyes wide and studied his very attractive breakfast partner. He wasn't going to miss this softball. "Oh, I like your *style* a lot, Danni. It's just your *method* I was wondering about."

She rolled her eyes. "Such as."

"Such as why didn't you just stay there and watch Huff instead of following me? Heck, you could have gone into the Irish pub yourself and talked with him face to face."

She pursed her lips. "I have reasons. I was getting cold, and, well, I thought you'd be able to tell me something useful first, before I see him directly."

Jason nodded. "I see." What she said might have been true, but it didn't sound wholly plausible to him. He tried to tell himself he didn't care, that it wasn't his business. But still, he had questions. "Well, have you tried to contact him?"

"Oh, yes. For days, back in the U.S. and now here in Denmark." Danni sighed. "Cellphone, email, texts. I presume he's getting everything I try, but he doesn't respond to anything."

"Oh. So he seriously wants to be lost."

"I hadn't thought of it that way, but I suppose you're right."

Right and wrong, was that what the world was about? The big binary question? Jason cleared his throat. "There was one thing I did wrong last night," Jason said.

"Do I want to know?"

"Maybe not, but you should. I'm afraid I left you with the impression that I spend all my evening hours in bars. So I just wanted to say that I'm sorry about that because it's not true. Actually, when I'm home I usually spend my evenings quietly with a serious book. Or sometimes I watch a documentary on public TV or one of the science channels. It's all about improving the mind."

"Really," she said with some astonishment. "Well, first, I can't believe you told me that with a straight face. And second, I don't think you're a lush at all. But aside from all that, you were more valuable to me last night hanging out at bars than watching public TV. Besides, I was your willing accomplice on the second bar visit."

"I suppose you're right about that last point."

Danni said, "I had another question."

"I'm an open book."

"And a serious one at that."

"Touché."

Danni smiled. "Since we're setting the record straight, I wanted to say I'm a little embarrassed to admit I've been so focused on my own business in Denmark that I forgot to ask you what you're doing here. I didn't mean to be selfish."

Jason could see that she meant it. And it occurred to him now that a security agent probably should have found out something about him before talking about her work and her company's missing money. But he let it go and pushed his plate back and poured himself another cup of coffee. "Don't worry about it. Besides, you probably wouldn't be very interested in my business."

"Try me." She gave him a look of genuine interest, and a curious little smile at that. He decided he wouldn't mind spending more time with her, at least in Denmark. He didn't have any plans to visit Pittsburgh.

"Well, I'm in the food import business. I'm a food broker or account rep, whatever you want to call the job. And I guess I'm the troubleshooter as well. Anyway, we used to get a lot of cheese from Denmark, but now we don't. Havarti, actually, if that matters to you."

"Havarti. Oh, it's very good. I've had it."

"I noticed," Jason said. "You just ate some five minutes ago. So did I."

"What's the problem then? The Danes want higher prices?"

"Possibly, but it seems more like a supply issue. All I can say for sure is that it's very confusing and that my company isn't getting good answers."

"Your company?"

"Sunny Day Farms. You probably have ten things in your kitchen at home from Sunny Day Farms."

"More like twenty," she said. "I know that label by heart. Big golden sun, green fields, and trees. And the jingle." She sang softly: *Every day's a sunny day at Sunny Day Farms.*

"You're hired. Well, not really. But here, let me give you my card." He reached into his wallet and took one out. "By the way, I didn't get yours."

"Oh, sure." She reached for her purse, then pulled her hand back. "Sorry, Jason. You almost had me there. I told you last night that I can't say that much."

He shrugged. "Oh, well. One of these times."

A server came and cleared their plates. "What are you doing today?" Danni asked.

"Havarti hunting." He explained that he'd made arrangements to visit one of Denmark's largest cheese distributors. Because it was Saturday there wouldn't be many people at the office, but there would be somebody there to let him look at their facilities and possibly give him some insight about what to expect from his counterpart when he returned for the official visit Monday.

Jason really wanted to understand why havarti had become so scarce. "American grocery chains want a steady supply, or they'll just move on to a different distributor," he told Danni. He also hoped to find some other specialty products he could import.

"And you couldn't do this from Seattle?"

"We tried. Phone calls used to work, but after a while they became pointless. You think you're communicating, getting your message across, but later you find out that while you were speaking English, they were speaking Danglish. There's a big difference."

"What about email?"

"Well, that should be better, shouldn't it? Put everything down in black and white, and then they'd have time to get clear on the meaning. Don't get me wrong. I think it's wonderful that they know English, because my Danish is just about zero, but putting all this into practice in an important business situation sometimes isn't something you can count on." Jason pulled a sheet of folded paper from his pocket. "Here's an email they sent me about my ride this morning."

Danni looked at the paper:

Morning, Will see you 9:3 front hotel. Our company have a blu Ford. It will freesingcold bring hevvysweater.

Danni gave him back the paper. "Well, it's rough, but I get the idea."

He refolded the paper and put it back into his pocket. "Sure, because that's a good one. Sometimes I wonder if the missing letters and words are at the bottom of the Atlantic with the communications cables, or in the stratosphere between ground stations and satellites. On the other hand, they probably think my emails have too many letters and words. We're just not connecting. I wish I could be happier about this, but if the notes and phone calls actually worked, then I could do all this from my office at home."

"So you're going to go out there today and get things straightened out."

"I'm going to start. It probably won't happen in one day."

Jason frowned, and Danni picked up on his discontent. "I don't mean to pry, but it sounds as if you have a lot riding on this havarti deal."

"Financially, yes. Some of my paycheck comes from commissions, and even though the havarti deal isn't a huge percentage in the overall picture, it's still an important one for the numbers. And for my situation in general. I'm fairly new to the company, and this is shaping up to be a test of what I can actually do."

"The pressure is on."

"Oh, yeah. I don't know the odds, but they could throw me out next week if this trip doesn't turn out well."

"But it will," Danni said. "I have a feeling you'll figure out the problem and make the deal."

Jason smiled at that. "Welcome to my support group. On the positive side of the ledger, I can actually earn a nice bonus by making this Danish deal come through. I'd really like to get that bonus."

"So it's a big job, with risks and rewards, but something tells me it's not all about the finances. You're also doing this because you like the challenge."

Jason wondered if Danni was reading him better than he read himself. "I suppose there's something to that. It's a puzzle that needs to be solved." He looked at his watch, thinking it was time to change the subject. He had a half hour before his ride came. And he was grateful that had been arranged ahead of time, because the last thing he wanted to do this morning was take a taxi. The harrowing ride from the airport was still fresh in his mind. He finished his coffee and opened his eyes wide. "Awake at last."

"Good. Wouldn't want you to fall into a vat of havarti."

He laughed. "That would impress them. What about you? What are you doing today?"

"I thought about doing a little shopping. So I'm going over to Magasin."

"I've heard of it," he said. "Big department store. Looking for something special?"

"No. I just wanted to see what was there. A trip to Europe wouldn't be complete without a few minutes in the local department store."

"Well, that's a matter of opinion." And he thought it might be more than a few minutes. "But what about the mysterious Mr. Huff? Won't you be tracking him?"

"When I see him. But I doubt he'll be hanging around the Irish pub again."

"You don't know. He might be having breakfast there right now."

She grinned. "You're a little crazy, but I like your sense of humor."

"Thanks. Anything to help. Seriously, I know your company's business is not my concern, and I only met you last night, but I am a little worried about your safety. Do you have a gun or anything?"

Danni looked down and played with her empty coffee cup. "Well, I appreciate your concern. No, I don't have a gun. Do you really think I could have got a gun past TSA? Even if I were a cop, I doubt that I could have brought a gun into Denmark. Anyway, my mission isn't supposed to be about threats and violence. I know Huff could be dangerous, especially after what you told me last night, but now that I've got a better idea of what I'm dealing with, I think I'll be able to stay out of harm's way."

"All right, I guess you know what you're doing." He pushed back from the table and stood up. "I need to go back to my room for a minute and get my attaché case before the blue Ford arrives. Important cheese papers."

"Oh, sure. Don't let me keep you."

"Danni, I was, uh, wondering about tonight." He looked her in the eye. He had her attention. "Would you like to have dinner together? With me? If you're not too busy."

"Are you asking me for a date?"

Jason didn't expect the question, or at least the way she asked it. He thought he had something to offer: Six feet tall, decent build, trimmed brown hair, brown eyes, no disfiguring facial scars. Maybe he was wrong. "I'm sorry. Are you married? I didn't see a ring."

"I'm not married," Danni said. "Or attached. I just wanted to know if you were merely whiling away the hours in faraway Copenhagen or if you were actually thinking of this as a date."

Well, she had him there. Best be honest. "Well, yes. A date, yes, I was thinking of a date. You know, boy meets girl and all that. I'll pick up the check."

"Then I accept." There was a twinkle in her eye. "I've never had a Saturday night date in Copenhagen."

"Good. I'll stop by about six-thirty."

#

Danni went to her room, took out her smartphone and called the United States.

"It's Danni," she said.

"You're calling so late," the man said.

"I guess so. I'm sorry. I'm already forgetting what time it is there. I should have called earlier, but I found out something, and then this morning I wanted to make sure I was on the right track. You said you'd be up late."

"I did, yes. All right, what do you have, Danni?"

"I saw Craig. Briefly."

"You talked to him?"

"No, I didn't get that close."

"But you know where he is."

"He's in Copenhagen. I know he's staying downtown somewhere. I plan to find out where today."

"You're keeping your distance. Is that going to get the job done?"

"I had a hard choice last night. I decided to follow the man he was drinking with to see if I could pick up any information first."

"Yes?"

"The other guy turned out to be an American. From Seattle.

His name is Jason Stallings."

"And?"

"Jason, the Seattle guy, said Craig was talking crazy. He seems emotionally disturbed."

"We're all disturbed, Danni. The books are a mess and our backs are against the wall." His voice rose. "We had to skip an inventory order, for God's sake." The man paused now, gathering himself. "This crime he committed, he's lucky he's not in jail now. He might be yet."

"I know. It's just that he's apparently contemplating another crime, a violent one."

"I didn't know he was violent."

"Neither did I, but that's what he told Jason."

"And you believe this Jason?"

"I didn't want to. But I saw him again this morning at breakfast—he's staying at my hotel. He seems trustworthy. Much more than Craig right now."

"This violent crime. Who? What?"

"I don't know who the target might be. I wonder if he knows himself."

"Find him, Danni. Bring him back. Bring the money back."

"I'm trying, but...I don't know." Her voice tailed off.

"You're afraid."

"Yes, a little. After what I heard last night. I wasn't expecting that."

"Are you going to be safe? Do you need help?"

"I'm safe. And Jason will help if I need him."

"You shouldn't count too much on an outsider, but I'll trust your judgment. You've never let me down. Take care, Danni."

"I will. Bye."

"Thanks for calling. Good night."

#

The blue Ford was smaller than Jason had imagined. The seat forced his knees into a position they hadn't been in since birth, but the car delivered him to Bjorneby Foods and that was the important thing. The driver didn't know much of anything useful about the cheese business. He only wanted to talk about American TV shows and politics. Jason didn't watch much TV other than what he'd told Danni, and though he voted on a regular basis, he didn't care to discuss politics, especially in a foreign country, even if Denmark was an ally. You never knew when you'd step on a landmine.

A young man named Per was expecting him and met him at the warehouse and showed him around. Per mentioned that he had been asked by Poul Stubkjaer to show him a little of the operation and answer questions if he could. Stubkjaer was the Bjorneby specialist in export sales whom Jason was scheduled to meet Monday.

Jason was impressed by how many food products Bjorneby handled, and he began to develop some ideas on importing other items besides the noble havarti. He wouldn't say anything now to Per. Until he could get some details on prices and quantities, he would keep the ideas to himself.

But everywhere there was the smell of cheese, not only havarti but also a kind of blue cheese, a cheddar, and he didn't know what else. Being sensitive to the smells certainly didn't help here. He felt a twinge of nausea and was on the borderline of being sick. His head was also swimming from the sounds. Machinery clanged, packaging cookie tins and jelly jars, conveyor belts whirred, gadgets snapped and clapped. And then the languages of the workers were like a discordant symphony. He heard Danish, of course—he could already pick it out—but he wasn't expecting to hear the others: German, Russian and a couple more he couldn't identify. Jason thought about yesterday's taxi driver and decided it would be okay if he never saw or heard a Russian again.

Per didn't seem to have his heart in the tour, and though Jason was a little queasy, he pressed on. Where was the havarti?

"There's not much to see, Mr. Stallings." Per was clearly reluctant to show him anything.

"Don't worry." Jason was prepared for either a room stacked high with havarti that was unavailable to him or an empty room with no havarti. Zero times any number was still zero.

Per went down a hallway and slid open a tall door. It was a

large room, and Jason didn't hit either of his guesses. But the room was closer to empty. Much closer. Only a few pallets stood for inspection.

"That's all there is?" Jason asked.

"At the moment, yes, Mr. Stallings. It comes and it goes."

"Then you do have havarti sometimes, Per. Do you have lots of it?"

"Oh, not for long. It moves very fast."

It sounded as if Per didn't know much about the havarti issue, but Jason was determined to learn something useful. Finally, he was in Denmark looking at a few dozen loaves of the cheese at the end of the rainbow and he had to know what was happening.

"Where does the havarti go?"

"To India." Per nodded with satisfaction as if the explanation put everything in its place.

And maybe it did, Jason thought. "To India? The big country in Asia?"

"That's right. I'm sorry. This is new information to you?"

"Very new." Jason circled the precious pallets of cheese, counting them: seven. He couldn't help dwelling on their small number. And he couldn't help thinking about the substantial needs of Sunny Day Farms and how they were so at odds with the enormous population of India. "India," Jason repeated. He turned to Per. "Are you sure? India?"

"Oh, yes, very sure." Per's voice rose with an irritating enthusiasm. "It's just supply and demand, you know."

"And you are telling me that right now there is a great demand in India for Danish havarti," Jason said, seeing the coffin nailed shut on his business trip.

Per eyes lit up as he nodded. "It's very exciting."

"Not for me," Jason said with studied composure. But he really wanted to throttle Per. No one should be that pleased with another's misfortune. This wasn't just everyday schadenfreude that could be dissected and dismissed. And it certainly wasn't good sportsmanship. If it was anything besides utter nonsense, it was sadistic. Jason tried to pull himself together and reason with this unreasonable challenge. "You see, Per, with all this havarti going to India, almost nothing is coming to my company in the United States."

"Perfect." Per was simply beaming.

Meanwhile, Jason was boiling. "Excuse me, how can that be perfect?" He paused to bring his suddenly rising voice back under control. There was already one idiot in the room, and Jason knew he didn't need to stoop to that level. "My company has a contract," he said calmly.

"I don't know about contracts, Mr. Stallings. Contracts are usually broken, aren't they? They're like treaties. They last for a while, and then, boom, there's war. Anyway, I'm studying economics." He pronounced it *e-CON-o-mix.* "This is classic supply and demand. That why I say perfect. I couldn't find a better example. India demands the havarti, and there goes the supply."

"Couldn't have said it better myself." Jason tried to keep a civil tongue. "But I think we're still missing the point about the American demand, which is high, and the supply, which is infinitesimally low."

"Yes, I understand," Per agreed. "And sometimes the supply in Denmark is also not so good." Then he brightened. "But when demand from India declines, there will be a better supply for America and Denmark. You see how simple this is?"

"But, Per, when do you expect demand from India to decline? The country has so many people. It's huge." Jason made a quick mental calculation. "Denmark has about five million people, right? India is like two hundred Denmarks."

Per walked up to the pallets and put a hand on a loaf of havarti, admiring it. He turned back to Jason, his hand still on the cheese. "Bjorneby Foods is a large company. It doesn't tell me about forecasts. I only know what comes and goes day by day. When I graduate, then I can work on economic forecasts."

Jason could hardly wait. Was it possible that a university would honor such claptrap with a degree? Sadly, he already knew the answer. But now he wondered if there wasn't a flaw in this Mumbai bombshell. "I wasn't aware that Indians had much of a taste for cheese. Don't they prefer to make yogurt and butter with their milk?"

"Yogurt? We have yogurt here at Bjorneby," Per said. "Would you like to see the supplies. They're much more impressive than the havarti."

"I'm talking about what the Indians want," Jason said tersely.

"Well, I don't think they want yogurt," Per assured him. "To my knowledge, India hasn't ordered any yogurt from us. Besides, I wouldn't expect it to ship well in large quantities. Cheese travels much better."

Jason blinked. Where was this heading? He stepped closer to Per. "But back to my point. India traditionally hasn't had much interest in Western cheese. The people there make yogurt and butter with their milk."

Per's eyes opened wide. "With *their* milk, yes, yes, I agree. And that is why they want havarti from *Danish* milk. See, they have no milk left to make cheese. Wouldn't that be the case? And why import milk, which doesn't keep long, even with careful refrigeration? You see, it is better to make the cheese where the milk is, here in Denmark."

"Makes perfect sense." Jason could see a strange upside down logic in almost everything Per offered up. But he saw no truth in it. Besides, he was no longer clear whether Per was parroting the company line or simply improvising. But what did it matter? One possibility was as pointless and preposterous as the other.

"Thank you," Per said proudly. "Yes, it's all economics. So the Indians who wanted havarti decided to just buy the havarti where it's made. Besides, they probably thought, if they made it themselves they would have to start from the beginning because they don't have the recipe."

"Surely it's on the Internet." You could find a bomb recipe online. Why not cheese?

Per shook his head. "Cheap imitations."

"So the Indians had to have Danish havarti, the authentic stuff. I was wondering why they couldn't have taken an interest in Swiss, or Gouda. That way would have been so much better."

"No, no. It would not have been better. Denmark does not make Gouda. Then the Indians would have taken their business to Holland."

"Exactly what I meant."

"Ah, I see now you are joking. When I watch TV shows and movies from the U.S., I try to understand American humor, but sometimes it slips by me. Yes, havarti is special to us," Per said, his chest filling with pride. "As you know, true havarti must come from Denmark. It was invented here, and no one can take that away from us."

Jason agreed. True havarti. That's what Sunny Day Farms was after. And that was because so many consumers wanted the real Danish stuff, not something from some Johnny-come-lately who had back-engineered the recipe, or read it online, and could turn out havarti at half the price. Jason eyed the seven lonely pallets of havarti again. He was glad the loaves were wrapped in plastic. That was easier on his nose.

The irony of his quest was that his disturbed sense of smell transformed the aroma of the delectable havarti into something like a failed chemistry experiment. As he had quietly done that morning at breakfast with Danni, he ate the cheese only if he didn't let himself smell it closely.

"Is there anything else you would like to see?" Per asked.

"No, I think that will be all for today. I'm getting the picture." It was a foreboding picture with dark, menacing clouds, and Jason had a choice of standing defenseless in an open field and being drenched or taking cover under a lone tree and getting struck by lightning. There was nothing like a choice.

"Could I ask a favor, then?" Per looked so optimistic.

Jason nodded, still hearing the crack of the lightning bolt. He could almost smell it, too. The meaning of resignation became abundantly clear, and now his irritation with his appointed host morphed gently into kindness. Per was such an innocent in this harsh convolution of international trade. "Certainly. What would you like?"

"When you see Mr. Stubkjaer on Monday, could you put in a

good word for me? I'm trying to be helpful, but he's very busy, and I think sometimes he doesn't notice."

"I'll do that, Per. You've told me a lot."

As Jason headed out to the blue Ford that would return him to his hotel, he figured that if Sunny Day Farms called a breach of contract against Bjorneby Foods, his company would get no havarti at all. There were smaller suppliers of Danish havarti, but they were hardly worth the bother. Bjorneby had the lion's share of the market, and now India's intervention looked like a juggernaut. All the cows grazing across that big country apparently were unable to provide milk for cheese to satisfy the people. So daunting was the task that not even the sacred cows were up to it. The Indians wanted their cheese from Denmark. How could he, just one person from Seattle, compete against all of India when the teeming masses were starved for Danish havarti?

· 4 ·

The morning after, Huff was torn. How could the night have gone the direction it did? He sat in his room, the scene of his own participation in the erotic strangeness. There was no escaping the memories here. Now it was almost noon, and he'd hardly done a thing today except have a little breakfast down in the hotel coffee shop, and that more from habit than hunger.

He got up and lit a cigarette, inhaled, exhaled. The rush of nicotine calmed him a little. Calmness was good, he thought. Stay calm, stay on course. He wouldn't be seeing Square Jaw today, and though their business was incomplete, Huff didn't mind a quiet day on that front. There was too much else going on.

His mind returned to the night before. Part of him enjoyed the memories intensely. Cabrina was undeniably fantastic. He'd never met a woman with such a sensual appetite. In a way he got what he wanted, but who was in control? Cabrina certainly got what she wanted. Her command of the situation was so great that she almost had him thinking he was in charge. Of course, maybe it was neither of them. Gitte had dreamed up everything, hadn't she? But he would forgive her. No, he forgave her already. It was a moment of weakness on her part to let things get carried away. Still, he thought he loved her. He'd come all this way for her, not her wild friend, who had apparently lifted some extra cash from his wallet while seeking cab fare.

At twelve Huff went to the phone and called Gitte. There was no answer. He left a message and would try again in an hour.

At one he called, but there was no answer. He went out and had some lunch and called again at two. There was no answer.

He waited until three, then took a taxi over to her apartment. He rang the buzzer, but no one answered. He walked around, smoked, then caught another taxi back to the Commodore.

His sinuses were complaining again, so he washed them down with the saline spray. He'd gone to a doctor about his sinuses back in California, but was just told to cut back on his smoking. Another idiot, Huff thought, an idiot with three college degrees, a second home in Maui and no understanding about anything that really mattered.

At five he visualized Gitte answering the phone and rushed to punch in her number before the picture faded.

And he tried again at six. Where was she?

He called once more at seven, then seven-thirty.

A minute later, he gave up.

#

Danni sat across the table from Jason in the upper-floor dining room of a restaurant in the Nyhavn district, the quaint subject of postcards over the years. Jason realized that he'd seen the postcard pictures here and there without quite being sure what he was looking at. So at last here he was at the real thing. It was night now, but in the daylight photographers captured the image of colorful, narrow eighteenth-century buildings with sailboats snuggled in the canal in front. Although the pictures were understandable and even attractive, Jason was a little amused.

"You know," he told Danni, "the other parts of Copenhagen I've seen aren't nearly as bright and colorful as Nyhavn."

"Jason, you can't just throw red, blue, green and yellow paint on those other old landmarks."

"I know, but if the colors of Nyhavn are so valued, why didn't they show up elsewhere in the city?"

"I have no idea. Maybe this is all Copenhagen needs. Just a spot of color. Too much would be garish to the people here."

"Could be. I like the theory. So they've agreed that Nyhavn can be splashy, but don't anybody else get any ideas."

He heard the clump-clump of footsteps on the wooden stairs and turned and saw their entrees being carried up by the sturdy hands and legs of a fit and cheerful waitress.

After their food was in front of them, Jason said, "She must go up and down those stairs twenty-five times a night."

"It's her job," Danni said. "Obviously, you were never a waitress."

"Never. But you have a point. She gets paid to exercise and stay in shape. If that saved her a trip to the gym, she essentially would be getting extra pay because she wouldn't have to spend anything at the gym."

"You're thinking too much, Jason. We have some good looking food here. Why don't we try it?"

"I was getting to that."

#

At seven-forty Huff called Cabrina, but just as before with Gitte, there was no answer. Since she'd asked him to phone, he left a message. He had a feeling she was testing him, maybe was even sitting at home listening to his message, studying his tone of voice. Whatever. He didn't care. Get on with it. He didn't want to spend Saturday night alone. Back in California, there would be plenty to do. Here he was adrift. But where was Gitte? Was there some emergency? He worried about her.

At eight, Huff called Cabrina again.

"*Ja.*" Yes.

"Cabrina, it's Craig Huff."

"Oh, I just got in and listened to your message. I was hoping you would call back."

That gave him a charge. "Did you want to get together tonight?"

"Yes. Very much."

"Should I come to your place?"

"No, I have something better in mind. I want you to meet me at this dance club." She gave directions. "Be there at nine thirty and wait outside if you get there first."

Well, that was only a short time away. But he had questions. "What about Gitte? Is she coming? I don't know where she is. I've been calling all day."

Cabrina laughed. "Don't worry so much. See you soon."

\#

When Danni and Jason were well into their dinner and their hunger had ebbed, Jason said, "I was thinking about our waitress."

"Oh, is she your type?"

"I don't know. I've never had a whiskey sour with her."

"So that's your test?" She let a little smile creep out.

"It's optional, but it can be instructive."

"Really. So what did you learn last night—on your whiskey sour test?"

"Can't say. I would be giving away trade secrets if I did."

"Come on, that's not fair."

"All right, all right. Well, this is going to sound as if I'm stepping around the question, but I learned that there's still much to know."

"What are you, the Oracle of Copenhagen? Or was that supposed to make sense?"

"No to the first question, and yes to the second. I learned that there's a great deal you didn't tell me last night."

"We've been over that ground, Jason. You know I can't."

"Yes, I've heard that, but I don't necessarily agree. Who knows, I might even be useful to your mission."

Danni wasn't buying it. "But you said he—Huff—was unstable and you wanted to steer clear of him."

"Did I say that? Well, I've reconsidered. I'm now offering to help."

"You don't think I'm up to the job. That's it. You think a woman can't handle this," Danni said evenly. "Is there some reason I shouldn't be offended?"

"Only that it's not true," Jason said. "Anyway, I do have the advantage of having spoken with Mr. Huff in Copenhagen, which puts me one up."

"How do you know I didn't talk with him this afternoon?"

"Oh, did you? That would be a breakthrough."

Danni said nothing.

Jason nodded, trying not to be too glad he was right. "I see. So other than a little shopping, it was a fruitless day."

"I wouldn't put it that way. I saw some of the city, got to know my way around. And I'm having a pleasant dinner—I think."

"Okay, I'm dropping the subject, but my offer holds."

Danni smiled at that. "I'll let you know. You didn't tell me much about your search for the wild havarti. Was it fruitful or fruitless?"

"Well, fruit and cheese do go together, but if I can mix metaphors, or whatever I'm doing, I'd have to say the fruit was not too plentiful and hard to reach." At Danni's urging, Jason filled her in on his visit to Bjorneby Foods. "So you see, I'm up against all of India. At least until something else presents itself. Great odds, huh?"

Danni shrugged. "Only a billion to one. But you'll figure out something and get the deal. I'm beginning to know you. You're a smart guy. One minute you're backed into a corner, and the next you'll be Mr. Smarty Havarti."

"You have a lot of confidence. Myself, I plan to have something else. Like a Remy Martin and a piece of chocolate fluff. Care to join me?"

"Chocolate? Never touch it. Except on Saturday night."

Jason ordered cognac and dessert for both of them. While they were waiting, he realized he was beginning to like Danni more than a little. He had the idea that the feelings might be mutual, but he'd been wrong on such matters before.

A few minutes later while they were enjoying the drinks and dessert, Danni gave him an answer of sorts. "I know we're on a date, Jason, but I feel it's fair to tell you something important."

Oh, oh, here it comes. Jason tried to look attentive.

"I'm gay."

"What?"

"Gay. Lesbian."

"I heard you. I'm just in shock. But go on."

"Well, I was afraid you might be getting ideas, and I probably gave you ideas, agreeing to go on a date and all."

"You do this often? Go on dates with men?"

"Oh, frequently. It's a good way to meet their sisters."

"Of course. Why didn't I think of that? But I didn't bring my sister to Denmark."

"I was afraid of that. Do you have a sister?"

"Well, no."

Now what was he going to do? Sweep her off her feet, rush back to the hotel and seduce her? Fat chance. He looked at her again and thought he saw the truth trying to wiggle out. Then it came to him. She was putting him on. Or pushing him away. Well, he would let the subject drop for now. Sooner or later, it would hit bottom and he would know what was genuine.

It was about a quarter till nine when they left the restaurant. The cognac had put Jason in a mellow mood, but now with Danni's apparent news, there didn't seem to be much chance of sharing that mood. Oh, well. He'd known her for only twenty-four hours. Before that, he had no idea about the possibilities, or disappointments.

They had to walk back up the street a little to catch a taxi to the Kong Jacob. The distance to the hotel wasn't impossible on foot, but they'd both walked a lot during the day, and neither one was up to another long hike in the cold.

A little way up from the restaurant, Jason grabbed Danni's arm. "Stop. There he is."

"Who? Where am I looking?"

"Craig Huff. On the front steps of that blue building. I think it's a hotel. This guy is smoking. Does Huff smoke? Sure, he was smoking at the Irish pub last night."

"It's him, it's him!" Danni said quickly. "Yes, he smokes. Oh my God, it's him!"

Huff looked down the street, to where they would go to find a taxi. Then he pivoted their way. Danni turned toward Jason and moved close to hide her face. Jason looked away, but kept Huff in his peripheral vision.

"What's he doing?" Danni asked.

"Smoking. He doesn't even have a coat on. Must be going back in soon. Wait, he's finishing. He's putting the cigarette butt in some kind of ash can. He's turning, looking all around. He's moving, no, he's stopped. Now he's moving again. He going inside. He's gone."

"Keep watching a little. He might come back out."

Jason put an arm around her shoulders and moved a little closer as he held her. She didn't seem to mind. A wave of her perfume swept over him, a dusty citrus fragrance. "Are you afraid?" he asked.

"Of course not."

"Then why don't you just go talk to him?"

"Not now. The time isn't right."

Jason thought he'd heard that line before. "There's nothing going on. People are just walking by. He's not coming out. I see the sign now. It's the Commodore Hotel."

"The Commodore Hotel? Wow, we found him. And it was so easy. I don't believe it." She hugged Jason and gave him a peck on the cheek.

Jason caught her before she could move away. He took in her perfume and held her briefly until she relaxed, then turned her head toward him and kissed her on the lips. She didn't resist. In fact, she pressed back for a few seconds before pulling away. The kiss was better than he had imagined, though not as long as he had hoped. Still, the kiss had taken him, and maybe her, to a dreamy place he'd like to visit again, which was amazing considering that the situation had looked so bleak ten minutes earlier. Notwithstanding his offer to help Danni, he had little interest in Huff, but he did now see hope for Danni.

"Thanks so much," she said. "Wow, that was unbelievable the way you spotted him. And you just stood there like Mr. Cool, taking it all in."

So she was willing to talk about Huff, but not the kiss. "I didn't know what else to do," Jason said.

They walked past the Commodore, peering in, trying to learn its secrets from a safe distance, but nothing more yielded itself. Then they walked on to the end of the street and found a taxi. The driver was a young Danish guy in a black leather jacket and had them back at the Kong Jacob in a little more than five minutes. When they were on their floor, Jason said, "Come in for a nightcap? I haven't tried the mini-bar yet."

"I don't know. My head is already kind of funny, I think. It's been a big night."

"My thoughts exactly. After all the excitement you need to kick back a little."

"All right. But just for a little while."

They went into Jason's room and threw their coats on the bed. Danni thought she liked her room better. It was more rectangular, she told him, and it looked out on a plaza across the street.

"I'd like to see it sometime," Jason said. Danni didn't reply. He peered into the mini-bar and found two Courvoisiers and then went into the bathroom and picked up two ordinary glasses.

He poured and said, "My apologies for the snifters. The hotel seems to have hidden the good ones." He handed her a glass.

She took it and sat down in an armchair, the room's only chair. "This is wicked stuff, you know."

He remained standing. "Could be. But I'll make up for it tomorrow. Won't touch a drop."

"That's not what I meant." She rubbed the glass, then took a sip. "The cognac at the restaurant made me a little silly, and now you're trying to make me be that way again."

"Be what again?" He took a sip of the Courvoisier and waited for an answer.

"Hug you. Kiss you. That stuff."

"That stuff? I didn't mind. Really, I enjoyed it."

"I'm sure you did. That's what men do."

"Oh, we're back to that." He went to the bed and sat down.

"I wasn't myself, I was somebody else back there," she insisted. "I wasn't grounded."

"You were excited to see Huff. So you did what came naturally."

"You probably don't believe me. You don't believe I'm gay."

Slowly, he said, "No, I don't believe that."

"Would it matter?"

The answer he was going to give seemed as if it would be important. He thought about it. "I would still like you, Danni, but, yes, it would matter."

She got up from the chair and paced around. "You see, it's complicated."

"Now that I believe."

"It's worse than that. Sometimes I'm actually attracted to men."

"How does that feel? I mean, does it bother you?"

"Not the being attracted part. Being with the man is okay if that's what I want to do at the time. What bothers me is that when I think about it, I get really confused."

"That's two of us. Have some more cognac." She did, and he did.

Jason got off the bed and put his glass on the dresser. He took Danni's glass and put it down next to his. He stepped over and took her into his arms.

She let him and said, "You're trying to seduce me. Ply me with cognac and then—"

He kissed her. She kissed back. The give and take went on about twenty seconds. He luxuriated in Danni's soft lips and dusty citrus fragrance until she pulled back and said, "There's one thing more dangerous than cognac."

"What's that? Two cognacs?"

"No, it's you. You're dangerous."

"Me? I'm the good guy."

"That's what I meant." She broke from his embrace and went to the bed to pick up her coat. "Well, gotta scoot."

"So soon? It's barely past nine o'clock."

"Really? It seems later. I'm very tired." She yawned, almost convincingly.

"How about tomorrow?"

"Well, there's breakfast. Knock when you're ready."

"Sure, but after that..."

"After that, we'll just have to see." She smiled for a second, playing with him.

The door shut, leaving the dangerous man alone in his room. He stared at the two glasses of cognac, but had lost his taste. He eyed the serious book on his nightstand, then turned away.

Maybe there was a good movie on TV. He could use a big dose of that American humor he'd heard about earlier in the day from Per. And he could take it straight because he didn't even need subtitles.

#

Huff put out the cigarette and went back inside. It was frigid out there. He could have smoked in the bar, but he was always going outside to smoke in California because that seemed to be what society and the law demanded. He was just keeping himself busy until it was time to go to the nightclub and meet Cabrina.

He went up to his room for a few minutes and then grabbed his coat to go to the club. When he stepped back outside and began walking, the street was almost clear. And that was good, because he wasn't happy about what he'd seen earlier. First, it was that Jason guy from Seattle that he'd met at the Irish place. How the Seattle guy had figured out his location at the Commodore, Huff wasn't sure. But he didn't like it one bit. Just showed you couldn't trust anyone. Now he saw that he'd been a fool to even strike up a conversation with Jason.

But more than that, it appeared his diverting the company money had brought another visitor to Denmark. He saw the blondish hair but hadn't been able to get a really good look, so he wasn't absolutely sure. But thinking about it now, as he walked toward the club, it shouldn't have been a surprise. His old landlord had probably talked, telling somebody where he was going. So they wanted their money back. So what. He wasn't giving it back.

Huff arrived at the club a little before nine thirty. Cabrina wasn't there yet, so even though he wanted to go in and warm up, he waited outside as she'd told him. If he went in, she might not find him.

Besides, he needed a minute to get himself in the right frame of mind so he could handle her energy. It would be nice to call the shots tonight, not be somebody's pawn. He was tired of being pushed around, even by people who thought they were doing him a favor. Didn't they know he was a new man now? He'd made the big break, and now it was time to live it up, extend himself. God knew he couldn't go back.

Copenhagen was in some ways so strange to him, but the nice thing about the city was that nobody paid attention to him. People here didn't set some grand standard he had to live up to. If he was fairly quiet and didn't cause trouble, they left him alone.

He was about ready to hike around the block to generate some body heat when Cabrina strolled up. Well, there was a surprise. Again she wasn't alone. But this time her companion wasn't Gitte. Instead, Cabrina had an odd dark-haired girl in tow. She was waif-like, thin and fairly short, and looked a year or two younger than Cabrina. And she looked lost.

Huff straightened up. "Why didn't you come alone? Who's this?"

"This is Lene." Cabrina turned to the girl. "Lene, this is Craig. He's American, here on holiday."

He wasn't going to correct her on that. "Well, why don't we go in?" They went in, and Huff paid the cover charge, a little annoyed that he was paying for a third person he'd barely met. But he soon forgot that. The band was playing a catchy dance tune, and the throbbing beat gave him energy. If this was Copenhagen nightlife, he could get used to it really fast.

They found a table, and Cabrina took off her coat and sat down. Lene just sat down. Cabrina looked at her a few seconds and said something to her in Danish. Then Lene took off her coat. She looked at Huff shyly.

Cabrina turned to Huff now. "Lene's English isn't too strong yet. But she's learning Danish very well."

"Learning?" Huff glanced at Lene, who seemed more sweet than shy now. "Where's she from?"

"Estonia. She's only been in Denmark a year."

Huff nodded, still off balance from Cabrina's surprise. "I'm forgetting my manners. Would you and Lene like a drink?"

"Naturally. White wine, I think." She asked Lene, "Wine?"

"Ja, ja."

Huff took care of the orders, adding a wine for himself, then looked back at Cabrina and Lene. He felt like calling them *the girls*. They were markedly younger than he was, especially Lene. They were of legal age, of course, but in comparison Gitte seemed mature.

"What's going on here?" Huff asked Cabrina. "Why did you bring her?" Huff didn't care whether Lene understood or not.

"I thought we might use the company. Don't you like company?" Cabrina put a suggestive twist on the word that was new to Huff. But the meaning was clear enough.

For now, he ignored it. The wine came and they toasted. "To mystery and adventure," Cabrina said.

Huff once again felt himself losing direction. Cabrina seemed to have an agenda, and he was just part of it. She was as beautiful as the night before, but he had to put that aside for a moment and show some independence. He had to be firm. "I would like to have seen Gitte," he said. "I called her all day but got no answer. I even went over to her place, but she wasn't home. Do you know where she is? Is she okay?"

Cabrina brushed his hand the way she'd done the night before. Huff was wary, but couldn't help being excited by her touch. "Gitte is fine. But she had to go to the country for the weekend to be with her mother. The poor woman is very ill. She has kidney disease, the doctors say, and may need dialysis. Is that the word? Yes, I think so. She can't really get the treatment where she lives. She would have to travel to a hospital three times a week, Gitte said, and that would be very hard on her. So she may have to come and live in Copenhagen. Until she stabilizes."

"I had no idea," Huff said. "Gitte never said a word about her mother."

"Well, this has been fairly sudden. Maybe she didn't want to bother you. Until she knows for sure."

"Until she knows what?"

"If her mother is moving in with her."

Moving in. He drank some wine, hoping that it would help him absorb the shock. He couldn't believe it. Gitte's sick mother moving in with her? He wanted to reject the whole idea. It was ridiculous. Yeah, he knew he was cynical, but he still didn't accept it. If the sick mother moved in, Gitte would never have a minute for him. Sure, he was selfish, but who wouldn't be? "What about Gitte's father? Can't he take care of the woman?"

"I'm afraid not," Cabrina said. "He's just a poor, simple farmer. It isn't really the cost, because there's insurance and all, but he has the farm to run, the animals to feed, and then there's the stress. So much stress."

"Doesn't Gitte have a brother or sister to help out? I thought I heard her mention a brother."

"Yes, she has a brother. But he's married to a German woman. They live in Bonn, and he has kids and a job there. The job is pretty good considering he doesn't have much education, but it ties him down so much, especially at this time of year. It's no good, you see. Gitte has to be the one who helps."

Huff nodded but silently rejected the concept, if there was any truth to it at all. And what if there was no truth to it? He couldn't plan his life on somebody else's stories and fabrications. He drank more wine.

He turned to Lene and noticed she'd gone through her wine like water. Cabrina wasn't too far behind, so they ordered another round. Huff started looking at Lene, wondering about the plan, wondering what kind of person she was like, wondering how life was in Estonia. Estonia? He wasn't even sure he could find it on a map. He knew it used to be part of the old Soviet Union, and he guessed it wasn't too far from Denmark, but after that the picture got fuzzy.

When he tried to bring Lene into the conversation, she didn't say much, maybe couldn't say much that he would understand in English, but she had a cute little smile. And she made sure he noticed. She knew what she was doing all right. Shy but sly. So...he would play along, have some fun, see what happened, but he'd keep his eyes open. They couldn't manipulate him if he had his eyes open. Yeah, that was the secret, keep his eyes open.

The wine was probably doing it, but he had pretty good feelings about *the girls* now. They were looking for a fun time, and they must have known he could provide it. That made him feel special. Everybody wanted to feel special, right? Then the girls took turns holding his hands, flirting with him. It was a game, he knew, but he liked it.

In a few minutes, Cabrina said, "Craig, dance with me."

The song was of medium tempo, but Cabrina gave it a slow-dance treatment, like the night before. Her body melted into his. He could feel every curve, and without Gitte in the room she wasn't bashful in the least. He didn't usually think about perfume, but hers was different tonight, sexier. While they were dancing, he forgot about Lene. He saw her out of the corner of his eye, but she barely registered. Cabrina was so hot. If there was something else going on, he didn't have time for it.

Huff wasn't sure the song had changed, but before he figured out what was going on, Cabrina was pulling away from him and beckoning Lene to step in. The Estonian girl didn't need to be asked twice.

She wasn't a bad dancer, either. Cabrina was graceful but aggressive. Lene was more intuitive. She flowed to his moves more smoothly, knowing ahead of time where to put her body for maximum effect. They danced awhile, and he was really enjoying himself. Then his head finally plugged into what was happening: Lene was a hooker.

Why hadn't he figured that out before? God, he was so naive. He was the older one, the one with maturity, and the girls were snookering him. The more he thought about, the madder he got, until suddenly he stopped dancing. He dropped his arms away from Lene and confronted Cabrina, "Why didn't you tell me you hired her?"

"Craig, can't we just have some fun?"

"I want to know what's going on. You owe me that."

Cabrina crossed her arms. "Okay, so I hired her. Now you know."

"There were three hundred kroner missing from my wallet this morning. Last night you took the taxi fare and then turned your back on me and—"

"That's right, and now Lene has the money. Even at that, she's underpaid."

That was a little shy of sixty bucks, Huff calculated, so he would hardly miss it, but it was the gall, the effrontery, the whole bizarre idea.

Lene pushed gently into Huff, interrupting his train of thought, and put a gentle finger to her lips, then to his lips. She tried to kiss him, but she was so much shorter and it wasn't possible unless he bent over a little. So he bent over. He would try this, see what came of it. Fifty, sixty bucks? It was nothing. The other night he'd dropped fifty on a modest little dinner just for himself and gone home lonely.

Lene was a good kisser, which didn't really surprise him. What surprised him maybe was how much he responded, knowing the raw truth of the whole deal. Yeah, he was still mad he'd been set up, but Lene poured cold water on that and lit a fire elsewhere. He came around to Cabrina's idea that they should just have some fun.

They danced for an hour, Cabrina and Lene alternating with him. Then Cabrina said, "Why don't we all go back to your room, Craig?"

He thought that was a wonderful idea.

Hours later, after *the girls* had left, he walked his room restively, and a heaviness descended on him.

If Gitte was gone all weekend, then he'd have to call her Monday after her work. He just had to talk to her and get clear. She had pushed him at Cabrina, and now Cabrina was pushing anything that moved, and tonight he'd bounced around like a pinball. He'd pushed back a little and wangled both of their cellphone numbers, including the one Gitte didn't want to give him, but now he wondered if he even needed them.

If Gitte truly had no time for him, he would leave Denmark in the coming week if everything else was in order. Gitte didn't know, and Cabrina didn't have a clue, but this wasn't his only reason for coming to Copenhagen.

He'd tried to put the phrase out of his mind—it was so ridiculous and yet so chilling—but now it was ricocheting back whether he wanted to face it or not: *Operation Sierra.*

· 5 ·

Jason paused at Danni's door and considered going down to Sunday brunch without her. Who knew where her thoughts would be this morning? But then he knocked. Might as well play out the hand and see what surprises she had in store. Besides, his day was free. He could forget about havarti until tomorrow.

At first there was silence behind the door, then scuffling. The door cracked open and revealed Danni's half-shut eyes. Somehow she saw Jason. "Oh. What time is it?"

He looked at his watch. "A little after nine. Time to eat."

"I'm not ready yet. You go down without me. I'll catch up."

He shrugged and walked down to the breakfast courtyard. The food looked good, about the same as the day before. He piled a good selection on his plate, but skipped the herring again. And today he passed on the havarti.

For a while he wondered if Danni would show up at all. Even though he ate slowly to give her time, he was nearly done when she arrived. It must have been a hectic struggle just to get here, but now she seemed to be in one piece. She sat down and poured coffee.

"Good morning," Jason said. "You're looking as beautiful as ever." See what that would do.

She furrowed her brow and looked at him skeptically. "You're just saying that. I don't feel beautiful."

"Oversleep?"

"I guess so. Blame it on the cognac." She smiled a little. "Or delayed jet lag."

"Really? Now that you mention it, I seem to have made a

quick adjustment to the time. Didn't even give it a thought this morning. Anyway, you look together. Have some breakfast."

Danni glanced at Jason's plate and then over at the buffet table. "I never eat like this at home. It's usually just yogurt and coffee and a vitamin pill and I'm out of there. Except on weekends. Then I do more."

"Well, you're not at home and this is the weekend."

"I guess you're right about that." She took a sip of coffee and stood up. "You're not right all the time, are you?"

"Only in my own mind."

"Ha."

She went to the buffet table, surveyed the offerings and came back with considerably more than yogurt. She sat down and reacted to Jason eyeing her plate like a hungry dog. "What? Okay, so I developed an appetite."

"Oh, good. For a second, I thought you'd picked up someone else's plate."

"Keep that up and you'll get a plate over the head."

Jason had another cup of coffee and watched Danni eat. He'd been fine by himself but was glad she was here with him. She gave the morning something new and refreshing. Copenhagen, he had observed, was a curious mixture of ancient and modern, often with no apparent rationale for either. Danni was definitely part of the modern. But the breakfast room was a good example of what he was thinking about. Some older architecture of no special merit served as a backdrop for a modern restaurant setting.

Today, of course, the room had a Sunday atmosphere. There was a bounty of customers, accompanied by a healthy measure of happy chatter. Signs of haste he'd noticed yesterday were almost entirely absent. If anyone was moving fast, it was the food staff. Above the courtyard canopy there was blue sky. He would have to get out today even if it was freezing. Couldn't be cooped up in his room for hours and hours. "So. Have any plans for the day?" he asked Danni.

"Actually I'm making a plan right now. I'm thinking of a train ride."

"A train ride? Any place in particular?"

"To be or not to be."

"Now who's sounding like the Oracle of Copenhagen?"

"Elsinore. Hamlet's Castle," she said. "Interested?"

"Now why didn't I think of that? But, wait, I'll have to check my schedule. I'm awfully busy today. When's the train leave?"

"When we get to the station."

Thirty minutes later they were walking to the Central Railroad Station. Jason carried his digital camera, prepared to be a tourist. "It's just a few blocks," Danni said.

"You're sure?" He didn't see any signs.

"Quite sure. I took the train in from the airport, and that's where it stopped. Then I walked over to the hotel."

"No taxi? What about your suitcase?"

"It has wheels. And after that long plane ride I needed to stretch my legs."

Jason realized that if he'd come to the Kong Jacob first, instead of the Hotel Lorentsen, he could have taken the train and saved himself from the wild Russian driver. Even though there had been little for him to plan because his trip was put together quickly by the company travel department, he could have read his travel guide on the plane. "So when did you figure out that the hotel was so close to the train station?"

"Flying over. I had plenty of time to read my travel book on the plane."

Jason felt his IQ plummet by 20 points.

Then the station appeared in front of them and gave him something else to think about. They soon found the timetable, which said the next train to Helsingør, or Elsinore, would be leaving in about ten minutes. Quickly, they bought roundtrip tickets, and by the time they got themselves to the right track, the train was already loading. They jumped on and took their choice of several empty seats. Apparently there wouldn't be a stampede to Elsinore on this freezing winter morning. Danni sat by one of the big windows, but it looked as if all the seats would have good views. As a voice crackled over the speakers in incomprehensible Danish, the train eased out of the station. Then the crackling voice returned with a list of stops, also incomprehensible, at least to Jason, but Danni picked up something she'd heard. "Helsingør," she said. "Good, we're on the right train."

"Good? That's *really* good. You know, that's a wonderful quality about trains. They always seem to know where they're going and how long it will take. Too bad humans can't get on that track."

Danni wrinkled her nose and shook her head. "Are you kidding? That would take away all the fun."

"By the way, how long is this ride?"

"Oh, forty-five, fifty minutes," she said. "We'll have a nice little trip through the countryside."

They went mostly northwest from Copenhagen on the island of Sjaelland, or Zealand, and the sun continued to shine. Danni took a guidebook out of her purse and leafed through the pages until she came to the right place. The town was Helsingør, she told him, and Shakespeare had anglicized and transformed it into the castle of Elsinore. Jason had figured that out on his own, but Danni forged on with a little history lesson that he did find informative. The Danish name for the castle was actually Kronborg Slot, pronounced more like *sloot*. If he could remember that a *slot* was a castle, he was fine. As far as history went, there was a big trick, or at least that's the way Jason thought of it. The castle was first built in 1585, during Shakespeare's lifetime, not when the Prince of Denmark might have lived there about five hundred years earlier. Then most of it burned down, and it was rebuilt a few years after Shakespeare's death.

"Oh, well," Jason said. "What's a few hundred years?"

"Literary license," Danni offered.

"Right. Anyway, Hamlet was just a fiction of Shakespeare's imagination."

"Figment."

"What?"

"Figment of his imagination."

"That's what I said."

Danni sighed. "You're hopeless."

But he could see that her exasperation was only pretense. Whatever she'd told him the night before, she still seemed to like him. He had to smile at that.

The Danish countryside was another matter. It wasn't that it was drab with its brown fields peeking through patches of snow— he accepted that it was winter—but it soon became apparent that the countryside had cows. Not simply cows, but dairy cows. He should have anticipated this, of course, but he didn't really want to look at the cows that wouldn't yield their havarti to him and Sunny Day Farms. Okay, so it wasn't up to the dairy cows. If he had to be absolutely fair, and he wasn't sure that was required, the cows were neutral in the matter, and technically speaking they made milk, not cheese. It probably wasn't even the fault of the farmers who milked the cows because all they did was sell the milk to the processors. But after that there were the distributors, and then the business situation started getting sticky. All he needed was a little cooperation somewhere along the line so he could go home with a deal intact.

The sun was out, but his vision was clouded today. He knew lots of city people thought dairy cows were cute—explain those urban crowds at county fairs some other way—but today he saw nothing at all in these animals that he would call endearing.

Jason assessed his trip so far. First, there were the long plane rides with little sleep, not to mention a missed opportunity to study the Danish travel guide. And the flight into Copenhagen had led to the daredevil taxi driver. Then there was the body in his hotel room, followed by his forced move to another hotel and a disturbing interaction at an Irish pub with an unstable American guy who had taken a lot of money from his company. Oh, yes, and the *piece de resistance*: cheese for India. It would be pure denial to say that he hadn't already figured out that the business part of his trip could easily be a waste of time. So much for being a troubleshooter. Of course, he had eaten some good food, but even men on death row were served a fine meal.

And at last there was his seatmate, Danni Rossler. She was just about the only pleasing part of his trip. He would overlook the fact that she was gazing fondly at his nettlesome dairy cows, since he wasn't about to interject his opinion and diminish her enjoyment of the scene by even a tenth of a degree. He wanted to hold her hand, but the time wasn't right. (There was that bedeviling phrase again.) But the major realization was that she had rounded the sharp edges of his trip. What was he going to do about that? Did he have to do something? He'd much prefer to meet her back in the States when she wasn't tracking a bad guy. And that brought his mind back to her safety.

"Danni, I was thinking about what you're doing here in Denmark. About Huff."

"What?" She turned away from the dairy cows. "Oh, that was so exciting last night, wasn't it? Who would have guessed that we would have seen him at his hotel?"

"Yes, but that's not what was on my mind. I'm just concerned about your safety."

"Well, thank you. That's sweet." And so was her smile.

"I didn't mean it that way. No, I mean... Anyway, this guy is talking about killing people. Without remorse, apparently. Maybe it's some prepared talk he likes to spring on unsuspecting strangers, but I wouldn't go messing with him. Not without some help."

"Right. But you offered to help." She wrinkled her forehead. "Didn't you?"

"I did, and I will. What I'm thinking right now is that part of my help should come in the form of persuading you to get *more* help. From a pro, not just somebody who happens to be nearby."

"Jason, I'm well trained in security procedures. That's why I didn't make a move when we saw him last night."

Could that be right? "Well, have you contacted the Copenhagen police? There must be some kind of Danish authority to help out in these international cases."

"No, I haven't contacted the police. There wouldn't be any point to that because we haven't called the, uh, American police yet. Didn't I tell you we're trying to keep this quiet so the competition doesn't find out and take advantage? Anyhow, you worry too much. First, I want to get a feel for what he's doing here."

"We're on a train *out* of the city," Jason said. "How is this helping you understand what he's doing *in* the city?"

"Okay, I'm taking a chance that he won't skip out today. Somehow a Sunday escape doesn't seem right. It's a risk, I admit, and maybe I'm blowing it. But I needed a little time to figure this out. I thought a side trip to the castle would be relaxing and put my mind on other things. You know, give me a new perspective, new ideas."

"Hmm. Even if I buy that, there's something else you could do while you're waiting for inspiration to strike."

"What's that?" She looked genuinely interested.

"Maybe it's a goofy idea, but you could hire a private investigator. Find some knowledgeable local to track Huff while you're doing other things. Even if you're poking around Copenhagen, you can't be everywhere all the time, so if somebody else could tell you what he's up to, then you'd be ahead of the game. Anyhow, that's the way I see it."

"That might work I'll think about it. But if Huff leaves Denmark as you suggested, someone has to follow him, and I don't think a local investigator is going to do that."

For now, Jason had nothing else to say. Danni was being stubborn, he thought. So he would just have to back off and watch what she did. Maybe he didn't know much about tracking criminals, but he was pretty sure Danni was in over her head.

#

When Danni and Jason got off the train in Helsingør, the sun was still out, and for a little while that oh-so-faint hint of summer seemed to mitigate the sting of the Danish winter. If they had waited, they probably could have caught a bus from the train station. The town had more than forty thousand people, and so getting around might have presented at least some challenge, but they could already see Hamlet's Castle ahead so instead decided to make the fifteen-minute walk. Across the water, about two and half miles away on the other side of the Øresund, was Sweden.

Approaching the castle, they strolled through a corridor of leafless trees. After Jason paused to take a photo, they walked across a bridge over a moat and entered the castle of yellow sandstone through the Crownwork Gate.

There was no sign of Hamlet, his ghost, or anyone else's. But the castle did beat Jason's previous plans for filling the day, which probably would have consisted of strolling around closed downtown Copenhagen shops, reading the serious book that wasn't speaking to him just now, and watching reruns of Jerry Springer and American movies. No matter what, though, he wasn't going to watch, or warm to, those Norwegian sports shows about the thrill of competition on ice and snow.

At one point Danni said, "I'm glad you came along, Jason. It's nice to have someone to talk with, and now I won't get lonely and think too much about home."

What could he say? Even when he didn't see eye to eye with her about Huff, he did enjoy being with her. But there was no hint that she wanted to renew or even think about last night's interrupted intimacies. On the other hand, there was thankfully no further talk of being gay or other matters that might distance them. For the moment, Danni just seemed to be a sightseer. Jason thought he might as well forget last night and be a sightseer as well.

The castle was large, but not quite what he'd hoped. In fact, some of it looked more like a dreary palace than the classic notion of a castle. The coppery green roof, domes and pinnacles were impressive though, and Danni wondered how anyone had ever climbed that high in the old days to work on them. Jason assured her he wouldn't have volunteered. She said he probably would have been somebody's servant and wouldn't have had a choice.

Kronborg Castle was a Renaissance building of repetition and precision with wings and spaces where guests could stay and never be noticed until the royal reception. For that there was the Ballroom, Northern Europe's largest castle hall at eleven meters wide and sixty-two meters long. That was a little more than thirty-five feet by two hundred feet, Jason and Danni calculated, and it ran the length of the whole south wing.

Part of the castle looked like a movie set, and indeed it had been. Plummer, Gielgud, Olivier and others of dramatic skill and fame had graced the halls of Elsinore, their robust voices resonating around the stonework and exploring the depths of betrayal and melancholy.

In the basement, in a dark and dingy area called the Casemates, he and Danni found Holger Danske, a statue of a sleeping but larger than life character embodying the indomitable spirit of Denmark. So the story went, the power of Holger Danske could be summoned when Denmark's hour of need was critical. He would arouse from his slumber, uncross his arms and become flesh, take up his sword and defend the fatherland. The Danes had called on Holger during the dark days of Nazi oppression, and Holger and the Danes had at last prevailed.

Jason approached the statue from several angles, trying to pick up the vibrations that would extricate Danni from her mess with Huff, and himself from his havarti troubles. If the spirit of old Holger was working on these important matters, then Jason had to say he'd missed the clues. He didn't feel anything different except colder and damper for having spent too much time in a castle basement. Still, he wasn't going to lay the blame at Holger's stone feet. Jason thought that probably the appeal had to come from a true Dane to be valid. Apparently, limits had to be drawn on even the power and might of Holger Danske.

As they stepped outside, back into the fresh, but cold air, Jason could feel himself losing interest in playing tourist. This was Hamlet's Castle, for God's sake. Why wasn't he reveling in this? Worse, he thought his performance was about as empty as the skull in Hamlet's gravedigger scene. *Alas, poor Yorick.* But Jason caught himself. He knew this wasn't his show. No, he was here to support Danni, just be with her and give her whatever help he could. Of course, he wasn't at all convinced he was actually helping much, but maybe that satisfaction would come later. So he recharged his enthusiasm and took exterior photos of the castle from the courtyard and the ramparts and persuaded Danni to be in a couple of them. They passed on Danish beer at the castle—"Too cold," Jason objected—and instead had lunch in a warm café downtown.

They found a table in the back and put in their order. As they waited, Danni studied something on her smartphone for several minutes. "What's going on?" Jason eventually asked.

Danni looked up, distracted, as if surprised she wasn't alone. "Oh, nothing much. More trouble in Afghanistan, it looks like. And a moderate earthquake in Italy."

"Business as usual, I see." When he thought about it, Jason realized that even though he was half way around the globe he was actually taking a little vacation from world events and that he could probably continue doing that for a few more days and catch up when he got home.

When the vegetable soup came, it was decidedly the warmest thing Jason had encountered since breakfast and he attacked it with gusto. Danni kept tapping at her phone while eating a spoonful of soup here and there. Before long, she got up and said, "I have to make a call." She headed up by the front door, and, phone in hand, paced in the lobby area. She was partially hidden by a short wall, but Jason could see her head and shoulders pop back into view from time to time. From what he could tell, she punched in two or three calls, though possibly didn't connect on one. But certainly he could see her talking into the phone. Well, he wouldn't get nosy, but he would keep his eyes and ears open.

After lunch, they walked around Helsingør to get a feel for the town and in about fifteen minutes found themselves almost back at the train station. Close to the station was the port, and something large and eye-catching in it.

"Nice ship," Jason said, looking at a long and tall white vessel.

"That's a ferry," Danni said. "Scandlines. I read about it. It goes across the Øresund, over to Sweden."

To Jason it looked like a British Columbia ferry in Canada, more of a ship for open water than the somewhat smaller green and white ferries that sailed Puget Sound and other calmer waters of Western Washington.

"Sweden. It looks so close," Danni said as she studied the land

and the town across the water. "Four kilometers, the guidebook says. You know, we're actually facing east."

"Yeah, I noticed the map earlier, while we were looking at your guidebook on the train. It's one of those mind benders. From Denmark, you'd think Sweden would be north. Which it mostly is. But at this particular location, it's really east."

"It's kind of like Detroit, where you go south to Canada," Danni said.

"To Windsor, Ontario."

"Right," she said. "You must have done well in geography class."

"I suppose. Mostly I just try to pay attention."

"How were you in history? Remember when that guy said to go east, young man?"

"It was *west*," Jason corrected. "Go *west*, young man. Horace Greeley."

"Perhaps. But I was thinking *east*."

Jason cocked his head. "You're not suggesting…"

"Have you ever been to Sweden?" she asked.

"Not really. I've been to IKEA a couple times. Bought a Swedish bookcase, for my serious books. And I ate Swedish meatballs and lingonberries."

"Doesn't count," she told him.

"I didn't bring my passport," he lied.

"You won't need it for this crossing. They don't seem to care."

So she'd been planning this. Jason let out a deep, exaggerated breath. "Resistance is futile."

"I think it only takes about twenty minutes. And we have a little while this afternoon."

When Jason didn't object this time, Danni said, "Good, then it's settled. Let's get tickets."

When they were on board and under way, Danni insisted on standing outside. But as Kronborg Castle receded in the distance and the speed of the ferry threw a blast of winter into their faces, they went back inside and got hot coffee.

"I knew they put seats inside for a reason," Jason said.

"What? Can't take a little cold?"

"Actually, I have a lot of trouble with that." He sipped his coffee. "It's not as if I'm a wimp, but I had a heatstroke about three years ago and my thermostat hasn't been right since. I really like to stay warm, but sometimes I just have a lot of trouble."

"Doesn't sound if you're suited for winters on the Baltic. What happened?"

"I'll give you the short version of the story. Any more than that and you'll risk taking on my condition."

After Jason had gone ever the Bloomsday Run, hepatitis and heatstroke, Danni said, "So you have trouble staying warm, especially in the winter, and you have a heightened sense of smell."

"Only part of the time on the sense of smell. It's not as if it's all day long."

"What do you smell right now?"

"Diesel. And coffee. Your perfume. By the way, I like that one. What about you?"

"Diesel. And salt water."

"Yeah, I forgot to say that. Too obvious, I guess."

After they had arrived in Helsingborg on the Swedish side of the sound, Danni said, "You know, it would be pretty easy for Craig Huff to slip away to Sweden, or some other country."

Jason shrugged. "Sure. Why not."

"Nice to see that you're agreeing with me. I knew you'd come around." She gave him a mischievous smile.

"I always agree with you when you're right. But now that you mention it, Huff might already have slipped away while we were back at Elsinore. He could be disguised as a Shakespearean actor on his way to Germany."

"Sure, it's possible. And he might have left while I was asleep last night."

"You know what I think—"

"Yes, I know what you think, Jason. You've already told me. And I don't really need to hear it again right now."

What he wanted to say was that Danni was playing fast and loose with an explosive character. But no one was listening. At least Hamlet had an audience.

As they docked, Jason looked up and said, "Hello, Sweden." Once off the ferry, they strolled around Helsingborg, a substantial small city about three times the size of Helsingør back in Denmark. Close to the ferry port, they came across the Rådhuset, the imposing red brick city hall.

"It looks a little like the Kong Jacob," Danni said.

"Second cousin, I think. But our hotel didn't get a clock tower. Or turrets."

"We should file a complaint." And they laughed.

Because of the cold and the time of day, they chose to make a quick swing around the immediate vicinity and not range too far. So they passed up the museums and yet another castle and merely scratched the surface of shopping opportunities. Danni did find one artsy glass shop that intrigued her, but ultimately decided the green vase she liked was too pricey to ship and had a high chance of breaking before she got home if she took it herself.

Although Helsingborg was clean and bustling and might have been more exciting at another time, they both sensed something was missing on their little visit to Sweden.. But it was their problem, not Helsingborg's. Maybe Danni really had needed a break, but without saying it aloud, they knew now that their hearts weren't in this kind of tourism because they both felt the tug of unfinished business back in Copenhagen. Although Jason had been trying to play tourist today, he had certainly felt an emptiness at Hamlet's Castle, and now he could tell that Danni had arrived at more or less the same position. Finally, Jason said, "This would be more interesting if we ran across somebody famous. Say, Stieg Larsson."

Danni turned to look at Jason as they walked on. "The writer? Considering that he's dead, that would be interesting. Do you think he ever came here, to Helsingborg?"

"I don't know. He could have driven down from Stockholm if he'd really wanted. Or taken a train. Sweden's fairly large, but it's not huge. Or maybe we could just find the girl with..."

"...the dragon tattoo," Danni finished.

"You're too quick."

"That's one reason I read that book. The tattoo, I mean. I have one."

Jason grinned. "Really? I never would have guessed. What is it?"

"Not a dragon."

"Well, no. Something, uh, more peaceful and refined, I would imagine. Despite your security work. Or perhaps as a counterpoint. Hmm. Not a wolf, not a tiger. Not a T-rex, not a scorpion. How about a bird? A robin? No? A butterfly, a flower?"

Danni kept shaking her head as they moved down the street. "None of the above. It's a ladybug. Two of them, actually. Ladybugs."

"Ah. Pest eaters. Such innocent looks, but such voracious appetites. Vermin beware." Jason watched Danni roll her eyes. "What color?" he asked.

"Red, of course. And black."

Jason nodded, thinking.

Danni laughed. "You surprise me. You didn't ask where they are."

"I was trying to preserve your modesty. But since you raised the question—"

Danni opened her mouth as if to answer him, but no words came out at first. Then, "Can't tell you. It's, uh, sort of private."

"Darn, what a tease. You know, I was really hoping to see those ladybugs."

Danni's eyes brightened and she couldn't help smiling. "Oh, I bet you were."

They circled back toward the dock, bought more hot coffee and a few minutes later caught the next ferry back to Denmark and got on the train to Copenhagen.

Jason took out his smartphone and earbuds and listened to music he'd loaded back at home. He felt as if he and Danni had talked out everything for now, and he certainly didn't want to think about Huff. So the mp3s helped fill the time during the train ride and made him think he'd actually be home in a few days. Periodically,

Danni did more tapping on her phone, and soon Copenhagen was in sight.

By the time they were back in the city, the sun was low in the sky. Jason supposed Denmark had long summer days to compensate for these slim rations of winter sun, but this was ridiculous. What made it even worse was the knowledge that the winter solstice was almost two months back and that this represented an *improvement*.

After they had walked out of the station, Danni bolted ahead and hailed a taxi. "What are you doing?" he asked as he ran to catch up. "Now that you've demonstrated it's close enough to walk, you suddenly decide to ride?"

"Get in and I'll explain."

He got in, and before he could say a word to Danni, she was giving directions to the driver, telling him to stop at the Kong Jacob first and then they would go on from there. She settled back in the seat and turned to Jason beside her. "I thought you'd like a ride to the hotel since we've already done a lot of walking today. At least you can go get warm."

"Well, thanks for the considerate thoughts, but after you wrote out today's itinerary, you forgot to give me a copy."

"I need to look into something on my own."

He nodded in defeat. "Something about those phone calls. But you're not going to tell me, are you?"

She patted his shoulder. "It's better that way."

"Right. Because then I won't be bending your ear, advising you not to do it." This approach wasn't working. "Why don't I go along, keep you company? Like today at the castle."

"No, Jason, you've done enough today. Really. I was glad you went with me to Elsinore. And Sweden. You kept me company just the way I wanted, and I do appreciate that. You've been wonderful. But now I need to do something on my own."

Well, what could he say to that? She was on her way to Nyhavn to spy on their old friend Huff, and there wasn't much he could do about it. She was right about the cold, though. He wasn't totally frozen out, but as far as he could tell, the only thing missing on the ferry ride to Sweden was an iceberg. On top of that, the train ride back had been on the cool side. So he needed to watch himself, not test his limits. He had a little reserve, but not enough to stand outside for hours in frigid weather watching someone watch someone else. Yeah, and be so inconspicuous that Danni wouldn't see him. That would be some trick.

When the taxi pulled up to the Kong Jacob, Jason opened the door and edged one foot out to the pavement. Then he put a gloved hand on Danni's arm and said, "You take care out there. I'd like to see you again tomorrow."

She nodded and patted his hand. "You'll see me."

He stood on the street and watched Danni's taxi until it went around the corner. So much for a sweet good night. Last night had been another mixed ending. Maybe one of these times they'd get it right.

Jason went up to his room and hovered over the radiator until he felt reasonably warm. Standing there gave him a chance to think about Huff and his wild words in the Irish pub. Almost forty-eight hours later, those words were as fresh as the night Huff had said them. Jason wiggled his fingers, then took off his shoes and wiggled his toes. Progress.

Well, now that his appendages were close to moving properly again and his face could no longer double as an ice pack, he thought of reconsidering his decision not to follow Danni over to Nyhavn. He could follow in a taxi and stay warm a little longer. But how could he protect her? Wasn't that the idea? Jason didn't really care what she learned about Huff, but he did want her to be safe. On the other hand, since she was trained in security, perhaps she was more capable than he was. He didn't want to be the well-meaning but blundering amateur who ruined the mission. Before, he'd told himself that Danni's concern with Huff was none of his business, and now he felt he should get back to that position. Emotions were the problem here. He couldn't let himself get carried away just because he'd kissed an attractive young lady. His assignment was to bring home cheese, not criminals.

Once he had that straightened out and was convinced he'd

been overreacting, he put his shoes back on and walked a few blocks over to the Strøget. He was getting hungry. Maybe he'd try something different tonight, something very un-Scandinavian to clear his mind. Chinese sounded good.

6

Monday was a work day. So despite being on this topsy-turvy arrangement called Central European Time, Jason got going fairly early and was finished with breakfast by eight-thirty. He hadn't knocked on Danni's door. Partly, it was because he was up and moving earlier, and partly it was because of the way she'd dismissed him yesterday. He wasn't mad at her, but he wasn't sure they had much to talk about this morning. She hadn't exactly told him to get lost, but it was clear she wanted her own space to do whatever she was doing. So he would let the situation settle.

He was walking up to his room when he met her on the stairs.

"You're up early," she said.

"Yep. Already had breakfast."

"And you're wearing a tie."

"It's a big day in the cheese business. I'm going out to Bjorne-by this morning to see if I can make sense of things." He drew in a deep breath. "What's going on for you today?"

"Oh, a little of this and a little of that." She sounded cheerful but coy.

"Well, good. I'll check with you later today then."

"Sure," she said as he was already starting to move up the stairs. "And good luck."

Well, he would need that. No matter what your talent and skills, he thought, luck was a welcome partner anytime. He brushed his teeth, washed his hands and face to remove any signs of breakfast, then grabbed his coat and business papers and went down to the front desk. There was no choice about the transportation today. So he crossed his fingers and had the front desk call a taxi. It came within five minutes, and when Jason got into the back of the car, he sensed something different. The driver gave him a cheerful "*Morgen*" greeting, and as soon as Jason said "Morning" in return, the driver switched to English. "Where can I take you today?"

"Bjorneby Foods." Jason gave him the address.

The driver eased away from the hotel and merged into traffic carefully but efficiently. When there was a chance to speed up, he did, but within limits. There was no sense that every car on the road had to be passed. Jason soon relaxed and concluded that this taxi ride would not be hazardous to his health. When they arrived at Bjorneby, Jason asked for the driver's card so he could call him for the return trip. His name was Carsten, which was easy to pronounce and easy to remember. Jason gave him his own card so Carsten would know who was calling.

Jason thought of the Bjorneby Foods building as the cheese warehouse, but it was more than that. A two-story wing of modern offices joined several sections of the sprawling warehouse that held many foods other than cheese. Jason gave his name to the receptionist, and in a minute a man in his late forties with thinning grayish brown hair walked down the broad staircase.

"Jason Stallings," he said, extending his hand. "I'm Poul Stubkjaer, director of exports." Jason noticed that the *J* in the name was pronounced as a soft *E*. He would figure out these things if he hung around Denmark long enough. Of course, not hanging around a long time was one of his objectives.

They shook hands. "It's good to meet you, Mr. Stubkjaer."

"Call me Poul, if you don't mind."

"Poul. And Jason."

"Great, great. My office is just upstairs, but first we should look at the operation. I think you saw a little on Saturday. Or were you able to make it in?"

"Yes, I was here. Per showed me around some. He was quite helpful."

"Per?" Stubkjaer frowned. "Per, oh yes. I was trying to remember who that was. One of our junior people. He's still in school and has much to learn. Well, maybe today I can fill in the picture for you. It's always good to know what's in front of you."

This tour was much more complete and polished than the one he had taken Saturday. Jason had the feeling that Stubkjaer had led it many times. Bjorneby Foods was much larger than he'd thought after the Saturday visit, and he had a new appreciation for the complexity of the operation. Today the havarti room, as he called it, was fairly full. The seven pallets had been joined by about fifty more. The cheese was in the form of four-kilogram loaves, about nine pounds apiece. Much of the havarti was plain, but some loaves were mixed with dill, some with caraway seeds, and some with jalapenos. Some were creamy, and some were low-fat. He presumed even more combinations were available or being tested. Jason couldn't tell if the havarti display was pure spin or just typical of the daily fluctuation.

After the tour, they went up to Stubkjaer's office, which was neat and modern, though too sterile for Jason's taste. Stubkjaer had his secretary serve coffee and pastries.

"Some Danish?" he said, holding up a plate for Jason.

Jason was still full from breakfast but took one anyhow. "You actually call the pastries Danish?"

"No, not really. But I know you Americans call them that."

Jason had a bite. "Very good, even if they're not Danish."

Stubkjaer laughed. "Oh, they're Danish in that sense. We don't import them. Danes have a well-developed talent for making pastries, all right. But we call them *Viennas*, or *wienerbrod*."

"I had no idea."

"I don't know exactly how the Danish name got attached. But we don't object."

They enjoyed their coffee and Danish for a minute, and then Jason said, "Poul, as you know, my company, Sunny Day Farms, has not received many shipments of havarti lately. We are trying to understand this problem, and that's why I'm here, to bridge the gap in a way that I haven't been able to do from Seattle."

"It's very good of you to visit, especially in the winter. We don't get many guests in the winter. Everybody wants to see us in the summer, but then we have a conflict because people show up when we are on holiday. It's quite a predicament."

"Yes, I can appreciate the problem."

"So then it's actually good that you have come in the winter. We are here to help and we hope we can do business."

"Business, yes, that's why I'm here. The thing is, I heard something strange when I dropped by Saturday. Maybe strange isn't the right word, but I found it hard to believe." Jason looked at Stubkjaer but got no reaction. "Anyway, I was hoping you could clear that up for me."

"Of course. What kind of *strangeness* did you hear?"

"Well, I heard that India has a newfound taste for havarti and that the cheese that used to go to America, to Sunny Day Farms, is now somehow being diverted to India."

"More coffee?"

"Just a little. I had quite a lot at breakfast."

Stubkjaer got up, fetched the coffeepot and poured a full cup. "Then I would say that there is no strangeness in what you heard."

"It's not true, the story about India?"

"Oh, yes, it is true. It is not a story. But I don't find it strange. I think it's perfectly natural. The Indians were long overdue to put havarti on their plates, and Denmark is proud of it."

"I see. But Poul, aren't the Indians newcomers? Shouldn't their needs, their desires, for this cheese come second to established customers like Sunny Day Farms?"

"Do you think? I don't know that India is a newcomer, as you call it. India is a much older culture than America."

Jason saw he would have to take a different approach. "Of course you are right about the culture. However, I was thinking more of the business relationship. Sunny Day Farms has been doing business with Bjorneby Foods for many years."

"Quite true. I don't know how far back it goes, but many years."

"So the thing is," Jason said, holding his arms out, "we have a contract, a contract signed by representatives of your company and mine."

"Oh, yes. Well, it's the normal way of doing business, isn't it?"

Jason was beginning to wonder. "But you seem to be saying that our contract for havarti is worthless, that it takes a secondary position to some new fascination in India for Danish havarti. Meanwhile, you have many pallets of havarti in the warehouse."

"*Fascination* may be overstating the case. I would call it *interest*. Yes, the Indians are interested in havarti most definitely." Stubkjaer paused, working himself up to the next stage of defense. "As for the contract, it is not worthless. There will be havarti for you when there is enough to go around. I'm sure I don't have to remind you that a contract does not control supplies. And the pallets you saw in the warehouse today will be on a ship to India tomorrow."

"A contract can be enforced in court, especially when one party purposely does not fulfill its obligations." Jason was surprised to hear himself talking so forcefully. "Sunny Day Farms takes no position per se on India's *interest* in havarti. It is a good product, and we can understand the attraction. But Sunny Day Farms can't be secondary to India when we have a contract that is primary."

"Naturally, that is your position. Stubkjaer got up from his desk and looked out the window. "But it is a narrow position. You must look at India's huge population. So many mouths to feed, and perhaps we are running out of time. Denmark, although a very small country of only five and a half million people, is immensely proud that it is keeping India from the brink of starvation." He turned back to Jason. "Can you honestly say that a contract is more important than helping an entire country fight off hunger?"

Jason's Saturday visit to Bjorneby Foods should have prepared him for Stubkjaer's impassioned stance, but somehow it hadn't. Stubkjaer wasn't just being obstinate, Jason thought. The man was living in another world, a world where law and logic apparently were unknown.

"I know there are many mouths in India." Jason said slowly, "About a billion, I believe. But tell me, how did the Indians eat before they had Danish havarti?"

"Not well. A country can't live on rice and turmeric alone."

Jason stared out the window, then stood up for a closer look at Stubkjaer's inspiring view. It turned out to be a parking lot. It wasn't pretty, but at least it was useful. Which was more than Jason felt. Okay, he was disappointed. But that was only an emotional reaction. He would put that aside and focus on what to do next. He would leave the havarti contract to the lawyers and think about finding another job. This was going to be bad news at Sunny Day Farms. But if he could make a deal for some other specialty foods, he might save himself. It was a long shot, but since he was here at Bjorneby's headquarters, he might as well make an effort.

Jason sat back down. "Poul, I noticed you had many other products that Americans might buy. Tell me about your cookies. And your jellies."

Stubkjaer brightened and gave him a rundown of the products Jason asked about. The discussion also covered chocolates, canned pork and some gourmet form of walnuts that Jason did not totally comprehend or want to sample. He also asked about a chili olive paste and the sardines packed with asparagus. It would be good to have some products to reject so he wouldn't appear too eager to buy Bjorneby's entire line. He had a strong feeling Sunny Day Farms and American consumers wouldn't go crazy for the olive paste or exotic sardines. After the product review, he and Stubkjaer went over prices and put together a tentative deal for non-havarti items that was about half the dollar amount of Sunny Day Farms' normal havarti order.

When Jason asked about other cheeses, Stubkjaer suggested the Danablu, or Danish blue. Remarkably, unlike havarti, it was available. So India either had no interest in blue cheese or was buying it elsewhere. Jason was curious about this product, but supplies were limited. Fortunately, his interest was also limited. But he added some to the order. Stubkjaer then suggested a cheddar— "not top of the line but quite good on cheeseburgers and salads."

"I'll pass on that one," Jason said. "We can get all the cheddar we want from the United States." Oregon, California, and Wisconsin were big producers. "Besides, true cheddar is from England."

"Oh, that reminds me," Stubkjaer said. "Wasn't it awful about the Englishman getting killed?"

"Englishman? I hadn't heard about that. But since you mentioned the subject, there was a man killed at the hotel where I first had a reservation. I had to change hotels."

"What hotel was that? The first one, where the man was killed."

"The Lorentsen. Then I moved over to the Kong Jacob."

"What day? I mean, you haven't been in Copenhagen long, I take it."

"It was Friday. At least that's the day I arrived in Copenhagen and the day the police came and took away the body. I saw him being carried out. Under a cover, of course. I'm not sure when he died."

"It has to be the same man," Stubkjaer said. "That's remarkable, really remarkable. Here, let me show you."

Jason wondered what he was going to be shown—surely not the murder weapon—but his host reached for a newspaper. It was a tabloid, *Ekstra Bladet*. "The story was just in this morning. I don't recall why it wasn't in earlier. Here, let me find it." He leafed through the paper, turned it sideways so Jason could look, and started scanning the story. "Oh, I see now. The police didn't release his identity until Sunday. They wanted to notify the appropriate people in England first."

Jason didn't comprehend much of the Danish in the news story, but he was able to pick up a few words—Hotel Lorentsen, English, and Martin Weathersby, apparently the man's name. "Martin Weathersby? That's the victim?"

"Yes, that's right. It seems he was stabbed to death." Stubkjaer looked up from the paper. "You know, this could possibly benefit you."

"What? The man's death? I don't see how." Jason didn't feel comfortable profiting from a stranger's death, and the only effect he'd noticed was being forced to change hotels. Of course, if he hadn't done that, he wouldn't have met Danni, but that was his personal business, and he didn't think it was what Stubkjaer had in mind.

"Let me explain," Stubkjaer said. "Martin Weathersby wasn't just anybody from England. He wasn't a tourist. He was a businessman, like yourself." He paused for effect. "And he was the broker for Delhi Deli Mercantile."

"Delhi Deli?"

"Your competitor, the Indian company that is buying all the Danish havarti."

"You said Delhi Deli." Were these people mad?

"Don't worry. It's real." Stubkjaer wrote it out for him.

Jason felt himself falling into shock. First, there was the havarti problem. Then Delhi Deli. And now this bizarre link to the dead man. He tried to make sense of the whole business. "Then you know, or knew, Weathersby, the dead man I saw at the hotel."

"I knew him much as I know you, "Stubkjaer said. We did business together, but I can't say that I really knew him. We didn't socialize."

Maybe that had been Weathersby's choice. Stubkjaer didn't seem like the kind of person anybody socialized with. "So when did you last see him?"

"He was in Thursday to discuss exports. And he had an appointment this afternoon to come back and confirm the order."

"He couldn't have phoned?"

"He could have, but he chose to come in person. He was always meticulous that way, never left a detail to chance if he could avoid it."

Despite his previous discomfort, Jason now edged into the thought that the Indians might be buying a little less havarti and leaving some for Sunny Day Farms. Since the company's contract had been trampled like a doormat, what did he have to lose? He saw an opening and went for it. "Well, Poul, it seems to me that Delhi Deli Mercantile has no standing now that their representative is obviously going to miss his appointment—and the chance to order havarti."

Stubkjaer shook his head gently. "I think that's a little bold, considering the situation. After all, we must show a little respect for the dead."

"Then what did you mean? You're the one who brought this up. You're the one who raised the possibility of a benefit."

"What I had in mind was some change over time, certainly nothing as immediate as today. It's possible Mr. Weathersby was merely carrying out the wishes of his Indian client. In that case, I expect Delhi Deli will proceed with much the same level of havarti business that we've already seen."

"And that wouldn't help me at all."

"Not that I can tell. But it's also possible that Mr. Weathersby was arranging for more havarti deliveries than his client really wanted."

Jason could see how that would work. "Like a stockbroker talking a client into buying a stock that the client never knew he needed or wanted. No doubt that would sweeten the commission."

"It's just a theory. Bjorneby Foods would not endorse such a practice, but there is nothing we can do to prevent such things."

"Then how do we find out what the Indians really want in the way of cheese?"

"We wait, Jason, we wait. Eventually they will tell us. All in good time."

Time is what Jason didn't have. He had been given a week in Denmark to find a havarti solution, so anything beyond a few days might as well be considered a failure on his part.

It was almost noon when Jason left Bjorneby headquarters. He had declined an invitation to stay for lunch, though he had told Stubkjaer he would return in a day or two, once the order of the non-havarti items had firmed up. "If something urgent comes up in the meantime, you can phone or text me." After they had ex-changed business cards, Jason said, "As I mentioned, I'm at the Kong Jacob."

The mixed smell of all the different foods at Bjorneby was get-ting to Jason, even in the office. The warehouse wasn't exactly close but it was attached. Jason's nose sparked with an electrical burning sensation, and his stomach rolled over like a rock tumbler. Whether cheese was part of the Bjorneby aroma he couldn't immediately tell. Nor did he care to parse out the ingredients as if he were a wine connoisseur or perfume maker. What he knew for sure was that he was now desperate for fresh air, even if it was freezing. And he really wanted to think of something besides cheese. Such single-mindedness couldn't be healthy, could it? Meanwhile, the employees of Bjorneby and folks all across Denmark were sitting down to lunch. But Jason wasn't even slightly hungry.

Beyond his personal situation, he needed to call his boss in Seattle. After all, he was being paid to solve a problem here, and he had to pass on the bad news that he hadn't solved it. He wasn't really afraid of getting fired because he figured he would be leaving Sunny Day Farms fairly soon anyhow. But all that would have to wait. Denmark was nine hours ahead of Seattle, so it was only three in the morning back home. He would wait until evening to make the call.

The receptionist was happy to phone Carsten the taxi driver for the return trip. As Jason rode back downtown, he wondered what Danni was doing. How long would she hang around and wait for Huff to make a move? And what kind of move would that be?

Jason was full of questions. On the other hand, forget the move by Huff. The man could just sit tight for a week. Was Danni prepared to stay that long? Without calling in the police? And would she follow Huff to another country, maybe even India? Huff could investigate the havarti market there and tell Jason what was really going on. Danni would laugh when he told her about Delhi Deli, and he realized he was looking forward to that.

Maybe what was more important to Jason than all these questions was what he had been hearing from her, or not hearing. Obviously she was holding back. But even if he did get answers, her trip to Denmark probably wouldn't make total sense to him. Would a company send a thirty-year-old woman alone to Europe just to shadow a suspected embezzler? Well, Jason had already been accused of being a sexist. But the point wasn't what *he* would do. The point was what her *company* would do. Maybe he was underestimating feminine resources and Danni's investigative prowess, but he wondered if the effort and expense of her Danish trip was too great for Huff's crime. And her seemingly reluctant approach fell short of what he expected from someone who had come so far to find him.

Jason was still trying to wrap his head around Danni's situation when he arrived back at the hotel. He paid and thanked Carsten and went up to his room, thinking maybe that his first-day opinion of Copenhagen cab drivers had been a little hasty. He unlocked his door and went in. It was good to be back to someplace even slightly familiar. Fortunately, his nose and stomach had returned to normal. Thank God he wasn't bombarded by the smell of food here. But something was amiss.

He put down his attaché and took off his heavy coat. He looked around and saw the bed had been made. So it was probably just the visit from housekeeping that he detected. He was getting jumpy. And he thought he knew why. Too much thinking or hearing about Huff. He really wished Danni were here for some other reason. Then there was this morning's news that the dead man in the other hotel was not only a food broker like himself but also a competitor.

He needed a break, something pleasant to clear his mind. Well, what was he going to do this afternoon? Walk around the city probably and again demonstrate the wisdom of buying that heavy coat. He looked for his travel guide on top of the dresser where he'd left it. But it wasn't there. Had the housekeeper moved it? He crouched down. No, the book was on the floor beside the dresser. It had been knocked off. That didn't look like the work of a fastidious housekeeper. Then he noticed that other papers on the dresser had been moved.

In itself, the placement of papers was inconsequential, but it did make him wonder what else had been moved. And why. He looked in his suitcases, which he still hadn't totally unpacked. The clothes hadn't been tossed, but they had been handled roughly, even by his own loose standards. But nothing seemed to be missing. Of course, people didn't usually steal clothes unless they were hanging from a store rack. No, whoever had looked in his suitcase was looking for something else. Money? He hadn't left any cash, credit cards or anything else of great value. So whoever it was must have gone away empty-handed.

No, wait. What about his digital camera? He'd left it in a dresser drawer with his socks and underwear. Well, that wasn't very smart. He stood up and quickly went to the dresser and opened the top drawer. Where was the camera? Gone.

No, there it was. At the back, but right on top. He breathed a sigh of relief. Nothing to worry about.

Except he hadn't put the camera on top. He'd put it under the clothes. Well, well.

He stood at the dresser, drawer open, and took a breath. What was going on? Nothing of value appeared to have been taken, maybe nothing at all had been taken. But somebody had been looking for something. The work definitely didn't meet the housekeeping standards of a fine hotel.

He took another breath through his nose. What was that? A smell, one that shouldn't have been there. The hotel's lavender air freshener was circulating in the background, but this was something else. He tried to separate the two, to do what he hadn't been motivated to do at Bjorneby Foods.

It was a subtle scent. That's why he hadn't picked it up at first. And it wasn't entirely pleasant. He thought it was a little like faded perfume, but couldn't say for sure. Maybe it overlapped with one of the base scents of the hotel air freshener. That would muddy the picture, all right. He reached for the scent in his mind, but couldn't quite touch it. It was slightly familiar though, as if he had come across it unintentionally and put it aside. If he'd almost reached it in his mind, then it had to be familiar. It had to. Or did he just want it to be familiar? The mind did that, filling in the blanks to match something known and find a level of comfort. The mind didn't like chaos that couldn't be explained.

Jason picked up the camera, turned it on and scrolled through the pictures he'd taken. He didn't see how his photos of Hamlet's Castle could be of much interest to an outsider. If an intruder didn't want the camera, then maybe he, or she, wasn't after material possessions. Then what else was there besides the thrill of pawing through someone else's stuff, and pretty mundane stuff at that? He looked over toward the bed. If the serious book on his nightstand had rated a second glance from the intruder, there was no evidence. He put back the camera and closed the drawer.

Well, if the intruder—burglar?—wasn't looking for kicks or material goods, then what was left? Something he could take without anyone noticing because the original was still there. Information. The intruder could take a copy in his mind and pass through any checkpoint.

What information would that be? Jason walked around his room, stepped into the bathroom and stepped back. Nothing spoke to him. He couldn't imagine anyone would care enough about the cheese business to search his room. Besides, he had carried all of his critical business papers with him. Of course, it was possible the intruder had been looking for information that wasn't there—his business papers, for instance—and left frustrated. If it was anything else, Jason was drawing a blank.

He thought of complaining to the hotel management about the search, but since nothing was missing that he could tell, he decided against it for now. He would end up sounding like an idiot, and the management would switch his door lock and card key to another code that the intruder could overcome just as easily as the first one. He'd have better luck finding the intruder by taking a nap.

But he wasn't sleepy. The coffee he'd had at Bjorneby foods was still trickling through his veins so he would have to find something to do with his eyes open. Then maybe he should do some work, except he wasn't in the mood. He could and should call on some of the secondary cheese distributors in Denmark. That would be the diligent thing to do. But he didn't feel very diligent. No, other than his call to Seattle this evening, work would have to wait until tomorrow. Never set sail on an incoming tide.

Jason went back to the dresser and picked up his camera. If some third-rate burglar didn't want it, then he would take it. He grabbed the travel guide, too, and walked out of the hotel whistling. It occurred to him later that that was the first time he'd heard anyone whistling in Copenhagen. It felt good, and no one told him to stop.

Out of curiosity, he took a different direction from the hotel this time, away from the Strøget, and before long came across a snow-covered expanse with a pond. It was a park. He took a couple of pictures and imagined how the park would look in the green of summer.

He poked through an antique shop, but had no real interest and left without buying anything. If he had bought anything, he would have had to take it home, and the thought of carrying anything heavy was enough to dissuade him. Unless it was a Fabergé egg or a first edition Hans Christian Andersen marked down for clearance, he would leave it all for the next astute shopper.

He moved on. And that gave him a charge. Done with this, ready for that. Next. The energy was flowing now.

The travel guide directed him to Copenhagen's famous Round Tower. He took a picture from the outside, read about horses trekking up the spiral walkway in the old days and about the grand view from the top. He figured there would be an excellent panorama of a lot of white snow and decided that reading about the view was good enough for today. He moved on.

It appeared the Strøget was magnetic—not magnetic north, just magnetic. Without even trying, he found himself back on it. The guidebook suggested he was walking east or maybe northeast, but all he could tell was that he was going away from the Kong Jacob. Moving on.

He found a landmark called the Kongens Nytorv, which meant Kings New Square. Not a bad name for something only about three hundred years old. Of course, everybody was stuck with the name because the Old Square moniker had already been taken. That was the Gammeltorv farther back on the Strøget. Jason took a picture of the guy on horseback at Kongens Nytorv, a dead king he presumed, and resolved to snap the bookend photo of Gammeltorv on his way back to the hotel.

Moving on. From Kongens Nytorv it was just a quick turn to Nyhavn, scene of Saturday night's dinner with Danni and the all-important sighting of Craig Huff. Jason shuddered a little when he remembered Huff out front of his hotel smoking a cigarette. For almost two hours he had managed not to think about Huff, and now the scoundrel was interjecting himself into Jason's mind. It wasn't right.

Jason strolled down Nyhavn, which meant New Harbor, apparently another inside joke, considering that the place was more than two hundred years old. He read that Hans Christian Andersen had lived at a couple of addresses on Nyhavn so took pictures of those. Maybe he could sell them on eBay. Belatedly he realized that Andersen had also lived in Helsingør, but he had no thought of going back there for pictures. The restaurant where he'd eaten with Danni was much closer. And it was a natural, so he shot that one. Then there was the Commodore Hotel, Huff's presumed residence. What the heck. It might be evidence, so Jason clicked on that one, too. He stepped around the corner and found the big ferries for Oslo and Stockholm and took their pictures, and he walked back and forth along Nyhavn, shooting street scenes pointing back toward Kongens Nytorv and the other way out to the larger harbor. The only thing he missed was a sidewalk café, but he'd have to wait a few months for better weather to get one of those. When he was done, he had his own set of postcards. He'd make sure his mother got copies along with her amber. She'd like them.

Moving on. He left Nyhavn and walked up to the Little Mermaid and took her picture. Her head was on today, and that made for a better photo. He'd heard that vandals had decapitated her some time back but then returned her head.

He stopped in a little café to rest and warm up. Afterward he considered calling Carsten or one of his friends for a ride to the hotel, then remembered he needed a photo of the Gammeltorv statue for symmetry. And Gammeltorv was in the middle of the Strøget, so a cab ride to there would be difficult. Well, he might not have another chance, so he showed some discipline and walked back and got the picture. By then he wasn't far from his hotel so just kept moving on.

When Jason got to the hotel, he was tired and a little sleepy and lay down for a nap. No more moving on for a while. He was tired of moving on.

Twenty minutes later he woke up and then turned on his bedside light and reached for his serious book. He read two long chapters and felt much better. When it was six o'clock, he called his boss in Seattle.

Ben Novitsky, the purchasing director at Sunny Day Farms, would have been at his desk an hour now, since eight a.m. Seattle time, and had probably already touched bases with a few buyers and contacts in other time zones, though not necessarily Jason's time zone. For Novitsky, it was very important to *touch bases*. "Let's touch bases on that before you make a move." Jason thought it was a good thing Novitsky was a baseball fan. His boss had season tickets to the Mariners so he could watch the whole American League touch bases for six months a year.

Sunny Day Farms had upgraded Jason's smartphone for European calls so there was no need to bother with the room phone and his old company calling card. He punched in a series of numbers, and Novitsky answered on the second ring. "Ben, it's Jason. In Copenhagen."

"Hey, how are you doing?"

"Good, although it's pretty cold here."

"You need some of that Viking blood, Jason. Anyway, it's raining here." Now there was news, Jason thought. Rain in Seattle. "I'd sure like to be down in Arizona about now for spring training," Novitsky said.

"Eighty degrees? Who wouldn't."

"What time is it there?"

"Six p.m."

"That late, huh. Well, I'm glad you called to touch bases."

"Ben, I had to change hotels so let me give you the new number for the room if my smartphone's turned off." Jason could almost see Novitsky pulling on his right ear with his free hand.

After Novitsky had noted the information about the Kong Jacob, he said, "I may have some bad news for you, Jason." At this point Novitsky would be bending over the desk, running a hand through his crew cut.

Jason felt better. Now the conversation wouldn't be one-sided. They could trade bad news. "What is it?"

"Your trip may be a waste of time."

Jason scratched his head. Was Novitsky psychic? "That doesn't sound good, Ben. Why do you say that?"

"I have a fax here, an interesting fax. It's an offer for Danish havarti at a fairly good price. But before I accept it, I thought we should touch bases."

"Ben, who sent you the fax? Who's making that offer?"

"Some European dealer. He must have known we were in the market for havarti. So do you think we should accept the offer?"

Jason was annoyed. Apparently he'd come all this way for nothing while some stranger out of the blue turned up a cache of Danish havarti. Maybe it was black market havarti. Was there such a thing? Well, maybe gray market. But why should he care now? If he wasn't going to bring home the goods, Sunny Day Farms would still get its cheese. "You know, Ben, you just might want to accept that offer because it doesn't look as if I'm going to make a deal for havarti in Copenhagen."

"That bad, huh?"

"You wouldn't believe it." Jason told him about India's new interest in havarti.

Novitsky didn't believe it. "That's one helluva story, Jason. Are you still jet lagged? India? Delhi Deli? You've gotta be pulling my leg."

"We're up a creek on havarti, at least with Bjorneby Foods. But I am putting together a substitute deal?"

"Substitute deal? Jason, I had better like this."

"I think you will. It's a bunch of Danish specialty foods." Jason named the products he and Stubkjaer had put on the tentative order. "On top of that, the prices are decent and the supplies are good. Anyway, you just said last week that we should probably be getting into more specialty foods."

"I said *probably*."

"Ben, you aren't going to do that curmudgeon thing on me again, are you? Because if you are, you're going to miss some good deals on these products. This is your opportunity to make a move in that direction, and if I were you I wouldn't pass it up. And the thing is, you could come out of this looking pretty good yourself."

"Well, it does sound kind of interesting. But I need to think about this a day or two. Don't make a move until you hear from me."

"You got it, Ben. But I've already done the legwork so all you need to do is give me the go-ahead. And I'd sure like to take care of this while I'm here."

"That's fine, Jason. I'll let you know. But back to the havarti business, there's something else you might not be aware of."

"You don't like the caraway flavor?"

"I love the caraway. Unfortunately, I love all the flavors." Ben's waistline was bulging. "That's not what I was thinking of. What's going on is that I've noticed that some of our competitors are beginning to offer Danish havarti."

That was bad news. "They are?"

"You should look around a grocery store more often. You might see these things. Anyway, I'm just wondering where they're getting their supplies. If we're locked out, why aren't they?"

"Can't we find out?"

"Probably not legally," Novitsky said. "Besides, industrial espionage isn't in my job description."

"Well, maybe you should just take that havarti offer you have and not worry about it. No need to get stressed out."

"I'm going to look at it a little more, but that's probably what I'll do."

"By the way, you didn't give me the name of this European dealer." Jason half expected to hear that Poul Stubkjaer was knifing him out of the picture.

"It's an Englishman, I think. Let's see, the name is, uh, Martin Weathersby."

Jason broke out laughing.

"What is it? You know this guy?"

"In a way. I've seen him. When did you get that fax?"

"Sometime Thursday, I think. Here it is on the time stamp. Yeah, 12:05 p.m. Thursday. Of course, it got misplaced in the shuffle so I didn't look at until sometime Friday, and by then you had already left for Denmark. Anyway, you shouldn't be laughing at this Englishman because it looks like he's found the havarti that you haven't."

"Ben, things aren't what they seem. Besides, I thought you were on my side."

"I am, Jason. Really, I am. But we need this cheese—we've needed it for weeks—and now this guy is offering it to me. You think all the pressure's on you, but if it came out that I turned down this cheese from another source, I wouldn't be around long myself. So since you're having all this trouble, I think I'll have to go ahead and do business with him. At least I'll be getting something."

"I wouldn't be so sure of that, Ben. This guy is going to be really hard to work with."

"Why's that? You're just full of sour grapes now."

"It's not sour grapes. Listen, Ben, you can't make a deal with Martin Weathersby for one simple reason. He's dead."

7

The call to Seattle worked up Jason's appetite. He'd
barely eaten since breakfast, and now his stomach was
complaining. Last night he'd dined by himself at the
Chinese place, but tonight he preferred some company.

He crossed the hall and knocked on Danni's door. Their morning encounter on the stairway had been short and not too informative, and he was curious what she was up to. At first there was no
response to his knock, but finally she opened the door.

She pushed tousled hair off her forehead and looked at him.
"Oh, hi."

"Uh, is this a good time?"

She took a deep breath. "Sure. Come on in. I was just nap-
ping."

He followed her in. This was the first time he'd been in her
room. It was a regular rectangular room with green-striped wallpa-
per. The furnishings were about the same as what his room had,
but it was kind of strange looking out onto the street instead of the
courtyard. Then he realized he'd developed a comfort zone with
his room. That was a little frightening, having an attachment for
something he really didn't care about.

He brought himself back to the present moment and said, "I
had a little nap myself this afternoon. It really helped."

"I don't know whether my nap helped me or not." She
yawned. "What time is it?"

He looked at his watch. "Almost six-thirty."

"That late? Then I was out two hours. Wow, I must have needed it. I guess I didn't get in too early last night." She yawned again.

Jason almost didn't want to ask. "Investigating Mr. Huff, I

presume?"

She went into the bathroom and ran the faucet, then came back out with a glass and drank some water. "Very clever deduction."

"Wild guess," Jason said. "Any progress? Or dare I ask?"

"Go ahead and sit down." She pointed at the chair. "I'll just lounge over here while I wake up." She sat on the edge of the bed, then succumbed to gravity and leaned over on one elbow. The bedspread was pulled down and rumpled. "I saw him with two different women last night."

"Sounds as if he's an active guy."

"Too active, I'd say. He's probably throwing money around, my company's money, and that's not a good thing. He has a careless attitude."

"He must think he's rich. Why wouldn't he with all that money? What about the women? Young, old, sexy, plain, good-looking, what?"

"Both mid-twenties, I think. Both good-looking. He can't be too serious about them, though. He's only been here a few days. That's about all I know for now."

Something went ping in the back of Jason's mind, but he couldn't catch it. He looked at the carpet then back at Danni. "Hmm. Well, I guess that's something."

She put up a hand. "Don't tell me. You're disappointed. Well, maybe you'll like this. I checked with my, uh, boss and hired a Danish investigator today. He's already on the job." She tried to repress a smile but didn't do a very good job.

"Really? I think that's a great idea. Gives you another set of eyes on the situation. But don't you mean you hired him yesterday?"

"Why would you say that?"

"Because you made those calls yesterday. From the café up in Elsinore. Then we got back to Copenhagen you rushed off like a fire truck."

"I was impatient," she said.

"To meet your new investigator."

"Okay. You made a good suggestion and I went with it. Satisfied?"

"I was just trying to establish the facts. So what's your hired man dug up?"

"Nothing yet. He's watching Craig Huff only incidentally. What I asked him to do was track the women, find out who they are. We both saw them last night. If I know who they are, then maybe I'll know why Huff's in Denmark. You know, I can't understand that. At this time of year, he could have picked a lot of warmer places. Copenhagen doesn't make any sense in February."

"It apparently makes sense to him," Jason said, sensing that ping again. He stood up. "Wait. I just remembered something."

"What?"

"In fact, I told you Friday night after I met him. The girlfriend. He told me he had a girlfriend in Copenhagen."

"Oh my God. You're right. I completely forgot. How could I do that?"

"It was late. You were tired. I know I was."

"But not old Craig. He has energy for two women. So he came here because of the girlfriend. It wouldn't matter if it's winter. He just wanted to be with her. And that's why he's in no hurry to leave. What was her name? You told me, didn't you? Jeannie, Gina, Gigi, something like that."

"No, I think it was...Gitte. Yeah, I'm pretty sure. Gitte."

"Gitte. So now what? We know her first name. What good is that?"

"You wait for your investigator's report and see if you get a match on the name, maybe an address. If she does match..."

Danni nodded strongly. "Then the puzzle is starting to come together. Except for the second woman. Did Huff say he had *two* girlfriends?"

"No. Sorry. Has he been to Denmark before?"

"Hmm. Not that I know of."

"It's coming back to me now," Jason said. "At the Irish pub, Huff said he'd met Gitte in San Francisco. I don't recall any of the details about why she was there, but it seems now that he's returning the visit."

"Wow," Danni said. "Old Craig gets himself a Danish girl."

Something didn't register right with Jason. "The way you said that, Danni."

"Huh? Oh, I was just thinking that there's more to this than embezzlement now. He's building a nest egg. I wonder if Gitte knows."

"Now that's a good question. But think about this. Huff didn't move in with her. He's still living in a hotel, a pretty nice one, it appears."

"I know," Danni said. "The guidebook gives the Commodore four stars."

"So it's way too pricey for the long term, but it's working for him right now, while he's waiting to find out."

"Find out if they can live together? Right." Danni clapped her hands. "So maybe she's putting him off. But then there's the second woman. When the first hesitates, he picks up a second. Lord, it's the Craig Huff soap opera."

"Danni, how well—"

Abruptly, she got to her feet and started pulling the bedspread up. "This place is a mess. I need a maid."

"Didn't she stop by this morning?" Jason asked, walking over to help with the bedspread.

Danni threw a pillow at him. "Wise guy."

Jason laughed and threw the pillow back.

She caught it and put it back on the bed and turned to Jason. "Hey, how was your day?" she asked. "How's the cheese business?"

"Oh, a slice of this, a slice of that. I could tell you about it, but I need to eat first. Want to go to dinner with me?"

"Sure. But not like this." She held her hands up to her face and widened her eyes. "Not unless it's fright night."

Jason thought she looked pretty good even half asleep, but he played along. "Could you pull yourself together in a half hour?"

"It would be a rush job, but I could do it."

"Okay, let's synchronize watches and I'll meet you in the lobby in thirty minutes."

Jason went back to his room and watched CNN for fifteen or twenty minutes. This was the World channel, not what Americans usually see at home, so there was a little different focus and ultra-serious tone with a British accent. He caught a portion of the business news. The dollar was up and the Dow was down. Or was it the other way around? Anyway, there was no mention of volatility on the havarti market, which he took as a good sign. In general news, the rest of the world seemed about the way it did last night—in trouble, but hanging on. He turned off the TV, grabbed his heavy coat and went downstairs.

A hotel lobby is a great place to sit and relax and observe the human scene, provided the room is designed right. The Kong Jacob lobby wasn't designed right. There were chairs, but mostly in places where foot traffic brushed by. And at this time of day a lot of people were moving through the lobby, checking in or going to dinner or some other evening activity. Jason thought he might have encountered less traffic on the sidewalk outside. Of course, that would have been too cold, so he wasn't going to experiment.

He'd been sitting in the lobby five or ten minutes wishing he could call together the hotel renovation crew for a good look at the lobby's functionality when he saw a dirty white Hotel Lorentsen van pull up in front. Fond memories of the Lorentsen returned. The staff was polite and helpful and so efficient at having dead people removed from the premises. He would have to visit sometime to learn why the unfortunate Martin Weathersby had stayed there.

What happened next surprised Jason. The driver got out, opened a side door and took out a cart and went into the Kong Jacob. When the insulated apparatus went by Jason, he smelled food. The driver pushed the cart off to the kitchen area and disappeared. Jason looked at the van out front with its Lorentsen logo and then back at the kitchen, trying to make the connection but not entirely succeeding. It was one thing to transfer a needy guest to the other establishment, but to also send food was extremely charitable. There must be an arrangement. Maybe he'd look into that.

But the first thing he was going to look at was Danni, who was now standing cheerfully in front of him with black boots, gray pants, black coat, black hat and neat blonde-brown hair. He got to his feet and noticed she'd put on fresh lipstick and makeup and that captivating perfume. "You're looking like a million bucks." He meant it.

"Thanks. I'm feeling better. And I'm almost awake."

He checked the time. "All in less than thirty minutes. I'm impressed."

"Don't push your luck. This whole façade could fall apart in seconds."

"Hungry?" he asked.

"That's a fair statement. Where are we going?"

"I was out roaming around this afternoon and saw this Italian place. It had its menu posted in front and looked kind of interesting. It's not far, a little off the Strøget. We can walk, if you're not too tired."

"Lead the way."

Jason reached into his coat pocket and turned off his phone. Now wasn't the time to be interrupted.

The walk was brisk, as usual, and Danni said, "You're not complaining about the cold tonight."

"I noticed that. You don't suppose I'm getting used to it?"

"There's a scary thought."

"Well, keep an eye on me. If I start speaking Danish, call the authorities. I'm sure they'll know what to do."

"I've heard they have an antidote. If you speak in tongues, they give you a needle and you go back to where you were as if it never happened. *We now return you to your normal language.*"

"You know, Danni, after this week I don't think I can return to normal."

"I know." And she took his arm and held on all the way to the restaurant.

The Italian place was warm and cozy and smelled of fresh bread and roasted garlic. Danni ordered cannelloni and Jason had manicotti, and they added two glasses of Italian red. After Danni had a little of the wine, she began to seem looser. Jason felt pretty good himself.

They spooned down their minestrone starter, and then Danni said, "You were going to tell me about today's exciting news in the cheese business."

"So I was, though it's not especially good. But I can give you the story, if you don't mind hearing about how an American got aced out by a company from India with the help of a stubborn Dane and a dead Englishman."

"Are you trying to confuse me?"

"No, but I guess I'd better explain. You see, it turns out the havarti we want, and have a contract to buy, is actually going to India."

"I hope you're not making this up. India?"

"India. And it gets better, or worse. Apparently India is starved for havarti, and the company there that's handling the imports is Delhi Deli Mercantile."

Danni made the mistake of having a swallow of wine about half way down her throat as she received this information, so when she started laughing some of the wine went on down, though not smoothly, and some involuntarily came back up, spraying the white paper placemat in front of her with red speckles. At the same time she emitted a sound that came out like "Hooobuchhughh" and immediately everyone within earshot lifted their heads.

Jason jumped to his feet and patted her back until she started breathing normally. He sat down again. "Are you okay now?"

"I think so. Almost." Danni made a few more warbling noises then became quiet. "Just don't say that, that thing again."

"Delhi Deli Mercantile?"

"Yes, that. Don't say it again."

"Okay, I won't. Now drink some water."

When Danni appeared to be on an even keel, Jason continued the story of his havarti adventures. He began with Novitsky's plan to make a deal with the dead Englishmen.

"You have a weird company," she said, "working with the dead and all."

"Well the offer was made when the Englishman, Weathersby, was alive, but then he died before I got to Copenhagen."

"You know when he died?"

"I know the range, within a few hours. No earlier than nine p.m. Thursday, Danish time, when he sent a fax to Seattle, and no later than about two p.m. Friday, when I saw him on a stretcher. But probably it was during the night."

"You saw him on a stretcher? I don't know if I want to eat now." But she did drink some wine, which went down and stayed down.

"You'll eat. You're hungry and the human mind and body are remarkably resilient about absorbing stuff like this and then getting back to the task at hand."

"But you looked at him, the dead Englishman, on a stretcher. I don't see how."

"Well, that was at the Hotel Lorentsen, where I had really planned to stay in Copenhagen, but I couldn't, because the dead guy was in my room. So they moved me over to the Kong Jacob, and I met you."

"I got the part about meeting you, but you'd better back up and explain the rest."

So Jason recapped the story, including the newspaper report that said Weathersby was stabbed to death, though he did omit the part about the red stain on the man's sheet.

"I'm glad you didn't tell me earlier," Danni said. "I think it's easier to take it all in now that I know you." She paused and shook her head. "The thing is, for being a quiet food importer, you seem to be having an interesting time in Denmark."

"It does seem that way. Of course, I'd only been in the country an hour when I saw Weathersby's body, so I wasn't sure what to expect."

"Not that, I hope."

"I wasn't expecting to be nearly killed by a suicidal taxi driver, either. But here I am, unscathed."

"What driver was that?"

"Oh, I guess I didn't tell you about him. That was on the way from the airport, before I saw the dead guy in the hotel." Jason summarized the ride for Danni and said, "So right after that I was skittish about all Copenhagen cab drivers, but everybody but the first guy has turned out to be okay."

The waiter appeared and quietly replaced Danni's red-stained placemat and brought extra napkins and then served the entrees. As they ate, Jason told Danni a little more about his visit to Bjorneby Foods and how Stubkjaer was throwing the contract out the window to help the Indians. "It was a matter of national pride, he said, little Denmark helping feed big India."

"It sort of makes sense," Danni commented, "if you don't get too rational. But you said Stubkjaer was the one who told you about Weathersby and how he'd died."

"Right. He even showed me the story in a newspaper, and that's when I realized Weathersby was the dead man I'd seen at the Lorentsen. But now that you point that out, it was strange. Stubkjaer tantalized me by saying Weathersby's death could work to my advantage, then he slammed the door in my face."

"For now, for now. You're going to figure out something. I know you will."

"Well, if I don't, I'm probably looking for a new job. I doubt that even this substitute deal I put together will make much difference."

During the meal, it occurred to Jason that he and Danni were getting along pretty well. She was still guarded about her dealings with Huff, but otherwise was open, friendly and encouraging. And she hadn't brought up that unbelievable smokescreen she'd tried to use on him two nights earlier.

Toward the end of dinner, Jason said, "Stop me if I'm talking too much about cheese, but it seems to me there's a serious flaw in the story about India's great interest in havarti if Weathersby was trying to peddle the cheese to Sunny Day Farms instead of sending it on to—that Indian company." Jason thought the danger had passed, but he wasn't taking any chances. He wasn't going to say *Delhi Deli Mercantile* again.

Danni said, "Weathersby sounds like an opportunist. Not now, of course. But then."

"It seems that way, but I'm not too concerned about his business ethics now. The thing I'm looking at is that Weathersby must have known a fair amount about Sunny Day Farms because, well, two reasons—he was aware we wanted the cheese, and his fax offering the havarti to us actually got to the right person, my boss, the person who normally would make the decision about buying it."

"Then you're saying that Weathersby was tipped off."

"Something like that. He knew way too much."

"And that's why he was stabbed to death?"

"Oh, I don't have any idea about that. I suppose the police will figure it out. I'm just trying to find an angle to make this business deal work. It's supposed to work. You can't dump a contract simply because you feel like it." Jason could sense himself getting agitated.

"Jason, you're not going to find the solution tonight."

He looked into her soft eyes and took the hint. "Sorry, I got a little carried away. No, I guess the cheese business can wait until tomorrow."

"Good." She patted his hand. "I wanted to tell you that even if I don't know how to swallow my wine, dinner was great and I've had a wonderful time."

He laughed. "I've enjoyed it, too."

When the check came, Danni grabbed it before he could react. "You're not playing fair," he said.

"Yes, I am." She put down her credit card, and the hovering waiter scooped it up. "You paid Saturday, and I pay tonight. That's sounds fair to me."

"You leave me with no choice—but to concede."

When Danni and Jason left the restaurant, he turned right and started walking back to the Kong Jacob. But she turned left. He stopped and said, "This way."

"No, I'm going *this* way."

"But *this* is the way back to the hotel. Are you lost?"

"I'm headed to a hotel, but not the Kong Jacob. Not yet."

"Oh, no. No, no, no," he said, shaking his head.

She came back to him. "Why not?"

"Because I don't want to go to Nyhavn and spy on anybody."

"Is that what I'm going to do?"

"You tell me."

"I just wanted to go this way and see what's there. We've got time. Walk with me?"

Danni put her hands on his arms, then moved closer. There it was. Along with the sweet talk now came the *touch*. He tried to stand his ground and not go to Nyhavn, but she was hard to resist. With her face only six inches away, the sheen of her lipstick under the streetlight drew him closer. And there was that dusty citrus fragrance again. Why did she have to put on fresh perfume tonight? She was more charming than he'd given her credit for, way too charming. He considered the possibilities. Who knew what would happen when they went back home to America, but tonight he wanted to be with her. He reached out and held her at the waist. "I'm not agreeing to this, but since you're asking so nicely, I'll go with you. Provided you stay out of trouble."

"No trouble, mister. No trouble." Then she moved her face up and kissed him.

Talk about a surprise. Jason was used to making the first move, but he didn't object this time. He pulled her closer. This could last as long she liked. That was about ten seconds. "Thanks, Jason, you're a prince, a Prince of Denmark."

"No, I think that was Hamlet."

"Sure, but he's not here and you are. Let's go."

The walk wasn't as severe as he'd imagined. It was only about three blocks, and after the manicotti it wasn't a bad idea. Despite the cold, when they got to Nyhavn the foot traffic along the pedestrian-only street by the canal was fairly high. That was good, Jason thought. If you're going to be a spy, it's best not to stand out.

Danni took his arm so they would look like lovers, and the gesture warmed Jason because he was thinking now that wasn't entirely an act on her part. As for his part, he didn't know what they were, but he was willing to go along, at least for a while. The *while* lasted about twenty minutes. By then, they had walked past the Commodore Hotel twice and were simply standing out in the frigid night air at a safe distance from the hotel waiting for something to happen. Behind them water slapped against sailboats in the canal.

"I'm sorry, Danni, but I'm getting cold. Why don't we just head up the street here and catch a taxi back to the hotel?"

"We need to wait a little longer. I have a feeling we're going to see something."

"What would that be?"

"I don't know yet. Keep watching."

Jason watched but nothing happened. After a while, he said, "I think I'm developing a complex about hotels. At home, I never think about them, and here I'm thinking about them all the time."

"It's natural. You're sleeping in a hotel. It's your home away from home."

"It's more than that. It started with Weathersby's body in my first hotel room. Then my room at the Kong Jacob was searched this morning while I was out trying to buy cheese, and now I'm on a stakeout at Huff's hotel."

"You're making too much of it."

"Maybe." And maybe she was right. He would consider that.

"Wait a second. Did I hear you right? Did you say your room was searched?"

Jason clapped his gloved hands together to generate some heat. "It was searched, but nothing was taken. Guess I didn't have anything the burglar was looking for."

"All the same, it gives me a chill."

"I've already got the chills."

"I know you're cold, Jason, but listen. What if this has something to do with Craig Huff? If he knows where *you* are, then it won't be too long before he knows where *I* am, if he doesn't already."

"I don't think it's Huff. Doesn't fit somehow. Besides, nobody broke into your room."

"No. It's fine, or at least it was."

Then Jason remembered the fleeting scent around his dresser. Now he knew where he'd run across it before, and Huff wasn't involved. It was the same cologne he'd smelled riding in from the airport. It belonged to the Russian taxi driver, or at least someone who wore the same cologne. But perfumes and colognes had a way of interacting with the chemistry of the individual user, coming close to a unique scent for each person if the nose was sensitive enough. Jason had no doubts about his own olfactory sensitivity.

He didn't tell Danni this. It was too ephemeral—only a scent—and at the same time too confusing. He realized that lots of people could have worn that scent, but if his assumption was correct, then he had no idea why the taxi driver would have been snooping in his room or how he even figured out what hotel his room was in. The man had dropped Jason at the Lorentsen, and it wasn't any automatic assumption that he would end up at the Kong Jacob. The only conclusion he could make was the one he'd reached before. Whoever had been in his room probably wasn't looking for thrills or money. No, the objective was information.

Originally, Jason had thought the flow of information, whatever it was, was to the intruder. In fact, nothing else had occurred to him. But now he wondered if it might instead be the opposite, that the break-in artist had been trying to transmit information to him. Intentional or not, he had indeed left a message, and it was short. Fear. *Be afraid because I can come back anytime I want.* And it was possible, maybe even likely, that the information had gone both ways. Beside leaving his crude threat and a calling card of cheap cologne, the intruder could still have walked out with some useful detail or two. It was maddening to consider the possibilities because there didn't seem to be any. But Jason would have bet money he was wrong about that.

Now he really had a chill, and it wasn't from the cold. He put his arm around Danni's shoulders. She didn't react one way or the other. That was all right, he decided, because he was the one who needed comforting, not her. Danni suspected Huff was the focal point of every nefarious act, and who was he to say she was wrong? But Huff didn't feel right. To Jason, Huff seemed like an amateur, a child in a grownup's game.

They kept standing there. After a while, something fluttered onto Jason's nose, but he didn't pay much attention. He was still thinking about the break-in and the unsettling array of his Copenhagen adventures.

Eventually, Danni said, "It's snowing."

Jason looked up toward a light and saw the flakes. "So it is." This could be a long haul out here, he thought. Taken far enough, it could be downright miserable. "Maybe we should go inside the Commodore and warm up, have an Irish coffee or something."

"Are you serious? We can't do that."

Then Jason knew. "You're afraid Huff will notice you."

"Well, of course. What did you think?"

What Jason could plainly see was that Danni was putting off the encounter as long as possible because she no had no leverage against Huff. She couldn't just go ask him to give the money back. He'd laugh in her face and say forget it. Or worse.

"Here comes somebody," Danni said.

"Who? Where am I looking?"

"That woman with the long reddish hair. She's going straight into the hotel."

"Maybe she has a room there." The young woman didn't act furtive and didn't seem to care whether anyone noticed. She was pretty, even beautiful, Jason thought, and carried herself with confidence as she went up the stairs and opened the door. "I've never seen her before."

"I have," Danni said. "Last night. She and Huff were standing about where you and I are right now. They were, well, holding each other."

"Where were you?"

"Down toward the ferry terminal. I didn't see her face that well because I didn't want to get too close, but her hair I would recognize anywhere. It's gorgeous."

"So it's probably Gitte. No wonder he's so taken with her. I think Huff told me what she looked like, but I can't remember now. He definitely thought Gitte was good-looking, but of course he would say that. I 'm not sure, but he might have said she was blonde."

"Could be," Danni said. "I was probably too far away, but I think the other woman I saw with Huff last night was blonde, but then so were about ten thousand other Danish women I've seen in the past few days."

Jason was solemn. "That narrows it down."

"Immensely. Okay, so we don't know if the redhead we just saw is Gitte or not. Neither of us knows what she looks like yet. Maybe this one is Gitte, and maybe she's the other woman I saw last night."

"Well, your investigator will probably find this woman's name, and then we'll know." Jason wasn't sure what that would mean, but the identity seemed important to Danni. They continued to stand in the falling snow another couple of minutes. "Are we through now?" Jason asked.

"Yeah, I guess so. That may be all for tonight. We can go."

They found a taxi at the end of the street and rode shoulder to shoulder in the back seat toward the Kong Jacob. With a curtain of white flakes all around them, time seemed to stop. Fresh snow on the streets turned the normal sound of rolling car tires into soft little crunches. Copenhagen was still. And for the first time since his arrival, Jason was at peace with being in wintry Denmark.

He looked at Danni and said, "I'm still thinking about that Irish coffee."

"How can you when we just had Italian food?"

"That seems like a long time ago. Anyway, I'd like one."

"Only one?"

"Well, for me. If you're going along, then we could get two."

She considered that a moment. "Or we could get straws and share."

Share? This was getting interesting. "But then we'd have to order a second one because we each would have had only half of the first."

"Oh, this is complicated," she said. "Maybe we should just get two."

"I think you're on to something. But speaking of sharing, I have something I'd like to share with you."

"Really? Ohhhhh—" Jason's mouth covered hers. If she had something else to say, it would have to wait. The first move was Jason's this time, but the second was Danni's as she worked her tongue against his. They leaned into each other and enjoyed the moment. Coming out the other end of the kiss, Danni said, "—myyyyy." She looked into his eyes, smiled, and then rested her head on his shoulder all the way back to the Kong Jacob.

They went straight from the cab to the hotel bar and ordered two Irish coffees. A booth was available, so they sat side by side, staying as close to each other as possible. When they had tasted their drinks, Danni said, "That's so good. I haven't had one of these in a long time."

"Me neither. You know, I was just thinking that you first saw me in an Irish bar, and now you're having an Irish coffee with me."

"That must mean something. It kind of completes the circuit."

"In a way. But, as far as completion goes, there was one more thing I was thinking of." Jason waited to see if she would take the hint.

She narrowed her eyes. "What if the circuits are too hot to handle?"

"I'll take my chances. Give me your hand." He held on tightly. "Just tell me one thing. That stuff you said the other night, about being gay?"

"Was nonsense. I was being silly. I'm sorry. I was a little scared that things were going too fast, so it was a way to buy time. But it was unkind. I shouldn't have done that."

"Of course, I didn't believe you. Well, maybe for a few minutes."

"I know." She laughed nervously. "That made it better actually, knowing that you didn't take the idea seriously." She squeezed his hand. "Things are different now. I know you better, a lot better, I think. And the thing is, this whole business I'm involved in would be very lonely without you."

Jason looked at her face and thought she might tear up. He didn't want to see that. "Don't you call home and check in?"

She hesitated. "Yes, but you're here with me and nobody else is. You've seen Huff, you've talked with him, you know his state of mind. And you're more objective about him than anybody back home. Believe me, that helps."

Jason could have continued down Huff Street if he had wanted. Danni seemed about ready to open up on the subject, but that would have spoiled the mood. They were in a fantastic space together now, and Jason wasn't going to shatter that with more questions. So he simply said, "I'm glad to help. I may be on thin ice here, but I'm feeling there are a lot of things I wouldn't mind helping you with."

Danni kissed him on the cheek. "That's not thin ice, mister. You're standing on solid ground."

"Drink up," he said. They both felt an urgency and finished their Irish coffees rapidly and headed for the stairs. When they got to their floor, they stopped in front of Danni's room and kissed.

Jason said, "We're making a spectacle."

"I don't mind being a spectacle."

"*You* don't mind, but I was hoping this could be more...private."

"Now there's an idea. Okay, give me ten minutes. I'd like to freshen up and slip into something *more comfortable*."

"Comfort is good. Be back in ten." They kissed again, then Jason reluctantly stepped over to his room.

As he opened the door, the room phone was ringing. Jason picked up and said hello.

"Jason, it's Ben Novitsky. Glad I got you. Need to touch bases. You weren't answering your cellphone, and I tried your room earlier but I guess you were out."

The voice on the line was so jarring. Jason realized it was only early afternoon in Seattle and that his boss was obviously hard at work, but all the same he would rather have postponed the call. Still, Jason supposed he had to say something. "Just having dinner, Ben. And taking a walk."

"Staying in shape, huh? Wish I could do that."

Jason was too annoyed to respond to this chitchat.

Novitsky must have got the message. "The reason I called, Jason, is that I received a fax offering a very large supply of havarti."

"Ben, haven't I already heard this?"

"No, this is a new one. Completely new. It's from something called Delhi Deli Mercantile. Weird name, huh, but have you ever heard of this company?"

"Yes, sort of," Jason said. "In fact, I mentioned it to you earlier. It's not as if we haven't talked about this." So he was being totally undercut in the cheese market. Not all the sharks were swimming in the ocean.

"I thought it sounded familiar. I think it's Indian. I mean from India. It sounds Indian. Didn't you tell me something earlier about folks in India liking havarti?"

Jason took a deep breath. Did the man listen to anything he said? Well, maybe some, but only enough to get confused. "Something like that," Jason replied. "What I told you earlier was that the havarti we're trying to buy is unavailable because it's being diverted to India. Or at least that's the story Bjorneby gave me. And as far as I can tell, the cheese is being funneled through Delhi Deli Mercantile."

"This fax I got was signed by some Indian guy, I guess. Looks like...Sayon Kunder. You know him?"

"Never heard of him," Jason said. "Sayon Kunder?"

"Here, let me spell it."

Jason grabbed a pen and wrote the name on a hotel notepad. "Got it."

"Anyway, this Kunder says there's only a short time to make a deal."

"How much time, Ben?"

"He doesn't say exactly. Just a short time."

Jason wondered about the hungry masses of India being deprived of havarti. Did they even know that the shipload of cheese that was to leave Copenhagen tomorrow was about to change course? Did they actually know anything at all about Danish havarti?

"Ben, I want you to stall."

"Stall? And miss this deal?" Novitsky had to be pulling on his ear now, then running his hand over his crew cut. "Look, the price is pretty good, and the amount he's offering is more than generous. I don't know about delivery time."

"Ben, stall. I'm working on something here." Which wasn't strictly true, but it would be.

"Okay, okay. I don't like this, but I'll do it. How long?"

"End of the week."

"That's a long time. Oh, all right. Jason—"

"Ben, I have to go. Somebody here needs me. Talk to you."

Jason thought that was the first time he'd ever hung up on Novitsky, and it felt good. In fact, it felt overdue. A smile crossed Jason's face, and he went to the bathroom and washed up and put on a *good* cologne. After that, he had four or five minutes to wait. He sat down in the chair and calmed himself with deep breathing. He'd fallen out of practice, but now seemed like an excellent time to get back into it, and back to that wonderful space he'd been in with Danni. In thirty seconds or so, he felt the tension start to go. He breathed it right out and kept breathing it out another five minutes.

Then he calmly checked the time, opened his door, shut off the lights, and went over to Danni's room and knocked.

"What's the code?" she called out.

Code? Nobody said anything about a code. He thought a second or two and ventured, "Solid ground."

She opened the door. "Good choice."

His jaw dropped. She was wearing a thin red robe, an *open* thin red robe, and underneath it a revealing lacy black teddy.

"Danni?"

"Come in and shut the door if you don't want the neighbors to see a spectacle."

He did what he was told. "I think I'm seeing one right now."

Her eyes were bright. "We haven't even got started."

Jason took a step closer and breathed in her intoxicating perfume. He reached for her.

#

Later, after he'd found her ladybug tattoos, she asked him to stay the night. It didn't take long to agree.

· 8 ·

In the morning, Jason rolled over and reached for Danni.

But Danni wasn't in bed.

When he cracked his eyes open, he saw her by the dresser brushing her hair. No enticing lingerie was in view now. She was already conservatively dressed for the day, a sweater hiding even her neck.

She heard him stir and looked over. "Morning, sleepyhead."

He glanced at the window. Daylight was peeking around the curtain. "Morning? What time is it?"

"Oh, a little after eight."

"You got up early," he said with a mixture of surprise and admiration.

"Showered, dressed and ready to go. After last night, I'm all invigorated."

"Oh. I was hoping there could be a little more of last night."

Danni came over and sat down on the bed. "That was wonderful, Jason." When she bent over and kissed him, he tried to pull her down. She broke away. "But now you're being a bad boy, and I have things to do."

"You have an agenda?"

"Of sorts." She pulled away from him and stood up. "I'm going out today and also need to make some phone calls."

"I see. And you want to do all that alone."

"I think so. I'm sorry, Jason, but that's kind of the way it has to be."

"Kind of the way," he muttered to himself. Make yourself scarce, kid. "What about breakfast? I could hurry and get dressed and go down with you."

"I'm not going down to breakfast, so don't rush on my account. I'll pick up something a little later."

"Well." He sat up in bed and felt the faint brush of air against his bare chest. The ventilation system was doing its job. Now that Danni's perfume had receded some, he could detect the pervasive lavender scent of hotel air freshener wafting through the pipes just as it did in his room. "Sounds as if you have everything in order then."

"Not everything. But enough. How about you?"

"More like disorder, I'd say. Oh, I'll scratch around and find something. After I get some coffee. Believe it or not, my boss called last night right between the Irish coffee and the time I came over here. It sounds as if somebody from—I won't say it—that Indian company is trying to deal us some havarti."

"What? First they take it from you, then they try to sell it back to you? Am I missing something?"

"Only what I'm missing. A good explanation." Jason looked around. "Speaking of missing, have you seen my clothes? I don't suppose it would be a good idea to cross the hall in the buff."

"You could borrow my robe."

"The little red one? If that's the choice, I'll go naked. I can always say I lost my way to the sauna, but if I wore that robe I'd be the one in hot water."

"Oh, in that case...your clothes are folded down here at the end of the bed."

"Folded? Those clothes don't know the word. Are you one of those neatniks?"

Danni held her palms up. "I confess, it happens sometimes. But you know it's not illegal to be neat. In some circles it's even considered a virtue. Besides, you're not as rumpled as you'd like to pretend. I've been in your room, and I've seen a lot worse."

Jason threw back the covers, reached for his clothes and started getting dressed. He felt Danni staring at him. "Hey, don't look. I'm modest. Didn't I tell you?"

Danni laughed. "Modesty. That's another thing you should stop pretending about."

It crossed Jason's mind that he should tell Danni to stop pretending about bringing Huff to justice. Standing out in the snow wasn't going to do it. But he was having too much fun with her now to dive back into that old discussion. "I'm almost always modest," he said. "You just caught me at an extreme moment last night."

"An extremely good one, too, mister. Please don't change."

When Jason was dressed, he said, "Well, I guess I'll see you later today. Maybe we could hook up for dinner again. Something not so Italian this time. You know, stay away from the red wine."

"Don't say it." But she was smiling.

"All right, I'll leave that one alone. But about tonight..."

"Okay, yeah, probably. We'll see where we are, see how it's going."

Jason made a move toward the door, but Danni grabbed him. "Jason, you forgot something." As she pulled him in for the last kiss of the morning, he started thinking he could get used to this. She made the extra few seconds in her room worthwhile and then gave him a little punch in the chest. "Now get outta here, mister."

He went over to his room and showered leisurely, shaved leisurely and then leisurely mussed up the bed to make the housekeeper think he'd slept there last night. The odd thing about leisure, he decided, was that most people engaged in it only because they had nothing else to do. That was more or less his case this morning, and he didn't think that fit the definition. A real test would be to maintain leisure when a hundred things were clamoring to get on the schedule. It sounded like an admirable goal. He'd have to work on that. But would it be leisure if he had to work at it?

All the same, he ate breakfast in a leisurely manner, almost dawdling, because he had no pressing appointments and no burning ideas that would rescue his business trip. What Novitsky had told him last night only deepened the problem. Jason had hoped that some bright idea would occur to him this morning about Delhi Deli Mercantile's sudden entry into the havarti sweepstakes, but it hadn't.

Perhaps if he'd stuck by his phone last night, instead of slipping off to dreamland with Danni, he could have heard from Novitsky again. Wouldn't that have been great? Before sunrise, his boss might have gathered in two or three more havarti offers by fax, email or carrier pigeon, and what did Jason think about those?

His first answer in this imaginary conversation was, well, uncivil. Where was his love for humanity?

Okay, okay. The truth was that even though Danni's asking had been more than a sufficient reason for staying over, a definite side benefit had been avoiding more late-night business dealings. Any ideas about buying cheese would just have to wait. If the havarti ship left port without him, then he'd catch up when he could—in a speedboat if necessary.

He looked at his food without excitement.

The culinary offerings of the Kong Jacob breakfast, or *morgenmad* as the Danes called it, were predictable by now. He tried to play a game of putting different things on his plate so the meal would seem like some new adventure. But it didn't really work.

Not having Danni there gave him a kind of empty feeling no matter which foods he ate. He knew she wouldn't be with him when he went home to Seattle and that, one way or another, they would both finish their business in Denmark and then leave, probably within days. The problem was that he wasn't prepared to deal with that yet. He supposed he would adjust and guessed that he would have to—later.

Adjusting might be easier than it seemed, though, because in some ways Jason realized he hardly knew Danni. Sure, he'd spent a lot of concentrated time with her, made terrific love, shared drinks and meals and had some laughs, even some disagreements. So he felt he had a good start on knowing and appreciating her, but he was almost in as much denial as she was about her background. It was as if they'd decided together that she didn't have one and didn't need one. Danni Rossler from Pittsburgh worked in some unknown capacity—he'd pretty much rejected her security job story—for an electronics company. That was all he knew, and he had to admit there was no validation that even those scant details were correct.

He knew something of Danni's character and values and emotions, but obviously that wasn't enough. What were things like for
her in Pittsburgh? Had she grown up there? Did she have anyone
she would call a boyfriend? Did she have a cat, a dog, tropical
fish? Did she have a brother or sister? And what did they do? And
where were the parents? He had none of that knowledge about her
and, more than that, didn't feel comfortable in asking. And the
more he thought about that, the more that it bothered him. If he did
ask, probably the best he could expect was a shrug followed by
silence. The worst was angering her and risking everything, and he
couldn't make himself do that. Not yet.

Of course, she could always say she didn't know many of
those things about him, either, but she hadn't tried to find out
much. There was the goofy query about whether he had a sister,
but she had been playacting then so he didn't count it. He knew
Danni didn't ask about him because that would open up his right to
question her, and she didn't want that. Why? If a security agent
made love with him, it made no sense that she couldn't talk about
her private life, at least a little. She was doing a far better job of
keeping her secrets than of reining in Huff.

Jason wondered if he could ease into the issue. He could talk
about himself and see if that approach sprang loose any return information. On the other hand, he had a feeling it could end in a
monologue, not a dialogue. Well, something else then. Maybe he
could ask Danni something fairly mundane about college. She was
keen on Shakespeare, and he'd taken a year's worth of classes, so
they had that in common. Okay, he could try that tonight.

First, he supposed he had to think about work, at least for an
hour or two. He pushed back from the breakfast table and headed
up to his room.

After all, he was still on the payroll of Sunny Day Farms, and
he'd said he was working on a plan. It wasn't as if he was in a habit of slacking off in the office. In fact, he usually worked pretty
hard. But here in Denmark he felt so disconnected it was difficult
to keep an edge. Was European travel putting his job and life into

perspective? Or was it only giving him crazy ideas? He knew he wasn't going to settle that question this morning, but if a couple of hours of work would relieve some guilt about crazy ideas, then he would do it.

Jason saw that the housekeeper hadn't come by yet, so maybe he could do this before someone popped in and interrupted him. He opened his attaché case and took out a short list of Danish cheese distributors he'd brought from home. This was the secondary list of distributors, but of course that was the position he was in right now since the Bjorneby Foods situation was running on its own track. It was good that he had his own list, with phone numbers, because there was no phone book in the room. Besides, what was he going to do with a phone book in Danish? The only relevant word he knew was *ost*, cheese.

The calls were perfunctory. Jason tried to pour himself into them, but he knew he wasn't doing much of a job. Effort alone wouldn't give him a passing grade. His enthusiasm was as hard to find as a cheese loaf on a plum tree. After an hour and a half he was wrung out from fighting through the layers of people who answered the phone, in Danish, and transferred him to others, who transferred him to the right person, he hoped, who in the end didn't have much to offer but thanked him for calling. Certainly there was no havarti of any consequence worth discussing.

He did find three distributors who had sold cheese to Martin Weathersby, although they couldn't or wouldn't say if it was havarti. Two of those three distributors had heard of Sayon Kunder. Two others in the non-Weathersby column had also heard of Kunder. There was little information beyond that. They'd only heard of him in connection with the cheese business. Jason dutifully left his name, his Seattle contact number, his cellphone number and an email address in case any of these companies wanted to deal with Sunny Day Farms later. Then, he supposed, when somebody called and asked about him, they could say, yes, they had heard of Jason Stallings.

Jason put down the hotel room phone at last and got up and stretched. The housekeeper still hadn't arrived, so he looked at his cellphone. After a minute, a new idea worked its way into his head. He pursed his lips and considered it, then looked up something on the phone. Well, what do you know? He should have tried that before. But did he want to go down that road? Not on his cellphone, he decided. The little screen, or maybe the new idea, was giving him a headache. He needed to get out of the hotel and breathe some fresh air.

#

Danni sat in a little café sipping her second cup of coffee. She had already eaten a little breakfast and watched the morning rush clear out. She'd hinted to Jason that she had so much to do today, but that was only partly true. Yes, she'd called home, reluctantly, and she'd checked in with her private investigator. But she also needed space, time away from Jason, time to think.

He was so good, good to her, and just plain decent. Oh, yes. And she was falling for him like a rock, a ten-ton rock.

That was the problem, or at least one of her problems. Something that should have been so wonderful was tearing her apart. How much longer could she pretend? Jason was asking real questions that deserved real answers, but her spineless response was to dodge and weave and brush the questions aside. How could she be proud of that? She shook her head in dismay at her own behavior, and then looked up, hoping no one in the café was watching her. Lies and avoidance, what a crazy foundation for a relationship. Jason deserved better, and Danni thought maybe she did as well. She wasn't such a bad person. She'd just gone at this all wrong. But what choice did she have then? Friday night when they had first met seemed so long ago. Now she could trust Jason, trust him with her life, but she didn't know him then. He was just a stranger she'd followed on the street. *Hello, Jason, I'm Danni, and here's my whole sad story, so can you help me now*? Sure, that would have worked. And would you like to buy this bridge?

But today was a new day. It could be a new start. It really could. She could begin at the beginning and Jason would understand. Wouldn't he? She would have to be brave, and it would be hard, because she realized that as soon she'd seen Craig Huff in the

Irish pub that night her courage had started to erode. But Jason could hold her in his arms and caress the truth out of her and make her whole. If he would do that, if he wasn't totally disgusted with her, if nothing came between them...it was almost too much to hope for.

Then, she thought, she would finish what she'd come to Denmark to do. She would get all the money back, go home, drink fine wine, make love with Jason and sleep for a week.

She rubbed the white coffee cup handle thoughtfully, but knew it was no magic lamp. She raised the cup and tipped the last ounce of coffee into her mouth. And she laughed at herself. Dream on, girl. Live those fairy tales. And while you're at it, dust off those old glass slippers.

Danni paid and put on her coat and went outside, and then, as the cold air enveloped her face, her phone started ringing.

She dug the phone out of her purse and almost dropped everything when she saw whose number was on her screen. But she steadied herself and answered. "Craig?"

"Danni, I don't have time for small talk, so I'll be straight with you."

"I would like that."

"Maybe you'll like it, and maybe you won't. But here's the message. Stop snooping around, stop following me and tell your hired hands to back off."

"You know I can't do that."

"Yes you can. You have to. Otherwise, it won't be safe."

Danni closed her eyes, trying to make sense of what she'd just heard while simultaneously trying to make it all go away. Neither effort worked. She opened her eyes and became aware of her steamy breath as she struggled for words. "Craig, are you threatening me?"

"No, Danni, I'm trying to protect you. The world can be an evil place, and even though I'm trying, I can't guard against what everyone else wants to do. So I'm just warning you. For your own good. Back off and do it now."

"Craig!"

But there was no answer. The line was dead. Danni could feel her heart thumping, but she wasn't at all sure how much of her was still alive.

#

Some walkways had been shoveled clear of last night's snow, but many others hadn't. Only about two inches had fallen overnight, so walking was slow but not especially troublesome. A few places were slick because they'd been packed down to a glaze by foot traffic, and Jason tried to be careful with those or step around them.

As he put one foot in front of the other, his fresh-air stroll acquired speed and purpose. He headed up the Strøget, poked around, asked a few questions and in a few minutes found his way into an Internet café. He hadn't brought a laptop because he'd never imagined needing one for what he was about to do. Of course, he also hadn't imagined a dead man in his hotel room. At any rate, the Internet café was a pleasant change of scenery, and probably there were people around who could help him when he was ready.

He paid his fee, sat down at a computer, and did a search for Copenhagen newspapers. At first he clicked on *The Copenhagen Post* because it was an English-language site. But the Post was a weekly operation and wasn't up to date with what he wanted. Either that or it was just too sedate to publish a story on what some people might call a common murder. He moved on to *Ekstra Bladet*, which he knew was a tabloid with a little spice. He'd seen it on the street. The website looked promising with its livelier display, and Jason knew that this was the paper Stubkjaer had shown him, the paper that had reported Weathersby's death. Of course, it was all in Danish.

Now Jason needed help. There was no one seated next to him so he turned around and asked, "Do you speak English?"

A young guy with a black leather jacket and a scruffy beard said he did, and when it was established that he also read Danish, Jason explained what he wanted. The guy hopped out of his chair, clicked on a couple of links and found the story about Martin Weathersby. "That's the one," Jason said. "Could I ask you to read it to me—in English?"

"I think so. My translating may not be so good, but we'll see how it goes."

It went well, and Jason gave him a hundred kroner for his trouble. Nineteen, twenty bucks, it was worth it. But the guy's eyes lit up as if it had been a hundred dollars. He thanked Jason several times.

Jason went to other websites, in English, and took a few notes on paper. He hadn't brought any paper with him so had to ask for that, too. Although the sites told him more of what he'd started to get into on his smartphone, and what he'd half suspected for days, seeing the actual information in front of him was still an emotional jolt. After he got up from the computer, he had something to eat while he thought over what he'd learned online.

Afterward he walked back to the Kong Jacob. The weather hadn't improved, and it looked as if it could start snowing again. He zipped through the lobby and was headed to the stairway when he heard a woman call his name. Turning around, he saw a desk clerk holding an envelope while looking straight at him. He stepped over and took it. It was a plain white letter-size envelope with only his name printed on the front. Curious, he opened it on the spot. The handwritten note was from Sayon Kunder.

Mr. Stallings,

We haven't had the opportunity to meet yet, so I would like to invite you to enjoy a refreshment with me at the Hotel Lorentsen at five this afternoon. I think it would be useful if we discussed the unfortunate havarti problem. Please look for me in the lounge.

Jason thought of asking the desk clerk who had left the note and when, but knew the answer wouldn't matter. He would just have to go see Kunder. Besides, the meeting could be interesting, especially back at the Lorentsen. He recalled that he'd thought about dropping into the bar on his first visit to the hotel. There must have been at least a hundred hotels in Copenhagen, but the Lorentsen kept drawing him back.

He put the envelope in his coat pocket and went up to his room. The meeting with Kunder was several hours away, so he had plenty of time to think. Of course, maybe thinking wasn't what he needed to do now. It hadn't really helped him deal with the information he'd picked up on the Internet this morning. No, it hadn't helped at all.

The bed had been made, Jason noticed, and he was glad that he'd been able to provide work for someone. His eyes roamed the rest of the room. Everything seemed neat, and nothing was out of place. Exactly what he expected from a hotel housekeeper. There was no sign of an intruder. But then he began to wonder.

He went to the dresser and opened a drawer. Underneath the socks and underwear, his camera was still there. He probably should have taken it with him this morning, but hadn't thought about it. Idly, he picked it up and reviewed the pictures he'd taken in Denmark. He looked at the photos in reverse order. It took only a few clicks to navigate to the ones from Nyhavn he'd taken yesterday afternoon. He stopped.

Something about one of the pictures grabbed his attention. He studied it in the viewer on the back of the camera, looking with various degrees of magnification at various parts of the photo. A familiar silver Mercedes taxi was parked by Kongens Nytorv near the entrance to Nyhavn. That's where he'd caught the cab back with Danni last night. But this wasn't the same cab. For one thing, it was a different color. Maybe there were a lot of silver Mercedes taxis like this in Copenhagen—he'd heard that Mercedes were favored for taxis because the taxi companies didn't have to pay the ultra-steep sales tax that private Danish citizens did. But what interested Jason more than the car was the man leaning against it.

He appeared to be the mad Russian driver. Jason hadn't noticed that at the time he'd taken the picture. He'd just pressed the button, turned a few degrees and pressed it again. And who was the man a few feet away from the taxi guy? It was hard to say from what he could see in the small viewer, even zoomed in, but the scene did look suspicious. He had a hunch who the second guy was, but wasn't sure. He needed to see the picture on a computer monitor, or a printout.

Jason put on his heavy coat and went back to the Internet café.

"Can anyone on your staff download a digital camera? I only need one picture."

"Not here," said the spike-haired brunette running the front counter. "Around the corner." She pointed. "There's a camera shop."

Jason felt an urgency now. The camera shop was close by as described. Good. He was tired of long walks in the snow. He went in and explained what he wanted. Business was slow, so he was invited to step around the counter and show the technician which picture he needed and what he wanted to do with it. The tech looked at his camera and found the right cable to connect to his computer. On screen, all of Jason's pictures popped up as thumbnail images. He pointed at the taxi picture, and the tech opened it to full size.

Jason blinked, then leaned toward the monitor. "So."

"You like this one?" the tech asked.

"The quality is good enough, but there are things in the background I didn't expect."

"Delete it?"

"Oh, no. I want a print. But just this part." Jason indicated his desired crop in front of the monitor with a finger and then said, "An eight by ten, if you can."

"Oh, that's an American size," the tech said.

Jason didn't know how to convert that to centimeters or whatever the Danes used, so he demonstrated the size with his hands. "Like this."

The tech nodded and made a couple of clicks and the photo printer started. Jason had him copy all the pictures to a flash drive but left them on the camera's memory card. While the tech was taking care of those jobs, Jason took a business card out of his wallet and used his cellphone to call Carsten the taxi driver. The camera shop was too close to the Strøget for a taxi to get in, so Carsten gave him a meeting spot and told him how to get there.

In a few minutes, Jason had the print in hand. It some ways it was even better than the monitor view. The man leaning against the taxi was indeed the Russian driver. And the man he appeared to be talking with was none other than Craig Huff.

Huff and the Russian driver. Was this an incidental meeting? It was close to the Commodore. Or was there something important happening? It was hard to say exactly what was going on in the photo, but knowing the Russian's aversion to casual conversation, Jason could hardly believe they were just chewing the fat. Did Huff know Russian? Or Danish? Jason didn't think so. Danni had no knowledge that Huff had been to Denmark before. So they were probably speaking English. The Russian must have known more English than he'd let on.

Jason got his camera back and paid for the print and flash drive. The store put the picture into a large envelope to protect it, and Jason walked a block or so to the appointed meeting spot for his taxi. When Carsten drove up a few minutes later, Jason asked for a ride to the Hotel Lorentsen.

It was too early to meet Kunder, but Jason wanted to talk with someone else first. When Carsten headed up the hotel's driveway to the front entrance, Jason felt a flicker of nostalgia. It had only been four days since he'd moved to the Kong Jacob, and he'd never gotten past the lobby of the Lorentsen, but he still felt a connection.

He went inside. Luckily, his connection was still intact, though since Jason was standing today, the man in front of him seemed a little shorter than he had last Friday, maybe about five feet ten. Jason stepped over to the front desk and said, "Hello, Thomas."

"Sir?" Thomas looked at him, then said, "Oh, hello again. I didn't recognize you at first." Thomas was the desk clerk who had consoled him the day he'd arrived in Copenhagen. "You would like a room?"

"No, thank you. I have a fine room at the Kong Jacob. You may remember."

"I do remember. It was quite a day." Thomas hesitated, a little cautious now. "Then how may I help you?"

"I was wondering about the man who was, who died here, in

the room I was to have. I learned in the newspaper that his name was Martin Weathersby."

"This is true."

"And?"

"He was a guest of the hotel."

"Isn't there something more interesting?"

"The police didn't tell us much. I don't think the manager even knows a lot about this. It's really up to the police." Thomas held out his arms as if to absolve himself, and after Jason saw his small-ish, deformed hand, he began to think of Thomas as a real person now, not just a desk clerk who might have answers for him.

"Who's the investigating officer?"

Thomas turned and looked at a card on a bulletin board. "Detective Arne Dalvang."

Jason wrote that down and verified the spelling. "You know, if I'm going to solve the murder, I need to know which officer to call." Then he laughed, and Thomas joined him a beat later, his face showing that he wasn't sure if Jason was joking, but willing to play along with the idea. Jason went on in a more serious tone. "Thomas, I have to ask about something that's been bothering me about this whole room situation."

"Sir?"

"Well, from what I can tell, last Friday night I was supposed to get the room Mr. Weathersby had occupied the night before, last Thursday night, when it appears that he was going to stay in Copenhagen at least until Monday morning, maybe longer."

"I don't know how long he had planned to stay."

"Well, I do. Thomas, I assume you're familiar with havarti cheese, one of Denmark's finest assets?"

"It's one of my favorite foods, yes"

"Mr. Weathersby was, and I still am, in the business of buying havarti at the wholesale level. So I have a little inside information on the matter. As it turns out, Mr. Weathersby had an appointment with a Danish cheese distributor yesterday afternoon. He didn't keep it."

"I wouldn't imagine."

"Of course not. But the point is that he was obviously here at the Hotel Lorentsen last Thursday night and was probably planning to stay through the weekend so he could keep that Monday appointment. But yet I was to get the room that he was in."

"It sounds complicated, sir."

"Thomas, why don't you call me Jason? This *sir* thing makes me uncomfortable."

"All right. It sounds complicated, Jason."

"Good. But see, there's where you could help me out. Because I have a feeling that it only *sounds* complicated but is actually much simpler."

"I don't follow—Jason."

"Hmm. Well, let me come at this another way. Because I was supposed to get that room Friday night, Mr. Weathersby must have planned to go elsewhere."

"I don't know. Yes, maybe. It would seem so."

"Good. Stay with me on this, Thomas. Why would he leave for another hotel at all, especially since he already had a nice room here at the Lorentsen. I mean, I guess it was nice. Not that I really got to see it. Just pictures on the website."

"It is a very good room. All rooms at the Lorentsen are very good."

"Yes, well, I'll have to take your word on that."

"Jason? You're not still upset that you were forced to move, because we want our customers to be happy and the management would—"

"I'm very happy at the Kong Jacob, thank you. And I've had a chance to meet a lovely lady there. So I wouldn't change a thing now."

"I'm glad to hear that, Jason. Well, if you'll excuse me, I have some work to do in the back. We have several guests arriving this afternoon and—"

"But we haven't finished our discussion, Thomas."

"Sir, I'm really quite busy."

"There goes that *sir* thing again. Thomas, I want to show you something." Jason took out his wallet and opened it slightly and then closed it again. "Did you see anything, Thomas?"

"Yes, sir, I believe I saw three hundred kroner."

"And I believe you're right." He removed three bills, about sixty dollars worth. "I want to give you this, as a little tip for your help the other day in settling my nerves and showing kindness in a trying moment. I'm very grateful."

Jason put the folded bills on the counter, and Thomas' left hand quickly covered them. "My job is to be of service, sir. Jason."

"That's very kind of you. So perhaps you remember something about the police investigation, about Mr. Weathersby, God rest his soul."

"The detective interviewed a lot of us here at the hotel."

"Employees? Guests?"

"Mostly the staff. And some guests. At least everyone on that floor. Anyway, we were told not to talk about the investigation."

"Of course. We'll let the police do their work. I wouldn't even suggest interfering with that. But maybe you can tell me something about Mr. Weathersby's plans and that little scheduling question I raised."

Thomas leaned forward and lowered his voice. "He was originally scheduled to be at the Lorentsen several nights and not check out until Monday morning."

"But he changed his plans."

"Apparently. He checked in about four o'clock Thursday afternoon, but about seven that night he called the front desk asking to be moved."

"*He* called. You're sure?"

"Absolutely. I took the call myself. He wanted to be moved to the Kong Jacob, immediately if possible."

"But he didn't move."

"No, that wasn't possible until the next day. We checked and the Kong Jacob was full. They're undergoing some renovation this winter, as you probably know, and not all the rooms will be available until sometime this spring. So he reluctantly decided to stay here at the Lorentsen the one night and then move the next day, which would have been Friday."

"The day I arrived," Jason said. Of course, Weathersby did leave that day, though for a different resting place than the grand old Kong Jacob. "But he could have gone to a third hotel," Jason said.

"He could have. But he'd already paid here for the first night. I suppose he was trying to save his money."

"Had Mr. Weathersby ever stayed here at the Lorentsen before?"

"No, I don't believe so. Of course, I've been here only a few months myself. But when he called, he told me that he always preferred the Kong Jacob when he came to Copenhagen. He said he liked an older hotel, something with character and atmosphere. Modern conveniences apparently didn't interest him much."

"So why didn't he go there in the first place?"

"Because he couldn't. Because of the renovation. Reservations were extremely tight for last Thursday, that first day, at least on short notice, so he couldn't get in when he wanted. Instead, he decided to break with tradition and go with the Lorentsen for his entire stay in Copenhagen. At least that was his plan until seven that night, when he called me."

"He told you all that?"

"Oh, yes. Apparently he thought he would get better service if he told his personal story. But I couldn't get him moved to the Kong Jacob that night no matter how hard I tried."

All this talk about the Lorentsen and the Kong Jacob made it sound as if there were only two hotels in Copenhagen, which was ridiculous. But there seemed to be more than a casual connection between the two, Jason thought. He remembered the Lorentsen van bringing the food cart to the Kong Jacob last night.

"Thomas, about the Kong Jacob and the Lorentsen. What's the connection? Do they have the same ownership?"

"Yes, they do. We try not to highlight that, but, yes, we do work together."

"Which is why I was moved to the Kong Jacob instead of some other hotel." And why Thomas' fetching partner at the desk that afternoon spoke so highly of the Kong Jacob. Then a new insight struck Jason. He had to pursue it. "So I suppose that Mr. Weathersby was then booked at the Kong Jacob for Friday night and the rest of the weekend."

"Oh, yes. We set that up Thursday night shortly after he called the desk. After I checked with the Kong Jacob, I called him back and gave him the good news."

"Good news."

"Yes, fortunately there was one vacancy there for the weekend. But as I mentioned earlier, they had no vacancy for Thursday, which is why he came here."

"One vacancy for the weekend, you say."

"As I recall, yes."

"But when it was obvious he couldn't show up to claim the room, the Kong Jacob then had a new vacancy."

"I never thought of it that way," Thomas said.

"A vacancy that then went to me. So it seems that instead of occupying the room Mr. Weathersby had here at the Lorentsen, I now am occupying the room he was supposed to get at the Kong Jacob."

Thomas opened his eyes wide. "My, God. That's amazing."

Unsettling was the word Jason had in mind. Despite the heavy coat he was still wearing, chills raced up his arms.

Thomas was fascinated now. "And you said you were both in the same business. The police might want to know that. Do you think?"

"I doubt it, but it's possible that..." Jason was a little distracted by what he was seeing now. Less than a hundred feet away at the other side of the lobby was the striking cinnamon-haired young woman he and Danni had seen going into the Commodore Hotel. Of course, this was one of the women Danni had previously seen embracing Huff. But now not only was she here at the Lorentsen but she was also wearing a blue uniform-like dress. Was this Gitte? Almost instinctively, Jason reached for his camera and snapped a picture of her.

"Don't do that," Thomas said, too late.

"Don't do what?" Jason glanced at Thomas, then turned his

gaze back to the woman. The camera didn't flash, and she didn't seem to notice that she'd been photographed.

"I was about to tell you not to take that picture."

"Oh, that. Don't worry. I won't embarrass the hotel. It's just for my private collection. You know, pretty girls and all. I'm a pushover for a pretty girl like that."

"Well, that she is." The woman was moving around the background with a pushcart while talking with a man wearing a similar uniform.

"Maybe I'll ask her for a date," Jason said, giving her an appreciative sidelong look. Now he turned back to Thomas. "Does she work here?"

"She does. Food service."

"Ah. That explains the uniform. So she's a waitress?"

"Sometimes, but not exactly. Mostly she prepares trays and does room service."

"Of course. Then you know her."

"I've dated her myself," Thomas said, his eyes directed at the floor.

"Really? What's her name?"

"Cabrina. Cabrina Jorgensen."

Not Gitte. Jason looked back across the lobby at Cabrina. So this was Huff's new love interest. Did he know her before coming to Denmark? Probably not. He'd specifically mentioned Gitte, and with great passion. Maybe at the time in that Irish pub Huff hadn't even met Cabrina. So either Huff was fickle or things weren't going well with Gitte. And if the Gitte situation was less than satisfactory, maybe Huff wouldn't hang around Copenhagen for long. On the other hand, if it was simply a matter of looks, Cabrina would be hard to beat.

Jason turned back to Thomas. "Are you dating her now?"

"Off and on, I think you say. Sometimes."

"You're a good-looking guy, Thomas. She ought to like you."

"We're getting there. I do what I can to make her like me. She's quite a woman."

"A hot one?"

"Oh, yes. Jason, you should think twice about getting involved with Cabrina. I think she would, what's the word, *exhaust* you."

"Really? I'm in pretty good shape."

"I wasn't thinking of sports. It's something different. How do I say it? She never seems to get tired, and she always seems to get what she wants. Very, uh, *seductive*. Yes, that's it."

"I'm getting the picture, Thomas. And I appreciate the warning."

Jason thanked Thomas for his time and got ready to leave the hotel, but not before making a small detour. He wanted a closer look at Cabrina. The camera was in his hand, and it would have been great to take her picture up close, but he wasn't going to make a scene. Probably what he had was good enough. Instead, he turned briefly and took a picture of the front desk, where Thomas was now helping someone else. He turned back and walked closer to Cabrina. When Jason got to within five or six feet of her, she noticed him and smiled, and he felt the pull that Thomas had spoken of. Jason hesitated with a catch in his step, then resisted and walked away. But resisting wasn't easy. He could see that it was something Craig Huff hadn't been able to do.

The air was icy crisp. Jason didn't feel like another walk in the cold at the moment. Besides, he had certain things to do before coming back to the Lorentsen to meet Sayon Kunder, and the clock was a factor now. A call to Carsten would be in order. On the other hand, an empty taxi was idling at the hotel entrance. Jason got in and gave directions back to the spot Carsten had picked him up near the camera shop. He'd never seen this driver before, and that was fine with him.

They recognized him immediately at the camera shop. Business was still slow, so Jason again was invited back to help with the process. This time he wanted to zoom in on Cabrina and crop out most of the lobby. She was a little too far away in the picture for a quality enlargement, but the tech was able to come up with a print that clearly showed her face and identified her. That was all that mattered.

Jason had that picture and the Thomas picture copied to his

flash drive and then walked back to the Kong Jacob. When he got to his floor, he knocked on Danni's door. She might not be expecting him at this time of day, but that was all right. He just hoped she was in.

She opened the door with a pained expression. "Jason, come in." She turned and hobbled back to the bed.

"My God, what happened?"

"I fell down late this morning. I was up at Magasin—you know, the department store—and I walked out and slipped on the sidewalk. The snow in that one spot was packed down, and I guess a little icy."

"You're hurting. Is anything broken?"

"I don't think so. I'm just banged up—hips, lower back—but I'm feeling worse than I did right afterward."

"That's natural. What happened after you fell? You didn't walk back, did you?"

"No. Some people helped me to my feet and stayed with me a few minutes, and then after I got my bearings, I took a cab to the hotel. And I rode up the elevator. No stairs today."

Jason moved over to stand by her and gave her a hug. "I'm really sorry, Danni. Maybe I should take you to a hospital to get checked out. They could do X-rays."

"Thanks, but I don't think it's that bad. I took a couple of acetaminophen, and I just need a little rest now."

"Well, if you're sure."

"Okay, if things get worse, you let me know."

"I'll let you know. Don't worry."

"Okay." Jason took off his coat and put down his picture envelopes. He walked over to the window and looked out at the plaza across the street. "I was wondering what your investigator found. You talked to him, I assume."

"I did. Ooooh. Can you help with these pillows? I have to lie back."

Jason hurried to the bed and got Danni propped up in a half sitting position.

"Thanks. I'll be glad when this is over."

He sat on the bed besides her and patted her leg. "Hope it wasn't anything I said."

"No, it wasn't you. Yes, I talked to the investigator. The pieces are fitting together a little. One of the women I saw with Craig Huff is Gitte Benneker."

"Gitte. So Huff was telling the truth. And now you have the last name. Anything else?"

"She's twenty-six and works in a telephone office. Normally she's quiet, but the investigator, or one of his people, observed her arguing with him."

"Interesting." So the Gitte-Huff show was on rocky terrain. "Is this the one we saw Monday night? With the long hair, the cinnamon color?"

"No, that's the other one."

"I thought so. How about her? Did you get anything?"

"Not so much. Only a first name so far. Cabrina somebody."

"That's it? No job, age, favorite food? No astrological sign?"

Danni started to laugh, then grimaced. "Don't make me laugh. It hurts."

"Sorry. Just trying to lighten the mood."

"I know. But as for Cabrina, that's all I know at the moment. It's not much, is it?"

"It's a start," Jason said. "And it fits with something I ran across a little while ago." He stood up and grabbed one of the envelopes. "Have a look at this."

Danni took the picture out of the envelope and looked at the shot of Cabrina in profile. "That's her." She looked up at Jason. "Where did you get this?"

"I took the picture this afternoon. It was from a little distance, but the tech who made the print for me was able to zoom in on her."

"I'm impressed. So where was this? It's indoors. She's not wearing a coat."

"The Hotel Lorentsen. That's where I had my reservation before I got moved over here."

"So you just waltz in and snap her picture and she doesn't even know it? How did you know where to find her?"

"I didn't know where to find her. All I did was turn around in the lobby and there she was. And I don't think she noticed I took her picture. If she did, she didn't object."

"I don't get it," Danni said. "So why were you at this hotel?"

"Remember the dead Englishman? Something was bothering me about the whole thing, and I had time, so I thought I'd ask the desk clerk a few questions."

"And he answered?"

"Well, it took a minute or two to get him warmed up. But then it went much better. Of course, that was after I tipped him for helping me the other day."

"You bribed him? I won't even ask how much."

"Probably too much. But it worked. And he told me about Cabrina. Cabrina Jorgensen, to be precise."

"Your desk clerk knows her?"

"Better than that. He's dated her. So he has something in common with Huff. But the clerk warned me off. Said Cabrina would eat me alive."

Danni looked at the picture again. "Oh, I believe it. She's not your type. Too young and too wild."

"Do you think she's Huff's type?" There was no answer. "Anyway, you can keep the picture if it helps you. Maybe you'll want to contact her."

"How would I do that? She was just passing through a hotel lobby. She's not going to magically pop up there if I drop in."

"She might," Jason said. "Look at the picture again. She's wearing a uniform."

Danni studied the photo. "Some kind of waitress?"

"That's right. She works at the hotel. Sort of a waitress, room service, stuff like that."

"So wonder boy is dating a waitress. It's interesting, but I don't see how it helps me."

Jason walked around the room, too keyed up to stay in one place. "Think about this. Cabrina has a fairly low-paying service job. She meets Huff somehow, and he flashes some cash and spends a little on her, so she goes back for more."

"She's a gold digger?"

"Well, maybe. I don't know. That could be a little harsh. But you know, she likes a guy who spends money on her, she likes the attention. And to her he's a foreigner. So there might be a thrill factor there, something she wouldn't have with a local guy."

"So that's what she gets out of it," Danni said. "What about wonder boy?"

"That's not too hard to figure. Things aren't going well with Gitte, not what he hoped, so he hooks up with Cabrina so he won't be lonely here in Copenhagen. He can spend a little money on her, maybe even buy her affection. Look at her picture. She's a knockout. So Huff might feel important just being around her. And if my hotel desk clerk is right, their late night meetings involve a little more excitement than reading poetry by candlelight. You saw them together over at Nyhavn. They weren't discussing iambic pentameter."

"Yeah, I'd sort of assumed it was like that. It makes sense. But what do I do with this information?"

"I was afraid you'd ask. I don't know exactly. But it probably depends on how you want to go at it. You could talk to Cabrina, I suppose, see what she knows about Huff. Or you could have her put a question or two to him and then report back."

"A snitch? Could I trust her not to tell him?"

"That's something you would have to decide."

Danni moved uncomfortably on the bed. "I'll think about that tomorrow—when I feel better."

"I take it you're in no condition to go out for dinner."

"That's an understatement. I hadn't even thought about food. I guess when I'm ready I'll try room service. And then go to sleep early."

"Probably a good idea." Jason paused, not sure how to tell Danni what he had to say. Well, maybe he would wait. "I have to go out for a while. I'm going to meet a guy from that Indian company. Sayon Kunder. He's invited me for a drink at the Lorentsen."

"You sure are spending a lot of time at that hotel today. How did he find you?"

"No idea. But I'll be asking."

Jason stepped toward the door, then turned around. "Danni, I hate to bring this up now, when you're hurting like this, but I found out some other things today."

"Something about Gitte? Or is it the cheese business?"

"No, it's about *you*."

"Me?" She looked nervous. "I'm not that interesting."

"But I think you are. I found out you're not from Pittsburgh. You're not from Pennsylvania. You're from California."

"Jason, I, I, I never said I was from Pennsylvania. I didn't know if I could trust you at first, so I just left it, you know, open to interpretation. What I meant, what I really meant, is that I'm from Pittsburg, California. Pittsburg without the *H*. It's a suburb, east of San Francisco. You might not have heard of it."

Jason shook his head. "I know where it is, Danni. But you're not from there, either. I know a little about the Bay Area, and you and Pittsburg without the *H* just don't fit."

"Okay, you got me there." She looked as if she were about ready to cry. "But I didn't lie to you about my name. I gave you my real name."

"I know. That's how I found you on the Internet. You really live in Benicia. It's a good town, nice little boutiques and antique shops, used to be the state capital way back when. And it's just a few miles up the road from Pittsburg without the *H*. I even know your home phone number." He gave it to her and she nodded.

"You're right. And I shouldn't have deceived you. I thought I was doing the right thing, keeping it to myself. I thought a lot about this stuff this morning. I'm sorry I lied to you."

"Danni, there's something else you kept to yourself, your reason for following Huff."

"He's an embezzler!"

"Okay. But he's also something else, at least to you. If he were a common criminal, you would have turned him in the first night you saw him. You've made no move to confront him or contact the police. And you hired a private investigator only after I told you to do it."

"Jason, I..." She was almost in tears now.

"I'm sorry, Danni. I really am." He went over and tried to comfort her.

She jerked his arm off her shoulder. "Don't touch me."

"Look, I'll come back after I see this Indian guy. We can talk then, sort this out. That'll give you a chance to think things over."

Danni didn't say anything, so he took a deep breath and opened the door. Halfway out he turned back to see how she was doing, but she wouldn't look at him. He went ahead and closed the door after himself. Out in the hallway, he stopped and shut his eyes. Should he go back? Try to smooth it out now? Then he heard a huge sob and imagined her injured body shaking. He'd hurt her even more, and he'd never felt so bad about doing the right thing. Last night they'd made beautiful love, but now she probably thought he was the biggest jerk in the world.

Between gasps, her sobs echoed on. He had to get out of there before he started crying himself. Damn it, life was just so unfair.

· 9 ·

Late in the afternoon when the sunlight began to fade, two men waited in a car, watching the front door of the Kong Jacob. The car was a four-door, seven-year-old black Saab in need of a wash because of the normal winter street slush, a car especially valued by this afternoon's driver because it was reliable and unremarkable. It was the kind of car almost everyone in Copenhagen had seen and almost no one remembered.

The man watching the hotel from the driver's seat needed such an unremarkable car for an hour or two, and so he had arranged to *borrow* it. He was not particular about the brand or year as long as the car didn't attract attention. His passenger had no interest in the car's origins and didn't even know it was a Saab.

It was the perfect car for the job.

The two men in the Saab kept the engine running to stay warm.

From the passenger side of the front seat, Craig Huff peered through binoculars. "There he is. He's leaving."

They watched Jason Stallings get into a taxi and ride away.

"We'll wait ten more minutes to make sure he doesn't return," the driver said.

Huff turned to look at him and hardly recognized the man himself, so complete was his transformation. Instead of his normal casual wear, Andrei Baransky was now dressed in a dark suit and blue silk tie, fine gray wool overcoat and fashionable leather gloves. If the observer didn't know that underneath the suit jacket was a holstered 9 mm Glock, then he'd have to say that the driver looked every bit the professional. And for anyone who might still recognize him as that wild Russian taxi driver, the graying false mustache was an effective disguise, at least on first glance, though probably even a full beard couldn't hide the square jaw. The mustache also made him look six or seven years older, maybe in his early forties now. Of course, there were some things Baransky hadn't changed. One was his cologne. Even with his stuffed sinuses, Huff could pick up the too-sweet smell. Where did people get that junk? A discount store? Oh, well, he wouldn't mention it now, not with so many important things to talk about.

"I still don't like it," Huff said, figuring he'd already lost the battle but still determined to fight on against the madness. "You know, we could just drive away and let things be. We don't have to do this."

"You're nervous, that's all. This is your first time. Just do what I tell you." Baransky's English was very good, and he had no discernible accent, except, of course, when he wanted one. Besides English and his native Russian, he spoke fluent Danish, Swedish, Norwegian, German and Dutch. He knew French fairly well and was now working on Italian. Spanish would be next. Despite his credentials, he found the Romance languages more challenging, not the vocabularies or rules of syntax but the idioms and nuances. Even he admitted that he was not comfortable with nuances. Still, with his training in the KGB, taking more than six months to master a language was catamount to failure.

"Yeah, I'm nervous, Andrei. But that's not the point. The point is that it's unnecessary to abduct anyone. She's harmless. Listen, she's been hanging around Copenhagen for days and has barely made a move. You think she's suddenly going to become dangerous? I gave her a warning this morning, and she hasn't done anything since. So let's give this a little time. If she stays quiet another day or two, then none of this is necessary. Anyway, the biggest thing she's done all week is to hire some private eye to tail me and my girlfriend."

"You mean girlfriends, don't you, Craig? Even I know about Miss Gitte and the famous Miss Cabrina."

"Whatever." Huff didn't like it when Baransky called him Craig. It was too personal. "They don't mean anything to me anymore. It won't be long before I leave them both behind."

"Ah, the spurned lover."

"Andrei, I could really do without your commentary." Huff knew better than to call him Square Jaw but instead thought he'd throw the first name approach back at Baransky, but it just bounced off harmlessly.

"As you please, my friend."

"I'm not your friend." That was another thing Baransky couldn't change for a million dollars: his personality. Huff hesitated to think that the Russian even had one, but he conceded that Square Jaw did have something that *resembled* a personality, a mindset that would fascinate a psychologist specializing in deviant behavior. There was so much rich material to be mined, and it was so close to the surface. "Anyway," Huff said, "there's no harm whatsoever in leaving her alone. Besides, after that fall, she's probably too sore to move."

"But she's young and will heal. Soon. And then there's her boyfriend, our dear Mr. Stallings. He's sly, don't you think? He pretends he's in Denmark only to buy cheese, but he's like a coiled snake. Turn your back on him and he will strike, especially if Miss Danni gives him ideas. No, I don't trust him."

"Ease up, Andrei. Sure, he's fallen for the girl, and maybe he would try to help her out, but that doesn't mean he can. He's not trained for these things like you are. I've met him. He's just a regular guy. You could outwit him in thirty seconds. You already have."

Huff reached into his coat. When his hand came out with a pack of cigarettes, Baransky barked, "No smoking in the car."

Huff glared at him, then put the cigarettes back.

Baransky went on as if nothing had happened. "Don't underestimate Stallings. I don't know whether he has training or not. See how he changed hotels in the blink of an eye and got a room just down the hall from Miss Danni. I admit I don't know what he's up to, but he's no fool. I see something of myself in him."

"You're delusional."

"And you, Craig, are an innocent baby."

"Gee, thanks for the compliment."

"Forget it. We should be talking about Miss Danni, not ourselves." Baransky went silent a moment, then chortled. "You know, she just dropped into my hands."

"Oh, come on. It was sheer luck that you were around when she fell."

"I make my own luck. I intended to hang close in case something happened, and it did. I would have paid the taxi fare myself if the rules allowed. It was worth a thousand times that much to hear her complain just once about her pain."

"You enjoyed that? That's sick." Huff looked out the window at the winter landscape. He could hardly believe he was sitting in a car in Copenhagen with a Russian spy.

"As usual, you miss the point. I care nothing one way or the other about her pain. It was the idea she gave me about the wheelchair."

"I know. I've already heard about the brilliant idea."

"Of course. But being there when she fell, and then getting the idea—that tells me the plan is right."

"It tells me you're pushing too hard. Besides, this sounds like kidnapping to me."

"Then arrest me." Baransky laughed. "You are weak and softhearted. Just like her. But we're not going to hurt her. She's only *moving*—for just a little while."

"You could have taken her then, when she was in your taxi coming back from the store. Why didn't you? Then you could have skipped this hotel business."

Baransky nodded. "So you found my flaw, Craig. I'll give you credit. As a matter of fact, I didn't think of doing anything that fast. But in retrospect, this plan may prove to be better anyhow. True, we need to exercise care in the hotel, but waiting has provided several advantages. First, we're assured that Stallings will be gone for a while, something we couldn't have known earlier. Second, a screaming woman in the back of my taxi would have caused endless trouble and I couldn't have been certain of the outcome. Third, I hadn't made arrangements at the other end yet. And fourth, I have assistance now. You."

"Whoopdy-doo." The protest was feeble, Huff knew. So what. Baransky was probably right about all of it. "Okay then. So we get her out of the hotel. Then what? You said we'd talk to her, scare her off."

"Of course. Then we'll take her to a warehouse as I told you earlier. She'll be all stiff and sore, but in a day or two she'll be found and life will go on. And by that time we will have concluded our business, and I'll be out of the country. And you should be, too."

"And what if she isn't found?"

"You care about her that much?" Baransky eyed him with pity. "Don't worry. I know how to do these things. I haven't made a mistake yet."

"So you're perfect."

"If you want to get personal, no, I'm not perfect. As you noticed, I have flaws. But in these matters, yes, I'm very good. So if you care about Miss Danni's future, you should hope I'm perfect."

Huff wasn't convinced of anything. Early this morning, part of him had wanted to leave the country without "Miss Danni" even knowing it. Then he called to warn her because his conscience wouldn't let him stay quiet any longer. Sure, he had made mistakes, but he was still trying to do the right thing with Baransky even if it didn't look like it. Most of all, he hadn't bargained for any of this crap. They could shove their Operation Sierra. If there was a next time, he wouldn't try to be a hero.

But none of that took Gitte into account. Yes, he'd told Square Jaw she didn't matter anymore, but that was a deception. Huff might leave the country disappointed, but she would still matter. He couldn't give up on her so quickly. They'd just got off to a bad start when he'd come to Copenhagen. Wasn't that it? If only he could go back and do it over.

Then in the afternoon he'd checked in with Baransky, and once it was clear that the Russian was planning this kidnapping, then Huff knew he had to be here, ostensibly to help but really to make sure the worst didn't happen. Technically, that made him an accessory, he supposed, but this wasn't a time to argue the fine points. He just had to do what he could. There wouldn't be a second chance.

Feeling more resolute now, Huff threw Baransky a hard look. "How do you know so much about Danni Rossler?"

"Because it's my business. She's spent so much time poking around your hotel I could hardly be *unaware*. Even if she never calls the police on you, she's still getting in the road. And one of these times, she's going to talk her boyfriend into something rash. No, we can't sit idly by and wait for her to accidentally push over the apple cart."

"But if the sample flash drive I showed you is valuable, if your contacts would hurry up and approve the deal, then we could get out of here now and not wait for her or the boyfriend to do something."

Baransky shook his head. "Listen. Stallings has already taken our picture together. You didn't realize it, but I did."

"When was that?"

"Yesterday. Near Kongens Nytorv, at the end of Nyhavn. I saw him, but didn't say anything at the time. I didn't want you to get jumpy and spook him. Maybe he didn't even know we were in the background of his little tourist scene. Maybe he'll throw that picture away and never look at it closely. I don't know. But the point is that if he got that close by accident, he could do much better if he wanted. That's why I left so abruptly. I couldn't take any chances."

"I was wondering about that."

"Yes, that's the way it will be with you, always one step behind."

"You're so compassionate."

"Don't mention it." Baransky looked at his watch. "All right. It's been ten minutes. Let's do it." He shut off the engine, popped the trunk and removed the wheelchair and a small black bag. After clicking the door locks and checking to see if anyone was watching, he tossed the bag onto the wheelchair and pushed toward the front door of the Kong Jacob.

If he was going to make a run for it, Huff thought this was his chance. If he'd really killed the Russian as he'd contemplated aloud in the Irish pub, then he wouldn't be thinking about a kidnapping now. But despite his bravado about taking down Square Jaw, he'd been sensible and nonviolent and trusting. Nor did he have a weapon, which now put him at a major disadvantage.

He calculated he could be around the corner in three seconds if he sprinted off at full speed and never looked back. And he calculated it would take three and a half seconds for Baransky to lift his hands off the wheelchair, strip the glove from his shooting hand, then reach inside his two coats, pull out the Glock, aim and fire.

If Huff was wrong about the timing, a heavy, sharp pain would pierce his back and drive him face down into the asphalt, and then blood would fill his lungs and he would die on the street, just another road kill, no different from a slow squirrel crushed by a garbage truck. If he was right about the timing, Baransky would probably not give chase. Instead, with no one to keep him in check, he would do whatever he wanted in that hotel room, and later on he would do whatever he wanted with the woman he was going to carry out of that room in a wheelchair.

Huff made the decision that was hardly a decision at all and hurried to keep up with Baransky. "What's the rush?"

"We have a mission. I would like you to focus on it."

"You didn't tell me something. How'd you know Stallings was leaving the hotel, and when?"

"He has a meeting to attend at this moment across town. He's reliable and punctual and, therefore, predictable."

"All right. But how'd you know about the meeting?"

Baransky stopped the wheelchair in the middle of the street and stared at Huff. "Like a little mouse, I only have to follow the trail of cheese crumbs. Now no more questions." And he rammed the wheelchair on to the hotel while Huff ran after him.

Jason felt a certain comfort in riding with Carsten. He almost wanted to take him home to Seattle to fight through the daily headaches of Interstate 5 while he rode calmly in the backseat. The thing about Carsten was that Jason trusted him. Jason knew the driver wouldn't endanger his life, and he felt that there was more to the man's character than his ability to control the accelerator and steering wheel.

"Carsten, could you pull over a minute? I want you to look at this picture."

The taxi driver found a safe spot, then flipped on his map light as Jason handed him the picture he'd taken at Nyhavn.

"Carsten, do you recognize the man leaning on the taxi?"

"Oh, yes," he responded after only a brief look at the photo. "That's one of the Russian drivers. What's his name? Bensky? Barsky? No, wait, it's Baransky."

"No first name?"

"Sorry. I've just seen him here and there. We're not friends."

"I wouldn't expect that. What about the other man in the picture? They seem to be talking to each other."

"No, never saw him. Is he American?" Carsten handed back the picture and switched off the map light.

"We can go now." The taxi started moving again as Jason answered. "Yes, he's American. But you said something about Russian drivers. Are there a lot in the taxi business here in Copenhagen."

"A lot? No, I don't suppose there are a lot. But several. I don't know quite how to say it in English. I don't count them. And I keep away from them."

"Why? What do they do?"

"I don't know what they *do*. I only know what I *hear*."

"Carsten, what do you hear about the Russian drivers?" Maybe Jason wouldn't take him back to Seattle. The man's ability to leave him hanging was exasperating.

"Oh, it's only a rumor, I suppose. But the word is that some of them are spies."

Jason wanted an hour to think *that* over before he met with Sayon Kunder, but before he knew it the taxi was pulling up to the Hotel Lorentsen. Carsten said he would be off duty in a half hour and wished him luck and said perhaps they would meet again tomorrow.

With everything that was happening today, Jason thought to-morrow was a long way off. He walked into the Lorentsen lobby thinking about Russian spies. If that driver, Baransky, really was a spy, then why would Huff be messing around with him? He couldn't believe that Danni had any idea about how deep Huff's involvement ran.

Jason scanned the lobby. Thomas was at his post, a little wealthier than he had been when he'd reported to work today, but Cabrina was nowhere in sight, if indeed she was even working right now. He had no clear idea what hours she worked, though her late evening arrival at the Commodore Hotel suggested a swing shift or something like it. Since she was in food service, she might be expected to work through the primary dinner hours or even later.

Jason paused at the entrance to the bar. While he let his eyes adjust to the dim light, he tried to put spies out of his mind and think for a few seconds about the great havarti chase that had brought him here. The lounge, as Kunder had called it, wasn't as busy as he thought it would be for such a large hotel. But of course the renovation had closed several rooms, and it was still fairly early for the cocktail crowd. And maybe the recent murder was keeping some people away. So with only about a dozen people in the bar, Kunder was easy to spot.

Jason only toyed with the idea that he would be dressed in the loose, flowing attire of the tropics. Was that a kurta? Of course, that would have been ridiculously inadequate for a sub-polar Danish winter, no better than a white linen suit of British colonialism. Kunder wore neither. Instead, a freshly pressed dark gray suit with whitish chalk stripes draped his fortysomething form, which measured about six feet even when he stood to greet Jason.

"Mr. Stallings. So glad you could come."

"Yes, I very much wanted to meet you, Mr. Kunder. Thank you for inviting me." Jason shed his heavy coat and sat down across the table from his Indian rival. Or should he say colleague? It was something they would have to determine.

Jason peered at Kunder's glass with no ice and asked, "What are you drinking this evening, if I may be so bold."

"You may," Kunder said. "It's a single malt scotch. Aberlour. And I happen to prefer mine neat."

"Interesting. Then you don't have to bother with ice on a cold night."

"Precisely. Shall I order one for you?"

"Well, why not. It's been a day of adventure. No need to stop now."

Kunder laughed politely, and though it was apparent they had many differences, Jason felt comfortable in his presence. Still, he would be on guard.

Kunder signaled to the bartender, pointed at his drink, then toward Jason, and in almost no time Jason was raising a toast. "To havarti, Denmark's finest."

"To havarti."

Jason liked the scotch, though without ice he thought it tasted more like brandy. But it was smooth and warm, and since Kunder was picking up the tab, he couldn't complain. "It's very good. Apparently I've been missing something."

"Well, you're young," Kunder said. "You still have time to catch up."

"Ah, yes. But maybe not as much as before. I seemed to have aged this week."

"You're looking healthier than most people. If you're under stress, you're concealing it well."

"Speaking of hidden things, how did you find me?" Jason asked. "I'm not trying to evade anyone, but my presence in Copenhagen isn't exactly well known."

"It's known well enough. The answer is very simple. Yesterday morning, you told Poul Stubkjaer that you would be at the Kong Jacob."

"And you went out to Bjorneby Foods yesterday afternoon and talked with him?"

"I did. See, we have no secrets. But how did you know I talked with him then?"

"Because Weathersby's appointment was in the afternoon. I assumed that you just stepped in and filled it."

"Well, I can't argue that."

"So you knew when the appointment was, before he died, I mean."

"Yes, good deduction. He gave me a little of his itinerary last week."

Jason sipped on his Aberlour, unsure how to proceed, unsure who was trying to get what out of this meeting. "Buying Danish havarti must mean a lot to you."

Kunder raised an eyebrow. "It's important."

"Yes, but coming all the way from India, to Denmark, in the winter..."

Kunder laughed heartily. "Ah, I see what you are thinking. I came only from London, a short ride by air. I live in England these days and rarely travel to India."

Jason wasn't sure what to make of that. "Oh. Then does the havarti go to India?"

"Sometimes. But sometimes it gets diverted, if the price is right. You should not think that Delhi Deli Mercantile is so provincial that it deals with commodities only for India. Our scope is much broader."

"All right. But what about the starving masses?"

"Well, I'm not sure what you mean, but I would guess they know nothing about Danish havarti. Is there some reason you ask?"

"Just something I heard," Jason said. "It's not important."

"It sounds like something Stubkjaer would say. Sometimes his eloquence precedes his mental preparation. But I think we should be clear that I am running a business, not a charity. And for that reason, I see my position as an intermediary between your company..."

"Sunny Day Farms."

"...Sunny Day Farms and Bjorneby Foods. In fact, I have already submitted an offer to your home office. In Seattle, I believe. Tell me, does it really rain there all the time?"

"It's much like London, though perhaps wetter in the spring. We celebrate summer with fireworks and umbrellas."

"Yes, and those dreadful hot dogs. Americans have such peculiar tastes."

"Well, we do have a taste for Danish havarti. But I don't understand why we need a middleman. I came to Denmark thinking I would deal directly with Bjorneby Foods. I know about your offer to Sunny Day Farms, and I know Weathersby is dead, but I don't understand why Bjorneby would sell cheese to you if it knew you were just going to resell it to my company."

Kunder laughed again and emptied his glass while Jason tried to keep up. "It seems so simple doesn't it," Kunder said. "For one thing, Bjorneby Foods doesn't care what your company or my company pays as long as it gets its price. If there's a small handling fee along the way, then so be it. Did your company object to my offer?"

"Sunny Day Farms is considering the offer. I haven't heard an actual objection yet." Of course, Novitsky was salivating over it, but Kunder would never hear that.

"Good. Taking the offer would perhaps pave a new road for other transactions. In fact, you should know that since Mr. Weathersby is gone, I plan to expand and take over much of his territory. Grand things are in store for Delhi Deli Mercantile, I'm sure. I believe you would call my company—what is the term?—yes, a *superbroker* for several suppliers. Naturally, Bjorneby Foods will be one of them."

"That's an interesting ambition," Jason said, "but backing up a moment, I'm afraid I don't see the substance in your position with Bjorneby Foods. It seems they would have no particular reason to work with you."

Kunder studied the bottom of his single malt scotch, possibly musing about a second round. "I have a special relationship with Stubkjaer. He knows it's in his best interest to deal with me, especially since I recently acquired some information from Mr. Weathersby—before his passing, of course."

"Did Weathersby have this same special relationship?"

"No. He didn't think his information was of much importance. He mentioned it to me only incidentally. The man was an excellent number counter, but he really had no vision."

Jason was stunned. "What? Are you blackmailing Stubkjaer?"

"That's a harsh word," Kunder scoffed.

"Then how you would state it?"

"Business. What else? I'm simply doing business." Kunder examined his decidedly empty glass. "Mr. Stallings. I'm in the mood for another. How about you?"

#

Huff and Baransky went through the front door of the Kong Jacob and were headed to the elevator when a front desk clerk said something in Danish, followed by "Wait" in English.

"What's wrong?" asked the clerk, a young man with short brown hair combed forward. "You have a wheelchair."

Baransky began to move toward the desk with the wheelchair, but Huff put out a hand and stopped him. He wasn't going to leave this entirely to the Russian. "We've come to help my sister," Huff told the clerk, improvising as he went. "She's suffered a bad fall on some ice today, and I've brought a doctor and a wheelchair to take her to a hospital. Most likely she will need X-rays to see if there's a broken bone. The doctor..."

Baransky spoke briefly in Danish, then they headed to the elevator unimpeded.

On the elevator, Baransky said, "That wasn't bad. I especially liked the part about the sister. Danes like to think they're so tough, but they're really so damn sentimental."

They went down the hall and stopped in front of the room. Huff had already asked how he knew which room it was, and Baransky had responded, as if to a child who wasn't quite capable of understanding, that he had friends who worked in the hotel. And these friends, who were also Russian, had given him Miss Danni's room number just as they had given him the number of Jason Stallings' room, as well as the key.

Baransky stopped in the hallway and took a small bottle of chloroform from his black bag. Huff knew what it was because they had gone over the actual abduction scene again and again like actors getting their parts down. But now that it was time for the curtains to lift, Huff couldn't think clearly at all. He could only watch. Baransky put a disposable medical glove on his right hand and with his bare left hand poured a little chloroform on the cloth, which he then held in a fist behind his back. "Now, remember," he told Huff, "stay back out of sight with the wheelchair in case she recognizes you. I'll give you the all clear when she's out. Here we go. Showtime."

#

Danni sat on the edge of the bed tapping her feet anxiously. She couldn't wait for Jason to return. She had just called her little brother Eddie in California, even though it was early morning there. Danni had talked with Craig Huff's former landlord, but Eddie had gone back for more information and learned that Gitte was an old flame he'd met the summer before in San Francisco, Pier 39 to be exact. She thought that jibed with what Jason had told her last Friday, though she was hurting too much now to remember clearly. But there was more. Apparently Craig had confided a lot in the landlord, and the landlord, a gregarious old Scandinavian type, had met Gitte and approved of her mightily. They'd even sat down for a glass of aquavit. Now Danni realized that the emotional attraction for Gitte ran stronger than she'd figured earlier, so that was at least one compelling reason for him to hang around.

Danni preferred talking to Eddie instead of her father about these things. Her father had too much at stake now, and after that one intimidating call she had made back home, she had decided to work with Eddie instead. *He* could talk to their parents and sort out the details in person.

Now she had something to sort out here with Jason. Until now, she hadn't been able to make herself tell him what was really going on. He'd already called her bluff on part of it, and the rest probably wouldn't be long in coming. So now she might as well finish the job, no matter how it made her look. She realized she'd made a big mistake but delaying the inevitable, and the longer she waited the worse it seemed to get. Ever since she'd met Jason, he'd been kind and helpful, and obviously he was no threat to her. Of course, she'd grown extremely fond of him. Fond? What a wimpy word. Who was she kidding? Her feelings redlined far beyond that, even if she had pushed him away and treated him like dirt after he'd told her that her Pittsburgh story was a big fib. It was just that she was in shock from hearing that he'd discovered part of her real life. After the revelations had been piled on to her physical pain from the fall, she just broke down and cried like a baby.

Once she had a grip and thought over her situation, she could see that she'd been foolish to expect him to swallow everything without question and not do a little digging. She wondered if she'd been too caught up in playing the elusive Copenhagen Danni. And she wondered if subconsciously she hadn't been worried that the regular California Danni would be a little dull by comparison, at least to a nice guy like Jason, who probably had his pick of women.

In addition to all that, there was the practical consideration of getting the money back, with or without Craig Huff's cooperation. His warning call that morning had knocked her off her foundation, and two hours later she was literally knocked off her foundation, slipping on the ice and crashing onto the sidewalk. If he hadn't called, maybe she would have been paying more attention to the ice instead of her own chaotic thoughts. His warning about the evils of the world and trying to protect her still made no sense, but his ominous tone had succeeded magnificently in scaring the wits out of her. So now she desperately needed Jason's help in figuring out what the warning meant and what to do about it.

As for the money, she knew she'd blown it and had never really had a useful plan. Even if she thought persuasion was the way to go, she hadn't been able to bring herself to try it. She was fearful because of the refusal she expected. And she had no contingency plan. Jason, she thought, would help her with that as well. If she laid out all the facts for him, he would step through the process rationally, unless she had totally alienated him.

There was a knock on her door. Was Jason back already? Surely he hadn't been gone long enough.

"Who is it?"

A slightly foreign-sounding voice said, "Hotel doctor."

Really? Maybe somebody had seen her hobbling through the lobby earlier today and asked the doctor to check on her. She'd tried to put aside her aches, but thought now she could probably use a doctor.

She got up and hobbled to the door, though she was a little foggy in the head after taking some pain pills that had done less to relieve her soreness than to cloud her mind. She unlocked the door and opened it.

"Miss Rossler?"

"Yes?" Somehow the doctor looked familiar, but maybe that was her imagination.

"I'm Doctor Andersen. The front desk called my clinic. It seems that several people noticed you limping in pain. I had another patient to see in the hotel so thought I would drop in and check on you."

"Oh, yes. I did fall on some ice today. I don't know how bad it is, Doctor. I don't think anything's broken but—"

"I should have a look while I'm here. The hotel would not want to have a problem. Please, we should go into your room."

Danni backed up, and the doctor moved forward, shutting the door behind him. There was something about his English that didn't sound like a Dane. Well, he didn't have to be a Dane. Maybe a German. But he said his name was Andersen. That wasn't German, maybe Swedish or...and then she looked at his hands. Or hand. Why was he holding his right hand behind his back?

Confused, she stopped moving, but he didn't. His face loomed closer with a determined expression, and she thought she might know him. Didn't he look like the taxi driver who had helped her this morning? No, it couldn't be. The clothes, the mustache...but now everything was going so fast, which is why she almost missed sight of the white cloth coming up to her face. She felt it squeeze hard over her nose. The smell was somewhat sweet and tangy, but something in her knew it was bad. Her arms and hands flailed harmlessly against the doctor's coat sleeve.

Oh, God. She wanted to scream, but a rough hand clamped over her mouth, forcing her to breathe the chemical through her nose. She tried to knock the doctor's hands away from her face, but now her arms only flailed weakly.

Danni felt the strength drain out of her. She was dizzy, but not quite out. She stumbled, and the floor lamp tipped and fell. She went down alongside it. Her elbow struck the floor, and her momentum rolled her onto her shoulder. Suddenly the sleeve of her sweater was jerked up, and she felt a sting in her arm. The floor started falling away underneath her. A contorted, menacing face glowered over her. The room swirled—and went dark.

10

Halfway through his second single malt scotch, Sayon Kunder invited Jason to stay for dinner. Jason, still nursing his first single malt, hesitated for a moment. He wondered if he should get back to check on Danni and figure out a dinner plan with her, but then remembered she was going to order room service. So he accepted Kunder's invitation. A little later, he considered phoning Danni to tell her he was going to be a while, but recalling the mood she was in when he left, he decided it would be best not to call just yet and stir up something new.

Kunder and Jason ordered steaks, and Kunder scanned the wine list and chose a French red without much deliberation.

"You'll like this one," Kunder said. "It's one of my favorites. Aggressive, yet smooth and well-balanced."

The description could have fit Kunder himself, Jason thought, but after tasting the wine, he had to agree that the commendation was apt. And the bottle definitely didn't come from the budget list. So Kunder knew how to choose a wine and spend money.

During dinner, Kunder moved away from the subject of cheese for a while and engaged Jason in a discussion of the world economy. After stating that the Third World had made only a centimeter of real progress in twenty years, Kunder said economic parity was necessary across the globe before political and military stability could be a realistic possibility.

Jason thought that sounded reasonable. "How much time do you think will be required for that?"

The Indian businessman took a sip of wine before he answered. "If we hurry, one hundred to two hundred years."

"Oh. I hope you have children."

"Three. Their mission awaits them."

"They have no choice?"

"Of course. For breakfast, they can choose porridge or corn flakes."

"I meant on the larger issues, their life's work."

"Life will tell them what their work is. And I am part of their life. They will save time by not thrashing about exploring useless alternatives."

"Then they will have no fun," Jason said.

"I'm sure they will not lack for fun. They find no end of things to distract them. But fun does not advance the cause of civilization."

"But it can make the tough days of advancement more palatable."

This time Kunder did not reply immediately. "I like you, Mr. Stallings. Even though you, at the back of your mind, are wondering how I might assist your quest for the holy havarti, you are still not afraid to disagree with me."

"Life is short. By spring, I might be selling shoes."

"You would not quit so easily, I think."

"Perhaps. Tell me, are you staying here at the Lorentsen?"

"Oh, yes. I didn't know of many hotels in Copenhagen. This one was mentioned, and I remembered it."

"You're following in Weathersby's footsteps."

"Only to a degree. Don't assume too much."

"What did you know about him? I keep hearing about him and keep talking about him, but I don't really know much except that he was a forty-nine-year-old Englishman."

"Maybe that's all that's worth knowing. I don't wish to defile the dead, but it's no secret that he wasn't a great businessman. He focused excessively on details, then often missed the larger business opportunities, especially here in Denmark. This little country is a beehive of potential, but our dear Mr. Weathersby seemed to prefer plodding when he came here."

"Plodding? He slowed down?"

"It wasn't so much a matter of speed as his penchant for repeating last week's activities without imagination."

"He was in a rut," Jason offered.

"Possibly. But it seemed more that he was distracted—by what, only God knows." Kunder shook his head. "In any case, it's probably just as well that he's not here. Progress was going to leave him behind."

"In other words, he wasn't useful to the cause of civilization."

Kunder eyed Jason skeptically. "You are trying to choose my words, yes? I would hesitate to use that phrasing, but to a large degree the analysis is correct. He was stuck in another time."

Jason took a sip of wine and then tried some other phrasing. "Did you kill him?"

Kunder laughed. "I knew you would ask. I thought little of his work, so therefore I'm a suspect. No, I didn't kill him. Murder is not my style."

"The police, no doubt, have a great interest in whose style it was."

"Ah. If we are getting down to cases, then I'm sure they also have an interest in where I was the night of the murder. I was at home in London last Thursday evening, entertaining business associates at my family's Kensington flat. After a lovely dinner organized by my wife, we all enjoyed several glasses of cognac and time slipped by. I saw my guests out at midnight, went straight to bed, then got up early Friday and was in my office before seven, where at least two people arrived before I did and observed me come in."

"So you had a few hours..."

"...To go to Heathrow, clear security, fly to Copenhagen in the middle of the night, take a cab into the city, stab Mr. Weathersby, wash my hands, dispose of the weapon, return to the airport, clear security again and fly home to wake up at six a.m. next to my wife and kiss her good morning. Yes, I can work fast, Mr. Stallings, but not that fast." He looked at Jason's glass. "More wine?"

"Thanks but no. My stomach's doing odd things." Jason ran a finger around the rim of the empty glass. "You mentioned family. Did Weathersby have one?"

"I wasn't close enough to know much about his private life, but I believe he had been divorced for several years."

"Any children?"

"Two, I think. Grown, or nearly grown. I heard once they were in Manchester, but I've never seen them."

"No lady friends for Weathersby?"

"I have no idea," Kunder said. "Nor am I much interested in those details. But since he traveled a lot in his work, I think it would be fair to say that he had plenty of chances. Anyway, I'm fairly confident the authorities contacted his family."

"And they contacted you, it seems."

"Oh, yes. There were business papers in his room with my name and number. Or so I'm told. After I gave my story, the police had no further interest in me except for identifying Mr. Weathersby from a photo, which I did. His relatives expect to take care of the rest." Kunder paused long enough to take a drink of wine. "You asked me about lady friends. I'm afraid I gave you an incomplete answer. I never saw any of these women, so I can only make assumptions on that point. But as I recall now, Mr. Weathersby did mention something to me a year or so ago. Let me think how that went. There was this woman, not his wife. He gave me no name or place or anything like that, but he did seemed burdened by something about her."

"What? He was giving her money?"

"Perhaps, though I don't think that was the major concern, if indeed that was the case at all. No, I believe it was a sense of longing. And guilt. Strange, I hadn't thought about that until now." Kunder looked Jason in the eye. "You know, you shouldn't believe everything you've heard tonight. I'm afraid I've been too hard on Mr. Weathersby. He failed, and I don't know why. It's sad. When there's a failure, I want to know what I can do to correct the situation."

Jason considered that. "Maybe somebody can explain Weathersby's situation, but nobody's going to fix it now."

#

Baransky worked Danni's limp body out of the wheelchair and

into the back seat of the Saab as Huff pulled on her from the other side. It had been amazingly easy to take her out through the hotel lobby. The desk clerks seem to be preoccupied with other matters and barely looked up.

Huff got into the front passenger seat, then the Russian came around to the driver's side and started the engine and got the heater going again. Huff said, "I can't believe we did that."

Baransky gave him a stern look. "Believe it."

"Wasn't there some other way? A phone call? A face to face warning?"

"I've heard your objections. Now be quiet."

Huff didn't say anything else, but he did wonder if Baransky wouldn't treat him even worse than Danni. The abduction was so according to form that it could have come out of a spy manual. If A, then B. Baransky was annoyed with Danni and Stallings, but not too emotionally involved, so it appeared he would just stick to his training. But what if he knew the person well enough to get vindictive and step outside the rules? And what if he, Craig Huff, was that person?

Huff turned back and looked at their unconscious captive. Again, he wished he'd never got involved with any of this, but remorse was just a sadness in his head if he didn't take action. He'd come along to do some good, and so far he wondered if he'd done anything toward that end. He had to try harder. He realized now he could have said something to the front desk crew at the hotel. He could have tipped them off, made a fuss, written a note, anything to stop the abduction. He might have been shot, but so what. He wasn't going to die a coward.

Huff turned back to Baransky. "You said you would talk to her and warn her off. How are you going to do that now? She's unconscious. You lied to me."

"Poor Craig, such a trusting, innocent soul."

"Enough. Just answer the question."

"You don't think she'll get the message now? When she wakes up, it'll be loud and clear."

As night set in, Baransky drove off, twisting and turning at excessive speeds, and Huff was pretty much lost. After about fifteen minutes, all he could say was that traffic was much lighter and they were now in an area of warehouses and light industry. Warehouses. They might be arriving at the destination soon, and Huff was still running options through his mind.

Suddenly, Baransky took a turn too wide and too fast. The tires were singing a high pitch on the bare pavement in the middle of the road, and Huff saw his chance. He snapped his left arm out, and the bony edge of his wrist smashed straight into Baransky's windpipe.

Baransky clearly wasn't expecting the blow, but managed to cough and say something foul and explosive in Russian while hanging on to the steering wheel. Now he was on full alert, so when Huff grabbed the wheel and tried to turn it even more to the left, going with the car's speed and centrifugal force, Baransky was able to counter the move by karate chopping at Huff's arms with his right hand.

A small truck flashed in front of them with horn blaring but didn't stop. The Saab was on the wrong side of the street, but they hadn't collided and there was no more traffic at the moment. Huff was out of his seatbelt now, almost standing, and throwing an elbow into Baransky's nose while continuing to try to steer the moving car across the street and into a building. There were no sidewalks or curbs, nothing to slow them before hitting the concrete.

But then the Saab did slow. Baransky was braking hard. Still, the tires couldn't grip the snow on the side of the road fast enough to completely avoid a crash. The left front bumper slammed into the building, and everything stopped.

Dazed by the impact, Huff looked down—into the barrel of Baransky's Glock.

Baransky calmly said, "I was just wondering about the size of the hole in your head after this 9 millimeter fires."

"Then you would have blood all over your fancy gray coat," Huff said.

"Fortunately for you, you are correct about that. So I'll try not to shoot you in the car." Baransky opened his door, stepped out and pulled Huff with him. Huff saw Baransky was slightly off balance so flipped the side of his left foot into Baransky's right Achilles tendon. They both fell to the ground and rolled in the snow, grappling for an advantage. Huff kept trying to keep the gun in sight, but it was too dark and the street light was too far away.

Huff felt Baransky push off his chest, and then there was no weight on him at all. The Russian was standing over him with the Glock pointed at Huff's heart. "You are a foolish boy, Craig. Did you really think you could take me?"

Huff tried to catch his breath.

"Get up."

Huff struggled to his feet.

"Against the wall," Baransky ordered.

Huff backed up. "So this is how it ends, huh, Andrei? The brave Russian spy executes his prey on a dark street with the weapon of a common criminal."

"Are you ready to die, Craig?"

"I've been ready since I knew I was alive."

"Good. But you might have to wait. You could be useful yet. When I get word on your data drive."

Operation Sierra. "Sure, Andrei. Business as usual."

"But tonight I need to get Miss Danni to her destination before she wakes up, and you are slowing me down."

"You broke a headlight. The cops will spot you now."

"I'll take my chances. Without you. You're staying here, Craig." Baransky then reached for Huff's head and banged the back of it into the wall. Twice. Huff was stunned momentarily. He felt the pain but didn't have time for it. Instead, he dropped his head and drove it into Baransky's midsection, pushing him back to the Saab.

Huff thought he could get the upper hand now, but when Baransky's hamstrings thumped the back fender, his right arm went up and the butt of the Glock went down. Huff felt a sharp blow above his left ear, and then his knees buckled and he dropped into the snow.

In his last moments of consciousness, he heard Baransky's

voice. "Catch you later, my friend."

Baransky observed the crumpled body at his feet, and he observed the sleeping body in the backseat of the car. He got in and fastened his seatbelt. Safety first, he thought, chuckling to himself. Who said spies didn't have a sense of humor? He started the car and drove off with a single headlight and a few minutes later turned into a wide driveway and stopped next to a large building with loading docks.

He pulled his unconscious passenger out of the backseat and into the wheelchair and entered the warehouse through an unlocked door. As Baransky pushed the wheelchair, he twice heard voices in the distance, but as expected his pathway had been cleared of any human obstructions.

When he got to an empty storage room in a remote part of the building, he slid open a big wooden door, then lifted his captive out of the wheelchair and propped her into a sitting position in a corner. Baransky took a roll of duct tape from his coat pocket and taped her ankles together. Then he taped her wrists to her thighs, sealed her mouth with tape and blindfolded her with tape. *There. She can still breathe. And she can wiggle around and roll over if she likes. But she won't get very far.*

Baransky closed the big wooden door behind him and pushed the wheelchair back to the car. Once he was a kilometer or so away from the warehouse, he got out and pitched the wheelchair to the side of the road. Then he drove another five kilometers to an area he recognized, jammed the already damaged front corner of the car into a tree and phoned a countryman for a ride. He had a few minutes to wait, which gave him time to wipe the Saab clean of fingerprints. By then his ride had shown up, and he began thinking about dinner.

#

Huff woke up to headlights in his eyes. A diesel engine rumbled close by. The pain in his head was excruciating, and he was cold, so cold. He reached up and touched the side of his head, but the pain remained. He looked at his glove and saw sticky blood.

A man said something to him in Danish, then threw a blanket

over him and propped something soft under his head. It hurt to lift his head, and it hurt to put it back down, but then he wasn't quite so cold.

More words in Danish.

Then Huff croaked out a word. "English."

The man's voice came back in a language Huff could understand. "I called for help. The police and medics are on the way."

Huff tried to force out a smile. His plan had failed, but he had a lot to be grateful for. He hadn't been shot, and it looked as if he was going to live. When his eyes stopped crossing and his head stopped hurting, he was going to get back out there and find Danni.

#

On the way back from dinner with Kunder, Jason paused at Danni's door and knocked lightly. When no answer came, he guessed she'd gone to sleep. He wouldn't bother her now.

He turned to go on to his own room, then stopped. There was something in the air. He breathed through his nose. The smell was faint but unusual. He wasn't sure he'd ever encountered it before. It was a little sweet, but not food or perfume, more like medicine. Probably it was something Danni had used, and maybe it was only his imagination. He was reluctant to make too much of his bloodhound prowess. It was too easy to be wrong. He took another breath through his nose to really identify the scent, and this time came up with nothing. If the smell had ever been there at all, it had now disappeared into the pervasive hotel air freshener. It must have been his imagination.

Jason walked down to his room and went in. It was too bad Danni was asleep. He really wanted to talk with her about Huff, but he supposed that could wait until morning. More than ever, he was convinced that Huff had some special meaning to her. He was more than an employee of her company who had slipped away with his pockets full of cash. And whatever she was doing, she was out of her element.

Jason walked around his room aimlessly. A few days ago none of Danni's problems would have meant a thing to him. But now there was a catch. He cared, and he cared a lot.

He grabbed the remote and flicked on the TV. Rolling over the channels, he stopped on a Steven Segal movie. Before long it became apparent that the cops and other people who were supposed to be the good guys were actually rotten, though not in Denmark. And the suspects turned out to have hearts of gold and grand schemes to steer society back on course. Too bad real life wasn't that simple, Jason thought.

But in a few seconds he wondered if there wasn't some kind of parallel with his Danish adventures because his Copenhagen cast of characters was also having a kind of identity crisis. Danni Rossler wasn't exactly who she said she was, and Craig Huff probably wasn't quite who she said he was, either. Poul Stubkjaer, the lord of havarti, acted like India's lord protector. Jason's boss, Ben Novitsky, though technically in Seattle, had fallen for a fax from a dead man in Copenhagen. Tonight's dinner partner, Sayon Kunder, was on one level a forthright businessman and on another a cunning manipulator, but in between the two extremes might be something else. And then there was Martin Weathersby, whose chief occupation had gone overnight from English food broker to dead man in Denmark, but perhaps not by chance. Oh, yes, and Huff's two girlfriends, Gitte Benneker and Cabrina Jorgensen, probably thought they were dealing with a regular guy on holiday instead of an embezzler on the lam. And how could he forget Mr. Baransky? Russian spy or taxi driver? Or probably both. Running against the grain, Thomas the hotel desk man and Carsten the taxi driver seemed to be themselves, but maybe that was only because he didn't know enough about them.

Jason yawned.

While he got up to brush his teeth, the movie played on. When he came back from the bathroom, another eight or ten people had been killed, and even more had donated blood to floors, streets and rivers. It was exhausting even trying to keep up. He shut off the TV and got ready for bed. As he drifted off to sleep, he held the thought that he and Danni would get squared away tomorrow. He hoped she wasn't in too much pain.

#

Huff blacked out again, then woke up on a gurney being wheeled into a hospital. The nurses removed his coat so they could take his blood pressure. They took his temperature, pressed his tongue down for a good look, checked for loose teeth and pointed strong little lights into his eyes. They asked him a lot of questions about what month it was and the day of the week and the president of the United States, and he thought he got some of the answers right. He figured he would pass if they graded on the curve. And they cleaned his head wounds and put on bandages with lots of white tape, though he couldn't see the one in the back when they got done. Somewhere along the way, they put an IV in his arm and gave him a drip and then put some drugs into that and he started thinking he didn't feel so bad at all. Later, when people stopped bothering him, he got very sleepy.

He woke up once and wished somebody would turn out the light. He remembered being out in front of the Kong Jacob and then going for a ride with Baransky. Where was Danni? Did they crash? It was all so confusing. Dimly lit warehouses pulsed in and out of his vision. Baransky was such a bad driver, didn't care about his passengers, just didn't care, no sympathy, no... Huff thought once of eating and couldn't remember if he'd had dinner. Must have. But when? He probably had the receipt in his wallet. But where was that. He was a little nauseous now so maybe he'd eat later. Yeah, later. Sure, sure.

He didn't know how long he'd been asleep when the nightmare woke him. Terrible three-foot-tall creatures with a dozen arms and a dozen hands were chasing him through a warehouse. There were so many he couldn't count them all. They spoke a strange unintelligible language and were bent on confusing him. When he cut one of them with a knife, a slimy green liquid gushed onto his hand and stung like hot peppers. They were closing in on him. It looked hopeless. He tried to scream, but only a moan emerged. His breath went faster and faster.

Then the little monsters were gone, but the lights were still on. The lights made his head hurt. If he could just reach the switch...

When both hands of the big clock next to his bed pointed

straight up, he asked a nice lady for a cigarette. She pushed more drugs into his IV and said, "Go back to sleep." And he did.

#

In the morning, Jason went down to breakfast. The Wednesday crowd looked like the Tuesday crowd, which had looked a lot like the Monday crowd. Except for Danni, who wasn't there this morning. Jason ate mechanically with one eye on the entrance, thinking she would show up a little later.

By the time he'd finished the meal, that notion had worn off, so he went upstairs to her room and knocked, not softly as he'd done last night, but loudly enough to wake her if she were still sleeping. He knocked repeatedly, but there was no answer, so he went back to his room and phoned her room. Still she didn't answer. But how could that be? She couldn't be gone. She was so bruised from the fall that she could barely walk.

Then he thought of the unusual smell he thought he'd detected in front of her door the night before. It wasn't there anymore, but now after his brain had processed it all night he knew it was chemical. Last night, he'd thought it was medical. But it didn't matter. Chemical, medical. Medical, chemical. It was all the same, and the vibes weren't good.

He picked up the phone again and called the front desk.

"Could you send the manager to my room?"

"Sir, how may we help you?" Jason thought the woman at the desk was hard of hearing.

"You can send the manager to my room."

"But, sir, what is the problem?"

"One of your guests may be missing. Now, do you want me to come down to the lobby and shout that out so everyone can hear, or are you going to send the manager up?"

"I'll get him now, sir."

Inside of ninety seconds, the day manager was knocking on the door. Jason let him in. The man wore his suit well and looked reasonably competent, so Jason explained Danni's injury the day before and told how he'd knocked on her door last night and again this morning without raising anyone.

"Well, she may have gone out, sir."

"Listen, she's a friend of mine, a close friend. She wouldn't have gone out without telling me. Something's wrong, I'm sure of it. She was injured. She may have fallen again and hurt herself, or worse. Now, can you just have a look?"

"I'll have to go by myself. Hotel policy."

"Fine. You know where to find me."

Jason stood in the doorway while the day manager went down the hallway and used his card key. Danni's room wasn't bolted from the inside, so he went right in. In a few seconds, he came back out. "There's no one here. She's gone. Come and see."

Jason took quick strides and looked in. A floor lamp was knocked over, but nothing else seemed unusual, except for Danni's absence. Her coat was hanging on the coat tree, and her purse was beside the bed, where he smelled her perfume. On top of the dresser Cabrina's photo was peeking out of the envelope he'd brought it in. He paused near the downed lamp. There must have been some kind of struggle. And that chemical smell came back, only much stronger this time. And there was a secondary chemical odor closer to the floor.

It couldn't be true, could it? But as soon as the possibility had occurred to him, he knew it was true. "She's been kidnapped. I'm sure of it." And she'd probably been knocked out with some kind of drugs while he'd been eating and drinking with Kunder at the Lorentsen. Of all the luck. But who knew she was here? Huff?

"Sir, I know you're upset but—"

Jason got in his face. "You're the manager. Tell me how was she taken from this hotel without anyone seeing her?"

"She might have walked out on her own."

"But she was injured, and she left her coat and purse."

"I'm very sorry, sir."

"Sorry?" The word was wholly inadequate.

"Yes, I'm sorry Miss Rossler has disappeared. I'm sorry she wasn't seen. Oh, this won't be good if it gets out to the press. We have to call the police."

"The police? Of course, we have to call the police."

"I'll go downstairs and do it now."

"Wait," Jason said. "I want you to ask for Detective Arne Dalvang."

"Dalvang. Very good, sir. Detective Dalvang."

After he'd gone and Jason was left standing in Danni's room alone, he didn't know why he'd done that. But it was a name he knew, a person he'd seen, he thought, not an anonymous cop who might not take this seriously.

God, where was Danni? And who had taken her?

Jason picked up the envelope with Cabrina's photo, then went back to his room and paced around with his door open so he wouldn't miss any activity. Jason was standing in the doorway when the manager came back down the hall. He peered into Danni's room, then shut the door. Seeing Jason, he said, "We need to preserve any evidence. The police are on the way."

"Detective Dalvang?"

"I gave them the message. That's all I could do."

The manager had obviously checked with the front desk on Jason's identity while downstairs. "Be assured that the Kong Jacob will cooperate fully with the investigation, Mr. Stallings. Did you know Miss Rossler well?"

That was an interesting question. "I've known her only a few days, but she's become special to me very fast. You know what I mean?"

"Yes sir. I think I understand."

"Good. Now, do you have security cameras in the lobby? I didn't see one."

The manager cleared his throat. "Not yet, unfortunately. Security cameras are coming with the renovation in the next few months, but there's nothing now."

"All right. Then do you know who was working at the front desk between four-thirty and nine last night?"

"I have an idea who was on duty, but I'd have to check the schedule."

"Then I suggest you check on that and call them at home and get them down here right away. The police will want to talk with them."

"Mr. Stallings, I understand your distress, but you just can't blame my staff."

"I thought you wanted to cooperate. Look, I'm not saying your people are responsible, but they might be witnesses. We need to know what they saw."

"I see your point, but why those hours?"

"Because I left this hotel for an appointment a little before five. Then I had dinner and returned here a little before nine. I knocked on Danni's door when I came back but didn't get an answer. I thought she'd gone to sleep so let it go. But at the time I smelled a chemical in the hall in front of her door. I didn't know what to make of it then, but a few minutes ago I smelled the same thing inside her room next to the lamp that was knocked over. Plus another chemical. So what I'm thinking is that these chemicals were used on her, and that she was taken while I was out, not during the night."

"Of course. I'll find out who was working and bring them in."

In a few minutes, Detective Dalvang arrived with two uniformed officers. As Jason suspected, Dalvang was the detective he'd seen at the Lorentsen the day Weathersby was carried out.

The police looked briefly at Danni's room, then closed the door. One of the uniformed officers stayed out in the hallway to stand guard and watch the room while the other, a woman, came into Jason's room with Dalvang and the manager.

After introductions, Dalvang said, "All right, Mr. Stallings, I've already heard a report from the manager here, so why don't you take me through the events as you remember them."

Jason started with Danni falling on the ice and his seeing her about four-thirty Tuesday afternoon. He told about going off to have a drink to talk about the cheese business with Kunder, and then staying for dinner with him at the Lorentsen. "I returned to the Kong Jacob a little before nine and knocked on her door lightly. I thought that because she'd been hurting from the fall that she'd gone to sleep early. So then I just went back to my room. It was only after she didn't go down to breakfast this morning that I had second thoughts."

Jason then told them that he sometimes had a heightened sense of smell and that he'd detected a chemical scent in front of Danni's door last night and again today. And he told about the chemical smells by the lamp when he'd gone into Danni's room with the manager. "I know it sounds goofy, and I can't prove it, but I think those chemicals were used on her."

"You smelled it by the lamp this morning?"

"That's right. Maybe half an hour ago."

"Then it may still be there. Stay here," he said to Jason. Then he turned to the manager and said, "Let's open up the room a minute."

Jason sat glumly and glanced at the female cop every now and then. She glanced back but didn't try to speak. Apparently her job didn't have a speaking part.

In a couple of minutes Dalvang and the manager came back. "You seem to be right," the detective said. "There was a faint chemical, very faint, but of course my nose isn't as good as yours. Anyhow, I would guess it's chloroform. If you know what you're doing, it works nicely for a knockout."

"How about the other chemical?" Jason asked.

"Well, having only a normal sense of smell, I didn't pick up anything, although if there was something there, it could be some patch or injection used after the chloroform. But we don't really need to know now. If it's chloroform, that tells me enough. But I'm wondering something else now. Miss Rossler is an American, like you?"

"That's right."

"What was she doing in Denmark?"

Jason knew the question was coming. "I'm going to have a hard time answering that. She's been somewhat secretive, so I can only tell you what she's told me in the past few days, since I met her last Friday. Anyway, she said a man from her company had embezzled a lot of money. I'm not sure about the amount, but probably two or three hundred thousand dollars. She was pretty sure he'd come to Copenhagen, so she flew over to find him."

"And did she find him?"

"She saw the man she was looking for, and so did I."

"Did she talk with him?"

"No, that was the strange thing. I talked with him by chance before I met Danni and before I knew who he was. Then the next day she accidentally found out where he was staying, but after that, she seemed afraid to move ahead and do much else. About all she did was learn that he was seeing a couple of young ladies."

"Strange that she would hold back like that. What was Miss Rossler's position in this company?"

"She implied she was a security agent, but I didn't believe it. She never acted tough enough to have a job like that."

"And the company?"

"She wouldn't tell me. Electronics is all she would say."

"Who was the man she was following?"

"Craig Huff." Jason spelled the name. "He's been staying at the Commodore Hotel in Nyhavn."

"You said *you* talked to him," Dalvang said. "Tell me about that."

"He approached me last Friday night at that Irish bar near the Strøget—you probably know the place—and once he knew I was an American he wanted to talk. Drink and talk. Mostly nothing of importance, but he mentioned a girlfriend here in Copenhagen, and he asked me if I'd ever thought of killing anyone. I thought he was unstable, and I left pretty quickly."

"So he sounded violent?"

"He sounded as if he were entertaining the idea of violence. I didn't know how serious he was and didn't really want to know."

"Do you think he kidnapped your friend?"

"I don't know. He's about the only one I can think of. Except..."

"Except who? Go on."

"Well, there was this Russian taxi driver." Jason summarized the ride from the airport and said he had taken a picture with Huff and the driver in the background without realizing it. "I used a digital camera, but I had a picture of that print made this afternoon. I was going to show it to Danni last night but never got the chance."

"May I see it?" Dalvang asked.

"Sure." Jason went to his dresser and pulled out the print. "The Russian driver is leaning on the taxi. The guy a few feet away is Huff."

"I'd like to make a copy of this," Dalvang said.

"By all means. I showed the picture to another taxi driver this evening, a driver I got to know and trust, and he said the Russian's name is Baransky."

"Baransky. Good. If he has a taxi license, we can track him. But what makes you think Baransky might have kidnapped Miss Rossler?"

"Not much, really. I'm scratching here. But I happened to ride in from the airport with him and he acted like a wild man. And he and Huff were talking together, which I don't understand. And then—there's a rumor I heard tonight, from a different taxi driver I showed the picture to." Jason looked at the floor. "You'll probably laugh, but he said the word was that some of the Russian drivers are spies." He raised his head to see how Dalvang took that and was surprised to see him trade knowing looks with the female cop.

"I've heard that rumor," Dalvang said. "But espionage is way above my pay grade. I deal in more down-to-earth crimes."

"Right. It's kind of out there, because Danni never gave a hint of any kind of international intrigue. She was just after Huff. Of course, maybe he had something to do with the spy business and she wasn't aware of it. I don't know, I'm thinking out loud, looking for reasons..."

A knock on the door brought the female cop to attention. Finally, she spoke—through the door, to the person on the other side, and in Danish. Then she opened the door. The other cop brought two people in, a man and a woman, both dressed casually.

The manager stood, and in English, thanked them for coming. "Detective, Mr. Stallings, these were the two main people at the front desk last evening, between four-thirty and nine."

Dalvang must have known they were coming because he didn't looked surprised. He stood, holding the picture of Huff and

Baransky, and talked to the hotel workers in Danish.

They studied the photo and pointed and began to nod as they replied, also in Danish.

"What are they saying?" Jason asked, frustrated by the language barrier.

Dalvang asked them to speak in English. The woman said, "I recognize this one," she said, pointing at Huff in the picture. "He was walking alongside the wheelchair while another man pushed the woman out."

"That's right," the man said. "There's something about that long nose I'd recognize anywhere. He said something earlier, before he went upstairs, about helping his sister."

Jason tried to absorb this quickly. Wheelchair? Huff and another man? "What time was that?" he asked.

"Five," said the man, looking at the woman for confirmation. "Maybe a little after."

"Damn, I'd just left."

"How about the one pushing the wheelchair?" Dalvang asked. "Is he in this picture?"

"That might be him leaning against the car," the front desk man said. "But the guy who came here to the hotel was dressed much different—nice suit and overcoat—and before they went upstairs, he said he was a doctor. He had a mustache, too."

The front desk woman looked again at the picture. "I don't know. It looks like him, but I can't say for sure. The sharp jaw line looks the same."

Dalvang nodded. "All right, we'll look for Huff and Baransky." He then asked the two front desk workers to describe the woman in the wheelchair. The man said she was nice-looking, about thirty years old, with dark blonde hair. "And she had her eyes closed." The woman could only describe the hair color, which agreed with what her colleague had said.

"That's Danni," Jason said. "God, she was unconscious, and they just wheeled her out." He went over to the window and looked down into the courtyard. Workers were clearing the breakfast setting.

Jason looked back at the manager, who had nothing to say, and at Dalvang, who wondered aloud, "I don't suppose you have a picture of your friend."

"No, but—wait, I do have a picture, a couple of them, on my camera." Jason rushed to the dresser and took out the camera and turned it on. He was so nervous he could hardly manipulate the small controls to scroll through the pictures he'd taken. "We went up to Hamlet's Castle on Sunday, and I took a couple of her there. Okay, here we are. These two." He showed them to Dalvang, then the hotel workers.

"That's her," said the man who had worked the front desk. The woman said the hair color was right.

"I'll need to borrow your camera for a while," Dalvang said to Jason.

"When I had the print made, I had copies of all the photos put on a flash drive. You can take that. It'll be faster."

"Great," Dalvang said. "We'll make prints of Miss Rossler and get them circulated."

"Is the picture of Huff and Baransky on here?"

"It is."

"Good. Maybe we can get a tighter crop and get prints of them to hand out."

Dalvang thanked the front desk workers and told them to leave their names with the female officer on the way out. He also thanked the manager and said he'd be searching Danni's room later and would be in touch if he needed something else. "And inform your night managers. You never know when I'll be calling."

Jason remembered Danni's purse was still in her room, and in it no doubt was her California driver's license. Probably there would be her business card, too, the card she'd almost shown him, and maybe there would be some papers related to her quest for Huff. Her phone would probably be there, too, but none of that really mattered at the moment. He and the police knew who one of the kidnappers was, if not both, so the manhunt for them had to be the priority, unless someone actually knew where to find Danni. Besides, how was he going to get into her room now and look around?

After the three hotel people had left, Dalvang went back to Jason. "Just another question or two, Mr. Stallings. You mentioned Huff having some girlfriends."

"Well, as far as we could tell."

"You were helping Miss Rossler investigate her embezzler?"

"In a way, I suppose. It was her show, and I more or less tried to stay out of it, but I kept getting drawn into it."

"I see. Then tell me what you know about the girlfriends. Huff may try to contact one of them."

Jason told him about the private investigator and gave him the names the investigator had come up with, Gitte Benneker and Cabrina, no last name. Jason said he didn't know who the investigator was.

"It might not be important. We'll come back to that later if we need to."

Jason didn't really want to get into the explanation of learning Cabrina's last name, but there was no good reason to hold back, especially if talking about it would help find Danni. So he told Dalvang how he and Danni had seen Cabrina at Nyhavn and how he'd later seen her at the Lorentsen Hotel and discovered her last name there from the front desk worker who had once dated her.

"You'll even see her picture on the flash drive. Long reddish hair and a kind of waitress uniform. I thought it might help Danni."

"This is complicated," Dalvang said, "but I guess it makes sense. Except for *why* you went to that hotel and *why* the desk guy talked to you at all."

"Well, I sort of knew him. Remember the wild taxi ride with Baransky? That was to the Lorentsen, because I had a reservation there. Of course, it turned out that I didn't really have a room there, so they sent me over here to the Kong Jacob. Anyway, while I was waiting there to come over here I talked to the front desk clerk. I had some time this afternoon so thought I would just drop in on him again."

Dalvang squinted. "Were you bored? The tourist sites and museums of our fair city didn't interest you?"

"That wasn't it," Jason said, wondering if he might be a suspect in some crime himself. "I wanted to follow up on something that turned out to be connected to the cheese business, which is why I came to Denmark."

"Cheese? I think you've lost me now."

So Jason explained a little about his food import job and the havarti problem. "And then it turned out that some of my troubles in getting enough havarti for the U.S. market were oddly connected to the reason I couldn't get a room at the Lorentsen."

"And now you're going to tell me what the connection is?"

"It's Martin Weathersby—your case, I believe."

Dalvang hardly blinked. "Tell me more."

"Well, that's about it. Weathersby was killed in the room I was supposed to get, and then later I learned from Bjorneby Foods that he was a food broker working on some of the same deals I was. So I wanted to satisfy my curiosity a little by talking to the desk clerk."

"Did you satisfy your curiosity?"

"No, not really. But the desk clerk did give me your name as the investigator. So I remembered it on the chance that I would call you if I heard something interesting about him, you know, from the food business."

"So that's why the hotel manager asked for me."

"That's it. I told him to ask. Your name was fresh in my mind, Detective, and I thought a detective capable of handling a murder case like that would be capable of finding Danni."

"Mr. Stallings, let me tell you how the police work here in Copenhagen. We have plenty of good detectives who can track down a variety of criminals and bring them to justice. But we tend to make our own assignments, and people don't usually ask for a certain officer as if they are ordering a hamburger."

"Well, yes, I can see now that was presumptuous of me, but you did come. And I'm glad you did. I have confidence in you."

"Well, thanks to you, and your camera, and those witnesses from the desk downstairs, we do have some decent leads to follow. I'll be frank with you. I'm going to work this case as hard as any.

But don't tell me how to do it."

"I'm sorry," Jason said. "I'm just trying to do the best thing for Danni. I don't think I could take it if..."

"You said you met her a few days ago?"

"That's right. Friday."

"And you care about her that much already?"

Jason nodded. "It's that obvious, huh?"

"Don't worry. It's okay to care. In my line of work, you see a lot of hardness in people. I wish more people cared."

11

Dalvang and Jason exchanged business cards. Then the police looked over Danni's room and left ten minutes later without telling Jason if they'd turned up any evidence or clues. He wasn't surprised or offended that they weren't sharing with him, but now he just felt useless and left out.

He walked around his little rented corner of Copenhagen like a caged lion and couldn't help thinking he should be doing something else to help find Danni. Sure, he'd given the police his pictures and told them where Huff was staying, and when they found Huff and Baransky maybe there would be some answers. But the reports of the front desk witnesses and his help with the pictures probably wouldn't be worth a thing if Huff and Baransky couldn't be tracked down.

Okay, so he felt useless—now what? He couldn't stay in his room all day doing nothing but pacing and waiting for the phone to ring. All right, he had his own phone, which meant he could pace somewhere else, maybe outside in the cold.

Arguing with himself like that wasn't helping. He had to do something better. It was painful to consider, but he wondered if he could go over the kidnapping again and see if he'd missed something.

He sat down with a pen and notepad and drew a timeline of the main events. He'd gone out a little before five, and Danni had been taken probably not more than a half hour later, maybe only ten or fifteen minutes later. The desk people had said five or a little after. Jason got chills. That was it, wasn't it? The timing was the clue. So maybe the reason she'd been taken while he was gone wasn't a matter of bad luck it all. It was beginning to look as if she'd been taken *because* they knew he'd left.

If Huff and Baransky had watched him leave the Kong Jacob, then they would have known exactly when he was out of the way. And they probably played it safe by waiting another five or ten minutes to begin their dirty work. But could they have been camped out all day watching his comings and goings? That was unlikely, and it sounded uncomfortable. It was cold, of course, and there weren't a lot of places near the hotel to park cars. Then maybe one of the perpetrators was inside, though the hotel itself didn't sound reasonable. Monday evening when Jason was waiting for Danni, he'd noticed he couldn't sit in the lobby without being seen at close range by everyone who walked by. The easiest thing would have been to keep the wait to a minimum. Then sitting out in a car for a few minutes wouldn't have taxed them much. So they must have had a good idea when he would be going and showed up not long before. And at that time of day on a late winter afternoon they would have had the cover of darkness.

So his drink and dinner meeting three kilometers away may not have been a coincidence at all. Still, he couldn't very well accuse Kunder of helping set up the crime. On the other hand, the man might be totally innocent but still have useful information that he didn't even realize.

Should he phone Kunder? Detective Dalvang didn't ask who he'd had dinner with, so Jason had to assume he didn't know anything about Kunder. Maybe he didn't care, either. Maybe the whole idea was a reach. Probably the best thing to do was wait for the police to bring in Huff and put the pressure on him. After all, eyewitnesses had seen Huff leaving the hotel with Danni. And with the picture and Huff's location at the Commodore, it should be easy to find him. So Jason wondered why he couldn't settle down. He couldn't really relax, but maybe he could get a grip on himself and let the police do their work. Hadn't he told Dalvang he had confidence in him? Well, he had confidence then, but now he'd had time to think over a thing or two.

Jason knew it was less a matter of losing faith in the police than of losing hope for an easy solution. Picking up Huff at his hotel would be way too easy. Crimes were hardly ever solved that way. *One, two, you're such a pest. Three, four, you're under arrest.* Sure, the police were probably the best bet for finding Danni, but that didn't mean they were the only bet. Jason thought of her hidden away, maybe tied up, maybe unconscious, or worse, and he couldn't bear the thought that someone had hurt her. Now he realized he couldn't just sit around. It was too frustrating. And most of all, she was far too important to him. An idea suddenly took shape. He had to do something, and he had something to do.

He went to the room phone and called the Lorentsen Hotel.

A few seconds later, he said, "Sayon Kunder, please."

As Kunder's phone rang, Jason had a flash of doubt about what he was doing. Then Kunder answered, and it was too late to back out. "Mr. Kunder. Jason Stallings here."

"Oh, good morning. How may I help you?"

"I wanted to thank you for the drinks and dinner last night." Stay patient, Jason told himself. Be polite and lay the groundwork. "I'm glad we got to know each other."

"Oh, I agree," Kunder said. "Now when these people at Bjorneby Foods mention your name, I won't be wondering who you are."

"Likewise. By the way, I have no news from Seattle on the company's position on your offer, so I can't say anything more about that today."

"Well, I wasn't expecting an answer this morning."

"Good, good. Say, I was curious about something else that may be important."

"Oh, I doubt that I have any special answers, but you can try."

"Right. The thing is, I was wondering who else knew that you and I were meeting yesterday evening."

"I don't know. I just wrote the note to you and brought it over to your hotel. I suppose the desk clerk could have read it. Wasn't the envelope sealed?"

"It was sealed," Jason said. "I wasn't thinking about hotel personnel. Anyone else come to mind?"

"Not really. No, wait. I did mention something to Poul

Stubkjaer at Bjorneby."

Stubkjaer? "I'm sorry to pry," Jason said, "but what exactly did you tell him?"

"Only that I was inviting you over for a drink to get to know you. Of course, I actually hadn't thought about dinner until after you'd arrived, so he couldn't possibly have known that."

"Did you give him the time?"

"I might have. I can't recall exactly now, but I probably said something about happy hour. Yes, that's it. I don't believe I mentioned a specific time. In fact, I didn't settle on a time until I wrote the note to you."

"Happy hour. That's sort of an American expression, isn't it? Or is it worldwide? Whatever it is, I wouldn't want to assume that Danes know a lot of American slang. Would Stubkjaer know what that meant, as far as time of day?"

"It's a question, but I think so. He's traveled a lot, and there's so much American TV here. Haven't you noticed? You can hardly escape it. What's this all about anyhow? Are you getting paranoid about the cheese business?"

"It's not that, Mr. Kunder. Perhaps I'll be able to explain it to you later. Could I ask you not to share this little conversation for a week or so? It could be a lifesaver."

"Certainly. You have my word."

Jason didn't know what Kunder's word was worth, but he would take it. Jason had another little question for Kunder, since he was staying at the Lorentsen, and the Indian assured him he would look into it.

Jason stayed in his room the rest of the morning. The housekeeper came and cleaned the bathroom and gave him fresh towels and made the bed, but he told her there was no need for anything else today and gave her fifty kroner just to leave.

A little later Dalvang called. There wasn't much to say. "Huff wasn't at his hotel, though he hasn't checked out, either. So there's still a chance there. The front desk will phone us the minute he comes in. Also, we have an officer in the area so we might see him ourselves. As for the taxi driver, he didn't report to work today, and he isn't in his apartment."

"Okay, thanks Detective."

So the police had already found Baransky's place. Was it any surprise that he'd skipped out so soon? That made Jason wonder again about Danni. How was she doing? Did she come out from the drugs safely? Was she breathing okay? Did she have anything to eat or drink? Had they hurt her, done terrible things to her? He stopped. No, he couldn't let his imagination run like that. It did no good.

When Jason thought about the Russian skipping out, it occurred to him that there hadn't been a ransom request. Didn't kidnappers want money? Maybe it was too early for that. It seemed like a long time, but really it had only been about eighteen hours. On the other hand, if the kidnappers didn't want money, what did they want? Huff already had taken three hundred grand from Danni's company, so money didn't seem to be the answer. Were they simply being malicious, or did they just want Danni out of the picture, at least for a while? Jason had to think of her disappearance as short term. It was the only way he could cope.

He went to the window and peered down at the courtyard where they'd eaten breakfast together. He could almost see her there, biting into a croissant. When the image shattered, he pounded a fist into the window casing and reeled around. There were no two ways about it. The bastards couldn't have her.

Time was excruciatingly slow. But eventually hunger grabbed his attention, so he ordered room service lunch. He wanted to stay close in case the police called the room phone again. Still, he felt guilty even eating. Again he wondered if Danni had any food. Was she warm? Did she have...? No, he couldn't ask these questions. It was ridiculous.

Later, when he put the lunch tray out in the hallway and looked down at Danni's room, a sign was hanging on the doorknob. It didn't matter what language it was in because he already knew it was the police warning to stay out. Stay out, stay away. He was tired of the message. He wanted to go find Danni.

Jason stepped back into his room and phoned the front desk to call him a taxi. He didn't have time to think about calling good old Carsten. The first ride available would be better, and he was pretty sure Baransky wouldn't be driving today. Jason grabbed his coat and went downstairs. In a minute the taxi came, and he told the driver to take him to Bjorneby Foods. He had a couple of questions for Poul Stubkjaer.

As Jason rode out to Bjorneby, he tried to fit together the pieces of the puzzle. It would be a surprise if Kunder or Stubkjaer had any connection with Huff, but he did wonder if Baransky wasn't involved with one of them somehow. Weren't there Russians working at the cheese warehouse? He thought he'd heard someone speak Russian there during his Saturday visit. It was a slim thread, but it might be a start.

At Bjorneby's front desk, Jason showed his business card and told the receptionist he wanted to see Stubkjaer.

"Do you have an appointment, sir?"

"Not today. We've been working on an export deal. I was in two days ago, and now something vital has come up."

"Normally, people call ahead for an appointment."

Jason nodded and accepted the chastisement. "Sorry. No time."

The receptionist grimaced and lifted her phone and spoke in Danish. Jason was able to hear his own name. Then the receptionist hung up and looked at him. "He'll see you in about fifteen minutes."

Jason sat down and looked at the magazines on the table. Most of them were in Danish, and one was in German. Then he found a *Newsweek* in English. It was a week old, so maybe it was *News Last Week*, or *News the Week Before*, but he leafed through it and avidly tried to find something to occupy his mind. He found a piece on the new international cuisine, which mentioned jalapenos but not havarti, and he found something on a Russian spy who had defected to Italy. Just what he needed.

The wait turned out to be twenty minutes. Apparently Stubkjaer had added another five minutes of detention time for not calling ahead, but Jason pretended he hadn't noticed. They shook hands and went up to Stubkjaer's office.

"Something rather urgent has come up," Jason said as he took a chair.

"So I gather. I still have no havarti to offer you."

"Poul, this isn't necessarily about havarti. Tell me about the Russians."

"Russians? In what regard?"

"In regard to your dealings with them."

"I see." Stubkjaer paused. "Well, we don't ordinarily disclose the sales of one customer to another customer."

"Fair enough, but you have Russian customers?"

"Of course, we sell to many parts of the world. Danish products are well respected."

Jason ignored the spin. "And you have Russians working here, right here in this building. I've heard them."

"A few. Mostly warehouse crews. Sometimes they're more willing to do the heavy lifting, or so I'm told. But that's another department. They don't work directly for me."

"So if it's an issue of readiness to do manual labor, then you should also have Turks and Moroccans and half of Asia and Africa. I didn't notice any of those people."

"Jason, I really can't see what you're getting at."

"Never mind. I'm having a bad day." Jason saw he wasn't going to budge Stubkjaer on this point, but the company's willingness to hire Russians and a few Germans, but not a wide range of other foreigners, made him wonder. Was there pressure from a certain Russian? Jason's head was spinning. He couldn't see how that would work.

"Have you heard from your company?" Stubkjaer asked.

"Company? Oh, yes I have. You mean about the order. Well, we seem to be in a holding pattern for a few more days. I don't know what the problem is." Of course, he did know what the problem was, but he wasn't going to say so. "You know, I think I'm a little distracted. The business of food imports and exports isn't really uppermost in my mind right now."

A silence fell over Stubkjaer's office.

Then it's principal occupant said, "Jason, I seem to be missing something. You show up unannounced, you tell me something is urgent, you don't want to talk about the food business, and all we do talk about is Russians. I'm not making the connections. What's going on, and what is so urgent?"

"Forget the connections," Jason said. "As for urgency, a friend of mine has disappeared from her hotel room. She was kidnapped last night."

"Kidnapped? My God."

"And apparently all because I went off to have a drink with Sayon Kunder."

"Kunder, yes. I did hear you were meeting last night. You're blaming Kunder?"

"No," Jason said. "But I learned a few things from him. Maybe the important thing, which I actually learned this morning, is that besides the two of us, only you knew we were meeting, and where and when."

"What are you saying, Jason?"

"I'm wondering if you mentioned this to someone else yesterday."

Stubkjaer hesitated. "I don't recall. I might have."

Jason said, "Well, if you did, that person might have used the information against my friend. And against me."

"That's a serious charge."

"Poul, this is a serious situation. My friend has been kidnapped."

"I'm sorry. I understand. I didn't mean to—"

"Good. Does the name Baransky mean anything to you?"

"No, I don't think so. It does sound Russian. Who is this Baransky?"

Jason couldn't detect anything in Stubkjaer's response or body language, so maybe he didn't know the Russian. "Just I guy I met. Taxi driver." Jason looked blankly at a mountain landscape on Stubkjaer's wall. He knew it wasn't the mountains of Denmark because there weren't any. "You know, Poul, I think I'm wasting your time. I should get going." There was no proof of anything that could link Stubkjaer to Baransky. He was wasting his own time.

"No problem," Stubkjaer said. "I think you needed someone to talk with about your friend."

"Yes, that was probably it. Thanks for listening."

"I wish I could do more. I assume the police are investigating."

"Oh, yes. They have some good leads. But it's been almost twenty-four hours now, and I'm beginning to worry."

"Of course."

Jason stood. "Well, I should go. I'll be back when the order is firmed up. It shouldn't be long."

Stubkjaer was already up and moving toward the door. "That would be good."

Together they walked downstairs to the lobby. At the bottom of the stairs, Jason said, "You know, this probably sounds strange, but I'd like to have another look at some pallets of havarti. It's not something I get to see in Seattle." Jason added a smile for good measure.

Stubkjaer looked at him and tilted his head. "Well. I suppose we could do that. If it doesn't take long. I do have an appointment in a few minutes."

"Thanks. The thing is, if I can't buy this havarti for Sunny Day Farms, I at least want to remember it. How it looks, how it smells, things like that."

"Of course. Why don't we go this way?" Stubkjaer held out a hand pointing the way and Jason fell into step. They went through a doorway and down a narrow hallway to the warehouse and then stepped into a wider hallway. The temperature was at least ten degrees cooler than the office. Jason was carrying his overcoat, but it wasn't cold enough for him to put it on. A forklift could be heard in the distance, and workers were coming and going with purpose.

"What's down there?" Jason asked, pointing to the left.

"Just a loading dock. We aren't using it much this winter."

"And the other way?"

"Some storage rooms. That's where we'll find the havarti."

Jason took a deep breath and thought he smelled...Danni's perfume? Lord, he was going crazy. "All right. Lead the way."

After another hundred feet, they turned a corner, and something about the ventilating system didn't move the air here. Jason took a breath through his nose and stopped. There was that dusty citrus fragrance again, but also something different, something cheaper. He looked at Stubkjaer quizzically, and the man must have thought that he'd lost it. It wouldn't be long until he quietly called for the medics. But these scents were so provocative that they had to be imaginary, didn't they? "Baransky," he said to himself, then realized Stubkjaer had heard him.

"Jason, what's wrong? Are you not feeling well? You could sit down here. I'll get some water, first aid..."

"I'm not hurt. It was something I smelled. Odd."

"Ah. Probably all the food in the warehouse. Of course, the concrete itself carries a certain raw smell."

"No. I smell perfume. And not just any perfume. Here in this hallway. Right here at this spot. My friend's perfume shouldn't be here."

"We do have women working here. I wouldn't make too much of it."

"And I wouldn't make too little of it." Jason felt the possibility but couldn't quite grasp it mentally. Why would Danni be here? Because Huff and Baransky had brought her here? In a wheelchair? Baransky. That was the cheaper scent, the cologne he'd smelled after someone had gone through the things in his room. It had to be the Russian. "Poul, do you have parts of the warehouse you're not using?"

"I'm not sure. At this time of year, there are probably some far corners. What are you getting at?"

"My friend. What if she's here in the warehouse? Her perfume is here. We've got to look."

"Jason, I don't know. The staff has so much work."

"Don't you have security people?"

"A few, yes. But we're not prepared for a full-scale search. This is a large building. Really, you can't be serious. The implications..."

"I know. You think I'm crazy." Jason felt his emotions building, half afraid he was arguing against the truth. "Another crazy person comes to your place and flips out right in front of your eyes. Happens all the time, but today you've reached your limit and can't take anymore. So you'll call the authorities to have me removed."

"Jason, I—"

"I think we should. We should call the authorities. Would you mind? I know a police detective right here in Copenhagen. Let's call him."

"Jason—"

"Oh, you want to see a search warrant first?"

"I don't think that will be necessary."

"Good." Jason pulled out his cellphone and saw he had no bars. "Let's find one of your phones. We'll need a landline in here."

"I don't know what to say. This is so strange. You think the kidnappers put your friend in the Bjorneby warehouse?"

"Now you're talking. That's exactly what I think."

"The good name of Bjorneby Foods can't be sullied. If you are wrong..."

"I know. I might as well never come back. My chances of making a deal with you will be as good as flying to the moon."

Stubkjaer sighed. "All right. Follow me. There's a phone in that office straight ahead."

#

Jason called Dalvang's mobile phone with the number Dalvang had given him. The detective answered right away but was clearly not excited about organizing a search of a warehouse.

"Give me one reason why I should do this."

"I'll give you three or four reasons. One, if I'm right, you can say you got an anonymous tip and instinct led you to solve the case. Two, you'll never have to see me again."

"That does have some appeal. But those are only two reasons."

"All right. Three, if I'm right, you'll be the hero of the Kong Jacob management and they'll probably comp you with drinks and dinner."

"Mr. Stallings, police officers can't accept bribes."

"Of course not. This would be more like a thank you note. I'll even put in a good word."

"You're too kind. Got another reason?"

"My nose."

Seconds passed. "Your nose."

"I told you I had a heightened sense of smell, and you did indicate there was probably chloroform in Danni's room."

"There was a faint indication, yes—to my nose."

"Well, it's happened again. Right here in the warehouse."

"What? Chloroform?"

"No. Danni's perfume. I smelled it in the hallway. It's a dusty citrus scent. I'd know it anywhere."

"Perfume? It could have been some other woman, almost anyone."

Jason sighed. "I know. I've been told that. But I don't think so. Detective, I'm asking you to come out. Human to human, I'm making my appeal. Besides, if you don't come out, I'll tear this place apart myself." Jason checked Stubkjaer's reaction, which was an official frown. "And then you'll have to come out anyhow and arrest me."

"Okay, okay. It may take me a few minutes to call in more officers. In the meantime, try to behave yourself. I'd like to say something good about you in my report."

Jason put down the phone and looked at Stubkjaer. "The police are coming."

"So I understand. Give me a minute. I have to cancel the appointment I mentioned, and I need to alert security to be ready for the police." Stubkjaer made his calls. Jason didn't understand any of what he said in Danish, but the man's voice sounded authoritative, which gave Jason the idea that Stubkjaer had even more influence at Bjorneby Foods than he'd indicated.

After the call, Stubkjaer said, "All right. Security will meet us in the reception area. That's also the way the police will come in."

"Thanks, Poul. I appreciate this."

"Jason, I don't know why I'm doing this. Tell me you

wouldn't have torn the place apart."

"No, probably not." He paused. "But I would have searched every nook and cranny of this building, and I would have made you go with me."

Stubkjaer swallowed. "Well, now that the police are coming, I guess they will take care of that."

They went back to the receptionist's desk where a couple of uniformed security guards were waiting. Stubkjaer spoke to them brusquely in Danish. They nodded in assent but looked unsure of themselves and eyed Jason as an intruder. After Stubkjaer stepped away to a nearby room, one of the guards kept a watch on the front door while the other made sure Jason didn't wander away or do something radical. If the situation weren't so serious, Jason would have laughed. Now he was a dangerous man—and maybe somewhat feared, too.

Without his asking, the receptionist appeared in front of him with a cup of coffee and asked if Jason wanted cream or sugar. He accepted the coffee in a paper cup but declined the additions. While Jason sat there on tenterhooks and sipped coffee, Stubkjaer made himself absent and the guards made sure Jason knew he was being watched.

His coffee cup was half full when Dalvang and six other officers arrived. Two of them were women, including the one who had barely spoken at the hotel, and altogether four of them were in uniform. Dalvang flashed his badge and brushed by the first security guard as he headed toward Jason. The second security guard stepped in front of Dalvang, which was a big mistake. The detective, with his badge still out, barked an order at the guard, who quickly stepped aside.

At this point Stubkjaer emerged from cover and said, in English, "Detective."

"Are you in charge?" Dalvang asked, also in English. Apparently both of them had decided Jason should be in on the conversation.

"In a manner of speaking," Stubkjaer said. "I'm Poul Stubkjaer, the director of exports at Bjorneby Foods. I've been working with Jason on a food order for his company. I was with him when he called you."

"Good. Then we won't have to go over all that again. Mr. Stubkjaer, I want you and Mr. Stallings to lead us to the place where he smelled the perfume."

"Actually, there were two places," Jason said. "Both in a hallway."

"Even better." Dalvang surveyed the two guards as if he had just picked up two wood splinters in his hand. Then he turned to Stubkjaer. "Your security people can come along, but they'll have to stay out of the way. All right, let's go."

Stubkjaer led the way, and Jason fell in behind him and Dalvang moved up on his shoulder. Jason was about to thank him for coming when Dalvang said, "We got a mug shot of Baransky from the taxi people. It matches the picture you took."

"No sign of him?"

"None. Don't be surprised if you never see him again."

In a minute or so, they were in the warehouse hallway, and Jason said. "Stop. This is the first place I smelled the perfume. It wasn't too strong, so at this point I wasn't sure." He glanced at Stubkjaer, who kept a stone face while hearing this for the first time. Then to Dalvang, he said, pointing to the left, "Up that way is a loading dock, apparently one not being used much right now."

Dalvang peered down the hallway. "Is that where your second spot is?"

"No, it's the other way, to the right. About a hundred feet."

"Then let's go."

This time Jason led the group. When they got to the right place, he said, "This is it." He breathed through his nose. "And I can still smell her perfume here."

Most of the others tried smelling, but then either shook their heads or shrugged their shoulders.

"Don't worry about it," Dalvang said to Jason. "I'll take your word for it. I didn't mention this earlier, but I've actually heard of someone like you, someone with hypersensitivity who could smell things other people couldn't." He looked back where they had been, then farther on. "All right, if they brought Miss Rossler from the loading dock and came this way, then they headed on to some place where they could put her without being noticed." He turned to Stubkjaer. "What's up this way?"

"Mostly food storage rooms. A few offices. More loading docks."

"Anything not in use right now? Hiding places? Spare offices?"

"No spare offices," Stubkjaer said, "but probably several storage rooms not in use at this time of year. I'm not sure exactly which ones because I haven't walked the whole warehouse for a while."

"Well, I guess we'll all be getting our exercise today." Dalvang turned around and spoke to the whole group in Danish, then English. "We will stay together until we get to the storage rooms. Then we'll break into three groups." Dalvang made the assignments. "I don't expect the kidnappers to be around, but be on guard. Mr. Stubkjaer, you and your security people should split up and each go with a group so we'll have some guidance on where we are. But I want *you* to stay with Mr. Stallings and me."

"Yes, sir. We'll be glad to help."

The way he said it, Jason believed him. So maybe the man did have some sympathy for Danni.

The next hour was a mixture of tedium and anxiety as they walked down wide hallways and slid open one heavy metal door after another, flipped on the lights and found either pallets of food or nothing at all. But where there were pallets that hid the view of the entire room, the police and Jason and even Stubkjaer and the guards stopped and looked around each one to be sure. As they progressed along, the doors were now wooden instead of metal. "This is the older part of the warehouse," Stubkjaer said. "We don't use it when we don't have to."

More doors were opened and closed, and more and more rooms were entirely empty. Not only that, but cool and empty. And some of them were refrigerated or set to freezer temperatures. It wasn't freezing most places, but to Jason the predominant temperature seemed to be no higher than the low fifties. He'd been carrying his overcoat but now put it on. He worried that Danni would be chilled, especially after the drugs she'd been given. He also worried that she wouldn't be here at all. She had been here, he was almost sure, but he realized she could have been moved later.

"How far along are we?" Dalvang asked Stubkjaer.

"At this rate, we will have seen everything in another twenty or twenty-five minutes."

"And if we find nothing," Dalvang said, "we'll have to decide then if we missed anything and whether we should go back and look again."

If we find nothing. The possibility was unacceptable to Jason.

He was getting weary himself when he stopped at another big door and sighed.

"Hang in there," Dalvang advised, putting a friendly hand on his shoulder. "Nobody said this would be easy."

"Right." Jason took a deep breath and—he thought he smelled something. He sniffed lightly, turning his head this way and that, taking a few steps either way. The scent wasn't strong, but it had to be. "Here," he said. "I think I smell her perfume here."

"Open this door," Dalvang shouted. Officers came from another group and assisted, but when the lights were turned on, the room was empty.

"Okay," Dalvang said. "Maybe we're getting close."

The groups broke apart again, and the search continued. Up ahead, Jason could see what looked like the end of the warehouse. He separated himself from Dalvang and went walking ahead down the hallway and tried to find the perfume. But either it wasn't there or he was so stressed his super-sensory powers weren't functioning. He desperately wanted a shortcut, but would have to settle for looking the hard way. He trudged back.

A few minutes later Jason was walking with Dalvang and Stubkjaer through yet another chilly room with stacks of pallets when the female officer who didn't talk much came running in and shouted something in Danish.

Jason was immediately alert. "What'd she say?" he asked Dalvang. "What'd she say?"

"They found your friend. She's alive."

· 12 ·

The other policewoman was taking the tape off Danni's eyes and mouth when Jason ran into the room. "Danni, Danni, my God."

"Jason, you found me." She was sitting on the floor leaning against the far wall near a corner. The policewoman quickly cut the tape from Danni's wrists and ankles and said, "Don't try to get up yet. We have to get medical help first."

Seeing Jason over her shoulder, the policewoman moved aside, and he stepped in and hugged Danni. "You're going to be okay, Danni."

She was crying. "I thought I was going to die here. I really did."

"Never. I would never have let that happen."

"I know, I know."

The room swelled into a hubbub of voices and activity. More people came in, and two-way radios beeped and seemed to speak of their own accord.

Jason looked at the woman in front of him with unrestrained appreciation. She was pale, but in her eyes he saw life and hope. "Danni, how are you?"

"Cold. And thirsty. And I have a headache."

He took off his coat and threw it over her. He could see that her white turtleneck wasn't nearly warm enough when she'd been sitting bound with tape on a chilly concrete floor all night and half the day.

Behind them an order was given in Danish. Then Dalvang came forward and said, "We're getting water and blankets."

"Thank you," Danni said to him, and then she turned back to

Jason. "And I'm so sore. From the fall—and sitting here so long. I don't know where I am." Her voice cracked.

"You're in a warehouse, the Bjorneby Foods warehouse."

"Isn't that..." A quizzical look spread over her face.

"Yes, it's where the cheese is. But don't think about that. It's a long story. We'll catch up on that later."

"How did you find me?"

"Your perfume. I smelled your perfume." And he hugged her again and kissed her on the cheek, and then on the lips. "You're wearing it now."

"Oh, Jason, that's so amazing."

"Miss Rossler?"

Dalvang's voice came from behind Jason. He turned to look at the detective, then back at Danni. "The police are here, you know."

"The police. I saw uniforms. The police, yes."

"Miss Rossler, we have an ambulance on the way. The paramedics will check you over and then take you to a hospital for a more thorough look."

"Good," Danni said. "I think I'll be okay, but that's good."

Someone brought blankets and water. Jason took his coat back while the policewoman who had announced the discovery stepped in and covered Danni and put another blanket behind her head and shoulders. Then someone else handed a bottle of water to Danni. Jason unscrewed the cap, and she drank. "That's better," she said.

"Keep sipping," Jason said. "You're probably dehydrated."

"Could I step in for a minute?" Dalvang asked.

Jason moved to the side, and held Danni's hand while Dalvang crouched beside her. "Miss Rossler. I'm Detective Arne Dalvang of the Copenhagen police. I'd like to ask you a few questions before the paramedics come. Do you know what happened to you?"

"Someone brought me here. I don't remember."

"Before that. At the hotel. Do you remember anything from the hotel?"

"Oh. Yes. I think so. A man knocked on my door. He said he was a doctor and he was going to check on me because I'd fallen—on the ice, you know. I believed him at first, but he really wasn't a doctor. He put a white cloth over my nose. It smelled funny, a weird kind of sweet smell, and it made me sleepy."

"Chloroform," Dalvang said.

"I tried to fight him off but my arms didn't work, and I was getting so sleepy. Then I fell down, and he pushed up my sleeve and put something in my arm, a needle, and—that's all I remember. It happened so fast."

"That's good information and will help us a lot." Dalvang smiled at Danni and nodded toward Jason as the facts fell into place. "Do you remember anything about the man who said he was a doctor?"

"I think so. I think I'd seen him before. He looked like the taxi driver who brought me back after my fall. But only a little bit. There was something different about him. He was all dressed up, something different." She shook her head. "I don't know."

"That's fine," Dalvang said. "Drink a little more water. It won't be long until we get you out of here. I don't want to move you until we're sure it's safe." Dalvang reached into a pocket and pulled out a piece of paper. "I have a picture here. Can you tell me if you recognize this man?"

Jason knew Baransky's mug immediately. This had to be his taxi license photo.

"That's the driver," Danni said. "And...he's the man who made me unconscious. Now I remember. At the hotel he had a mustache, sort of gray, and nice dressy clothes, but it's the same man."

"How many men came into your room?" Dalvang asked.

"Just him. Just the one. Was there another?"

Dalvang stood up. "There was another, we think. But it doesn't matter right now. You just rest. And drink the water."

The policewoman who had been with Danni at first now crouched down beside her, and Jason recognized the woman. She'd been Dalvang's partner at the Lorentsen investigating the Weathersby murder.

Seeing that Danni was in good hands, Jason stood up with Dalvang. "May I?" he asked, pointing to the photo.

Dalvang handed it to him. "Yeah, that's Baransky," Jason said.

Stubkjaer stepped forward and looked at the picture. "Hmm."

"Do you know him?" Dalvang asked.

"Don't really know him. But he looks familiar. I may have seen him here in the warehouse once or twice. I probably thought he was an employee. Or maybe a truck driver."

"There are several Russians working here," Jason told Dalvang.

"We may want to talk with them," Dalvang said. "Mr. Stubkjaer, I was wondering. How could this Baransky have come into your warehouse at five-thirty or six o'clock in the evening without anyone seeing him? How could he even gain access?"

"I don't know, I really don't. I work mostly in sales, so I'm not sure about the access. "

Dalvang went on. "We know that Miss Rossler was taken out of her hotel in a wheelchair. For the sake of argument, let's assume that Baransky brought his car to that loading dock near the point Mr. Stallings first smelled the perfume. Then Baransky put her back in the wheelchair and brought her way down here. That's a long way to be pushing a wheelchair in a food warehouse without being noticed."

Stubkjaer sighed and shook his head. "I agree. And I can't explain it except that after five we have only a few people working in the winter. In the summer there would have been more people around."

"What about a camera at that loading dock?"

"We don't have one. The managers have talked about putting cameras at all the entry points, but haven't done it yet. There hasn't been a problem. Until now. The guards drive around the perimeters and check all the doors."

"Well, apparently they didn't see anything," Dalvang said. "And a locked door is no problem if you have a key, or somebody on the inside lets you in."

"Detective, what are you suggesting?"

"Only the obvious, Mr. Stubkjaer. That it seemed a little too easy for Baransky to come and go with a wheelchair. It's not your ordinary warehouse vehicle, is it?"

#

The paramedics arrived sooner than Jason had thought possible. Three of them rushed in, breathing hard from running down the warehouse hallway pushing a gurney. Unlike the police and himself, at least they had known where they were going in the warehouse. Jason assumed there had been police or guards along the way to direct them.

They checked Danni's pulse and temperature and blood pressure. Her blood pressure was a little low, which was to be expected considering what she'd been through. Meanwhile, Dalvang told them that it appeared she had been chloroformed and then injected with some other drug. The paramedics thought they found the point where the needle had gone into her arm, but didn't see anything to worry about.

"At least it wasn't heroin," Dalvang told Jason. "Probably just a painkiller that would have made her sleep. As if the chloroform wasn't enough."

Jason had never thought about heroin. He appreciated the fact that Dalvang had spared him that possibility earlier.

Dalvang's partner came up and told him something in Danish, which Dalvang then shared with Jason. "There's no sign of any evidence here. They apparently just dumped her and left."

The paramedics also pointed a flashlight into Danni's eyes and checked her head for cuts, bruises and other signs of abuse but found nothing. Danni told them about her fall on the ice and that her back and hips were sore before she'd been taken out of the hotel, and now she'd been sitting on concrete for what seemed like forever. They helped her to her feet, one on each side and one in front. The two on her sides had her put her arms around their shoulders and then asked her to walk if she could. She took three tentative steps, and then her legs buckled. They pulled her up straight, and the other paramedic moved the gurney into position behind her. She sat down, and then they had her lie down and pulled a blanket over her.

They put an oxygen mask on her face and turned a dial on the green tank. Once again they took her pulse and blood pressure, which they said had gone lower than before. They were concerned but not panicked. She was ready to go to the hospital now. Jason could ride along in the ambulance. Dalvang would follow in his own car.

While two-way radios crackled with activity, the gurney moved into the hallway. When Jason looked back into the storage room that had been Danni's prison, a Bjorneby security guard was standing next to Stubkjaer, who was holding one of the blankets that had been brought to warm up Danni. He looked helpless and dejected, and Jason couldn't find anything in himself to care.

#

At the emergency room, the nurses made all the checks on Danni that the paramedics had done, and more. She was embarrassed that her clothes were a mess, so they gave her a gown and robe and said they'd wash up what she'd been wearing. After all, the police had requested the best possible care for her. She was warmer now, and her blood pressure was nearly back up to normal, but she still felt weak. A young doctor came in and checked her heart and lungs with a stethoscope and gave her a good look in the eye and asked her what Jason's name was and what month it was and what holiday was celebrated in December and a few other questions like that. Danni gave him all the right answers, but the doctor said he wanted to take X-rays of her lower back and hips in case she'd broken something in her fall on the ice.

After the X-rays, she had to wait for the doctor to come back so Jason sat with her in a curtained examining area while she drank hot chicken broth and ate little crackers that one of the nurses had brought in. At least she was able to sit up on her own, and her color looked better. "How's the pain?" he asked.

"Not bad. My head's better, and my back isn't too sore if I don't move the wrong way."

"Sounds as if you're on the mend. But no tours of castles for at least a day."

She laughed a little and squeezed his hand.

In a few minutes the doctor came back and said, "Nothing's broken, so I'll have to turn you loose. If you like, I could give you a painkiller to help you sleep tonight."

"No drugs," she said. "I've had enough of that for a while. I just want to be me."

"All right, then. It's up to you."

"Doctor, I want to thank you." Danni said.

"Well, you're welcome, but it's my job to help people."

"I know, but I want to thank you for being a real doctor. Yesterday I met this pretender, and he had no class at all. Not like you."

The doctor laughed. "I'm going to pass that on to my other patients. They don't know lucky they are."

A nurse brought Danni's clothes back, clean and dry, so she changed and put on her shoes. A few minutes later another nurse came in and had her sign a release form.

Then a head poked around the curtain. "Ready?"

Jason looked up. "Detective Dalvang."

"I came to give you a ride back to your hotel. That way you won't get hooked up with any Russian taxi drivers."

"There are more of them?"

"So I hear. And as for you, young lady, you have to ride to my car in a wheelchair. The nurses insisted, but they're going to let me push. I've got a better sense of direction than those characters who wheeled you out last night. Not only that, I'll let you keep your eyes open."

Danni laughed. "Oh, don't I feel special."

"You are special. I'll even take your boyfriend along. Of course, you get to ride in the front while he sits in the back."

"Has he been giving you a bad time?"

"Oh, no, but I've seen a little too much of him today and not nearly enough of you. Besides, you're much better looking."

Jason smiled. "Well, there's something we can agree on."

#

Dalvang had Danni and Jason wait in his car while he went into the Kong Jacob and talked to the day manager. The policeman had given Jason back his flash drive. Dalvang had retrieved it from the police station while Danni was being checked out in the hospital and assured him it had served a good purpose.

Now it was almost five o'clock, and Jason said, "It was only twenty-four ago that I was leaving the hotel and Baransky was sitting out here someplace waiting for me to leave so he could come in and get you."

"My God," Danni said. "I can't imagine how the man lives with himself."

"Rumor is he's a spy. KGB or something."

"And he gets his kicks by kidnapping women?"

"I don't know about kicks. I think he had a reason. We'll have to talk about that later."

"Not now?"

"No, maybe later. I'm still thinking about it." That wasn't strictly true. What he was thinking about was finding a good way to explain it to Danni. They had a lot to talk about, all right, but it was too soon. First, they needed to get back to a comfort zone, even if it was just the Kong Jacob.

It wasn't long before Dalvang popped back out of the hotel and got into the car. "Okay, I think they're ready for you."

"Ready?" Jason asked from the back seat. "What's that mean? There's a reception with tea and creampuffs?"

"Not exactly. But it's good. Our friend the manager is much relieved and delighted that you're returning safely. He'd like to apologize, but I said not right now, maybe tomorrow. At the moment I thought you'd like to get back to your room without any fuss and just relax. Someone on the staff ran up there a few minutes ago to tidy up and should be done about now. You didn't get regular maid service this morning because of the investigation."

"I'm going to complain," Danni said.

"Well, you could," Dalvang replied, "but in the end you'd be complaining to me because I'm the one who kept the maid out."

"Oh, in that case..."

"Right. So what you both want to do is quietly go to the elevator and don't even look at the front desk, and the staff people will studiously avoid interfering with your privacy."

"I like it," Danni said.

"Then in about an hour, you can call the dining room and let them know you're coming down. Here's the extension," Dalvang said, handing Jason a hotel business card with a number written on it. "The maitre d' will meet you and escort you to your table, and dinner will be on the house. So now be on your way, before I go in and eat that dinner myself."

"Detective," Danni said. "Thank you so much." And she leaned across the front seat and kissed him on the cheek.

"Well," Dalvang said, looking a little flustered while Danni was clearly amused at his reaction. "You're recovering faster than I expected."

Jason said, "I'm not kissing you, Detective, but I will shake your hand."

"All's well that ends well," Dalvang said, reaching back to Jason.

"I've heard that line before. Somewhere."

Danni was safe now, but Jason knew that Dalvang's investigation would continue.

#

After Danni had gone into her room to shower and change clothes, Jason went on down the hall to regroup in his own room. He would go back to Danni's place in an hour, and then they would call the dining room for arrangements.

He threw his coat on the bed, switched on a lamp and saw that the room phone was blinking red. He lifted the receiver and punched in the number to retrieve the message. It was Novitsky in Seattle, wanting to know why Jason didn't answer his cellphone and was he ready to pull the trigger on the cheese deal from Kunder. It was morning in Seattle, a perfect time to call back, but Jason had nothing to say. So he just listened and hung up.

There was another phone message, this one from Sayon Kunder answering his earlier question about a little detail at the Lorentsen. Jason listened to it and then sat down in the armchair. Clearing his head is what he wanted to do now. He held still as random thoughts toyed with his mind, and he gently pushed them aside. Now he remembered that the breathing was important. Half closing his eyes, he concentrated on his breath until he thought only of his breath. This was the classic way, because it worked. Gradually he felt himself grow calmer, and he let the calmness envelop him. Later there was a tingle up his spine, a good sign, he'd been told. He continued following his breath. In, out, in out. Follow the breath.

In about ten minutes he eased his eyes open, and he continued breathing calmly while he re-entered the 3-D world. He turned and looked down at the courtyard. It was fallow now with low light, waiting for another breakfast, another energetic start of a new day.

The new day. Where would he begin? Where would Danni begin? But he was getting ahead of himself. If there was an opportunity, and he thought there would be, they would have to discuss a few things tonight. He resolved to get to the bottom of her quest, and her kidnapping. He felt now that the two couldn't be separated. Along the way, he would have to share his misgivings. It might be hard on Danni, but it was a chance he would have to take.

Jason got up and went to the bathroom and washed up, then came out and changed into a crew neck sweater. It wasn't time to go over to Danni's room yet, so he picked up his camera and scrolled through his pictures. Holding the camera in both hands, he sat on the bed as he viewed each frame. He had some nice shots of Copenhagen scenes, but the ones that interested him now were the ones with people he knew. Huff and Baransky and Danni. Jason went back a couple of days to the time he thought someone had broken into his room but not taken anything except possibly information. And then later he realized it had been the fading whisper of Baransky's cologne he'd detected.

Now he figured he knew what Baransky had taken, and that was the knowledge that he and Danni were linked. The evidence was on the camera, two pictures from Hamlet's Castle with Danni in the foreground. Pictures of Danni on *his* camera. It was so obvious. And they were in the same hotel. Baransky must have seen Danni poking around Nyhavn and then made the connection when he looked at the camera himself. Baransky knew that hurting one of them would hurt the other.

Then the goon had gone after Danni directly, traumatically, but with strangely restrained violence. No lasting marks, no broken bones, no physical abuse beyond the carefully planned application of the knockout drugs. Not only was she the easier mark, but she was also the primary target, Jason figured. So Baransky had wanted Danni out of the way for a while. Whether she knew it or not, she was getting in his way. With her kidnapping, the Russian had bought time, maybe only a day or so in his thinking, until he'd accomplished what he wanted. But what was that?

It was hard to say, but Jason was convinced the objective had something to do with Huff. Danni's embezzler had participated in the kidnapping, too, though maybe not with the gusto of Baransky. Though Huff had demonstrated his wild streak in that Irish pub, and Jason had passed on the information to Dalvang, Jason now didn't feel that the kidnapping had Huff's touch. Huff was too nervous and he would have bungled it somewhere along the line, but the abduction itself had been flawless, almost professional, especially the wheelchair. Huff would never have thought of that. The wheelchair was too clever for a guy who couldn't focus.

What if Huff had been more or less forced to join in? What if he'd even resisted the idea for a while but hadn't been able to stand up to Baransky's strong will? Okay, Baransky really could be a KGB operative, a rogue, but the real thing. That could explain the nearly masterful kidnapping. But what was he doing in Denmark? And why was he driving a taxi?

Jason scrolled through his pictures again and studied the one of Baransky and Huff together near Kongens Nytorv. They weren't standing face to face having a conversation. No, Baransky was leaning against the Mercedes, relaxed, seemingly in charge, while Huff kept a little distance, maybe unsure of himself as he stood uncomfortably, tentative about his relationship with Baransky. Which was what? Some kind of spy business? Huff the mild-mannered embezzler who'd never been to Denmark, or maybe anywhere in Europe, was now an international spy dealing with the KGB? Jason shook his head rapidly, as if trapped by cobwebs.

That didn't make sense, and yet it was the best he could come up with.

It was almost too much to think about. Jason shut off the camera and got up and put it in the dresser drawer. Enough of that. It was nearly time to go see Danni and have dinner. What he needed to do was get himself in the right frame of mind. There would be no problem in being sympathetic with Danni, because he truly was, and there would be no problem in rekindling romance, because even this afternoon in the hospital when she hadn't looked her best he had been as attracted as much as ever. No, the danger was that he would let sympathy and romance take the upper hand and put a sugarcoated but insufficient kindness ahead of bearing down and asking the questions that should be answered. What he'd like to do, he thought, was just be the sympathetic and romantic guy and let some hardened pro like Dalvang handle the interrogation. Unfortunately, that was not an option. Besides, Dalvang didn't have the background to know what to ask.

#

As soon as Danni's door opened, Jason said, "You look great." She had looked haggard this afternoon after she had been found in the warehouse and gone to the hospital, but now she had washed her hair and put on makeup and different clothes. More than that, her face was vibrant. Yes, she looked a little tired, but it appeared to be a temporary situation. A good night's sleep in a real bed would probably do wonders.

After he had stepped into the room and closed the door, Danni offered a kiss, which he gladly accepted. After the kiss he continued to hold her.

"Oh, Jason, that feels so good."

"Hey, that's what I was going to say."

"I got there first. But I guess we can share."

Jason pulled back from the embrace. "I'd like that. Now what about dinner?"

"I'm hungry. Except for that broth and those crackers, it's been a while."

"Shame, shame. Weren't you told not to skip meals?"

"Constantly," Danni said. "But apparently I didn't listen." Her voice was lively now, with tease and charm.

"Well, there'll be no skipping tonight. Let's get started. Dalvang said to call the dining room first. So here goes." Jason made the call, and they went downstairs. The maitre d' greeted them. "Welcome, Miss Rossler, Mr. Stallings. We're so glad you could join us tonight."

"Thank you," Danni said. "I hope you haven't gone to much trouble."

"No trouble at all," he said. "Would you follow me?" He led them past diners, and tables with candles, and white tablecloths to a table in the back. The tablecloth, and the candles were the same here, but this one also had a large vase of flowers of red, yellow, orange, white, and blue.

"They're beautiful," Danni said.

"Yes, they are," said the maitre d', and after dinner you should take them to your room. The hotel management insists."

"Oh my gosh. That's so nice. Thank you."

"You're welcome," said the maitre d'. "Now if you'll be seated..." And he pulled the table away from the wall. Danni and Jason slid behind the table onto the booth-like padded seat.

"As I assume you know," the maitre d' continued, "both of you are our special guests tonight, and there will be no charge for your dinners."

"Thank you," Jason said.

"Very good. Now, if you'd like to look over the menu," the maitre d' said as he handed them the glossy booklets. "Your waiter will be with you shortly."

Danni sighed and then smiled. "This seems so unreal."

"What? A free dinner?"

"No, not that, though it's very nice. The special attention is like a birthday party. No, what I meant was it's unreal to be sitting here in a place like this, a comfortable, pleasant place, so soon after..." She started to choke up, and Jason put an arm around her.

"So soon after we found you," Jason said. "Is that what you meant?"

"Yes," Danni recovered. "So soon after you found me."

"You know, I was thinking the same thing. But it's only going to be for a little while that you have this strange feeling, maybe even just tonight, or tonight and tomorrow. In a day or two there'll be new things to think about."

"I suppose so. Of course, in a day or two I might be going home." She reached for Jason's hand and held it tight. "And then I don't know what will happen."

Jason squeezed back. "Nobody knows. But right now, I think we should enjoy this dinner, and enjoy the moment."

"Is that an order?" Danni threw him a playful look.

They settled in for a fabulous dinner. Danni ordered the London broil. Jason went along with the beef trend and ordered the tournedos, and a bottle of Bordeaux. For an appetizer, they ordered coconut prawns. As expected, Danni had a good appetite. But she was a little cautious with the wine, still working on her first glass halfway through the meal.

Jason didn't feel that it was time yet to push for answers, maybe after dinner when he was fairly sure Danni was psychologically strong enough. So he was surprised when she was the one who wanted to ask the questions, not his questions, but at least a good start. "You were going to tell me about why I was put in that particular warehouse where the cheese is. Can you do that now? Does it have something to do with you?"

"No. I don't think it has anything to do with me, though my connection with Bjorneby Foods put me in the building at the right time. I still haven't figured it out totally, but it seems the Russian, Baransky, had some connections there. I know there were several Russians working there, and the circumstances seem kind of strange. It might all be on the up and up, but if he really is a spy, the warehouse might be some kind of base or jumping off point for whatever he, and maybe the other Russians, were doing. On the other hand, Baransky might have been using the other Russians as cover. It probably doesn't matter now, but I'd guess he was using his influence to get them hired. Why, I don't know, but the how might be more interesting. The guy I've been working with out there, Poul Stubkjaer, denies any connection with Baransky, but I'm not so sure."

"You're sure Stubkjaer wasn't behind kidnapping me?"

"Yes, fairly certain. Stubkjaer would have nothing to gain from it. If anything, he's embarrassed that Baransky chose his warehouse the way he did. If he knew Baransky, and I wouldn't doubt that he did, he's feeling now that he didn't know the Russian very well. In a way, he's a victim, too, but maybe not quite an innocent one."

"Hmm. So where does that leave your cheese negotiations?"

"I have no idea. You knew I met with the Indian guy, Sayon Kunder. Well, it turns out that Kunder is just another opportunist, and apparently a successful one. He's now offering to sell havarti to my company."

"But what about all the starving Indians?"

"Oh, that. It turns out that India's interest in Danish havarti is mostly an invention of Stubkjaer's."

"Those are two weird guys," Danni said. "So how do you feel about the cheese business now?"

"After today, indifferent, I guess. I haven't spent more than five minutes all day thinking about my job. There was a message from my boss in Seattle, but I haven't bothered to return the call. Thinking that you were gone, and then finding you, has made work seem pretty insignificant."

"Then you're okay with going home without the havarti?"

"Perfectly," Jason said. "Oh, it'll cost me some commission and bonus, but I haven't given up yet. And I won't go home without a sizable food order of some kind. That's already in the pipeline now. But if I don't get the havarti, I can live with the consequences."

"And your boss?"

"If he can't live with what I deliver, he'll have to live without me altogether."

"You're brave."

"Or foolhardy. Sometimes it's hard to tell the difference."

The waiter suddenly appeared with the appetizer they had ordered, and so they put aside the questions and answers as dinner took precedence. When they were all done in the dining room, Danni picked up the vase of multicolored flowers and they went off toward the elevator. Jason was reaching out to press the button when Danni said, "I'd like to take the stairs."

"You're sure?"

"I could use the exercise, and I don't want to get too stiff. As long as we're in no hurry, I can make it."

"All right. But let me carry the flowers. That way you can hang on to the railing, and to me, if you need to."

Danni was slow up the stairs, but no one else was using them as they went up and she made it to the top without incident. They went on down the hallway to her room, and Danni said, "I want you to come in. I think we should talk now."

This was a little surprise to Jason. He expected to be invited in, but was relieved that a serious talk was her idea. Now he wouldn't have to look like the bad guy just because he also wanted a serious talk.

Danni turned on two lamps, and Jason put the vase down on the dresser. She came over and rearranged the flowers to her satisfaction and then turned to Jason. "Something from the mini-bar?"

"No, thanks. The wine was more than enough, especially since you weren't able to drink that much."

"I've had plenty. But I think now that I'd like to lie down and rest."

Jason helped her get into a good sitting position on the bed and placed pillows behind her back. "There," she said. "Now we can talk. You sit down, too."

He went around to the other side and perched in the middle of the bed so he could have a good look at her and not be too far away. "All right. Go for it."

"I have some questions," Danni said. "First, are we done with the police?"

"I don't know. Maybe, maybe not. It depends on what else they find."

"The kidnappers, you mean."

"Yeah, I guess so. Or some kind of evidence."

"Hmm. I've noticed nobody wants to talk to me about *why* this happened."

"Well, I don't think the police know that."

"Fair enough. But you do. You know this Russian character. Was it because he brought me back in his taxi?"

"Possibly," Jason said. "More likely, he brought you back in his taxi because he was following you and was all ready to take advantage of some opportunity."

"He was following me? I don't get it."

"I think it was because of the other kidnapper."

"Yeah, that guy. Somebody else no one wants to talk about."

"Danni, I was going to get to that. But I wanted to have a nice dinner first and make sure you were stable enough to hear what I had to say."

"Stable? You mean mentally?"

"Mentally, physically, any way you want to look at it."

"And how am I, Jason? Am I stable?"

"Very stable," Jason said. "I know you're a little sore yet from the fall and so much time on that hard floor, but obviously nothing is escaping you. You're thinking clearly and your emotions are in check."

"Well, thanks, doc. So give me the news about this guy."

Jason reached out and held her hand. "Danni, this is a tough one. But I'll tell it to you straight. The hotel staff made a positive ID on the other kidnapper from a picture I took at Nyhavn. The other kidnapper is Craig Huff."

Danni slumped forward. "My God. That can't be. I don't believe it."

"I'm sorry. It can be, and it is. The police are still looking for him, but he hasn't shown up yet at his hotel room."

She raised her head back up and looked Jason in the eye. "But I never saw him—here, in this room. When I opened the door, it was only the taxi driver, the Russian."

"By design. Baransky pretended to be a doctor, to fool you temporarily, and Huff stayed out of sight until you were unconscious. They weren't taking any chances that you'd see Huff and raise your voice in recognition or cause some kind of ruckus. So Baransky put you out as fast as possible."

"And you told me they used a wheelchair to take me out of the hotel. I never saw that, either."

"Huff was probably standing out in the hall with the wheelchair. Until it was time, which apparently wasn't long."

Danni shook her head. "So who was in charge?"

"I'm pretty sure it was Baransky. This operation doesn't sound like Huff to me."

"Me either. In so many ways I feel sorry for him. He was an ordinary guy who did something foolish with the money, and now he's a kidnapper running around with a Russian goofball."

"A very calculating goofball."

"You don't have to convince me."

"So the police are still looking for them?"

"Both of them, yeah. Though it appears Baransky has left the country. I don't know about Huff. He didn't check out of his hotel, but he hasn't turned up yet, either."

"What's going to happen to him?"

"If he's caught, he'll probably be charged. Two people at the front desk saw him. He could go to prison."

"My God."

Jason was about to lose his patience. "Danni, he helped kidnap you."

"I know, but..."

Jason circled back to what he'd suspected before. Huff wasn't just an embezzler, or even a kidnapper. He meant something more to Danni—in a fractured sort of way. That's why she felt sorry for him and didn't want him to go to prison. She was the victim, but she took pity on this guy. And that's why she had never asked the police for help earlier. She didn't want the police involved at all. And now they were.

Huff wasn't going to wiggle out of this easily. He could argue that Baransky gave him no choice, but the front desk people had seen him cooperating with the Russian. Before the kidnapping they'd heard him say he was going upstairs to, what? To help? Yes, but there was more.

And then Jason remembered what the front desk people had told Dalvang. Huff had said he was going upstairs to help his *sister*. "Oh, my God," Jason said. "I get it. I finally get it. Now I know why you feel sorry for him."

"Jason, no." Danni didn't want to hear what he was going to say.

But he said it anyway. "Craig Huff is your brother. He's your brother."

Danni nodded and began to cry. Jason moved closer and hugged her, and she put her arms around his back. Amidst the sobs that racked her whole body, he felt the release coming. It was going to be a long cry.

· 13 ·

Sitting on the bed with Jason holding her tight, Danni gradually regained control of herself. When little spaces started to develop, she spoke in bursts and fragments. "Jason...I wanted...to tell you. I was going...to tell you. I couldn't figure out...how to do it. I was going to do it...last night...then... Could you get me a tissue?"

Jason hopped off the bed, went into the bathroom, grabbed the whole box of tissues, and brought it back to Danni. She took it and began blowing her nose. After she had reached some degree of composure, he sat down on the bed again. She looked at him with a wan smile. "You probably think I cry all the time."

"No, I don't. But I don't blame you now. I'm almost crying myself."

"Oh, don't do that." She took a deep breath. "All right, here we go." She took a deep breath.." I was going to tell you the whole story tonight, I really was. That's why I asked you in to talk."

"I believe you, Danni."

"I know, I know. It's just been so hard."

"What? Not telling me? Maybe you should have told me in the beginning."

Danni nodded. Her eyes were red from the crying. "That sounds good now, doesn't it. But it wasn't that simple. I, I don't know."

"Take your time," Jason said. "We have plenty of time."

"I didn't know you at first. And when you told me about Craig talking that crazy stuff about killing people, I couldn't have told you then."

"I see. But then you did get to know me, and trust me."

"That's right. And there's one more thing. I got to like you. And I wanted you to like me."

"Well, I did. And I do. I like you a lot, Danni." He brushed the back of her hand with his fingers. "But it's out now, and it doesn't make me think any less of you. Hearing all this, I can see how hard it's been for you."

"It has been hard, Jason. It's been hard to live with the knowledge of what he's done. And I wanted you to like me, so I couldn't tell you my brother is an embezzler. That would really have impressed you."

"Danni, I wouldn't have run away. I would have helped. I didn't want to interfere in your business, but if I had known that, I would have helped."

"How?"

"I would have gone to see him. To talk. We'd already talked once, so he knew me. He would have done it again. Apparently things haven't gone so well with his girlfriend Gitte, so he was lonely here in Denmark. He would have opened up with an American. Maybe after some time, he would have agreed to give the money back, go back home and start over. Isn't that what you want? Isn't that why you didn't want the police involved? You want to keep it in the family."

"Of course, I didn't want the police involved. I didn't want to turn in my own brother. But when I got here and saw him, and you helped me find out where he was staying, and all that stuff about his girlfriends came out, I got so confused I didn't know what to do. And after you left last night to go see the Indian guy, I decided I would tell you everything when you got back. I was going to come clean. It wasn't fair to you, and I didn't want to deceive you anymore. But I didn't get a chance to tell you."

"Danni, Danni. But you've told me now."

"Not everything," Danni said. "Get me some water, and I'll begin at the beginning."

Jason got a glass of water for Danni, and one for himself. They each drank some, and he said, "All right. Whenever you're ready."

"I'm ready now. Are you going to sit down?"

"Not just yet. I may need to walk around a little. To help absorb the news."

"If that helps, sure. Well, first of all," she said, "some of what I told you before is true. I mean most of it was true, I think. Except for the Pittsburgh stuff. I don't know why I said that except that before I knew you, when I saw you at the Irish pub and out in the hallway, I thought maybe you were in league with Craig somehow so I didn't see the harm. I thought it would be better if you didn't know too much about me."

"Protective covering," Jason said.

"I suppose. Like some furry little animal on one of those nature shows. *The California marmot takes on the coloration of her Pennsylvania cousins to protect herself from strangers.* That's what the narrator would say. Anyway, as for the rest of what I told you, I think I left out so much that nobody could tell what was going on."

"Well, you're right about that."

"Okay, so here goes. First, Craig isn't exactly my brother."

Jason froze and raised his eyebrows. "No?"

"He's my half brother."

"Ah. That's why I had trouble figuring this out. Your last names are different."

"Right. We have the same mother, but different fathers. Anyway, he did take a lot of money from the company where we both work."

"So are you a security agent?"

"Not even close. I just made that up and let you believe I was something grander than I really am. No, it's a small company, a family company."

"Electronics, you said."

"That's true. I didn't make up that part. My mother and father own a small chain of electronics stores in the East Bay and Contra Costa areas. Actually, we have six stores. The main one is in Walnut Creek."

"Not too far down the road from your place in Benicia," Jason said.

"No, not far at all. My folks live in Walnut Creek, but I wanted to be separate a little. Besides, we have a store up in Vallejo, so I'm the closest one to that location and tend to keep track of it more than my dad does. It saves him some travel, and I even have a part-time office there."

"What do you do for the company?"

"I'm the marketing director."

"So it's a successful company. Your dad's the electronics genius? Always tinkering with little parts to come up with something miraculous?"

Danni laughed. "How'd you guess?"

"And your mom does the finances."

"She used to, when the company was smaller. Now she's the inventory manager and buyer. She has a lot to do just keeping merchandise on the shelf. And my little brother, Eddie, manages one of the stores."

"So it's really a family company. But six stores—you need more managers, sales people, technicians, drivers, accountants."

"I know. That's where Craig came in. About a year ago he was hired as our chief accountant. He has a fair understanding of electronics, too. His predecessor left to start his own business, so we really needed someone who could step in quickly without much training. Craig seemed like a really good fit."

"Whose idea was it to hire him?"

"Well, it started with my mom," Danni said. "And it made a lot of sense to me."

"But your dad resisted."

"At first. It wasn't a matter of competence. He figured Craig could do the job all right. Dad didn't want to stir up old troubles, but after a while he came around and then Craig moved up from Southern California."

Jason walked back and forth by the end of the bed. "Old troubles. That sounds interesting. So how did Craig work out, as an accountant?"

"Oh, he was very efficient. The books were always in order. Taxes and payroll went smoothly, and nobody had any complaints on that score."

"Right. On that score. So I suppose we're back to the old troubles."

"Well, it's hard to say whether they were new troubles or old ones. After a while, Craig started quarreling with Mom and Dad. Little stuff, nothing major about the company, but there was tension. Mom would defend him, to a point, and Dad would start to criticize him, then clam up. More tension."

"Okay. So did you grow up with Craig? Or was he someplace else?"

"He lived in Colorado mostly. Near Denver. Of course, he's six years older than I am, so early on either I wasn't on the scene yet or I was too young to know any different. I remember him coming to visit sometimes, and I thought it was strange that my little brother lived with me but my big brother lived in another state."

"How did Craig feel about that, living with his dad in Colorado?"

"Oh, living with his dad was fine. But not living with his mother, our mother, wasn't so good. Craig was four years old when the divorce came, and I guess his dad had a good job and my mom didn't, so they agreed ahead of time that Craig would live with his dad most of the time, and his dad would pay some alimony but not child support. That kind of worked in the beginning, because Craig could still visit fairly often, but then his dad got transferred to Colorado, and since he had custody, he took Craig."

"Did his dad remarry?" Jason asked. "When he got to Colorado?"

"He did. So Craig had a stepmother, who I think liked him a lot and took good care of him, but it wasn't the same, you know. She wasn't his real mother."

"I can see that. But then your mother remarried. She was probably more financially stable later on. Couldn't she have taken Craig back?"

"I don't know for sure. It's still fuzzy to me. I've talked with Mom about this, but I get vague answers, and I can't exactly give her the third degree. I suspect Dad wasn't too enthused about taking in Craig. When they first knew each other, Craig wasn't around much. Of course, then they got married, and it wasn't too long before Mom was pregnant with me, and bringing Craig back then was the last thing on their minds."

"And your little brother. Eddie?"

"He came along about eighteen months after me. So, yeah, it was getting to be a houseful."

"Then how did your mom feel about Craig?"

"Oh, I don't know. She had Eddie and me, which was probably more than enough. Oh, I'm sure she missed him, but she'd started a new life with Dad and she knew she'd made a mistake with her first husband and she couldn't put all the pieces back together. She couldn't ask for Craig back, even if that could have been arranged, and still take care of Eddie and me as well as she wanted. I guess it was just too much."

Jason sat down on the edge of the bed, sideways to Danni. "So Craig was wanted but not wanted. And he didn't take it well."

"No. Later on, when I was about twelve years old, and he was eighteen and getting ready to go to college, he still felt as if our mother had rejected him, which in a way she had. Even as an adult, he never forgot that, never really moved past it." Danni sighed. "You know, Jason, when I try to explain all this to you, it sounds so messy."

"I guess that's life. Messy."

"Well, my family is right in the thick of that mess."

"How do you feel about what your mom, and your dad, did in regard to Craig? Do you blame them?"

"I can't. They took care of me really well. And Eddie. I know they made mistakes, but I can't blame them. I can see how Craig felt. If that happened now, maybe he could get counseling, something to help him understand. But I know he didn't get it then. And if he had lived in California instead of so far away, he could have come to visit more often. The way it was, he was almost a stranger."

"So all these years he's been convinced that your mom, and

maybe your dad, just didn't care. He's let this fester."

"That's pretty much it."

"He's how old now?"

"Thirty-five."

"Well, I suppose you could say he's way too old to hang on to this kind of issue, but he obviously still needs some help in moving past it. So I'd say it's not too late for some sort of counseling." Jason had heard a lot of good answers from Danni, but he still had more questions. "But back to the time when your dad hired him, didn't anybody think about this stuff?"

"Well, Dad did. That's why I said he didn't want to stir up old troubles. He certainly wasn't against giving Craig an opportunity, but he had his doubts about the wisdom of it. He had doubts about things working out."

"Right. But your mother prevailed."

"I guess I helped, too. I'm sure Mom thought that offering him a good job was a way to put some salve on old wounds. Actually, I thought pretty much the same. And I wanted to be close to Craig as an adult. I think I wanted him to be the big brother I never really had. So when the job was coming open, it didn't take us long to invite Craig back into the family nest."

"I wonder what Craig thought then."

"It's hard to say now. Maybe he bought into Mom's idea, and my idea, and maybe he was only kidding himself. Anyway, it didn't take too long to find out that his old resentment was still bubbling and that he couldn't keep a lid on it."

"Obviously," Jason said. "You know, this is a lot more complicated than I thought it would be. So what kind of terms were you on with him? Since you haven't talked with him since you got to Denmark, I assume that things weren't the greatest."

"Actually, I did talk with him yesterday morning. But only for a minute. Then...I never had a chance to tell you."

"You called him again? I thought he wasn't answering."

"Craig called me. I'd just had breakfast at a little café and then my phone rang. I was absolutely stunned when I saw it was Craig."

Jason was a little stunned himself. "So what did he say?"

"He told me to back off and leave him alone. He didn't want anyone following him around, and I guess he was also talking about you and the private investigator."

"Of course, he would say that. So is that all?"

Danni shook her head. "The worst part is that he said there was evil in the world and that he was trying to protect me but didn't know how much he could do."

"My God," Jason said. "He knew. He knew Baransky would try something."

"I think so. Craig didn't get specific, but that does seem to be the story. But then he hung up and I was in such a scattered state the rest of the morning that I wasn't watching what I was doing and slipped on the ice."

"Wow. I'm still taking in what you just told me, but, you know, I'm feeling a little more positive about Craig now. He was at least thinking about protecting you."

"I can see that now. Jason? Can you help me move? I'm getting all stiff."

He went over and rearranged the pillows and gave her a hug and kissed her on the lips. "You're doing great," he said. "Things are starting to make sense now. Do you feel like going on?"

"I don't *feel* like it, but that doesn't matter. I need to get this out so you'll know everything, and I might as well do it now."

"All right. You're tough. So, we'll just talk a little more and see how it goes." Getting a nod from Danni, Jason said, "I was wondering how you and Craig got along when he started working for the family company, or even before."

"I would say our relationship was more neutral than anything else. At least from his point of view. It wasn't warm and fuzzy, even though I'd sort of wanted that. But he wasn't hostile either. I'm not saying this right. It's not as if anyone pretended we weren't related, but the family thing never really developed. He envied my relatively calm upbringing, but he didn't blame me for what happened. When I tried the brother-sister routine with him, he was kind of puzzled at first and let me take charge and think I was making headway, but after a while it became apparent he wanted to keep his distance."

"Did you ask him about your mother? What he felt?"

"Sure. But he said it wasn't my concern. He was polite, but he didn't want to talk about it. Not with me anyhow."

"And how about with Eddie?"

"Well, kind of the same. Eddie recognized the situation, and he was civil, but he didn't try to bond or anything. Eddie is enough younger that he has his own interests, his own friends. He could work with Craig, or he could work without him. It didn't matter much. But Eddie has tried to help me. He's a good kid."

"Wow, Danni, you do have some family."

"And now maybe you see why I didn't tell you all this at first. I just couldn't."

"Oh, I understand. Anyway, so Craig decides to divert a few hundred thousand dollars. Out of spite? Why did he do it?"

"I can only guess," Danni said. "But spite probably isn't far off the mark. I think he wanted to punish Mom and Dad. Or maybe he thought he deserved it."

"Mission accomplished, then." Jason put his hand to his chin. "Okay, so he knows how the company's books work, and he could find a pigeon hole for the money where nobody would notice, at least long enough to pull off the deed and get out of town. And so he not only got out of town, he got out of the country, and here you are trying to get the money back and save your family's company."

"And Craig, too. Maybe for my Dad it's more about the money and keeping the company in one piece. But for me, and Mom, and probably even Dad, we don't want Craig to disappear and be some fugitive. We love him, we really do. He's part of the family. We want him back."

"It doesn't look as if he wants to go back," Jason said.

"Oh, I know how it looks. But he's confused now. And when you're confused, you're easily manipulated."

"I suppose. But what about the money? What's the loss doing to the company?"

"The loss has definitely put a financial strain on the company. And Dad had to hire an accounting agency temporarily to step in just to keep things running. Worse than that, he's had to sell some stock from his retirement fund to make up at least part of the difference. Of course, it was a very sensitive issue when he had to tell the new accountants that he was short three hundred thousand dollars. But he had to do it so everyone knew where they stood. He told them it was a loan to Craig, but I don't think they bought that for a minute."

"And your parents never reported the loss to the police?"

"No. Dad was thinking hard about it, and Mom went off the deep end when the subject was mentioned. So that's when I volunteered to go to Denmark and try to find him. We got information from his landlord that he was headed to Copenhagen. Anyway, my parents have said that if Craig returns the money, they won't pursue legal action. If he wants his job back, they will talk with him and at least consider it. That makes Dad pretty nervous, but he's agreed to the plan."

"And here you are in Denmark," Jason said. "It's all coming together now. But, of course, you could have told Craig all that the first time you saw him here in Copenhagen. Over at the Irish pub."

"I could have. I could have walked in and said, 'Hi, Craig.' And he would have run the other way."

"Oh, he would have listened to you."

"I don't think so, or didn't think so then. But it doesn't matter now what I thought that night. I got scared. I didn't want to blow my big chance. I wanted to warm up to it. Then there was the girlfriend issue. Once you told me about Gitte, I didn't know how serious he was about her. But I thought that after he got her out of his system, he might be open to talking to me and forgetting about Denmark. Now I don't know where he is, and the police are looking for him."

Jason wondered if Huff's mission in Denmark was so simple. Just get the girl. His connection with Baransky was still puzzling and didn't seem to have anything to do with Gitte.

"Danni, I have to ask you a pointed question. You would take Craig back into the family even though he helped kidnap you?"

"If he helped, he was forced. By that Russian spy. Didn't I tell you that?"

"I don't know how much he was forced. But he did help. Doesn't that bother you?"

"Craig didn't hurt me, I know that. Yes, I would still take him back into the family. And whatever he did wrong, I forgive him."

"Really? Even if he doesn't deserve that?"

"I don't know what Craig deserves. But I'm forgiving him for myself, my own benefit. I don't want a lifelong burden of seeking justice, I don't want to play the victim, and I don't want my own limited understanding of all this to get in the road of a better life for him or me."

Jason listened with attention and tried to comprehend the deep heart of this lovely woman he'd come to know. "And would you tell your mom and dad about the kidnapping?"

Danni looked startled by the question. "No. No, I wouldn't tell them. They've been hurt enough. I made it through, with your help. I survived. Oh, Jason, you've done so much for me. I don't know how to thank you."

"Just keep your chin up. That's all I ask."

Danni and Jason hugged again and continued to talk, but the conversation drifted elsewhere. Jason wanted to know what kind of place Danni lived in, and she wanted to know the same about him. It turned out they both had small condos, and while Jason had a view of green fir trees and a peek-a-boo view of Puget Sound, Danni had a view of bare brown hills and Carquinez Strait. They talked about other things, too, which weren't remarkable in themselves, but were part of the settling in process, their way of telling each other that they could still be together after the Craig Huff truth was out and Danni had told her story.

After a while, they watched some TV, a lightweight American comedy about finding gold in a wacky New Mexico scavenger hunt, and then Danni said she was getting sleepy and Jason said he would trundle off to his own room and Danni said, "Not on your life, mister. You can go get your book and your toothbrush, but I want you to stay with me tonight. I'll sleep a lot better."

Jason thought if he'd just been rescued from a kidnapping he might want a little company, too, so he agreed. Danni went to sleep early, with the bedside lamp still on, and Jason delved into his serious book. It served his purpose, sharpening his mind while simultaneously acting as a sedative. And that was good, because it allowed him to turn off the light and close his sandbagged eyes an hour or so sooner than he might have otherwise.

#

They went down to breakfast together in the morning, and Danni felt better and was moving more easily and with less pain. Her appetite was good, and after they came back up Jason went to his room and called Dalvang. The police still hadn't seen Baransky.

Jason listened, then said, "I didn't hear you mention Craig Huff. Something going on?"

"Something," Dalvang said, with some disgust.

"What? He slipped through the manhunt?"

"In a way. It turns out we knew where he was yesterday. That was Wednesday. We even knew where he was Tuesday night. When I say *we*, I mean the police."

"And now he's escaped?"

"I wouldn't put it exactly that way. But he walked away late yesterday afternoon, with expert help. He had medical assistance and police assistance."

"I'm not sure what you just told me, Detective, but you don't sound happy."

"I'm spitting nails," Dalvang said. "And if I were in charge, heads would roll. But okay, here's the story. About seven o'clock Tuesday night, a trucker calls for emergency medical help and says he's found a guy lying unconscious in the snow beside a road in the warehouse district."

"Craig Huff."

"Excellent guess. So Huff's lying there with a concussion, and he's bleeding from the back of his skull and also above one ear."

"Baransky."

"Probably," Dalvang said, "but we don't know for sure how Huff got hurt or how he got to that particular place. If we draw a line between your hotel and the Bjorneby Foods building, Huff's location was more or less on the way."

"So it was close to Bjorneby's warehouse?"

"Six or seven minutes by car maybe, if you don't get lost in that maze."

Jason tried to put together the picture. "So either Baransky stops the car and forces Huff out and beats him up, or Huff tries to take control of the car and then Huff whacks him."

"Mr. Stallings, I know where you're headed with this, and I'm not in a real charitable mood about Huff right now, but the tire tracks and shoe prints in the snow and a mark on the concrete building from a black car bumper actually do suggest that the car was forced off the road. By the way, we found the car as well, several kilometers away. Stolen, of course. There was left front bumper damage and a trace of chloroform in the backseat."

"Well," Jason said. "I guess all that fits. But what happened to Huff?"

"He was in a hospital close to twenty-four hours, and he got bandaged up and doped up with painkillers and they let him go when he could finally see straight. The problem is that now I can't see straight because a policeman investigated the scene of the crime and watched the medics load Huff into the ambulance, and then the policemen went to the hospital later and saw that Huff wasn't going to be talking coherently that night, and when his shift ended, he passed the word for someone else to check on Huff and nobody ever went back."

"I can see why you're upset."

"Right. And on top of that, the first investigating officer didn't ever get to see Huff's picture or even know he was wanted—until his shift the next day, and by then Huff had been released."

"Oh, God. I do see the problem now."

"It gets worse. We know Huff left the hospital in a taxi, and we got the taxi records and know the driver took him to the Commodore Hotel. We had the staff there on alert to notify us when he came in, but he never came in. So he spent the night somewhere else with his bandaged head, and we don't know where."

"With that concussion, he still might have been dazed, not thinking straight."

"Or he could have been thinking very well and knew we'd be looking for him."

"You're looking on the dark side, Detective."

"Ha. I carry a flashlight and follow the bad guys wherever they go."

"Fair enough. Believe it or not, I'd like to stop talking about Craig Huff, but I actually have some new information for you, which is one reason I called." Jason explained that he'd found out last night that Huff was Danni's half brother and some of what that entailed. Even so, she didn't want her brother to go to prison. The family wanted the money back, of course, but they wanted Huff, too.

"That all makes sense now, the way you said she was holding back. But I don't know that it means I should take pity on him." Dalvang cleared his throat. "We have eyewitnesses that he helped with the kidnapping. Being related to the victim won't earn him any special treatment with the judge. It could even be worse."

"Right. I wouldn't expect you to see it differently. But I've done a lot of thinking on this, even before I knew he was Danni's half brother, and it doesn't add up that he was an equal participant in the kidnapping. She told me last night that Huff called her yesterday morning and told her he was trying to protect her and then warned her to stay away because of evil forces in the world."

"Evil forces? Sounds like Baransky. But Huff is still a kidnapper. They did it together."

"I know. But I think he was forced into it and may be a victim as much as Danni."

"Interesting theory."

"It's more than a theory. My personal experience with Baransky is that he's a madman. If he's really a spy, too, then he's doubly dangerous. He's got the personality of a demon, knows all the tricks of his trade, and doesn't mind using them. He enjoys seeing people suffer and holds back only because going too far would have bad consequences for himself. He scared the hell out of me in his taxi, but for him it was probably fun in his twisted way. Ever since Huff took the money, his compass has been spinning. He doesn't know which way is up and probably couldn't say no to Baransky. He may have even feared for his own life. And he was too afraid to tell Baransky that Danni is his sister."

"Okay," Dalvang said. "Let's say Huff was dragged into the kidnapping. If he forced the collision that got him beat up, it's half believable. But what do you want me to do about it? I still have to bring him in. And I'd like to find the explanation behind this. Even if Baransky is the devil himself, he had a motive."

"I've been wondering about that. All I could think of is that he wanted Danni out of the way for a while. Until—"

"Until what? Yeah, that's the question. Well, we'll see what happens when Huff shows up. In the meantime, I have a murder to solve over at another hotel. You may have heard about it."

The call ended, and Jason sat down and tried to think. Dalvang clearly didn't think much of Huff, but Jason was changing his mind, and it wasn't just because of Huff's newly revealed link with Danni. Danni had confidence he was a victim, and Huff's mysterious beating in the snow gave credence to that. What if Huff had really tried to save Danni from Baransky? What if Huff had risked his life to save his sister? If the truck driver hadn't found him so soon afterward, he would have died from exposure. That told Jason there was hope for the man, assuming the concussion hadn't totally messed up his head.

Jason got up and went back to Danni's room and updated her. She was up and down, nerves dancing on high voltage. The story of her brother's injuries horrified her, but like Jason, she wanted to think that he'd tried to stop Baransky from taking her to the warehouse. But she worried now that he'd been released from the hospital too soon and had hurt himself again or maybe got himself mixed up with Baransky's associates, whoever they were.

It was all plausible, but Jason was on edge himself and couldn't sit there and listen to Danni theorize without foundation. He needed to step away and break the pattern. But where? He didn't want to take a walk or go back to his room. So he stood up and said, "Breakfast is still being served, so I think I'll go down and have another cup of coffee. Want to come along?"

"No more coffee right now, thanks. I already have the jitters."

"Okay, lock your door. I won't be long, but call if you need something. I have my phone."

Jason expected Danni's answer on the coffee, and he was actually glad to have a few minutes alone. He could have gone either way on the caffeine, but what he really wanted was some down time.

He got his coffee and sat down with his phone and plugged in earbuds. Then he listened to music he'd brought from home, and it reminded him of normal times and relaxed him. Even with the high-test java in his cup, he felt more at ease. After while, a plan began to form. He just needed one thing to fall in place first. And a few minutes later, as if on command, it did.

His phone rang. Dalvang.

Jason switched off his music and answered. "You found Huff?"

"We did. His head seems to be better. At least he's not wearing bandages. I have an officer walking a half block behind him now. Huff is on foot and appears to be headed back to the Commodore Hotel."

"You're going to arrest him?"

"That's the plan. The officer is just waiting for my signal. But I thought you'd appreciate an update and courtesy call first. You can pass the word to Miss Rossler as you see fit."

"Detective, I've been thinking."

"Thinking. Now why do I have the feeling that you're going to propose some wild idea?"

"Not wild, Detective. Just different. Here's the deal. I'd like you to let me talk with him first. Pull your people out of Nyhavn, or at least back closer to their normal routines. Tell the hotel staff to let him pass as if nothing's wrong. When he returns to his room, I don't want him to feel threatened. With his concussion, he probably isn't clear how he got injured and he might not even remember the kidnapping."

"Possibly. We'll find out when I take him in and ask him."

"Later, if you need to. But first, I want to talk to him. Have the hotel people notify you when they see him, but then stay back until you hear from me. If I fail miserably, if he turns violent, then he's all yours."

"You know, Mr. Stallings, normally I wouldn't even listen to a crackpot idea like that. But since we wouldn't have found Miss Rossler today without you..."

"Thank you, Detective."

"This won't go in my report. Not yet anyhow. In fact, if some-one asks, I'm probably going to forget I even called you. I must have fallen out of bed this morning and had a concussion myself."

"Good. I mean I wish you a speedy recovery. But while we're waiting for Huff to get back to his room and before you forget you're talking to me now, I was wondering if you could tell me something else, about your other case."

Dalvang's voice hardened. "What other case?"

"The Martin Weathersby murder."

"Oh, that one. Not much to say. We have a lot of leads and about two hundred suspects. At the rate we're going, it should be solved in about two years. Unless, of course, we get a break. Is that why you're asking? You're going to give me the break?"

"Well, I actually might have some information for you. But I've learned I have this rather strange connection with Weathersby. If you have a minute, I can explain it. Then you'll know why I'm curious about the case."

"In my work, I get used to strangeness. So what's your story?"

Jason took a deep breath and began. There was the first day at the Hotel Lorentsen, seeing the body, seeing Dalvang himself, finding out that he was supposed to get the room that Weathersby died in, and then getting shuffled off to the Kong Jacob and later realizing that he probably got Weathersby's room there, too, since the Englishman had planned to transfer to the Kong Jacob that night. And then there were the intersecting lines of the cheese business, where Jason was trying to arrange a large havarti pur-chase, but Weathersby, in his capacity as a food broker, snared the havarti first, then offered it to Jason's company with a fax only hours before he died.

"I didn't know about the fax," Dalvang said. "You're sure?"

"It was sent to Seattle so I can't give it to you verbatim, but it was sent five minutes after nine o'clock Thursday night, Copenhagen time. I could probably get it later for your file."

"So he died after that. Unless the killer sent the fax for him, but that seems unlikely. All right, this could be helpful."

Then Dalvang agreed to share some information. He told Jason about interviewing all the staff at work that night, plus all the guests on the floor where Weathersby was killed.

"That must have taken days."

"It did take a while, but I didn't do it all myself. We had teams."

"All the guests on that floor?"

"All we could find. A few foreigners had checked out by the time we were notified and probably left the country."

"So the murderer could have merrily gone to the airport and flown away."

"It's possible. Of course, it's also possible that the murderer walked in off the street, took the elevator up to the room, did his deed, washed his hands and then walked back out with none the wiser."

"Well, that wouldn't help your odds," Jason said.

"Not at all. Wait a minute, you said something back there."

"Back where?"

"You said something about getting Weathersby's room at the Kong Jacob. What did I miss? He was booked at the Lorentsen for four nights."

"Originally, yes. Maybe what you were told was about the old booking. But my new friend Thomas, the desk clerk, said Weathersby called up about seven that first night and asked to be transferred to the Kong Jacob immediately. I shouldn't say asked. It was more like a demand, according to Thomas. Among other things, Weathersby usually stayed at the Kong Jacob on his visits to Copenhagen and preferred the old world charm."

"But he was at the Lorentsen," Dalvang said.

"Right. Thomas said the Kong Jacob didn't have a room for him until Friday night."

"So he stayed on. Unfortunately. But something changed his mind about the Lorentsen. Something spooked him after he checked in. Any idea what?"

"No clue. But maybe something will come up."

"Maybe. You know, Mr. Stallings, I see why you're curious about the Weathersby case, how you might even feel this connection, but I wouldn't worry much about it, and I wouldn't spend any more time talking with desk clerks. I appreciate your help and your information, but frankly, the odds on this one stink, and we might never catch anyone."

"Weathersby's family won't like that."

"I know, but my job is to investigate, not to play to the emotions of families."

"Of course, I hear he was divorced," Jason said. "Kids grown up."

"Who told you that?"

"Another guy in the food business. Sayon Kunder. He lives in London, but he's staying at the Lorentsen this week. I guess you've talked with him."

"Oh, yes. A slippery fellow. But he seems to have a solid alibi."

"I've heard it," Jason said. "He was pretty strong about defending his position."

"That's a nice way of putting it," Dalvang said. He paused, then went on. "You know, now that you mentioned family, there was something curious in Weathersby's room. I don't suppose it would do any harm to tell you. There was something in his suitcase, a picture of a young woman and a little girl, about two years old, probably her daughter. It was an old picture, in an old wooden frame with glass, all wrapped in plastic like a slice of bread. It seemed odd the way he was protecting it, and it seemed odd that he would even have it with him, traveling like that."

"Maybe his wife and daughter in England? I guess that would

be ex-wife."

"I don't know," the detective said. "I'll check it out. Of course, I was thinking he had two sons, but we'll see. I could be wrong."

"No names on the picture?"

"No. Only a date on the back. Twenty-one years ago."

"Curious," Jason said. "I don't suppose I could have a copy."

"What? That's evidence."

"I said a copy, Detective. You keep the evidence."

"You want me to break all the rules?"

"Of course not. But you do distribute copies of photos now and then as part of an investigation, don't you? You did it with Huff and Baransky."

"All right, all right. Anything else? Knowing you, I imagine there's more."

"Is it in color?"

"It's a little faded, but yes it's in color."

"Great. Could I have the copy today?"

"Good Lord. Today? Okay, okay. And I suppose you want me to send it to your hotel.."

"Detective, you read my mind."

"Hold on." Dalvang put down the phone, then came back. "I just got a note. Huff has entered his hotel and gone up to his room."

"I'm on my way."

"Mr. Stallings?"

"Sir?"

"Tonight before I go to sleep I want to look back on the day's events and feel *really good* about what we're doing here. Because if I don't feel *really good*, I'll be cranky and won't sleep well. And then tomorrow, I'll be even crankier with just about everybody I run across, people I know and people I don't know."

"That's a lot of people. So I guess that would include me."

"Oh, yes. Especially you."

14

Jason went up to his room, fetched his heavy coat and then stopped to see Danni. "Two things," he said. "Craig's back in his hotel, and I'm going over to see him."

Danni's face lit up. "What? What? Tell me." She grabbed his arm and made him sit down with her on the bed. "Tell me the whole thing."

So Jason filled her in on what Dalvang had told him. He went over how her brother had been found unconscious in the snow, and he told her what he knew about the hospital and then Craig's temporary disappearance. And he told her about the police agreeing to let him go see Craig first. Danni's face went on a roller coaster ride of expressions while she gripped Jason's arm harder than he thought she had the strength to do.

When he was done, Danni sat quietly a moment, looking sideways at him. "This isn't real."

He raised his hand. "I swear to tell the truth, the whole—"

"No, I believe what you said. It's just that everything has changed so fast. I don't know how you do it. You go out for coffee and fifteen minutes later the whole situation is different. Is there something you do to make this happen?"

"I don't know, Danni. There's no magic dust. All I do is ask questions, get answers, think through how things might work out. Then I make plans, dive in and hope for the best. It's just about what anyone would do."

"It's what anyone might *try* to do, but you actually *do* it."

"Don't give me too much credit. I might disappoint you."

"I understand. I'll try to keep my feet on the ground." She took a deep breath and shook her head. "Tell me if I'm wrong, but it really sounds as if Craig tried to stop the Russian."

"That's what I think, but we really don't know. Not yet. But even Dalvang seems to be warming to the idea. That might be why he's letting me go over there."

"You're very persuasive." Danni smiled, a twinkle in her eye. Jason thought she was looking much better than she did last night.

"Let's hope I'm persuasive with Craig. He has some strong ideas I don't understand. There's still a lot going on with him and a lot we don't know yet."

"My head's spinning. Either I'm still recovering or you're going too fast. What have I missed? So you guys talk and then what happens?"

"I'm still working on that, but I'm hoping the police will let him go."

"Just let him go? Wow, that would be something. But why would they?"

"Because when you leave the country, it's going to be harder to prosecute him. And I mean *you*, Danni. When *you* leave the country."

"I never thought of that." Then she wrinkled her nose. "So are you telling me to leave Denmark?"

"Be ready to go home. If I can pull this off, you might be out of here in less than twenty-four hours. With your brother." Jason raised his eyebrows.

"You're kidding me. The police agreed to that?"

"No. The police don't know about that part of the plan yet. And let's be honest, I may be kidding myself. It's a long shot, but who knows, Dalvang might go for it. First I have to talk with Craig. So are you game?"

"Of course. What about the money?"

"Well, it's probably in some safe place. Maybe in a bank in the Bahamas, or the Cayman Islands or Switzerland. Heck, maybe even in California. I don't know, but I doubt that it's here in Denmark. Craig has a credit card or two and maybe a couple thousand in travel cash, but I think the serious money is someplace else."

"Actually, that makes sense," Danni said. "An accountant

wouldn't be lugging around a suitcase full of that kind of money."

Jason stood up. "All right. Lock your door and don't let anybody in until I get back. This probably won't take long. But if something starts to pop, I'll give you a call. You may need to make arrangements in a hurry."

Danni had a sad smile. "It's so weird. I traveled almost ten thousand miles to find Craig and persuade him to come home, and now that we've reached this point it's you who's going to talk to him while I'll sit in this hotel room like a bundle of nerves."

"It's better this way."

"I know, I know. That's why I'm not objecting. You've been right about a whole bunch of things since I met you, and now that I'm coming to my senses I think I'll listen to you."

Jason smiled. "You're putting the pressure on."

"You can take it." Danni gave him a hug. "There's one thing you haven't told me, though."

"What's that?" Jason knew what was coming, but he didn't want to talk about it yet.

"What about you? If I go home, and by some miracle Craig goes with me, then where will you be?"

"I need to stay here another day to wrap up the cheese business, if I can." Here it comes now, he thought.

"And then you'll go back to Seattle?"

"Yes. I have a return plane ticket."

"But then what?"

"I don't know, Danni. We'll just have to see. Now wish me luck. I'm going to go do something I've never tried before."

"You got it, mister." She gave him a quick kiss, and her eyes watered. "Now get going before I make a fool of myself."

#

The taxi dropped Jason at the entrance to Nyhavn, and he walked straight to the Commodore Hotel and on in to the front desk. "Hello," he said to the desk clerk, thinking that he'd seen one too many hotel desk clerks in the past week. "I'd like to visit one of your guests, Craig Huff. Could you tell him Jason is here?"

The clerk, a dark-haired woman in her twenties said, "Just a moment, sir." She glanced at her colleague, who simply nodded, and then she picked up the phone and punched in his number.

"Mr. Huff," the desk clerk said, "there's a man here to see you. His name is Jason." She listened a moment, then said, "All right. Thank you." She put down the phone and looked at Jason. "Mr. Huff would like you to go on up. He's in Room 312."

Jason smiled and walked to the elevator, pressed a button, found his way to the right door and knocked twice.

Craig Huff opened right away, looked out into the hallway, and invited him in. "I never thought I would see you again. Not this close anyhow."

"Well, you never know. And don't worry. I came alone. The police know I'm here, but it's all right. They won't bother us, at least not right away."

"I don't know. I've probably made a mistake in having you up."

"Nonsense, Craig. It's one of the best moves you've made since coming to Copenhagen." For days Jason had been calling him Huff, even thinking of him as Huff, but ever since he'd found out that the man was Danni's half brother, Jason knew he should use the first name. He'd done that for Danni this morning, and he could do it now. At least Jason wasn't going to call him Greg Hunt, the name he'd been told the day he arrived in Copenhagen.

Craig eyed Jason as if he were a pushy life insurance salesman. "So why are you here?"

"Well, we could start with Danni. You haven't asked me about her."

"Well, I know that she's been found and that she seems to be okay," Craig said. "I heard it last night. Believe it or not, I'm really glad. I mean *really* glad."

"Well, good. But how did you know?"

"Baransky. That guy seems to know everything."

Jason thought about that a little and then looked at Craig's head. "And how are you doing? I heard you had a rough time the other night." Jason paused, then said. "Oh, don't look at me like that. I've been talking with the police. They know all about your

concussion. The thing is, you weren't supposed to leave the hospital on your own, but fortunately for you, the police bungled your
case and you walked out a free man, at least for a while."

"Well, I'm doing better. The headaches have mostly stopped,
but I need to be careful for a while. No bumps, no sudden move-
ments. I don't have much energy yet. But what you said about the
police, I didn't know any of that. But it sort of makes sense now."

They talked about Craig's head wounds a minute and he let Jason have a close look at the red gashes on his scalp. "So how much
do you remember?" Jason asked.

When Craig hesitated, Jason said. "Look, I'm not the police.
I'm just trying to help Danni. And maybe I can help you, too. The
hotel staff saw you and Baransky leaving with her in the wheelchair. And the next day we found Danni, of course. It's the parts in
between that you could tell me about."

"Only some of it," Craig said. "Only what I remember. All
right, Baransky was driving the car, not his taxi, but some other
car. Probably stolen, I guess. I mean, a guy like that wouldn't *buy* a
car if he didn't have to. Danni's in the back, knocked out, and
we're headed to this warehouse he's got all planned for her. So he
does his usual stunt driver routine, trying to scare the crap out of
me, and then when we're out in the warehouse district and I figure
we're getting close to where we're going, he takes a corner too
wide, even for him, and the tires are screaming and it seems like he
might be losing control of the car."

"So you help him out a little and steer into a building."

Craig shrugged. "I guess so. I remember thinking I had to do
something for Danni and this was my best chance. He had a gun,
you know, so he could have just shot me whenever he felt like it.
Anyway, we're going around the corner like we're in some movie
and I grab the wheel, and we're both holding on, and I elbow him
in the nose, and that's about all I remember. We must have hit a
wall, but I can't tell you. This morning a little more started to come
back. I think we fought in the snow. I don't know, he probably hit
my head with his gun. The next thing I knew, some trucker has his
headlights in my eyes and my head hurts like hell and I'm freezing

to death and he's throwing a blanket over me and telling me he's called for help. I owe that guy."

Jason nodded. So Craig had tried to save Danni. And he'd almost died for his trouble. At the very least, Jason could now honestly give Danni the report she wanted to believe, and maybe Dalvang would believe it, too.

"Craig, there's another reason I'm here. To find out how you feel about things. Not your head wounds, but inside your head, your heart."

"How I feel? What are you, a psychologist?"

"No. Come on, Craig. How do you feel about your family? It's a simple question."

"Well, the answer isn't simple. It's actually pretty complicated. Let's say I'm confused."

"*You're* confused? Mind if I make myself at home?" Getting no answer, Jason peeled off his overcoat and helped himself to the armchair. "First you tell me your name is Greg Hunt, but then Danni tells me it's Craig Huff. She sounds pretty sure about it so I go with her on that. Then she tells me a bunch of other things that we'll get to, some of which I believe and some of which I don't, and then last night she stops keeping secrets and tells me that you're her half brother."

Craig sighed. "It's true. Why did it take her so long to tell you?"

"I guess she had her reasons, " Jason said. "Something to do with why she came to Denmark to find you."

"Yeah, I can see how that would have worked. When it comes to me, family pride goes out the window. I'm sure she told you that. Now I'm officially the black sheep."

"Don't be so hard on yourself, Craig. Okay, so it is complicated. Danni didn't know me at first and didn't know how much she could trust me, so she held back. It turned out not to be a wise thing to do, but I can understand it. By the way, when you first saw me at the Irish place, I wasn't working with Danni. I hadn't even met her yet. But she saw us through the window and afterward followed me back to my hotel, her hotel, and then we met."

Craig nodded. "Interesting, interesting. And now your know her a whole lot better." Craig gave Jason a knowing smile.

"True. She's a lovely lady."

"Well, I think there's more going on than that. I can add two and two, Jason. After all, I'm an accountant. But I can see why she likes you. You're smart, decent, good looking—"

"Enough, Craig. I appreciate the good words, but I didn't come over here to meet the family." Jason raised his eyebrows.

Craig got the point. "Okay. So now what? The police are after me, right?"

"For the kidnapping? Yes, and no. I've persuaded them to hold off until I had a chance to talk with you."

"God, I'm so sorry about that. You've got to know that, Jason." Craig turned away and looked out the window. "Only an idiot would kidnap his own sister, but that's what I did. It was a terrible idea, but I couldn't stop Baransky." Now he turned back to Jason. "He might have killed me if I'd crossed him too much. You can't reason with someone like that. I guess you'd have to meet him to understand."

"Actually, we have met. And I do understand. He's a wild man."

"You've met?" Craig had a strange look on his face.

"By chance, I took his taxi in from the airport the day I arrived in Copenhagen. I don't think his car even had brakes. The ride was kind of a near death experience."

"Oh, yeah, I can imagine. He's got a sadistic streak, all right. When it became obvious he could have taken me out and that I couldn't see a way to prevent the kidnapping, it seemed like a good idea to play along, you know, to make sure Baransky didn't do anything terribly violent on his own. I would have stopped that. I don't know how, but I would have."

"You don't think knocking Danni out with drugs and then dumping her in a cold warehouse wasn't violent?"

Craig pursed his lips. "I, I know there's no defense for what I did, or helped do. I'm just trying to explain. Yes, it was bad for Danni. Absolutely. No doubt whatsoever. But I see now that it could have been much worse if Baransky had wanted it to be."

The possibilities had weighed heavily on Jason, but he'd brushed them aside when Danni had been found with no major physical harm. He didn't want to think of them now, either, but Craig did have a point. Jason could see where Craig was going with this line of reasoning, but something about it still didn't sit right. "Yes, I realize it could have been much worse. So you acted as Baransky's conscience, if that's possible. You held him in check a little. Maybe so. But are you sure that's the only reason you went along?"

Craig was pacing now. "Yes. No. Damn it, what are you doing asking questions like that?"

"This is nothing compared with what the police have in mind for you."

"All right, all right. Well, I knew Danni was following me around. You too. I saw you guys out front that night. Saturday. I tried to shake it off, but I couldn't. Then I saw her another time or two. I knew what she was doing, but after a while, it began to stick in my craw. You know? Being tailed like that? Like I needed some kind of chaperone."

"Craig, she just wanted to know what you were doing."

"Then she should have asked," he barked.

"She called you, she said. Sent texts. You didn't respond. Then later, I think she was—afraid."

"Afraid? Of me? Oh, Jesus." Craig stopped pacing for a moment, wiped his brow and took a deep breath. Then he started walking again, resuming his one-man assault on the carpet. "Anyway, what I was going to tell you was that, right or wrong, I resented her following me and for one crazy moment after Baransky brought up the idea I thought that hauling her out of that hotel room might teach her not to snoop around and tell me what to do."

Jason's head jerked back. "That's a hell of a lesson."

"I know, I know. It's indefensible. Totally disgusting." Craig stopped moving around the room and looked directly at Jason. "I don't know what came over me. Of course, a minute later I saw how horribly bad the idea was, but by then Baransky had it between his teeth like a vicious dog and I couldn't stop it, or him. I could have run away, if he wouldn't have shot me, but then I got the idea it would be best if I went along, to make sure nothing terrible happened. Of course, I didn't do a very good job of that. I kept telling Baransky the whole kidnapping was unnecessary, but I didn't know it was going to turn out that way. I thought he was only going to warn Danni, not dump her in a warehouse." Craig's voice softened. "It must have been awful for her. Was she tied up?"

"Duct tape. Arms, legs, eyes, mouth. Yes, from what she said, it was pretty awful. But fortunately, for all of us, she checked out okay at the hospital."

"That's good news, *fantastically* good news." Craig took another deep breath, gathering himself. "You know, I was going to phone the police and tell them. Not where she was so much, because I didn't know exactly. But about Baransky."

"If I understand the timing, you were still in the hospital when we found her. You probably weren't in any position to call the police"

"Yeah, I guess so. I was so groggy when the hospital let me go that I couldn't think straight for a while. Then later I turned on my cellphone and heard the message Baransky had left."

Now they were back to the all-knowing Russian, and Jason was perplexed. So Baransky had information, rapid information, maybe from someone inside Bjorneby Foods. The question was, who was the source? Stubkjaer? Or one of those Russians who just happened to be working there? "How did Baransky feel about that?"

"I don't know. It's hard to tell if the guy even has emotions. Anger's about the only one I ever saw. But he told me straight. Didn't seem upset. Didn't even mention our fight, or whatever we had, didn't mention hitting me in the head. I guess he felt he'd proved his point."

"Which was what?"

"That Danni and you should keep your distance."

"Keep our distance? From you and Baransky? Why?"

"Oh, boy. That's really complicated. Maybe you should ask him."

"He doesn't seem to be around today. At least that's what the police say. They think he skipped out of the country, maybe back to Russia."

"What a surprise. Yeah, he's probably in St. Petersburg by now." Craig went to his nightstand and picked up a pack of cigarettes. He took one out and put it to his lips.

"I would prefer you didn't smoke."

"It's my room."

"Well, my lungs are in your room, and I'm your guest. Actually, I'm getting enough smoke just breathing the stale air in here. I have a pretty keen sense of smell, and I'd say you had a cigarette about ten minutes before I got here."

"Well, then, you know everything, don't you?"

"I know about the money you took from the family business."

This froze Craig in place. "I figured we'd get to that."

"Craig, I want to make you an offer."

"What kind of offer?"

"Staying out of jail, for one thing. If you'll agree to go back to California with Danni, I'll try to get the police to let you go."

"What? They would do that?"

"They might. I haven't asked yet, but I have a good connection and I think there's a chance. But there's one condition to my offer."

"The money," Craig said. "It's in a Cayman Islands account, by the way."

"That was one of my guesses. Anyway, you have to give it back."

"I already decided last night that I would. But the transfer will be a little tricky and I need to wait for my head to clear up before I handle anything that sensitive."

"That's great news, Craig. I'll tell Danni."

"That's good. And it's good that you'll do that for me. I'm not sure I could talk about that with her right now. But I'm curious. What if I didn't give it back?"

"As far as the money goes, that's up to your conscience. If you get to California with Danni and then disappear again, nobody can stop you, I guess. As far as agreeing to get on the plane with her—well, if you don't do that, the Copenhagen police will certainly arrest you for kidnapping. And they have eyewitnesses from the hotel. It could be rough."

Craig sat down on the bed. "You know, I should go back to California. It was a mistake to come here to Denmark. I don't belong here. You remember that girlfriend I was talking about? Gitte? Well, things haven't gone so well with Gitte."

"So I figured."

"Yeah, I thought we were one hot item. The only problem was that I was the only one thinking that. Whatever she felt for me once is gone now. I think she'd be glad to see me go."

"Then she's not going to be a problem. Craig, why don't you go downstairs for that smoke you wanted? I'd like to make a phone call, and it would be better if you weren't around for a few minutes. After you come back up I have a few questions about another thing or two."

"You think I'll come back?"

"You'll come back. Unless you want to be in prison until all your hair falls out."

15

Jason waited a minute, thinking about how he was going to do this, then stood up and went to the phone. He punched in Dalvang's number. "Detective, this is Jason Stallings again. I'm over at Craig Huff's hotel. In his room actually."

"Where is Huff?"

"Oh, I sent him out for a smoke. One of your stakeout officers might see him lighting up on the front step about now. Anyway, I thought we might have a word in private."

"Big secret?"

"No, not really. But he's a little skittish at the moment. No point in stressing him even more."

"And how would you do that?"

"I have a little proposition."

"Somehow I knew you were getting to that. All right, I'm listening."

Jason gave him his plan. Dalvang had to think it over a minute, then reluctantly agreed.

Jason hung up and sat back down in the armchair. His conversation with Dalvang had been short, so he figured he had a few minutes. Craig would be about halfway through his cigarette about now. Jason closed his eyes and took a deep breath. Then he started tracking his breath. Going deep now. He felt the tension leave his body with the carbon dioxide.

In a couple of minutes Craig opened the door again, and Jason opened his eyes. "Taking a nap?" Craig asked.

"Oh, not really. Just resting my eyes. How was your smoke?"

"I don't know. I hardly even thought about the cigarette. I had other things on my mind, wondering what you were doing, wondering about Danni, my family, Gitte, wondering about a lot of stuff."

"Danni's fine, really. She's still recovering from everything, of course, but she's going to be okay. As for what I was doing, well, we'll get to that soon enough. Actually, I'm thinking of someone else right now. Your buddy Baransky."

"Buddy? I never want to see him again."

"And you probably won't. As we discussed, he's apparently left the country."

"There you go. Why don't you go after him if you want to know about him?"

"Too inconvenient," Jason said. "Especially if he went back to Russia. But what is convenient is *you*. Tell me about your connection to Baransky."

"It's not much. I just ran into him. Besides, this has nothing to do with Danni."

"On the contrary, Craig. It has a lot to do with Danni. You were partners in kidnapping her, and do I have to remind you that kidnapping is a crime?"

Craig stared at Jason, then turned, and let out a groan. "Okay, I'll tell you. But it's probably more than you're expecting, and if you don't understand everything, I could look really bad, even worse than you're probably thinking about me right now. So make sure you get the whole picture before you judge me. And think twice about telling the cops."

"Well, that depends on what you tell me. But if it helps, my motivation is more personal than legal."

Craig frowned at him, then said, "Okay, okay. Where do you want to start?"

"How about the beginning? I have a little time."

"Yeah, well, this could take a few minutes." Craig sat down on the bed. "You know about my job—old job—with the family company, in Walnut Creek?"

"Right. Chief accountant."

"Well, to a large degree, I took the job to get out of the mega-company rat race."

"You were in Southern California, Danni said."

"That's right. I was working for a big defense contractor. I'd been there eight years. It seemed like a hundred."

"Defense contractor? I didn't know that." Danni had never mentioned that, and it hadn't occurred to Jason that Craig's previous job might be relevant.

"Yeah, naturally we had tight security. Everybody presumed we did stuff that would be of interest to China and Russia and maybe a bunch of other countries. Maybe terrorists, I don't know. But we had things worth keeping secret."

"Most defense contractors do."

"Well, one night after work I was in a tavern having a few beers with some guys from the plant, and this engineer said he'd heard of a Russian who would pay for information. I thought he'd just had too much to drink, and was bluffing, so I challenged him to prove it. I never much liked guys who talked big but couldn't back it up."

"You wanted to shut him up."

"Something like that. It did shut up him, for about ten minutes, but before we left the tavern he took me aside, away from the other guys."

"Did they believe him? The other guys?"

"It seems like they thought he was only mouthing off. Or maybe they didn't hear him. But this guy told me he'd prove it. I said go ahead, I had fifty bucks that said he was blowing hot air. So he told me to show up in this park at two o'clock the next Sunday afternoon and I could find out for myself. 'By the way,' he said as he was leaving, 'thanks for the fifty.'"

"So you met Baransky?"

"No, that was later. Anyway, I thought the engineer was still bluffing, and I didn't think much about it until that Sunday. It wasn't about the fifty bucks. I just wanted to shut this guy up— you know, prove that he was a windbag. So when I went down to the park, the engineer was there, and he had this guy with him, a Russian. The guy sort of looked Russian anyhow, but his accent wasn't heavy, so I couldn't really tell. I asked him to speak some

Russian to me, so he blurted out some words, and I asked him what they meant, and he said that he'd told me I should be careful who I met in parks. And here's the kicker, the Russian guy called himself Steve."

"Steve?"

Craig rubbed his hands together nervously. "Yeah, he had this regular job, said he worked at a shipping company in Long Beach and his name was Steve. So we walked around and talked, and before I knew it, the engineer who hooked me up with the Russian sort of dropped away and sat on a bench. So I walked around with Steve a little and went back home."

"He didn't ask you to do anything?"

"No, I was expecting that, but thinking back, he was sizing me up first, seeing if I might be able to help his cause later."

"But it didn't end there, did it?"

"No, I paid off my bet with the engineer, but he wouldn't let me forget about Steve. So I met him a couple more times. I was kind of fascinated with the spy game, just taking it all in. It was scary but exciting at the same time."

"You didn't think it was wrong, spying for the Russians?"

"I wasn't spying, only learning about it. And the more I thought about it, the more disgusting it sounded, and the more I thought about it the more disgusted I became with myself for thinking about it. I mean, I'm as patriotic as the next guy."

"But you overcame your objections and went along with the Russians anyhow?"

"Wrong," Craig said. "I overcame my initial stupidity and began to think of turning this thing upside down. There was a thrill factor to that, too, but I was also getting mad at the Russians for thinking they could just come in and exploit a defense contractor and take whatever they wanted. I mean, Steve was really kind of an ordinary fellow, he didn't seem very threatening, but it's what he represented."

Jason was trying to comprehend the information, but having a little trouble assigning a value to everything he was hearing. So he kept asking questions. "Did Steve ask you to spy for him?"

"Not in so many words. Once he found out I was an account-ant, he told me things he would be interested in, things that would be worth money. I thought over what he said and decided most of those things would be too hard for me to find. But there was one set of data on his shopping list that I figured I knew how to get without a whole lot of trouble."

"So you were still thinking of helping the Russians with their spy game."

"No, absolutely not. What I realized instead is that I could help the United States in ways that the FBI, CIA and other agencies would have trouble doing. Without trying very hard, I had become a contact that the Russians seemed to trust. It might take years and some elaborate setup for a government agent to do even half of what I'd done in just a few weeks."

Jason studied Craig. He could sort of see where Danni's broth-er was going with this story, but he wasn't convinced yet that it was anything more than a story. So far, the account seemed to have too much detail to be made of whole cloth, but since Jason knew next to nothing about spies and defense contractors, he couldn't check out the facts and realized he'd just have to go with his in-stincts.

Craig picked up on Jason's skepticism. "You think this is a lot of B.S., don't you."

Jason tilted his head. "I think it could be, but I have an open mind. Really, all I want to know is what you were doing with Ba-ransky."

"I'm getting there. But it's not easy. You know, I've never told anybody about this the way I'm telling you."

"I appreciate that, Craig. Go on, then."

"All right, I called the FBI, and we set up a meeting. At the beginning, I guess they thought I was nuts. But they listened and went back to corroborate a few things, and when we met again, I could see we were getting somewhere. Something I'd told them must have jibed with other information their office already had, and so now I had some credibility."

"You told them about Steve?"

"About Steve. And about the engineer. I started to hate that guy, because I figured over the years he must have gotten who knows how many people to cooperate with him and the Russians, and that made me sick. You know, I don't agree with everything the government does. I don't think too hard about what percentage I agree with or political parties or that whole circus, but I do think it's wrong to give away our hard work and endanger the country. That's just wrong."

"Okay, the FBI arrested those two guys and told you to go to Denmark?"

"The arrests might be coming about now. Today, maybe to-morrow, maybe next week. It's hard to say. They don't tell me everything. But the main thing, what you want to know leading up to Baransky, is what I proposed to the FBI."

"That you become a government agent?"

"Bingo. But not in a regular way. I didn't go on the payroll. Anyway, when Steve insisted that the deal be finished outside the country, the FBI eventually passed me on to the CIA. That's when the real plan started to take shape. The CIA went to the defense contractor's internal security people about my ideas, and finally we all met and figured out what they could do and what I could do. If I wanted. They told me they appreciated my initiative, that they liked the plan, but that I didn't have to do it. I could walk away at any time. No hard feelings."

"So you're still in Southern California when all this is happening." Jason said.

"Right. But despite the secret agent maneuvers, I was finding it harder and harder to work for the defense contractor. I mean, you've never seen such a bureaucracy. Endless rules, endless memos, endless meetings. To me, it was downright oppressive. I don't know how anyone makes it out alive. I know some people love it, but I sure wasn't one of them. Then about this time, I got the offer to go up to Walnut Creek for the family electronics com-pany. The pay was almost as good, and it sounded like a change I needed. Sure, I had misgivings about working for my stepfather, but the whole thing, the job and the move, was like a breath of fresh air."

"Okay, but you didn't forget the CIA and the Russians and all that."

"No, I told the CIA contacts I was going to take the new job up north with the family company, and they said that was great for me and would look even better to the Russians if I went ahead. I hadn't thought of it that way, but it's true that by quitting I could pretend to be the disgruntled worker with an ax to grind and willing to seek some kind of revenge."

"But you didn't do anything right away."

"No, I put the CIA on hold and I moved and got involved with the new job and was doing really well for a while. Later on, the arguments started and I wondered if I'd made a big mistake. Danni, God bless her, was so positive and just wanted the whole family to get along, but her dad and I were like oil and water, and then everything just went downhill. So I started thinking about leaving, and with Gitte in the picture and the CIA and Steve waiting I thought maybe I could go to Denmark and put it all together. So I went back to the CIA and the contractor's security team and said I'd help if I could deliver the package to Copenhagen. They scratched their heads because they'd been thinking we'd do the transfer in Canada or maybe Mexico or someplace else in Central America, but then they approved Denmark. They actually thought my interest in Gitte was a great cover. Anyway, we were on. They started calling it Operation Sierra."

"Catchy." Operation Sierra. Jason had read about the birth of spy projects, but until now he'd never heard a first-hand account. And even though he didn't understand it all yet, he thought Craig's story was sounding coherent.

"Yeah. At least it was easy to remember. Too easy, actually. It stuck in my head when I didn't want to think about it." Craig cleared his throat. "Anyway, the next step was to work it out with Steve. So I found him again, told him what I could do and told him I wanted to do it in Denmark. He said great, they had an agent in Copenhagen I could meet and work with."

"Baransky," Jason said.

"That's our boy."

"Steve didn't figure out what you were doing?"

"I don't think so. You probably don't know it, but when I was in college I did some live theater. It was fun and gave me a change of pace from those stuffy business classes. So I learned how to act, be somebody else in a convincing way."

"Are you acting right now? With me?"

"No, but the night I first met you, I was into it. Of course, I'd had a little too much to drink. Fuel on the fire, so to speak."

Jason nodded as he remembered that night in the pub. "I get it now. So tell me about the package," Jason said. "What exactly did you deliver to Baransky?"

"It was a two-step plan," Craig said. "First I gave him a flash drive with sample data from the defense contractor. This was financial information I had access to, not engineering plans or hardware or anything like that, but stuff they would think was in my wheelhouse as an accountant. In a way, it was just a taste, but it demonstrated my bona fides. It was real stuff, fairly up to date, mostly innocuous data everybody assumed the Russians already had, but with enough new data thrown in to pique their interest."

"The bait."

"Exactly. The CIA and the contractor and I worked out what we'd put on that sample disk, what everyone would be okay with handing over, and I made sure it was in a form that someone in my accounting position would have reasonably dealt with. It was all carefully constructed for the Russians, but it didn't appear slick or polished. Instead, it looked a little scattered and haphazard. I figured that way the Russians were more likely to think it was authentic."

"So Baransky took the flash drive and sent it up the line for approval."

"Yeah, but it took way too long. That's when I told you I was thinking of killing somebody. That day I actually might have killed him if he'd provoked me one more time, and I'd had a weapon. So I had to stay in touch with him while I waited. I didn't know what the hang-up was. Was it Moscow, or was it Baransky, or was it something else? I worried that the Russians would figure out the plan and that Baransky would shoot me if I looked at him wrong."

Jason was feeling better about Craig, but there were still loose ends. "Now Baransky is gone. So what good was all that effort you went to, all that risk you subjected yourself to?"

"The risk and effort paid off, Jason. As for Baransky, he wasn't the only Russian spy in Copenhagen. This morning, before I walked back here to the hotel, I delivered a second flash drive to a different Russian—a fisherman, or at least that's his cover. But he looked over the data and made the big call. And now the deal is done."

"The drive was like the first one?"

"Close. As with the sample disk, the defense contractor's security team helped me put it together. It took a while. I had to keep flying back to Southern California for meetings and access to their computers. And then finally the CIA approved the data. It was just about everything Steve asked for and just about everything Baransky's supervisors thought they wanted. It was an ice cream sundae with a cherry on top. But it was almost entirely fabricated. Fake. There was only enough truth in it to make it seem real. It was a classic disinformation campaign and in a way was just more theater."

Now Jason started to worry. "But the Russians will find out eventually."

"Eventually. In the meantime, they'll spin their wheels. Here's how it works. There are four parts to the data. One part is real information, just not terribly valuable. But you have to mix it in to help make them think everything else is equally as real. A second part looks just as real, but is actually a worthless time-waster. The Russians will spend valuable resources pursuing that phantom. A third part will cause their own systems real harm. It'll be like a computer virus, not from malicious code on the flash drive itself, but it will act as a self-induced virus as the Russians reach their conclusions from the data and then apply those conclusions to their own intelligence apparatus. Think of poison in Halloween candy. It tastes good at first, but then the ghouls really come out." Craig laughed loudly at his own visualization of chaos.

Now he looked at Jason squarely and said, "Finally, the fourth part will send the CIA and other American agencies valuable data on what the Russians are doing. I wasn't the computer genius who built the mechanism, but I'm proud to say the idea was all mine. You know those red dye packs banks use? When the bank robber takes the strap off the cash, the red dye explodes and makes the money worthless and sometimes the dye even blows up in the robber's face. All fun stuff. Well, this will be kind of an *infrared* dye pack. The Russians won't see it because they won't be looking at it in the right way, but over time American agents will notice it floating into the electronic data stream, and they'll know exactly what the Russians are trying to do with all this wonderful bogus data."

Jason waited a moment before speaking, collecting himself. "I don't know what to say, Craig. I had no idea about any of this. I can see now that I saw only a small part of you before. I guess you're some kind of American hero. Operation Sierra."

"I'm not a hero," Craig said.

"Really? I mean you risked your safety and did the whole crazy spy drop business for free."

"No. Not for free."

"You said you weren't on the government payroll."

"I'm not. And after I got my final regular paycheck from the defense contractor, I wasn't on their payroll either."

"That leaves…"

"Baransky. The Russians."

"You scammed Baransky?"

"Damn right. The way he treated me, he deserved it."

"How much," Jason asked, thinking maybe a hundred grand.

"Only a half million."

Jason's head involuntarily snapped up. "A half million? Craig, I've underestimated you."

"Yeah? Well, so did Baransky." Craig laughed to himself. "He thought he knew everything, acting like the lord and master of the universe."

"And you get to keep the half million? Tell me."

"This morning it went into a Swiss bank account, my Swiss bank account, at the same time I handed over the flash drive. It's my payout. In this particular venture, the CIA is interested only in what Russia does with the data, not making a profit. The money has to go to someone, so the CIA said I could keep the proceeds for my troubles. Tax free, of course. Then they calculated what the drive might be worth if it was totally real and told me the value could easily be a hundred times what I got today. But since I'm just a small, rogue operator in the eyes of the Russians, I couldn't price the flash drive anything close to that and be taken seriously. Or kept alive. So they advised me to just ask for a million and settle for half."

Jason repeated the words as if in a trance. "Ask for a million and settle for half."

They grinned at each other until their faces hurt.

After a time, Jason said, "Danni and I talked about why you took the company money. Speculated actually, because you're the only one who really knows. She told me all about your family, so some answers seem pretty apparent. But now the question comes up again, this time with a twist. Why did you embezzle from the family company, especially when the big Russian payoff was close at hand?"

Craig sat quietly for a moment, looking at Jason, then at the floor, then back at Jason. "I was angry at my mother and stepfather, for sending me away."

"Danni told me about the whole thing. You were well taken care of in Colorado, but you felt abandoned."

"I suppose that's the simple explanation. But it went a lot deeper." Craig paused a few seconds. "Anyway, I thought taking the money would be a good way to even the score."

"All right. Then at the same time you were gearing up to get paid by the Russians. Why take your family's money if you were in line to get a half million here in Denmark?"

"I see what you mean," Craig said. "When I left California, I'd only put in my bid for the payoff. That's when I told Steve I wanted a million. Then Baransky and I did the final negotiations here in

Copenhagen. So when I was still working in Walnut Creek, I didn't know what I'd get paid in Denmark, if anything. Despite all the trouble we'd gone to set up the data package and transfer, nobody knew if Operation Sierra would even work. There was no guarantee."

"I think I get it now. So you said a while ago that you decided last night to return the family money. That was before you knew the Russians would come through with the half million."

"That's right. I saw what I needed to do. And I wouldn't have changed my mind if the whole Russian deal had gone south. Crazy, huh?"

"Not at all," Jason said. "It sounds to me as if you finally have a clear vision of how to go about setting things right." Jason rubbed his chin and thought of the danger Craig might be in. "You're not afraid of Baransky now? Afraid that some Russian will try to take revenge?"

"A little maybe. But that's a chance I'll have to take. I think it'll actually go worse for Baransky, throwing away someone else's money like that. As for me, I can alert the FBI if I feel in danger. There's always a chance of a bullet, and then there's always a chance of a car wreck. But if I die now, I'll go out knowing I've done the right thing for our country."

Jason thought of the kidnapping again, wondering about Craig's attempt to stop it. "You mentioned *car wreck*. You intentionally caused one the other day, Craig. If you'd actually stopped Baransky from taking Danni to the warehouse, you would have blown the deal with the Russians. Did you realize that at the time?"

"Sure, I knew it, but I didn't think too hard about it. Danni was far more important then. I'm the one who put her in harm's way by taking the company's money, so I needed to do what I could to help her and make amends. If Operation Sierra had just evaporated then with Baransky out of the way, I still would have been very happy because Danni would have been safe. Of course, I failed, but then you stepped in."

"Well, I guess we both had an idea of what Baransky was capable of. So he decided to kidnap Danni to keep her from stumbling across his spy business?"

"Until the deal with me was final, yes" Craig said. "He was buying time, he thought, while he waited for his own people to come through. To me, Danni's snooping around was annoying, more than annoying, but still not much of a surprise. I mean, I knew she had to be here about the money. But I didn't want to tell Baransky that she was part of the family and had come to Copenhagen to nag her big brother to come home and play nice."

"You wanted to look tougher."

"In a way, yeah. But there was more. When Baransky noticed Danni poking around, I had to say something, to protect her, to keep him from doing anything extreme. By that time, I knew it wouldn't take much to set him off. So I told him I'd embezzled some company money and that she was here in Copenhagen to try to get it back. Total truth there. Baransky actually thought that was cool. It was one of the few times he gave me any respect. Of course, as I mentioned, I wasn't about to tell him who she really was. Anyway, to Baransky, Danni represented trouble, someone who was going to stumble onto our deal and blow the lid off."

"It must have been very important to him."

"Very important to his mission here in Denmark, yes. In Baransky's mind, the deal had to go through. He dropped a hint that it would mean some kind of promotion for him. He wouldn't have to drive a taxi in Denmark anymore. He didn't like his cover job, so that's probably one reason he drove like a maniac. Of course, knowing how much he wanted the deal to succeed gave me a little advantage, but there was still a huge threat of danger. I called Danni Tuesday morning to warn her off, but then things started happening very fast. She fell on the ice, and Baransky was following her and took her back to the hotel in his taxi, and the next thing I know he's planning to kidnap her so she won't interfere."

"My God," Jason said. He remembered Danni all taped up on that cold warehouse floor and couldn't help shuddering himself.

Craig went on. "Somewhere about that time he let me know that kidnapping her was also a way to slow you down. You know, divert your attention in case you'd figured out anything."

"I'm not sure I was close to figuring out much of anything then," Jason said. "But even if I had been, Baransky had no cause to kidnap Danni. It's insane."

"I know, I know. That's the worst part of everything that happened. I tried to talk him out of it, but he was too paranoid. At the same time, he considered you a threat to him. He thought that when you put your mind to it that you could ruin the deal. I know that sounds goofy now, but I'm pretty sure your quick action in the warehouse to find Danni is what made him pack up for Russia in a hurry. And then you called in the police and he didn't like the odds. He didn't want to mess with you anymore. So give yourself a little credit."

Jason didn't know that he deserved any credit. He could think about that in a week or two back in Seattle when he had a slow day at the office. "You know, Craig, you could have stopped this whole thing earlier," he said. "You could have just answered Danni's messages and then told her straight that Baransky was a menace and then made her leave Copenhagen right away. You would have lost Operation Sierra, but you just told me you were willing to lose it when you tried to crash the car."

"I know. It sounds simple now. And I actually wish I had done that. But so much was happening all at once I didn't see it as clearly then as I do now. Not at all." Craig alternately squeezed his hands together then released them as he tried to explain. "I had a lot of stuff going. I was still mad at Danni for following me here, and I was involved with Gitte and her friends, and I was all nerves about the data transfer. I figured the CIA had someone here watching me, but I never knew who or what help I could get if I needed it or even if I'd get any help at all. When I asked about that back in California, I got only vague assurances. And by the way, I never did see the CIA, so maybe I just imagined there was somebody out there. And Baransky—even though he was an absolute jerk from day one, I honestly didn't expect him to do what he did. Then on Tuesday things happened so fast. I called Danni, as I told you, and hoped that would be enough. But I was soon overwhelmed by Baransky's intensity. The guy was half KGB and half robot. I was no match for him. Sure, I had chances to head this off, but in the middle of it I didn't think on my feet and act quickly enough. God, I wish I had."

Craig's jaw was quivering, and Jason could see he had worked himself into an anxious state that wasn't serving anyone. Jason stood up and went to the window. When he'd asked about Baransky, he'd gotten more than he'd anticipated. And Craig Huff was more complicated than he'd ever thought likely, more complicated than Danni knew. Jason didn't know how to tell Danni about the CIA intrigue. And then he decided she didn't have to know, at least right away, and she wasn't going to hear it from him. If Craig decided to tell his sister, that would be his business.

"Okay, Craig, you've played a dangerous game, but enough about the Russians." He turned back to Danni's brother, still sitting on the bed. "Here's the deal. You can leave Denmark with Danni—tonight, if necessary, but I'd prefer you wait until tomorrow. I have a little plan. The police are on board with it as long you stay on track and do what I tell you."

Craig narrowed his eyes. "No cops, huh? Wow. I'd love to go tonight, but tomorrow works. Maybe that will give me a chance to say goodbye to Gitte."

"Gitte. Right. Hold that thought, Craig. What I'd like you to do now is get me your return airline ticket. You need to make a reservation."

When Craig had given him his ticket, Jason got on the phone and called Danni. "You're going home tomorrow," he said. "With your brother."

"Oh, my God, Jason. Yes, yes."

"As far as the company money goes, it's in an off-shore account, so he'll have to live up to his word to me and return it. That's all I can do for now."

"I understand. This is incredible."

"No, this is almost the easy part. Maybe what's incredible is everything that's happened up to this point. Okay, now listen. I want to you to play travel agent or get a travel agent or whatever it takes. I'm going to give you Craig's ticket information, and you need to figure out how to get both of you on the same plane back to San Francisco tomorrow."

When Danni had the information, Jason said, "Okay, now I'm going to put a stranger on to talk with you."

He handed the phone to Craig, who took it gingerly. "Danni?"

"Craig, how are you? I've been so worried about you. We all have."

"I know. I've hurt you. I'm really, really sorry. I've hurt Mom. I've hurt a lot of people. And I've made a lot of mistakes."

"Well, going back with me isn't one of them. I'm so glad you're doing this."

They talked another minute or so, and then Craig hung up and spoke to Jason. "You know, other than that little warning call Tuesday, that's the first time I've talked with Danni in several weeks. It felt good. In fact, I *feel* good, doing what I'm doing now."

"Great, Craig. Okay, I hate to rush you, but there's one more thing we need to do."

"What's that?"

"Arrange a farewell dinner. For tonight."

"Farewell? I don't get it."

"With Gitte," Jason said. "Didn't you mention something about wanting to say goodbye to her?"

"Well, yeah. Sure. Yeah, it would be good to see her again. Even if it's the last time. You know, I've been so busy thinking about Baransky and Danni and—"

"That's fine. First, we'll need a place to eat. There's a nice restaurant I saw the other day." Jason told him where it was. "I'll make the reservation, in your name." Jason got on the phone and called the front desk for the number.

After Jason had phoned the restaurant, Craig got a strange look on his face. "Not so fast. You made the reservation for *four*. What's going on?"

"Oh, that. Well, I'll be joining you."

Craig frowned. "Well, won't that be romantic."

"This isn't about romance, Craig. For one thing, we know it's the end of the line with Gitte. But if you want to stay and have a drink with her, that's okay with me. I'll probably be skipping dessert and leaving early."

"So who's the fourth?" Craig asked. "You said four. Danni?"

"No, Danni still needs to rest tonight. And pack."

"So it's a mystery person. I have to wait and see?"

"Not at all. In fact, you should call her up right now and invite her. And Gitte, of course."

"You said *her*. A woman?"

"Cabrina."

"Cabrina?" Craig did a double take. "Wait a minute? How do you know about Cabrina?"

"Well, I've seen her. Beautiful cinnamon-colored hair. Drop-dead gorgeous. She went into your hotel one night. And Danni saw her with you. You two were in some kind of embrace. And then Danni hired a private detective and got her first name. And later I came across her where she works, at another hotel, you know, and learned her last name. Let's see, there was something else. Oh, yes. I took her picture."

Craig was stunned. "Her picture?"

"Would you like to see it? I have it right here." Jason took his camera out of his coat pocket and turned on the viewer and scrolled to the shot of Cabrina. "It's from a little distance, but not too bad, I think. I'll zoom in for you."

Craig took the camera and examined the photo in the viewer. "That's her, all right." He looked up as he handed the camera back. "I don't get it. You know, Gitte introduced me to Cabrina, literally pushed me toward her. They're friends, so if you think you're going to stir up something..."

"Don't worry," Jason said. "I won't embarrass you. Now call those two ladies and make sure they can go to dinner. Tell them that they're expected at seven and that they should make their own arrangements to get there. Tell them you're sorry you can't meet them earlier because you're getting ready to leave Denmark tomorrow."

"Anything else?" Craig asked with a little exasperation.

"Hmm. Well, two things. You'll be picking up the tab. Anyone who made a half million this morning can afford to buy dinner. And the other thing is that I need your picture."

Jason pointed his camera at Craig and pressed the button. "Nice. Good close-up."

"You're full of surprises, aren't you? Why did you need my picture?"

"Actually, I don't But the police might want it. If you don't show up for dinner tonight, and at the airport tomorrow."

Craig smiled wryly. "Leverage."

"Never hurts." Jason got up and put on his coat. "I'm going now, so you'd better get busy and call the ladies."

#

It was as cold as ever, but the sun was out, so Jason walked through the Strøget all the way back to the Kong Jacob. Tonight there would be the farewell dinner, and now there was the farewell tour of downtown Copenhagen. It would be good to get home, but in a way he would miss this.

When he got back to the Kong Jacob he went straight to Danni's room and knocked.

Her voice came through the door. "Who is it?"

"Jason, Prince of Denmark."

"What's your favorite cheese?"

He thought for a second." Gouda."

Danni opened the door in mock disgust. "No, no. It's havarti."

"Sorry. I was a little out of character."

"You *are* a character. Come on in."

Jason shut the door and looked around. Danni seemed to be in fairly good shape and the lamps were standing upright. "Anything happen?"

"Well, I did open the door earlier," Danni said.

He frowned. "I told you not to do that."

"I know, but it was the hotel manager. He wanted to apologize to me. He didn't really need to, I told him, but I let him anyhow. He really wanted to. Actually, it was touching."

"Well, in that case."

"I thanked him for the flowers, and dinner. And then I made his day."

Jason squinted. "You took off your—ooof." Danni's punch cut him off. He rubbed his now tender ribs, vowing to let her finish before speaking again.

"No, silly. I simply told him I wouldn't sue."

"I'd like to have seen that."

Danni nodded. "It was something. His smile was as wide as the room. Oh, and I made the reservations," she said, handing him her notes. "We're flying out a little after eleven but need to be at the ticket counter by nine-thirty. Should I call Craig back?"

"No, I can tell him. And I'll arrange a ride for everyone. Be ready by nine."

"So you're all done at Craig's place?"

"All done at his hotel, yes, but not all done with Craig. We're going to dinner tonight."

"Really," Danni said. Disappointment crossed her face. "Without me?"

"I'm sorry. I told him you were still resting and needed to pack."

"Yeah, that's what you told him. What's the real reason?"

"Saw right through that, huh? Danni, the real reason is that it's a farewell dinner so Craig can say goodbye to his girlfriends."

"Gitte's going to dinner with Craig?"

"And Cabrina."

Danni glared at him, pretending to be jealous. "You just want to meet her, don't you? Admit it, you lecher."

"I would like to meet her, but not for the reason you're suggesting."

"Then what's the story?"

"Can't say. Maybe tomorrow. Anyway, this might not be the most pleasant dinner in Copenhagen tonight. I'd hate for you to get indigestion."

"So it's room service again?"

"Well, you could go down to the dining room. They know you, and I think it's safe. Baransky has disappeared. Probably gone back to Russia."

"Then maybe I will. The manager offered another free dinner. And I'm going a little stir crazy in here."

"Okay, then you're set for dinner. But right now, I'd like to take you to lunch. I know this Chinese place, if you're up for a walk."

"A *slow* walk," Danni said. "I'm still feeling a little stiff."

"I've got all afternoon," Jason said.

"And all you want to do is have Chinese food?"

"Well, we could shop a little. You like to shop, don't you? Isn't that what women like to do? I know a place you can get some very nice amber."

"Oh, I could shop all right. But I was thinking..." She stepped up to him and put her arms around his waist. "If we had all afternoon..."

Jason pulled her closer. "Oh, you naughty girl, surely you're not..."

"I am."

"Well, in that case, let's go have lunch first because I need to build up my energy. I have a lot to do this afternoon."

"Mister, I hope I'm on your agenda," Danni said, looking him in the eye.

"Top of the list. Let me show you." They kissed long and hard. For Jason, it was like that first great kiss outside the Italian restaurant. "And there'll be more of that, but only after lunch."

"You're one tough negotiator."

"Get your coat. I'm outta here."

The Chinese place was noisy and crowded, but the food smelled good, and there was a table for Danni and Jason. They sat and looked over the menus, and Danni said, "I've never seen a Chinese menu in Danish. It's not right."

"Don't bother with it," Jason said, still studying the menu. "Just flip it over and read the English version."

"Oh, but that's no fun. Then I would know what I was ordering."

Jason looked up. "Isn't that the idea?"

"Not always. Sometimes I want to fling caution to the wind."

"I think you already have, running around with me all week. Good thing your father is back in California so he can't object."

"No, he'd like you. You get things done. You found me in the warehouse. You steered Craig away from disaster."

"Well, the first I absolutely had to do, and the second, well, let's see if it turns out as well as I think it will. But the reason I originally came to Denmark is still hanging over my head."

"The cheese. Any hope?"

"I have a little plan. For tomorrow. One more trip out to Bjorneby Foods and I'll know."

"I don't even want to think about that place."

He squeezed her hand. "I know. I'm not so fond of it myself, but I'll keep breathing and get through it."

They ordered in English, and the waitress wrote something on a pad, then walked away with the menus. Jason said, "I think we're both flinging caution to the wind. Let's hope it's edible."

"But you said you'd been here before."

"I have. That was Sunday night, after we got back from Hamlet's Castle and you ran off and left me alone. I was hungry."

"I shouldn't have left you that night," Danni said. "I shouldn't have done a lot of things the past few days."

"Forget it. Anyway, I think it's going to work out okay."

After lunch, which measured high on the edibility scale, they stood out on the street. "Left to shopping," Jason said, pointing the way. "Or right to hotel."

"Right. Most definitely right." Danni took his arm. "Remember, you've got a full schedule. This is no time to be looking for trinkets."

"Oh, I couldn't agree more."

Back at the hotel, they were crossing the lobby when a voice sang out. "Mr. Stallings." Jason turned to the front desk, and the clerk said, "A letter for you."

"Ah. *Mange tak.*" Thank you very much. The letter was actually a large manila envelope.

"What's that?" Danni asked.

Jason opened it. "A copy of a photo. The police found a photo in Martin Weathersby's suitcase. I persuaded Detective Dalvang to share a copy with me."

Danni looked at the studio shot of a young woman and a little girl. "Cute girl. Who are they?"

"Don't know. But apparently they meant something to Weathersby."

Jason put the photo back into the envelope, and they went to the elevator. "Ride or walk?" he asked.

"I'll take the stairs. That outing to the restaurant has loosened me up. I feel good."

"Then you're recovering. Just in time."

Halfway up the stairs to their floor, Danni stopped.

"What is it?" Jason asked. "Are you in pain? Should we go back down? I thought you were feeling better."

"I'm fine," Danni said. "You almost got that one by me."

"Almost got what by you?"

"The picture, of the woman and girl. You're trying to solve that murder case, aren't you? The Englishman, Weathersby."

"I'm curious, that's all. Let's keep walking." Jason took slow steps in parallel with Danni, who was now more interested in his response than getting to the top of the stairs. "All right, if you really have to know… Dalvang and I were talking this morning about this and that, and I told him some things I knew about Weathersby, about a fax he'd sent to our company in Seattle and some other things the hotel desk clerk told me, and then Dalvang decided to talk about this picture. He ended up agreeing to send me a copy. That's all."

They reached the top of the stairs and turned down the hall toward their rooms. "Oh, yeah. That's all. Like this police detective hands out copies of evidence from murder cases to every American who happens through Copenhagen."

"Well, I've developed a special connection. You know about that. Besides, I'm not a cop. It's Dalvang's job to solve the case."

"What are you going to do with that picture then?"

"I don't know. Think about it, I guess. See if something breaks loose."

"It will," Danni said. "I can see those little wheels turning in your head."

They stopped at Danni's door.

"So how's your schedule looking?" she asked.

He put a hand on each side of the door frame, pretending to trap her. "I'm booked solid for the afternoon. I'll be lucky to come up for air."

"Sounds exciting. Anybody I know?"

"This nice lady from California. Benicia, I believe. She needs help."

Danni blinked. "What kind of help?"

"A massage. For starters."

"A massage? Hmm. And then?"

"And then we'll have to figure it out."

Danni's breath was short. "We will, won't we. I mean, you will. You and the lady from Benicia."

"There's just one question," he said. "Whose room?"

"Oh. I like yours. I mean I think the lady from Benicia would like your room. Change of scenery, you know."

"I think you're right. If you'll follow me..."

They went into Jason's room. "Nice view of the courtyard," he said, reaching for the curtains, "but much too bright. And too public." He slid the fabric shut, leaving only a sliver of light. Around the corner the bathroom was still in sunshine, so he closed the door. Then as their eyes were adjusting to near darkness, he switched on the lamp sitting on the dresser and threw his coat onto the chair. He helped Danni out of her coat and threw it over his.

She said, "Now, about that massage..."

In a few minutes, as she lay on her chest feeling Jason's healing touch at work, he pressed a thumb lightly into each exposed hip and paused.

"What's wrong?" She mumbled lazily into the bed. "You can't stop now."

"I'm not stopping. I'm just admiring two of the cutest little ladybugs I've ever seen."

She sighed dreamily. "I have no more secrets."

He bent over and kissed her lips while lightly stroking the tat-toos. "It's okay. I'll never tell."

Hours later, the languorous winter day began to fade into an-other early sunset. As only long, thin traces of daylight slipped by the almost closed curtains and fell across the bed, Danni lay on her back and said, "This is so amazingly beautiful. I'm the most re-laxed I've ever been since I came to Denmark."

Lying next to her on his back, the length of their bare arms and legs touching, Jason said, "You stole my lines."

And they both laughed. It felt so good to laugh.

16

Jason arrived at the restaurant a few minutes early. He didn't see Craig right away, but had an idea where he was. The bar was separated from the dining room by a wooden partition about four feet high topped by etched glass windows with gold paint in a filigree style. Anyone close enough to the windows could see through to the other side. Jason took the shortcut, however, and peered through the doorway. Craig was already there, at a table in the bar with a nearly empty glass. Jason went in. "You made it," he said.

Craig looked up with a grin. "You were worried, weren't you?"

"Not really. But it's nice to see that you're following through." Jason sat down across the table from Craig.

"I intend to follow through. Now that I've had a few hours to think about this, I realize I haven't thanked you properly. You've done me a big favor."

"Don't take offense, Craig, but I did it more for Danni. I don't think she'd be too keen on visiting her brother in a Danish prison."

Craig hovered over his glass. "Hey, I'm smart enough to see that my sister is a big part of this. All the same, I owe you. At least I can buy you a drink."

"Why not," Jason said. "Scotch on the rocks, like the first time we met."

"Sure." Craig got up and took care of the order, getting another one for himself.

When Craig came back with the drinks, Jason had a piece of paper waiting for him. "Here's your flight information. Danni has it all worked out. You need to be at the ticket counter by nine-thirty, so she and I will come by about nine to pick you up. Be down at the taxi pickup spot at the end of your street by nine and we'll find you."

Craig looked at the paper. "This is really great. You're flying out, too?"

"No, I'm staying another day, for my work. But I'll see you guys off."

"You don't have to. I mean, you can trust me."

"I'm doing it for Danni," Jason said. "And for myself."

"Maybe this isn't the end of things for you two."

Jason gave him a tight smile. "What's important right now is that she needs to go home with you. Your family has a lot of work ahead of it, and I can't be part of that."

"I understand."

Jason took a sip of the scotch. It was smooth. He thought of Sayon Kunder and his single malt neat. Maybe he'd try that when he got back home. He looked at Craig and said, "You know, the last time we drank together, you had a different name."

"You had to remind me." Craig had a sheepish look. "Well, it was a crazy night and I was doing crazy stuff. I told you I was doing a little acting, trying out the possibility that I was somebody else."

"Well, I can't tell you to forget it," Jason said, "because I know you won't. But when you get back home, I hope you can try to put your life back together and feel good about yourself."

"That's going to take a while."

"I know. But put some effort into it. Just don't sit around and mope."

"I'll have to get a job. Get back in the saddle. Since I have the half mil, it wouldn't be for the money, at least right away, but I need to feel I'm contributing to something."

"A job with the family company?"

"I doubt that. Pretty much burned my bridges there. Besides, it might be kind of painful—for everyone."

"I don't know. They might be the forgiving kind, if they get the money back."

"They'll get the money back, don't worry, but I wouldn't count on forgiveness. You don't know Danni's father."

"No, I don't, except he sounds a little like my father. He's human, too. Give him a chance. Anyway, Danni's already forgiven you, and in such a genuine way I can hardly describe it. If anybody should be upset with you, it's Danni. I can't say I totally understand it, but she also has a tremendous amount of love for you. I haven't told her about Operation Sierra and your connection with Baransky. So you'll have to decide what and when you're going to tell her, and though I know now that there was a greater purpose, you've got to tell me you would never do anything to let her down. Never."

"No, I can't let her down now. Truthfully, she's been really good to me this past year, but I kept pushing her away. I think I didn't want to get too close because if I did I'd be admitting the possibility that I could put aside my family grudges."

"You liked those grudges, didn't you?"

"I still do, I guess. I own them."

"Have you thought about some kind of counseling, Craig? Seems to me you need somebody to talk to, at least about some of this stuff, the family history especially. I don't know that it needs to be formal, on a shrink's couch with appointments and all that, but I really think you could benefit from some kind of help."

"No, I haven't thought about that, but maybe I should. I guess right now my only counselor is what's in this glass. I've just been a case of nerves the last couple of hours, thinking about Gitte, and Cabrina, thinking how this would go."

Jason looked at his watch. "It's almost seven. Maybe we should get our table and wait for the ladies in the dining room."

"Okay. Sounds good. Well, bottoms up." Craig drained his glass. "They don't call this stuff courage for nothing."

The dining room was decorated in cherry-stained paneling topped with brass rails. The restaurant was a classy steak and fish place with oversized menus and fine carpeting of muted reds, blues and browns. The hostess seated them, and Jason asked her to send the ladies to the table when they arrived. He didn't know if they would be traveling together, but had his question answered in only about two minutes when he saw Gitte walking alone toward them.

She and Craig kissed politely, and he introduced her to Jason. "And, Gitte, this is Jason Stallings. He's a friend of my sister's, visiting Copenhagen on business."

Jason had wondered how that introduction would go and thought Craig handled it nicely. Jason and Craig were sitting opposite of each other, so Gitte took the chair next to Craig on his right. He told Gitte of his travel plans, and she nodded solemnly. Jason couldn't tell if she was disguising her pleasure that he was leaving Denmark or that she was truly sad to see him leave. Maybe it was a little of both.

Meanwhile, Jason had been perusing the wine list, and when a waiter came around, he ordered a Bordeaux and hoped it was as good as the one he and Danni had shared.

The waiter returned with the wine quickly, showed Jason the label, opened the bottle and poured a little into his glass. Jason swirled the dark red liquid delicately, then tasted it and said it was an excellent Bordeaux. "*Tak.*" After the waiter had poured four glasses and gone away, the three of them seated at the table toasted to a safe journey.

A few minutes later, Cabrina arrived, a little breathless, but fairly cheerful, though perhaps slightly wary of Jason. The men stood, and Craig made introductions again without much change in the script, and then Cabrina sat down next to Jason on his left. He noticed that no kisses were offered this time. He had studied his picture of her closely before he'd left the Kong Jacob and reaffirmed his opinion that she was striking in three-dimensional form. Of course, he had had a few looks at her on the street in Nyhavn and back in the Hotel Lorentsen, mostly from a distance, but sitting next to her was a totally different experience. If she remembered him from the brief lobby encounter, it was hard to tell.

Cabrina was stunning, and no wonder Danni had pretended to be a little jealous about this dinner. Gitte was a pretty blonde in the classic Scandinavian mold, but Cabrina was in a class by herself. Jason compared the picture, which stuck in his mind, to the real thing. The red hair couldn't be ignored, and her facial bones seemed to be finer in real life than in the picture. Thinking about the characterization he'd heard from Thomas the desk clerk, Jason hadn't expected her to appear quite so delicate and even fragile in person. Yet glancing sideways at her as she sipped her wine, he saw details that the picture he'd shot from across the lobby hadn't quite revealed. He could understand why Craig was taken with her, but wasn't so sure what she saw in Craig. But Jason realized he would never really know what a woman thought.

When the waiter came around, the men ordered in English, and the women in Danish. If that amused the waiter, he handled the situation with aplomb.

As the food began to arrive and dinner proceeded, Jason steered the conversation to families. He mentioned having two brothers but no sisters and more or less normal parents. Gitte said she had a brother, who was married to a German woman and living in Bonn. Her parents lived on a farm, but her mother had been sick and might need kidney dialysis. Craig and Cabrina exchanged glances about that, but Gitte didn't seem to notice.

About the time a second bottle of wine arrived, Craig told about his split family, a half brother and half sister in California and a half brother in Colorado, a father and stepmother in Colorado and a mother and stepfather in California. Jason almost got whiplash listening to the recitation as it bounced across the Sierras and the Rockies and back again, and he wasn't sure how the ladies were sorting out the American geography or what they knew already. He did know that Gitte had been to San Francisco, and he asked Cabrina if she'd traveled to the United States, but she hadn't. She'd only been to other parts of Scandinavia, and Germany, France and England.

"Cabrina, what about your family?" Craig asked.

Cabrina's shoulders fell. "It's not a very happy story," she said. "My father, my real father, left my mother and me when I was a baby."

Gitte let out a gasp. "Cabrina, I never knew that."

"Well, it's never come up, I suppose, but it's true. So my

mother raised me by herself, working a little here in Copenhagen and getting some help from the government. Then when I was seven, she remarried, but my stepfather didn't really like children, especially me, I think, and after about two years he also left."

Craig listened attentively, comparing her situation to his own. "I can see how that would hurt a child. It sounds worse than what I went through."

Cabrina pushed on. "I really hated my father. He rejected me then, and he..." She paused. "I hated my stepfather, too. I still hate them both."

Gloom settled over the table like a debilitating dust. "I never knew any of this," Gitte said. "Did you ever know who your real father was?"

"Not at first. But gradually I learned. My mother didn't want to tell me until I was older, but I pried the details out of her."

"So who was he?" Gitte asked.

"He was a two-timer, that's what he was. He was already married and had a family in England while he had an affair with my mother. After a few months with me as a baby, he packed up and went back to England. Later, he sent a little money now and then, but not nearly enough to raise a family."

Craig said, "I felt bad when my mother let my father take me away to Colorado."

Cabrina ignored him, and Gitte gave him a withering look. Jason read it loud and clear: *This is Cabrina's time to tell her story so just let her tell it.*

Jason quietly drank his wine, so he didn't have to say anything. He reached into the inside breast pocket of his sports jacket with his right hand and felt the folded picture between his fingers. It was the copy that Dalvang had given him, and Jason was on the edge of taking it out and showing Cabrina and asking her if she was the little girl in the picture. But he didn't see an opening, not a decent one anyhow. Cabrina had told them the story would be sad, and now that he'd heard it, it struck him as even sadder. It would have been utter cruelty at this point to confront her with the picture, he thought, and so removed his hand from his pocket and rested it on the table.

They all tried to eat a little more, but by now everyone had pretty much lost their appetite, and the wine went down better than the food. After a minute, Gitte asked, "How is your mother now?"

"Oh, she works. She has a cat to keep her company. She gets by. I see her at least once a week. Here, I have a picture of her, of both of us, when I was little." She reached for her purse on the floor and took out a leather-bound picture and showed it to Gitte. "I was two years old then."

Jason didn't really have to look. He already knew. But to be absolutely sure, he peered over and saw that Cabrina's picture was the same as the photo he had in his pocket, the photo Dalvang had taken from Martin Weathersby's suitcase. Cabrina's print was more like a three-by-five, or whatever the Danish dimensions were, and Jason's was the equivalent of a five-by-seven, but other than size, the picture was the same.

"Your mother was beautiful," Jason said.

"Yes, she was," Cabrina said. "Of course, she's older now and has been through a lot and lost some of her looks, but I still want to think of her this way. That's why I carry this picture with me. She's always beautiful in this picture."

"Your father," Gitte said. "I wonder what he's doing now."

Cabrina closed her eyes and took a deep breath. When she opened them again, she said, "He's dead. For years, I hated him and wanted him dead. And now he is dead."

Gitte was flushed. "Oh, I'm sorry. I'm really sorry."

"He was murdered." Cabrina started crying.

"What? Murdered?"

But Cabrina didn't seem to hear Gitte now. The crying had exploded into outright sobs. Jason put a hand on her back, and Gitte jumped out of her chair and came around the table to comfort her. Craig half rose, wondering what to do, and muttered, "Cabrina, Cabrina." As Gitte's arm went around Cabrina's shoulders, trying to re-establish composure, Jason let his hand fall away.

Gitte said, "Cabrina, come with me." Gitte pulled her to her feet, and they went off to the ladies room as other diners turned to stare.

Craig shook his head. "I never knew, I never knew any of this."

Jason grimaced. "That was an amazing story. And so painful."

Craig and Jason toyed with their remaining food, but eating didn't seem right. Craig poured himself more wine and offered some to Jason, but he waved off the refill.

In a couple of minutes, Gitte hurried back to the table, alone, and grabbed Cabrina's coat and purse. "She has to leave," Gitte said. "I'm sorry."

Jason and Craig stood up, speechless, and Gitte said, "I'll be back in a minute."

It was more like five minutes, but when Gitte did come back, she seemed almost as sad as Cabrina had been. The spring had gone out of her step, and gravity pulled at her mouth. She sat down and said, "That poor girl. Doesn't your heart go out to her?"

"She kept it to herself all this time," Craig said. "She hid it so well."

"That's what I was thinking. Oh, Craig." She turned and put her arms around him, looking for her own peace of mind. Craig held her and gently patted her back, and glanced at Jason with a helpless expression.

Jason shrugged and finally backed his chair away from the table and stood up and reached for his coat. "I need to be going, you guys. I'll leave you now to say your goodbyes. It was nice to meet you, Gitte. And, Craig, thanks for dinner, and I'll see you in the morning. About nine."

"Sure thing."

Gitte looked up at him. "Goodbye, Jason. Thanks for coming."

Jason found a taxi a half block away and took it back to the Kong Jacob. It was too cold and too far to walk tonight, and he wasn't in the mood for self-reflection, which is what those long walks usually produced.

When he got back to the Kong Jacob, he stopped at Danni's room and checked on her. She'd gone to the hotel dining room but hadn't eaten much. "I barely touch my food when I eat alone," she said. "And no fresh flowers this time. I had to come back up here to see flowers." They talked about the taxi in the morning. Jason had arranged for Carsten to pick up Danni and himself about eight forty-five and then swing by Nyhavn to load up Craig for the trip to the airport.

"You're so efficient," Danni said. "But I appreciate the custom service."

"Well, I'm glad to do what I can."

"How was Craig tonight?"

"I'd say he's adjusting. He finds a lot of things to be nervous about, and he drinks too much, or at least relies too much on the booze. But his heart seems to be in the right place. And this time I think he'd like to give you a chance to be his sister."

"You're not sugarcoating this, are you?"

"Maybe he was, but I'm not. You can see for yourself tomorrow."

"I guess so. I called home, to California. Everybody's excited, even Dad."

"Now you're the one doing the sugarcoating," Jason said.

"Well, maybe a little." Danni gave him a crooked little smile. "Anyway, he's pleased. And he told me to give you a big thank you for your part."

"Already got that," Jason said. "Free dinner tonight. Craig paid."

"Oh, yes, the dinner. How were the ladies?"

"Interesting. And very nice looking. Craig has good taste."

"Oh, does he? And how would you know, mister?" Danni was almost laughing.

"Casual observation."

"Casual. Hmm. I bet. You didn't stay long, though."

"Cabrina had a little problem and had to leave early. So I left soon afterward. That way Craig could have some time with Gitte. But I had a good steak. It was a nice dinner."

"Mmm."

"You look tired, Danni."

"Weary," she said. "And nervous at the same time, like Craig."

"About tomorrow?"

She nodded. "And the next day, and the next."

"Well, better get some sleep. I think I'll turn in early myself." He turned to go.

"Jason, come and get me for breakfast?"

"Sure. Say seven-thirty?"

"I'll be ready."

He turned to go again, then was stopped by Danni's expression. It was a night of sad looks by the young women in his life. "What is it?"

"I was just thinking about a good-night kiss."

"Oh, you were? Well, I didn't want to press my luck."

"We're way past that, mister. Get over here."

"Sounds like an order," Jason said. "But I'll take it."

The kiss was as good as the first time, as good as the ones they had shared a few hours earlier making love in his room, as good as all of them. And that was the problem. He didn't want to stop.

But at least Danni had some discipline. She pulled away. "Now go to your room," she said, "before you get me started again."

"Okay." He backpedaled to the door. "Seven-thirty."

He went out and down the hall to his room. It seemed empty without Danni, though her perfume still lingered from the afternoon. But they both knew that tonight wasn't the night. They had enjoyed a full afternoon of indulgence, and now they needed to rest. Jason washed up and brushed his teeth. He sat down on the bed and adjusted his alarm clock. Then he reached for something to read. It was a good time for a serious book. He read for fifteen minutes, long enough for Danni to slip from the front of his mind to the back. Then just when he felt the book was imparting incredible wisdom, his eyes grew heavy and somebody shut out the light.

#

Danni was perky at breakfast, and Jason said, "You're eating well this morning."

"That's because I have company now."

Jason nodded. "Are you excited about seeing Craig? I mean

really seeing him?"

"I'm anxious. Excited, yes, but nervous and maybe a little embarrassed. I've been spying on him for a week, and he knows it."

"Of course, he knows it. He totally understands. But he's the one who ought to be embarrassed. Anyway, just be yourself."

"Okay. I needed to hear that. By the way, I've been wondering about something."

"What's that?"

"Why you went to dinner with Craig last night. Couldn't he have said goodbye to his girlfriends by himself?"

Jason took a drink of his coffee. "Of course, of course. I was a little curious about Gitte, I admit, and wanted to see her, but mostly it was Cabrina."

"What a shock." Danni had a playful smirk on her face.

"No, not that. You already know she's beautiful. That's no surprise. I had to find out something about her. And seeing her in person was the only way I could do it for sure. I thought the best way might be a dinner at Craig's invitation."

"And what did you find out about her?"

"That she colors her hair. It isn't really that beautiful cinnamon color. It's brown."

"Brown?" Danni considered that a moment. "Well, that's a woman's prerogative. I mean some women even frost their hair." Danni flipped a few strands of her own. "How do you know it's brown?"

"I saw the roots. The color wasn't really in the picture I took of her, but in person, three feet away, I could tell."

"So her hair's brown. So what? There's something you're not saying, mister."

"That's true. How about this? I'll save my breath for now, but when we pick up Craig, I'll tell you both together. I'm sure he'll find it interesting."

"Speaking of Craig. We'd better get moving. The cab will be here in thirty minutes."

After Danni and Jason finished breakfast, he made a phone call to Detective Dalvang and then went over to Danni's room and hung around as she finished packing. When she was ready, he carried her suitcases downstairs and stood to the side while she turned in her card key and checked out. As they waited for Carsten and his taxi, they stood together awkwardly inside the front door of the hotel. Neither of them knew how to say goodbye, and so they said nothing about going their own ways. There would be a tomorrow, but it was bound to be different. Finally Danni asked, "Have you found a way to get your havarti? You haven't said much about it, but I bet you've been thinking about it."

"I have an idea," Jason said, drawing out the word. "And I'm going out to Bjorneby Foods this afternoon to see how it works."

"You want to tell me how it might turn out? I guess I won't be around to hear the ending."

When Danni started to get that sad look again, Jason couldn't stand it. "Fair enough. Here's my plan."

After Danni heard it, she said, "If that doesn't work, nothing will—if you have the courage to pull it off. And I think you do."

"What have I got to lose? Ah, there's Carsten."

The taxi pulled up in front, and Danni went out first into the sunshine, holding the door for Jason as he carried her bags. They loaded up and Jason asked Carsten to drive over to Nyhavn to pick up Craig. "Danni's brother is visiting Copenhagen at the same time, but they ended up in different hotels, and they haven't seen each other properly for a few days."

"Too bad," Carsten said, turning to them in the back seat. "That's the way these reservations go. But at least you're riding together today."

"That we are, and it's a beautiful day for flying," Danni said, looking out the window at the cloudless winter sky.

The cab went through traffic effortlessly and was soon at the entrance to Nyhavn. "There he is," Danni shouted. "There's Craig."

He was standing next to the curb, and as soon as Carsten stopped the taxi, Danni pushed open her door and bounded out to hug her brother. Craig looked surprised, but pleased as Danni rushed into his arms. Jason got out of the car at a more relaxed pace, but in time to hear Craig say, "Wow."

Danni and Craig exchanged sentimental greetings and kisses on the cheek while Jason looked on and Carsten loaded Craig's bags into the trunk.

After Danni had checked out his head wounds and asked about his health, Craig held his sister at arm's length and said, "Danni, this may not be the last time I apologize to you, but I want to do it now before we get into the car, I want to do it right this time. I am so sorry for the trouble I've caused you, the trouble I've caused everyone, but especially you. You came over here to help me, and I treated you in an unthinkable way, but I just want to say that it's over, and from now on—"

Danni cut him off with a smile. "Craig, you big loon. Enough of this. I know you're sorry, but you don't have to go on all day. Anyway, I'm sorry, too, for spying on you and all that stuff. It was silly."

Jason stepped up to them. "And both of you will be sorry if you miss your flight. Come on, our driver is waiting."

The all-American contingent sat together in the back seat, Danni in the middle, Jason on the left, Craig on the right. As they drove off from Nyhavn, Carsten said, "Jason, I have news about that Baransky fellow you rode with. The word among the drivers is that he's gone back to Russia."

"Hallelujah," Jason said.

Danni and Craig smiled. Then Danni said, "Well, on that pleasing note, let's hear the rest of your Cabrina story, Jason. So why is it so darned important that she really had brown hair?"

"Yeah, that's right," Craig said. "That beautiful coloring came out of a bottle."

"So you both knew it. Why didn't you ask Craig then, Jason?"

Jason sighed. "Because I didn't think of that right away. Anyway, I still needed to see it for myself, and it didn't really matter until she brought out the picture."

Craig said, "Man, that was so weird. And really sad."

Danni was turning her head back and forth. "What's going on here? I'm going to strain my neck if you guys don't stop talking in riddles. What picture? Jason, you didn't show her that picture you took, did you?"

"Of course not. We're talking about the picture she showed us. Tell her, Craig."

"All right. Well, we were talking about families, and it turns out Jason is as close to normal as anyone."

"It only seems that way because I didn't tell you much. But go on."

"Right. Well, then Gitte told her story, and I told mine, which I thought would be about as much as anyone would want to hear, and after that Cabrina told hers. Reluctantly, I guess. Anyway, her father left her and her mother when Cabrina was a baby, which was pretty awful. And then there was this picture of Cabrina and her mother when Cabrina was about two years old. Cabrina apparently carries it with her all the time, and that's what she showed us."

"That is weird," Danni said. "Just yesterday Jason showed me a picture of a young mother and a little girl. What a strange coincidence."

"Not a coincidence," Jason said, removing his copy of the photo from his inside jacket pocket. "You mean this picture, Danni?"

"Yeah, that's the one."

And Craig said, "What the..."

Jason waited for the words that didn't come, then laughed. "What's that, Craig?"

Craig recovered his voice. "That's the picture she showed us. That's Cabrina. Look at the little girl's face." He reached across Danni and took the picture from Jason. "It's Cabrina. You can see it plain as day. Where'd you get this?"

"Jason, I'm—" Danni said.

"One at a time," Jason said. "How about ladies first?"

Danni said, "Well, I was going to say that I'm confused now. Jason, you got this photo yesterday afternoon, right after we came back from lunch. You opened the envelope in the lobby of the Kong Jacob, and you showed me the photo. So how did you know it was Cabrina before you had dinner with her last night?"

"I didn't know it in the afternoon," Jason said, "although I did suspect it. One of the problems, of course, was the color of the little girl's hair and the mother's hair. Neither was red. Both were brown."

"Oh, my God!" Danni said. "And Cabrina's hair is really brown."

"But that wasn't enough evidence," Jason said. "Those two in the photo still could have been a lot of people. I had to know for certain that it was Cabrina and her mother. So when she started talking about her family, I thought I would pull out the old photo and spring it on her. But I couldn't make myself do it. I was almost sure then, but considering the condition Cabrina was in last night, it would have been cruel to show her that picture. And then there would have been the explaining, how I came to have a copy."

Craig said, "But then, she took out her own picture, like this one, but a little smaller, and told us about her mother, and her scoundrel father, and her jerk of a stepfather. We were all about to start crying, I think."

Carsten took the taxi through traffic smoothly as they traveled out of the city into an industrial area. Jason watched buildings go by at a reasonable pace, and he wondered how different this week would have been if he hadn't stepped into Baransky's taxi at the airport a week before.

Danni turned to Jason. "You told me Cabrina had a little problem and left early. So that was it?"

"Close, but not quite. Gitte asked where Cabrina's real father was now, and Cabrina said he'd been murdered. That's when she totally broke down. She hurried off to the ladies room with Gitte, then Gitte came and got Cabrina's purse and coat and we didn't see Cabrina again."

Danni's mouth was hanging open. "Murdered? Oh, now I get. I get it, I get it! Oh, God, Jason, you figured it out!"

"Wait a minute," Craig said. "Now I'm the one who's confused, and I don't think it's from my concussion. Figured out what? But first, where did you get this picture, Jason? Like Danni mentioned, you had it in the afternoon. Who sent it to you?"

"The police. Detective Dalvang," Jason said. "We were swapping stories yesterday morning, and he decided to tell me about this old photo, and I had a hunch so I asked him to send me a copy."

"A hunch," Danni said. "Sure."

"Well, yeah. Well, a little more than that. I knew Weathersby was divorced, and Sayon Kunder, the Indian food broker, gave me the clue, which didn't totally make sense until last night."

"Who's Weathersby?" Craig asked.

"An Englishman killed in a hotel here in Copenhagen a week ago, a hotel where I was supposed to stay, the room where I was originally supposed to stay. Anyway, according to Kunder, it seemed that Weathersby longed for a woman he didn't have, maybe couldn't have, but someone he'd been close to once. Not only that, he felt guilty. And I began to wonder if the object of his emotions wasn't more than a woman. Maybe it was a woman *and* a child. Then last night Cabrina said that her father had abandoned her and her mother and had gone home to his family in England. And short of the photo, that cinched it for me. Weathersby was already married with a family in England when he had an affair with Cabrina's mother and fathered Cabrina."

"That makes sense," Craig said.

"I agree," Jason said, "but keep listening. A few months after Cabrina was born, Weathersby went back to his family in England. Commendable on one count, but he abandoned his new family in Denmark. So he sent a little money sometimes, but not nearly enough. He was caught between two families and couldn't win. He stayed in England, but he kept thinking about his lover in Denmark, and his little girl, a little girl he couldn't see if he was going to stay with his wife and children in England. Then years later, after those kids were grown up, he divorced. But along the way, probably when Cabrina was two years old, the mother sent Weathersby the picture."

"Okay," Craig said. "You said the police gave you a copy of the picture. Where did the police get the original? From Weathersby?"

"From Weathersby's suitcase," Jason said. "It was part of the evidence, and Dalvang felt that it was important, but he didn't know exactly how. So when it struck a chord with me, and I asked for a copy, I'm thinking he's the one who had a hunch, that I might be able to make a connection that had eluded him."

"Amazing," Danni said. "So this guy Weathersby you've been obsessing about turns out to have a daughter named Cabrina, who knows Craig."

"And Gitte." Jason looked over at Craig. "I assume that it was Gitte who introduced you to Cabrina," Jason said.

"That's right."

"But you haven't told us everything," Danni said. "There's more."

Jason tried to look innocent. "Is there?"

"Of course there is. Weathersby was killed in the Hotel Lorentsen, and you said that's where you snapped that picture of Cabrina."

Craig was instantly alert. "The Lorentsen? That's where Cabrina works."

"Right," Jason said. "In food service. And the desk clerk told me that one of the things she does is room service."

"I knew that," Craig said.

Jason checked the road. They were almost to the airport. "And the police knew that. They interviewed Cabrina, as far as I can tell, along with the other staff. But I don't think they connected her with that picture in Weathersby's suitcase."

"Jason," Danni said slowly. "Are you saying Cabrina did room service for her own father?"

"Well, I don't have that information, and I haven't asked Dalvang yet, but it seems quite likely. Danni, remember I told you that something unnerved Weathersby last Thursday evening. When he came to Copenhagen, he normally stayed at the Kong Jacob, but since he couldn't get reservations when he wanted, he agreed to stay at the Lorentsen, for four nights. Then on Thursday evening, about seven o'clock, only about three hours after he'd checked in, he called the front desk in an agitated state and almost demanded to be moved out of the Lorentsen. Well, because of the space problem with the renovation at the Kong Jacob, the hotel people couldn't do that until Friday night. So instead of packing up and going to a third hotel and having to pay double that one night, he decided to ride out the night at the Lorentsen. Except he didn't ride it out. Sometime after nine o'clock, when he sent a fax offering cheese to my company in Seattle, he was stabbed to death."

"Cabrina?" Craig asked.

"Imagine this," Jason said. "Weathersby was still working on business deals into the evening and didn't want to go out to dinner or even down to the dining room. So Cabrina delivered his dinner around six. Maybe she saw the name of the hotel guest on the food order and volunteered to take it up because she knew Weathersby's name, and maybe she delivered it by chance. Dalvang will figure it out. In either case, Weathersby recognized her. Cabrina looks quite a bit like her mother looked in that picture, and even though Weathersby carried the old picture around, seeing Cabrina in the flesh could have sent him into some kind of panic."

Danni said, "You might think he would want to see his daughter."

"You and I might think that, but I wonder when push came to shove if he didn't prefer to live with the picture and his old memories, a kind of harmless, innocent fantasy that would never require personal involvement. He'd been to Denmark often and had plenty of chances to look up his old flame and her daughter. Maybe he'd tried, I don't know, but at this point I would guess that the adult Cabrina was a little too real for him and reminded him of his mistakes."

"He was in some sort of denial," Danni said. "He wasn't taking responsibility."

"That could have been it, yes. Anyhow, let's say Cabrina sensed something was wrong and put two and two together on the spot if she knew the name before she went up to the room, or added things up a little later if she didn't already know it. In any case, imagine that she thought things over and made a few preparations and returned to Weathersby's room a few hours later. Last night at our dinner she said she hated her father and had hated him for years for abandoning her and her mother. And I think she started to say that he'd rejected her recently. In one way she hated him, but in another she still wanted a father. Then, unexpectedly, she saw a chance for revenge."

"That wouldn't surprise me a bit," Craig said. "The way she talked last night."

"Right. The way I'm looking at this, it was getting late, past nine, and Weathersby wasn't expecting Cabrina to return, but let's say she knocked on the door and he let her in. He was still dressed, wearing shoes. I saw he was wearing black shoes when the police removed his body last Friday, so the shoes told me he hadn't gone to bed yet. He didn't know what to say to her at first, but probably they clarified who they were. Maybe they argued. Maybe for a little while she held out some hope for reconciliation, but at the same time she had a knife. And then when he was off guard and defenseless...well, you can imagine the rest."

Craig spoke. "You said he was stabbed."

"Multiple times."

Danni slumped in her seat. "Oh, Lord."

"But you can't prove Cabrina did it," Craig said.

"No, I can't. Last night Cabrina showed us guilt. But proof is another matter. You can make your own conclusion. You and the police."

"You'll talk to Dalvang again?" Danni asked.

"I suppose so, if I have a chance before I leave."

"You're not turning her in?" Craig asked. "She's such a beautiful person. I admit she's pretty aggressive sometimes, but I really liked her. It's hard to believe all this."

"Then you shouldn't believe it, Craig. She has outer beauty but inner turmoil. No, I'm not turning her in. I've only put a few strands of information together and come up with a possibility, a scenario."

"More than that, I think," Danni said. "But it also sounds as if there was no idea that she would hurt anyone else, like Craig. She just hated her father so much."

"Yes, it could be like that," Jason said. "One and done. It's possible, but I'm not betting the farm yet."

The taxi was almost at the terminal now, and as they pulled into the airport grounds, the subject of Cabrina was dropped. Jason began to tense up, and Danni must have felt the same because she moved even closer to him and held his arm and took his hand. At the international terminal, Carsten stopped the taxi and took out the bags. Another car pulled in not far behind, and a man in an overcoat got out. Jason looked back at him a second, then told Carsten to go on because he would be a while and would find his way back to town on his own. Jason fetched a baggage cart for Danni, and Craig got one for himself, and they pushed into the terminal.

While Danni and Jason went to the ticket counter, checked their bags and got squared away with their flight details, Jason waited quietly behind the lines. He kept trying to think of something clever to say, but all his scenarios were as flat and tasteless as dry bread.

After Craig and Danni had finished checking in, they found Jason again. "We're sitting together," Danni said. "I guess we'll have plenty of time to talk."

"That's good. I'm sure you two have a lot to catch up on, and plans to make."

"We do," Craig said. "I only wish there was some way to thank you for everything you've done."

Danni said, "I've brought up the same thing, Craig, but I didn't get very far."

"Knowing that you two are going to go back to California and put that family company back together and get a fresh start is good enough for me."

"Mr. Modesty," Danni said.

Jason checked the time. "Maybe you guys should be moving toward the gate."

"Where do we go?" Danni asked, scanning the terminal. "This looks so different from the way I came in."

"Up the escalator, I think," Jason said. "You have to get on the upper level."

They walked to the escalator and rode up. When they got off, they could see the metal detectors not far ahead. From that point forward, only ticketed passengers were allowed.

Craig said, "I'll go on through and wait for you on the other side, Danni."

She nodded and turned to Jason.

"This is as far as I can go," he said. "At least for today."

"You're flying back tomorrow?" Danni asked.

"That's when my reservation is and I plan to keep it. It'll work out nicely for what I have left to do here in Copenhagen."

"Oh, Jason. I don't want to leave. No, that's not right. What I mean is that I want to leave, but I don't want to leave you."

He took Danni in his arms. "I know. It's been quite a week. And you're an exceptional woman. It's going to be rough on me, too."

She lifted her head. "Will I ever see you again, Jason?"

"I don't know, Danni. Time will tell. But when you get back home, you'll have plenty to think about with your job, and Craig, and the rest of your family."

"I know, I know. But I won't forget about you. Never,"

"No, and I won't forget about you either, Danni. Now give me a big kiss and don't keep your brother waiting."

It was a kind of heaven, and simultaneously a kind of torture. He didn't want to let her go, and he was glad when she broke loose first.

"Bye, Jason. You take care."

"Bye, Danni." And he turned and went back down the escalator before she even got up to the screening machines. He didn't want her to see that his eyes were wet.

17

Jason wasn't going to turn into a pillar of salt, but if he did look back, he didn't know that he could handle the situation. It had been hard enough to get this far. So if he looked back, he might just end up saying goodbye all over again, and that would be one time too many.

He rode down the escalator, walked around the terminal a little, then looked up to the second level when he thought it was safe. Danni would be through the security check by now and with her brother, and they would be on their way to the gate for their flight. At least she had somebody to talk with. He stopped at a snack counter and bought a coffee, not because he wanted to pep himself up but because he needed something physical to do, something to hang on to. The coffee tasted good and was a pleasant distraction.

He was in no particular hurry, but he didn't feel good hanging around an airport when he wasn't flying anywhere and the emotions were all too intense. Now he needed to take the train back into the city. To get to the tracks he had to go down a level on another escalator. The train wasn't there yet, so he bought his ticket, sipped his coffee and waited. The underground level was clean and tidy, as he would have expected in Denmark, and served Jason as a refuge from the activity on the levels above. Only a few people were waiting for the train, and though the view was of station walls and dark tunnels, at least nothing much would bother him here.

The wait was about ten minutes, long enough for him to finish his coffee and reframe his thinking for the task ahead. But as soon as the train left the station, Jason couldn't help realizing that he was on it only because Danni had taken it and indirectly suggested it. And, of course, if he had taken the train that first day, he might never have made the Baransky connection. There were a lot of ifs, and though some people believed that every fork in the road took a person to exactly where he should be, Jason wasn't quite ready to believe that.

By the time he arrived downtown at the Central Station, he was getting hungry, so found a nearby eatery for a quick and early lunch. Afterward, he walked over to the Kong Jacob to pick up some work papers from his room, and then he called for a cab. He didn't phone Carsten this time. He didn't want to drive the poor fellow crazy hauling him around, and right now he didn't feel much like explaining who those other two Americans were and what they'd been talking about. But he would call Carsten tomorrow for his own trip to the airport. Then it would be easier. It would be his own farewell to Denmark.

First, though, he had to visit Poul Stubkjaer at Bjorneby Foods. There was the little matter of the missing havarti order, and he intended to have it. No dead Englishman or Indian opportunist was going to take that away.

When Jason arrived, the receptionist gave him a wary look, perhaps having seen him once too often. Even so, she tried to pretend he was a stranger and even greeted him in Danish. Jason ignored her act and asked for Stubkjaer in plain English.

"I'll see if he's in," she said crisply.

Of course, Stubkjaer wasn't immediately available. As Jason expected, he would have to cool his heels in the lobby. He didn't have an appointment, though it could hardly be a surprise to Stubkjaer that he would return. In ten minutes or so, Stubkjaer came to get him. "Jason, nice to see you today. I wasn't expecting you. You should have called."

"Too many things going on," Jason said. "I wasn't sure when I could get here. When I had a break, I hopped into a taxi and came out."

"Well, no mind. I have a few minutes, so we can talk."

They walked into his office and Stubkjaer shut the door. "We don't want to be disturbed."

"No, we don't."

They sat down, Stubkjaer behind his desk. "Jason, first of all, let me ask about your friend, the young lady."

"She's recovering nicely, thank you. And I took her to the airport this morning. She's flying home today."

"Oh, good. I'm relieved."

"She has a strong will," Jason said. "No matter what happened here, she's going to be all right."

"Yes, of course. That's excellent news." Stubkjaer paused. "So what brings you back, Jason?"

"Business, Poul. I'm here to do business."

Stubkjaer spread his hands. "Well, nothing's new. You have the tentative order we wrote the other day. We should confirm that, I suppose, but that's all I can offer you. At least at this time."

"No, it isn't."

"Pardon?" Stubkjaer looked shocked.

Jason put his elbows on Stubkjaer's desk. "You know what I want."

"You must be reasonable, Jason. If this is the way you do business in America..."

"I tell you what, Poul. If Bjorneby Foods starts honoring its contract commitment to send a substantial amount of havarti to Sunny Day Farms, I won't tell the police about your connection with Andrei Baransky."

"Now look here, Jason, I won't be threatened."

"And you look, Poul. I have a pretty good working relationship with Detective Dalvang, and if I asked him to take a close look at your operation here with perhaps an inexplicable number of undocumented Russian workers—well, you might want to reconsider."

"You would do that?"

"My friend Danni, the young lady, was put through a terrible ordeal on these premises, and I don't think Baransky picked the Bjorneby warehouse by accident. To him, this was a safe haven. What I'm suggesting is that the police might want to take a closer look at why it was a safe haven. The investigation is still open. Of course, there could be a way to avoid that. I'm sure it would be unpleasant for you, as well as many of your staff, for the police to be poking around for days on end, asking pointed questions, searching for documents, investigating your personal background, your travel, your income, your connections."

"Enough."

"Then you've reached a decision?"

"Bjorneby Foods has an agreement with Delhi Deli Mercantile, which I understand has a havarti offer on the table for your company. You're going to get the cheese anyhow."

"It's a bogus agreement."

"Must we quibble?"

"Besides, I can't stand middlemen. Especially Sayon Kunder. He's holding something over you, and I think I know what it is. He learned from Weathersby that the Russian connection here is no accident. Am I right?"

Stubkjaer worked one thumb against the other rapidly, but said nothing.

Jason went on. "Of course, Kunder himself is not to be trusted. He hardly gives his own children room to move. It's tantamount to abuse. Surely, your scruples rise above that."

"I had no idea."

"It's true. They're like slaves. They might as well be wearing shackles. He gives them no freedom at all. The only things he doesn't tell them how to do are breathe and go to the bathroom, although he's probably tried."

"Jason, you drive a hard bargain. If you get the havarti directly, what about the tentative order, the substitute order?"

"No problem. I would sign for it."

"And in the future?"

"You would get even more business. But I never want to set eyes on you again. Something about your face turns my stomach. So if I ever have to come back to Copenhagen to fix a problem, I will be in a bad mood. You can count on it."

Stubkjaer shook his head. "I don't know, I just don't know."

"No, of course not. It's tough to decide. But that's all right." Jason reached into his coat pocket and took out his phone. "I'll just give the police a ring."

"That's blackmail," Stubkjaer barked. "And you know it."

"Poul, I hardly think telling the police about immigration violations is a crime. Don't you think they would be interested? And by the way, Baransky has gone back to Russia. If he ever sets foot in Denmark again, he'll be arrested. You don't owe him anything. You can send those Russians packing. All of them. Baransky has no leverage against you now."

Stubkjaer looked worried. "It's not that easy. You don't know him."

"Actually, I do. He's not a normal man. He's a sadist. You should wash your hands of him, and you can start today. Clean house and the police won't look your way again."

Stubkjaer sighed and nodded slowly. "All right, all right. I know it's the decent thing to do. Let's get to work on that havarti order."

"Excellent. And we'll fax the whole thing to Seattle, and it will be on my boss' desk when he comes to work in a few hours."

Stubkjaer looked Jason in the eye. "You had this whole thing planned, didn't you?"

Jason shrugged. "Not every word. I improvised here and there."

#

Late that afternoon, when Seattle's morning commute was at full throttle and Jason knew Ben Novitsky was at his desk early as usual, Jason phoned the office.

"Ben, it's Jason, calling from Copenhagen."

"Jason, I got the fax. Been looking it over." Jason imagined his boss pulling on his right ear with his free hand.

"Glad to hear it."

"I don't know how you got that havarti order, but it's what you went over there for, so it's really nice to see that you came through."

"Thanks, Ben."

"But these other items—the chocolates, the canned pork, all that—I don't know. The order is too much. It'll put us over budget.

I wish you had touched bases with me earlier."

Jason knew this was coming. "You know, I told you about those things a few days ago. You liked them then."

"That was in a different context. We were talking about a substitute for the havarti, but now we're getting the havarti. So we don't need this stuff."

"Ben, you don't know what I went through."

"And that's supposed to make a difference?"

"Yes, it is. Anyway, it's an all or nothing deal. If you're over budget, cut back on something else. Take bananas, for instance. When I was in the grocery store last week, I saw bunches and bunches of overripe bananas. People aren't buying as many bananas these days, Ben. So there's a good place to cut back."

"What?"

"Haven't you heard about these low-carb diets? Bananas are suspect. So you could cut back there, way back."

"And buy chocolates instead?"

"They have Made in Denmark labels. They're exotic."

"Bananas are imported, too."

"What're you going to say, Ben? Made in Costa Rica? That'll really sell."

"Jason, sometimes I think I made a mistake in recommending your hiring. Has that ever occurred to you?"

"Daily. But let's talk about that next week. I'm flying home tomorrow, Saturday, and I'll be back in the office Wednesday after a couple of days of vacation."

"Vacation?" Jason could see Novitsky's scalp turn red under his crew cut. "May I remind you, Mr. Stallings, that you are still new with Sunny Day Farms and haven't earned vacation time yet? Besides, you got a trip to Europe on the company's dime."

Mr. Stallings? Ouch. "Fine," Jason said, "then call it comp time. That's even better. I'll save my vacation time for warm weather. I'm flying thirteen hours on my day off, and I'll be in Wednesday."

"Jason, this is no time to be insubordinate."

"What? You want me to cancel that havarti order?"

"Of course not."

"Then I'll see you Wednesday. Have a nice weekend, Ben."

Jason kicked off his shoes, lay down on his bed, and put Novitsky out of his mind. Jason thought he should never have let Novitsky into his mind anyhow. There wasn't enough room in there for both of them. Jason looked at the ceiling, then at the windows. It was dark outside now, and the faint illumination coming through was from the courtyard, where a few security lights would burn all night. He took a couple of deep breaths and calmed himself, and then began following his breath.

About five minutes later he came to the surface just as the room phone began to ring. Refreshed, he got up and answered it.

"This is Dalvang. I'm in the lobby. If you want to come down, I'll buy you a drink."

"Sounds good, Detective. See you in a minute."

Jason splashed water on his face and put on his shoes and jacket. At the last second, he grabbed his camera. When he got to the bar, Dalvang was already seated at a table with a glass in front of him.

Jason sat down. "What's that you're drinking?"

"Aquavit."

"I almost tried it once. You like it?"

"In a way. I like to believe it's good for the soul. If I had a beer, well, it's only a beer. But with aquavit, you know you're drinking. It's kind of like vodka, but made from potatoes, with a little flavoring. I prefer mine with caraway seeds."

"You're a brave man." The bartender came by, and Jason ordered a whiskey sour, for old time's sake. "So what's on your mind? Celebrating with a shot of aquavit?"

"Something like that. I figured you were about ready to go back to America, so I thought we'd catch up on this and that before you left."

"A social call."

"Partly. By the way, I know it's late in the game, Jason, but I'd like you to call me Arne. Then maybe I wouldn't feel that I'm working right now."

"Arne. I like that name. So what's new, Arne?"

"Well, for one thing, I told you that this Russian, Baransky, had left the country. I might have been a little ahead of myself then, but I can confirm it now. I probably shouldn't be telling you, but one of our Danish agents saw him in St. Petersburg today."

"I thought as much. The taxi drivers seemed to know that he'd left."

"Well, if you ever want to know something, ask a taxi driver."

They both laughed, happy to skewer an old cliché, even if there was some basis for it. The whiskey sour arrived, and Jason took a sip, with memories of his first drink at the Kong Jacob.

"By the way," Dalvang said, "I really appreciate your call this morning explaining the Huff-Baransky connection. You probably have a lot more details, but the CIA angle is good enough for me. As I told you the other day, that sort of thing is above my pay grade. Now I don't have to lose any sleep wondering what was going on."

Jason said, "I don't suppose you'll lose any sleep wondering about Craig Huff's welfare, either, but I should tell you that he seems to be okay. He and Danni have begun to patch up their differences, and he's flying to San Francisco with her right now."

"I know, not about getting along with his sister, but about his leaving. When you called this morning, I put a tail on your taxi."

"I thought I saw your man at the airport. He got out right behind us. No one but me seemed to notice, though."

"That's good. Didn't want to scare anyone," Dalvang said. "You stopped at the security checkpoint and said your goodbyes, but my man went clear to the gate and didn't leave until he saw Huff get on the plane and the plane took off."

"So you left nothing to chance. Were you afraid he wouldn't get on the flight? That was our agreement, that he would leave."

"I wasn't afraid." Dalvang said. "I've been a cop too long to be afraid about these things. But I wanted confirmation. I wanted a tidy case."

"So now the kidnapping victim has left the country, and the two suspects have left the country. Case closed?"

"I would say so. But there's one case that isn't closed."

"Weathersby. Well, I figured out a few things, but I'm not sure I solved it."

Dalvang sighed. "Too bad, I was counting on you. You showed a knack. It would have made my job easier."

"On the other hand," Jason said, "I'm not sure that I didn't solve it."

Dalvang tilted his head. "That's more like it. What did you do with the picture?"

"Not much, I guess." He took it out of his jacket pocket and put it on the table. "You should take it back. I never got a chance to show it, at least not to who I had in mind."

"Jason, you can do better than that."

"No, not really."

Dalvang held up the copy of the photo. "Then let me tell you the way I see it. I think this is a picture of Weathersby's old lover, and her daughter, their daughter."

"I guess I didn't want to go first, but that's the way I saw it, too. It's about the only reasonable explanation. The picture obviously meant something to him."

"And I think you had dinner with that daughter last night, twenty-one years after that two-year-old girl was photographed."

Jason raised an eyebrow. "You know, Arne, I've been trying to anticipate things—events, attitudes, words—the whole week I've been in Denmark. And I think I've done a decent job. But this one got by me. I have to say that I'm surprised that you knew that much about last night. Maybe I'm getting tired."

"It's okay. And it's nice to know that the pros can do a guy like you one better. I had a colleague follow Huff from his hotel last night."

"Of course, when I called you from his hotel yesterday morning I told you we were going out to dinner."

"You did, but you didn't say where. Anyway, the surprise wasn't where you went—nice place, by the way—but who your guests were."

"Where was your man?"

"In the bar, drinking tea. You know, you can see right through those partitions if you get close enough." Dalvang wore an amused look.

"I should have known."

"Don't worry. Anyway, one of your guests left early, somebody I've seen before. Cabrina Jorgensen. Of course, her picture was on your camera. You mentioned that earlier."

"The beautiful Cabrina, one of Craig Huff's Danish lovers."

Dalvang grunted. "Tell me."

"I ran across her at the hotel by chance. So I thought if I took her photo, I could help Danni identify which girlfriend was which. And later I wondered if Cabrina couldn't help Danni some way, such as gain leverage on her brother. You know, maybe the girlfriend could tell Danni something useful. But we never got to that point."

"Well, all that explains why Cabrina was at your dinner, but not what happened. The report I got is that she looked pretty upset. So I wondered why. And since you were right there..."

"Okay, why not? We were talking about our families, and when it was Cabrina's turn, she said her father had abandoned her and her mother when Cabrina was three months old and gone back to his family in England, his real family."

"Nice."

"Extremely. But it was one family or the other. Over the years as Cabrina grew up she became bitter and maybe even obsessive about not having a father. There was a stepfather in the picture for a couple of years, but that was another bad experience. Cabrina pestered her mother for details about her father until she got them. Cabrina really hated her father. She took what he did as a personal rejection, and she dwelled on it. On one hand she wanted a father, but on the other it seems she also wanted revenge. My guess is that she and Weathersby each figured out who the other was that night at the hotel and that he rejected her again. At the dinner last night, she even hinted at that, then stopped herself before she said too much."

"So you don't think Weathersby had seen his daughter in all

these years?"

"No, I don't. After all, he had made plenty of business trips to Denmark so had had plenty of chances to look her up long ago. He could have defused her, but it looks as if she still had everything bottled up. The way I see it, Weathersby liked the old picture he carried around, the captured memory of his lover, but he was not nearly as excited about the current reality of his adult daughter. So last Thursday night when she delivered a meal to his hotel room, anything less than a warm embrace from her father could have been the last straw for Cabrina. Let that kind of emotion cook for twenty-some years and anything could happen."

"And it did happen," Dalvang said, "violently, one night in the Lorentsen a few hours after Cabrina took a dinner tray to a certain room."

"So she really was the one who did the room service. I wasn't absolutely sure."

"We interviewed her. She admitted that part. And it's on the hotel kitchen records."

"Did she volunteer?"

Dalvang raised an eyebrow. "Actually, she did. You suspected, then. But it doesn't seem to help the case. Only she knows why. She just says she volunteers a lot, that it's her style. She's young and energetic and tries to be a good worker, tries to be helpful."

"Okay, but you don't know what happened later."

"No, not really. I have an idea, a scenario, but I haven't been able to do much with it. The forensics don't tell us a whole lot we didn't already know. Apparently the attack surprised Weathersby. There was no sign he resisted, or had a chance to fight back. No cuts on his hands or anything like that. The autopsy said he died about four hours after eating, but that's about all we can say. So, basically, I don't have a solid case to present to the prosecutor."

"I know what you mean. There's guilt—and then there's proof."

Dalvang poured some aquavit down his throat, so Jason took the opportunity to put away a little of his whiskey sour. The detective wiped his lips and smiled wryly. "Guilt—and proof. Yes, that's about the way I see it."

"Then there's the knife."

"We never found it. Not a trace."

"But what did forensics say?"

"The blade went into the body about 15 centimeters, six inches in your measurement. It was maybe an inch wide, sharp on only one side. A sharp, smooth blade, not serrated. Three separate stab wounds in the back. Probably the first one killed him, but any one of them could have been fatal. Then there was another stab wound in the chest, but he apparently was already dead by then."

"So, not a steak knife," Jason said, "but something easily found in a big hotel kitchen. I don't suppose they keep inventory."

"No chance there. Assuming the knife was from the kitchen, we narrowed it down to two or three different styles. But for all we know, the knife isn't even missing."

"Never thought of that. Sure, why not. Wipe off the knife, rinse it off, put it into the dishwasher and there goes your evidence."

"That's right. One of the cooks might have used that knife the next day. And the next."

Jason thought about his dinner with Kunder at the Lorentsen and let that sink in. "Arne, that's just disgusting."

Dalvang nodded in agreement. "Best not to think about it too much."

They both worked on their drinks, and then Jason asked, "What do the forensics say about whether the killer used the right hand or the left?"

Dalvang pursed his lips, frowned for a few seconds and said, "I'm sorry, I don't know. I never read anything about that in the report. But let me check." He took out his cellphone and made a call. He spoke in Danish, of course, so Jason didn't hear anything understandable except the name Weathersby. When the conversation paused, the detective looked up at Jason. "They're getting the pathologist. Just be a second." Then Dalvang was speaking Danish again for a minute or so and then ended the call. "Well, I guess I need to get eyeglasses so I can read those reports better."

"Something new?"

"Not to the pathologist, I guess. He's never been wrong in his life. Just ask him. Anyway, he calculates the killer was about five feet ten, if he or she was wearing shoes of normal height."

"Hmm. That's close but maybe not close enough," Jason said. "I'd estimate Cabrina at five feet seven in low heels."

"Okay, a three-inch difference sounds like a lot, but it might not matter that much. There could be other factors that affect the height equation—high heels, the victim slumping down, anything that would have made one person taller or the other shorter for a moment or two. And no one was there with a measuring tape. So the question could go either way, especially with a jury. But the other thing is what you actually asked about, which hand did the killer use."

"It has to be the dominant hand. You pick up papers or something light with your non-dominant hand, but if you're doing serious work with a knife, you use your dominant hand. What did your pathologist say?"

"The killer was left-handed," Dalvang said, making a fist with this right hand and pounding the table moderately in controlled anger with himself. "Damn, I should have known that."

"Cabrina is right-handed," Jason said. "Just like you."

Dalvang appraised his fist as if it were someone else's, then said, "You sure about Cabrina?"

"I sat next to her at dinner for almost two hours. She's right-handed."

Dalvang squinted. "You were already wondering about the hand question last night at dinner, weren't you? That's why you're asking now. Most people wouldn't think of noticing."

"Yes, I was wondering a little. It wasn't a big deal last night, but I paid attention. Anyway, there was no doubt. It was the way she ate, drank wine, drank water, the whole thing."

"But she's not American. She'd used a knife and fork, not just a fork."

"Certainly. And if you're right-handed, you hold the fork in your left hand and the *knife* in your right. European or American, it doesn't matter. It's easier to maneuver a fork with your non-dominant hand than it is a knife."

"Don't *twist* that knife, Jason. I feel bad enough already. I should have known this. I was just becoming so sure Cabrina was our killer, even if I couldn't quite prove it. She was in the room, she had all the motivation. Now I have to start all over."

"Maybe not," Jason said. "There's another possibility, one that keeps her motivation."

"What are you getting at? She grew three inches that night and used her left hand to stab her father four times?"

"Doesn't sound likely, does it. No, I think Cabrina was as motivated as ever. You know those motivational speakers? They get you whipped up to make a million dollars in thirty days? And on the way you lift a three-thousand-pound car to save your child. What if Cabrina were that motivational speaker, powerfully persuading someone else to do the deed?"

"Hmm. Who?"

"A man, Arne. A left-handed man who's about five feet ten."

"Of course. The perfect suspect," Dalvang said with a touch of bitterness. "We know everything about him, everything except his name, face and fingerprints."

"I think I might know the name and face, and you could get his fingerprints tonight if you want, but you probably won't need them."

"You have me intrigued, Jason. But it seems that our glasses are empty. Another?"

"Why not. I'm off the clock."

Dalvang ordered another round and made a phone call while Jason waited. Then he made another quick call. When he got off the phone, a fresh aquavit and a fresh whiskey sour sat in front of them. "I just called my wife and said I'll probably be working a little late tonight on an important case."

"That's considerate. But you made *two* calls."

"Yes, I did. I called the station and said I would need a ride because I might be an impaired driver and also could they send backup because I'm about to make a big arrest."

"I've never seen you this confident, Arne."

"I'll be more confident in a minute or two, I think." He sipped a little aquavit. "Tell me about Cabrina's powers of persuasion."

"I think you're on to something, Arne. But the question isn't so much about her persuasive powers as about who would be susceptible to them. Who would do Cabrina's bidding to win her favor?" He sampled his new whiskey sour as he waited for the policeman's answer.

"You mean win her *heart*, don't you? I'd say we're probably looking at a younger guy who thinks he'd have everything he ever wanted if he could get a beauty like Cabrina to love him. Craig Huff?"

"No. Not Craig. Cabrina was too pushy for him, and besides, he wanted her friend Gitte. So why would this guy do anything Cabrina wanted?" Jason asked, already knowing the answer.

"Let's see. He's in love, and she's probably dated him and dropped enough hints to make him think the feeling could be mutual. Maybe they even went to bed once or twice."

"That sounds about right," Jason said. "There's one other reason he might do anything for Cabrina, especially if something came up quickly, such as Cabrina learning something hugely important last Thursday night and such as Cabrina learning her hated father was in the hotel. And then she concocted a hurry-up murder plot and served it up with a gallon of sugary syrup and he didn't have time to think over her demand rationally."

"I get the hurry-up plot, but what's the other reason?"

"This guy might think he'd be extremely lucky to win over a hot one like Cabrina because he doesn't have as much to offer as most guys his age. There's some factual basis to his attitude, but what he thinks is more important than the actual facts. Also, he's close by, ready to go. And you, Detective Arne Dalvang, know who he is."

"Me? No way."

"You do, because he's already dated Cabrina and he's still waiting for the big payoff and he's five feet ten and he's left-handed and that's because he only has one hand."

Dalvang's face lit up. "The desk clerk?"

"Thomas."

"His other hand? What happened?"

"I had our friend Sayon Kunder do a little checking around the hotel. Since he's probably even pushier than Cabrina, I knew he'd get me an answer. Thomas actually does have a vestige of a right hand, if you recall. I have his picture on my camera. Let's have a look." Jason turned on his camera and scrolled through to the Lorentsen pictures. When he'd walked near Cabrina in the hotel that day, he turned back toward the front desk, mostly to make Cabrina think he wasn't looking at her, but he'd also taken a picture of Thomas at work. Now he showed Dalvang. "See, his right arm is a normal length, but the right hand is not fully developed and barely functional, so he uses his left hand for almost everything." Jason turned off the camera.

"So Kunder told you what happened to Thomas?"

"He did. Thomas would probably be living in another country if there hadn't been a major accident. Twenty-five years ago he was in his mother's womb in the then-Soviet republic called Ukraine when the Chernobyl nuclear plant exploded. His mother was lucky to be alive, but somehow she brought Thomas to term. I don't have the final details, but I think we can speculate. Either his mother came to Denmark as a refugee from the radiation and he was born here, or he was brought here as a baby when it was obvious he would need special help."

"You suspected Thomas from the beginning?"

"Not at all. I went over to the Lorentsen to ask him about Weathersby's room and the room I didn't get. That whole business confused me, and I wanted to understand it. Okay, so I got the clarity I was after, and I talked with Thomas about his feelings toward Cabrina obviously. That's how I knew that they'd dated. But when I noticed that little right hand, I began to see Thomas not just as a hotel desk clerk but as a human in the most profound way. Like you, I was homing in on Cabrina, just by herself, but it was only last night at dinner, when I got to see her up close and learn more about her, that I saw how she was internally conflicted, that she truly wanted her father dead but probably couldn't quite kill him herself. And I saw not only her sex appeal but that certain magnetism that could draw in someone vulnerable. You know, the spider and the fly. Craig Huff had one foot in that territory probably, but ultimately wasn't interested enough in Cabrina. But I think Thomas went along for the whole ride."

"That's a very sad story," Dalvang said. "But now that you've laid it out so well, I have no choice but to take him in. And Cabrina. It'll be an interesting evening in the interrogation room." Dalvang glanced up and saw a fellow policeman at the door. "My ride is here. Time to go out in the cold and get to work."

He and Jason stood up. "Thanks for all your help, Jason. I have your card, so I'll send you a note and let you know how the Weathersby case turns out."

"I'd like that, Arne. If you ever get to Seattle, look me up."

"I'll do that, Jason."

They shook hands and Jason looked down at his own hand and then the table and his eye fell on his whiskey sour glass. For a second, his vision blurred and he saw two of them. He pulled his head up and looked the detective in the eye. "And, Arne, thank you for *everything* you did for Danni and me. *Mange tak.*"

18

As promised, Jason returned to work on Wednesday. Novitsky had some new assignments for him, but they were straightforward and could be handled by phone and email. Novitsky said nothing about budget excesses, and neither did anyone else.

Though Jason had been home a few days and had rested up from jet lag, it still seemed strange to be back in Seattle and actually working in an office again. It would take a few days for the mundane reality of that to set in.

Arne Dalvang sent him an email Thursday saying that both Thomas and Cabrina had confessed. They'd worked together just as Jason had suspected. Cabrina distracted her father by standing in front of him while Thomas willingly did the dirty work on the back side. Jason replied right away, thanking Arne for the update and wishing him well.

By Friday the reality of Jason's job was taking hold. Work was by the book and unexciting. About eleven o'clock the clerk brought around the mail. Jason sat at his desk and looked through the usual assortment of business letters and small packages of food from clients thanking him or looking to make deals.

In the middle of the stack was a plum-colored envelope. And it wasn't his birthday. The return address said *Danni Rossler, Benicia, CA.* Even before Jason opened the envelope, Danni's dusty citrus perfume percolated up to greet him. In the envelope was a greeting card with a European street scene. He unfolded it to handwritten words.

Jason,

Craig and Mom had a long heart to heart, and they're really trying to make things right and put the past behind them. Craig gave all the money back and even reimbursed me for my Denmark expenses. And someone twisted Dad's arm, so Craig will get his job back. Dad says I'm crazy, but that's no surprise to you.

The other thing is, I miss you. A lot. I'm not really sure what I want, but I was just thinking it would be nice to hear from you.

Jason now noticed Danni's business card had fallen out of the envelope and onto his desk. He picked up the card. Beside her printed business phone number, she had written her home and cell-phone numbers. He continued reading.

Anyway, thanks so much for everything, Mr. Smarty Havarti. Love, Danni

Jason went out to the hallway and down to the office kitchen for a cup of coffee. From ten feet away, he could smell that it was burned, but he poured a cup anyway. He needed to drink something. A tightness gripped his throat.

He returned to his office and picked up Danni's business card. On the back side, she'd drawn two red and black ladybugs. He smiled to himself and turned the card back to the front. As he dialed Danni's number, he was already on a plane to California.

About the Author

Walter Rice is the author of several books of fiction, most involving crime. Lengths vary from short stories to novellas to long novels. Rice is a former newspaper editor and reporter in the Pacific Northwest and lives near Seattle with his wife and several hungry pets. He also paints, often digitally, and plays the piano and writes music.

Visit the author's website at:
walterrice.yolasite.com

**More crime fiction
by Walter Rice**

Such a Cruel Month

The Last Prisoner

Holes in My Armor

The Kansas Cross-up

Dig